1

Cold Blooded

(The Nick McCarty Assassin Series)

Book III:

Sins and Sanctions

by

Bernard Lee DeLeo

*****

PUBLISHED BY:

Bernard Lee DeLeo and RJ Parker Publishing Inc

ISBN-13: 978-1503097070

ISBN-10: 1503097072

*****

License Notes

This ebook is licensed for your personal enjoyment only. This ebook may not be resold or given away to other people. Please respect the author's work. This is a work of fiction. Any resemblance to real life persons, events, or places is purely coincidental.

*****

The unauthorized reproduction or distribution of a copyrighted work is illegal. Criminal copyright infringement, including infringement without monetary gain, is investigated by the FBI and is punishable by fines and federal imprisonment.

In memory of my wife

Joyce Lynn Whitney DeLeo

Joyce was the finest woman and best friend I ever met. She was the greatest partner a man could ask for. Whenever trouble came, I had only to look at my side. There would be Joyce, fists up and game face on. She had no equal in my eyes. I wrote this to her for our 37th wedding anniversary. Joyce told me it was her favorite one I ever did for her.

We don't talk about love, because we own love.
We don't turn from trouble, because we own trouble
We don't need life examples - we are life examples.
We don't measure our success – we simply succeed.
We don't seek others' blessings – we count our own.
We don't demand respect from others – we earn it.
We don't cry when denied respect – we settle for fear.
When one of us needs help, we know who'll be at our side.
When we're in danger, we know who'll bring the shotgun.
When danger ends, we know who'll be at our side burying it.
We don't waste precious moments trying to turn back time.
We spend what time we have left making precious moments.
Our kids don't look for backup, because we are backup.
Our friends wonder how we're still together – we don't.

~Rest in peace, baby. You were the best.~

Chapter One

El Muerto Returns

Sweat ran salty and stinging into the young woman's eyes. The dripping byproduct not a consequence of effort, but one based in fear. Her head swiveled anxiously, checking for movement behind her. Each time she jogged with her attention on the sidewalk ahead, rasping footsteps sounded on the cement behind her. The hair on her neck tingled upwards with the chilling sixth sense of danger human beings experience when in spite of all visual proof to the contrary, they know their lives hang in the balance.

Sharon Tennington jogged on the streets around the same set of blocks, measuring four miles from her house round trip, each night between eleven and twelve since working the late shift at the Alltown Roxbury convenience store. Her jogging route took her along Franklin Park, where with winter still in full swing, the near freezing temperatures, snow covered ground, and later hours kept foot traffic sparse or nonexistent. Nobody bothered her during those hours at all, especially during the week; but lately, Sharon noticed anxiety creeping into her nightly run – noises sounding haphazardly, without visual sighting, or precise direction. Habit ruled the the young woman's life. She enjoyed routine to the point of obsession, and loathed the insecure uneasiness change threaded into her mind. Faced with the feeling of terror in competition with the angst of a lost routine, Sharon had vowed to carry pepper spray with her. Tonight found her in deadly danger due to procrastination.

At twenty-three, Sharon hoped to achieve her nursing degree from the College of Nursing in Boston, but paying her own way meant the grind of working the convenience store to supplement her parents' financial support for tuition. It also meant interaction with many hundreds of people on a monthly basis, the majority of whom were like her, striving to get by. A small percentage represented the seamier and darker side of humanity. One in particular poked around in the store night after night, shopping for nothing, but watching Sharon with half lidded eyes, a lopsided grin on his face. With a lean, well-endowed figure, and long auburn hair, Sharon expected as well as appreciated the attention of men. She flirted, her outgoing personality and ready smile made her an instant hit with everyone she met. So dedicated to her life's ambition, and independence, Sharon rarely dated unless in a group setting with her female friends from college. The flirtation she enjoyed employing with the men who frequented her place of employment had unfortunately drawn the attention of a deadly exception to the majority of harmless male customers.

* * *

Gavin Kroneg raped, mutilated, and murdered young women – all auburn haired, pretty victims very much like Sharon. Forty-three years old, with a tally of thirteen brutal slayings across the country behind him, the unobtrusive, quiet six footer moved from one location to another, never staying in one place for long, depending on his deadly vice. Kroneg limited himself to one victim in each area he lived in. Sharon haunted his every thought since seeing her at the convenience store. Her innocent flirtation with him as he paid for a six pack of beer unintentionally flipped his predator switch on. He hunted cautiously, picking his victims with patience. Stalking her home and habits became Kroneg's pastime after leaving his work as a carpet cleaning assistant. To his fellow workers and neighbors, Kroneg interacted with polite respect, never giving offense or shirking his duties.

Tonight, Kroneg smiled as he shadowed his intended victim, taking pleasure in Sharon's fearful glances. The next block bordered the park Kroneg planned to take her down near. He sped up, sticking closely to the houses along the way, racing ahead each moment she looked away until he passed her on the opposite side of Seaver Street bordering Franklin Park. Although in excellent shape, Kroneg sweated in the early March cold air. Snow still blanketed the ground in spots, making sudden acceleration a dangerous chore, but the stalker decided days ago the exact spot he would take Sharon down at.

After achieving nearly a hundred yard lead, Koneg slipped across darkened Seaver Street into the line of trees. Taking deep breaths, he waited in excited readiness to overwhelm his target, all thought of discomfort replaced by fevered anticipation. Each step in his deadly game flashed through his mind, now only seconds away from fruition. This hunt felt as near perfection as he could make it. Kroneg would move on immediately, after giving two weeks' notice to avoid suspicious discussion. His sudden disappearance in conjunction with the grisly headlines he was sure to engender might cause complications which would prove disastrous. He envisioned two weeks of heightened delirium, rejoicing in the bloody speculation the papers always reveled in, while commiserating with his neighbors and fellow employees about the tragic death of a young woman.

* * *

Sharon relaxed finally, slowing her pace. The feeling of something or someone behind her diminished with every step. Her feelings of dread threatening to turn the night jog into a terror race left her, leaving Sharon wondering at what she figured was silly paranoia. Beautiful Franklin Park lay ahead on her right, where the night stillness coupled with winter snow to suppress any anxiety from imagined danger.

Horror hit with cold efficiency, as a flurry of movement on her right preceded a blow to her head. Sharon gasped at the movement before Kroneg's fist struck her behind the right eye socket. Arms flailed in panic, but could not keep the woman on her feet. Wavering between murky darkness and unconsciousness, hands gripped her parka, dragging Sharon through the snow into

8

the park's tree lined parameter. In the ensuing moments, she blearily tried to claw at her attacker as he dragged her into the shadow of a structure within the park. Koneg's gloved left hand jammed her head down onto a hard surface near the structure by the throat, pinching off a terrified scream welling up within her. Kroneg's face pressed close to hers, while he straddled Sharon with a grunt of satisfaction bordering on sexual excitement.

"Hello pretty," Kroneg whispered, heat from Sharon's fear driving him insane with desire. Her wide eyed choking anguish worked like an aphrodisiac as his stalking hunt came to an end with prey in hand. "You and I are going to have such fun, my sweet. Just a few cuts to get you in the mood, baby." His right hand flicked the switchblade out to its deadly length, provoking a stifled agonized whine from his victim. As he slowly moved the blade toward Sharon's face, everything went suddenly very wrong.

* * *

"Shit! We're late, Gus," Nick whispered urgently, sighting on the Franklin Park tree lined perimeter he had watched for days, gauging his enemy with professional expertise. His night vision range finders located Kroneg in the spot where the killer practiced his approach each evening. Sharon Tennington's increased speed during her run made Nick's calculations crucial seconds off schedule.

Nick McCarty wrote bestselling novels about an international assassin named Diego. Even now, he and his partner, Gus Nason, stayed in Boston for a combination of a family reunion with Gus's brother, Gus's wedding, and book signings in the area. They traveled his publishing agent's book tour route to a planned family and friend gathering in Boston. Gus's brother and wife were due to meet Nick's family: wife Rachel, stepdaughter Jean, and Deke the dog, along with Gus's fiancé Tina. It would be an uneasy reunion, because at one point Gus had secured Nick's help to save his brother Phil, along with Phil's friend Damian, and Damian's sister, Julie. Nick had blasted his way into a Jamaican Posse hideout, freeing Phil, Damian, and Julie, killing without mercy. The event forever stained any relationship Gus tried to smooth into place between Nick and Phil, who married Julie after their ordeal. Their daughter Katie, only three years of age would see her Uncle Gus for only the second time. Gus reminded his brother of their debt to Nick, and the fact Nick was the reason Phil and his wife Julie still breathed.

Nick is an assassin, and in Gus's estimation, one of the most dangerous men on earth. A former Delta Force unit member, Nick killed people with startling efficiency and no conscience. During negotiations and breakup with a shadowy National Security Agency offshoot, Nick gained a family, but ended the NSA's black ops chapter while saving Rachel, Jean, and Deke the dog. After flirting with retirement, Gus talked Nick into returning to his deadly occupation, thinking his partner would be so out of his element simply writing, the inaction might drive Nick quietly nuts. In succeeding, Gus had unintentionally activated his partner's quirky side with a comic book reference, while Nick threaded his murderous way into CIA folds as a contract killer under new department chief Paul Gilbrech.

Gus listened to Nick's muffled movements, picturing him moving across the park to the interception point. "Do you still have your El Muerto mask on? Take it off, shoot that bastard in the head, and I'll pick you up along Seaver Street."

Gus heard Nick mutter something. "What?"

Nick sighed loud enough for Gus to hear. "I didn't bring my gun. El Muerto kills sometimes with a knife, and many times with his bare hands."

"Are you stupid? What the hell's gotten into you, Nick?"

"Quiet… Payaso, my disrespectful sidekick. El Muerto is thinking."

10

"I told you to quit calling me Payaso!" Gus bristled at Nick's new nickname for Gus in retaliation for Gus labeling him El Muerto (The Dead One) in Spanish. Payaso meant clown.

"Can't talk now, my loyal sidekick. El Muerto must save the damsel in distress," Nick whispered, watching Kroneg drag Tennington under a park structure eave. So intent on his terror inducing ploy with the knife, Kroneg neglected his own backside.

* * *

Sharon tried to scream, but her attacker's hand clamped off her throat, pinning her head in an unbreakable grip. As the knife descended toward her face slowly, an arm clamped around her attacker's neck, and a gloved hand gripped his knife wielding wrist. She heard the bones in the man's wrist crack. His anguished pain filled scream was choked off by the arm around his throat jerking him away from Sharon, and into the air. Sharon's vision cleared as she gasped and choked air into her tortured lungs. Someone with a black mask over his head with eyeholes cut into it, and tied in a knot at the back of his head yanked her attacker into the air while grinding his wrist bones without letup. He looked a little like the hero in a movie she saw as a kid: Zorro. Sharon scooted into the structure wall while watching the deadly struggle. It ended a minute later as Kroneg's body hung in limp submission to death, his eyes bulging in grim illustration of eternity. The masked man holding Kroneg held him for nearly a minute longer before allowing the body to drop from his arm's grip.

The deadly Reaper made placating gestures at Sharon. She had unconsciously skittered a few feet further away. "Your torture ended seconds ago, young woman. Are you in need of medical attention?"

"I...I'm fine." Sharon broke down into tears for a moment – rasping, aching renderings of shock and relief. Her savior remained silent, allowing her to regain control without moving. After many moments, Sharon used the structure wall to regain her

11

feet, a wobbly sensation passing through her as she faced the masked man with uneasy grace. "Who are you?"

"I… I am El Muerto!" The masked man struck a pose in crouched form with his right foot extended, and his right arm over the lower part of his face as if he had a cape.

Sharon giggled, but made conciliatory gestures at her savior. "I know you! You saved those two women in the news! Oh my God… you're real… a real super hero! Thank you, El Muerto!"

* * *

Gus watched the video cam pickup with his face twisted in anxiety as the low light cam portrayed Nick's hurried flight to prevent Tennington's death. He grinned as Nick clamped Kroneg around the neck while pulverizing his right wrist. Gus let his breath out slowly as Kroneg's scream ended in a throat choking arm vice. The aftermath entertained Gus to no end as he watched Nick play comic book super hero, his deadly assassin friend the only one he could ever imagine pulling something like this off. Tennington's giggle at Nick's posing prompted a guttural laugh from Gus, and a sigh as she continued on into hero worship.

"Get out of there, Muerto."

"Shut up, Payaso," Nick cautioned in a whisper. "El Muerto must make a statement here."

"What did you say, El Muerto?" Sharon stepped toward Nick.

Nick made a grandiose gesture of dismissal. "It is nothing young lady. El Muerto must flee the scene of this monster's death. I have here proof positive this man is a serial killer, who I have been hunting. He will never again terrorize, mutilate and murder. I apologize for arriving only a moment before he subjected you to further horrors."

Nick handed the woman a small memory disc. "Please call 911, and tell them what has happened. Give them the flash drive to prove what you will tell them is true. Thank you for your cooperation. El Muerto must leave… now!"

"Wait… El Muerto!" Sharon called out. "None of my… you know… friends will ever believe this. Please, can we take a picture with my phone?"

Nick hesitated with Gus laughing in his ear. "Very well, my lady. If it will add to your credibility, I will grant you a picture with me."

"What!" Gus nearly screamed in Nick's ear. "Are you out of your ever lovin' mind? You can't photobomb selfies on a whim like this! Get a grip, Nick!"

"Shut the hell up, Payaso."

"What did you say, El Muerto?"

"I merely had to remind my trusted sidekick, Payaso, that you are to be trusted with the secret of El Muerto."

"Of course… I would never betray you, El Muerto," Sharon stated. "Hey… doesn't Payaso mean clown?"

"Yes, but he is a deadly clown, a very dangerous clown – one to strike fear in the hearts of those criminals who do not know him," Nick explained with Gus making gagging noises in his ear. "Let us perform this selfie with El Muerto while we stand next to the body of this hideous killer of women!"

Sharon lifted her iPhone while huddling close to Nick. He covered the lower part of his face in a caped superhero pose with a right forearm, while draping his left arm around Sharon's shoulders. Nick then crouched in his all black leather outfit, again with his forearm pose, one foot on the throat of Kroneg's neck, angling so as to hide his actual height.

"Call 911," Nick/El Muerto urged Sharon. "Although El Muerto must leave, I will be watching from the shadows. You will be safe until the police arrive. El Muerto... away!"

"I love you, El Muerto!" Sharon called out as Nick fled into the park.

* * *

On the way to their hotel, Gus remained silent while Nick laughed his way through the video on Gus's iPad. "You know, Payaso... El Muerto doesn't think he has ever enjoyed killing someone as much as he did Kroneg. A few minutes earlier, and El Muerto could have prevented him from taking the girl. Capturing that scumbag alive for an hour in the park would have pleased El Muerto's hunger for justice."

"I doubt you've done anything dumber than what you did tonight, and for God's sake would you please stop referring to yourself in the third person... and quit calling me Payaso!"

"You started this El Muerto thing," Nick reminded him. "Remember, many people are in deadly fear of clowns. We should make you a costume, Payaso. You could assist El Muerto with an evil and deadly clown mask at times, where El Muerto doesn't need his trusty sidekick to act as getaway driver."

"No thanks."

"Okay then, think about this. If I hadn't walked into Sharon Tennington's store after Rachel's craving for chocolate chip ice cream, I would never have spotted Kroneg. She would be dead now, and Kroneg still on the loose if not for us. It was a miracle."

"It's not a miracle when one serial killer can spot another serial killer."

"That's hurtful, Payaso."

14

Gus chuckled. "I admit it. Your noticing Kroneg, and our research into his background turning up a trail of dead women across the country in the places he'd been was pretty cool. I had my doubts until these past few days watching Kroneg stalk her. How did you know tonight would be the night he moved on her?"

"He didn't go to the store for the first time. Did you have any luck with Phil? I have three more book signings scheduled, but then we have to move on. I could postpone the dates though if you want. At least you spent time with Katie. I don't have to be at the wedding anyway. Let Phil be your best man. You can't blame Phil and Julie for not wanting anything to do with seeing me again."

"Bullshit! I don't want Phil as my best man. If not for you, they'd both be dead. Yes, I loved seeing Katie, but it makes no sense for them not to meet you, Rachel, and Jean before the ceremony. He said they might stop by the book signing tomorrow at the Harvard Book Store with Katie."

"Neat. That's a nice venue to say hi in, and reassure them I'm not going to thread into their lives with my murderous but heroic Muerto tendencies."

Gus took a deep breath. "What the hell was I thinking when I tagged you with the El Muerto label as a joke. I should have known you'd take it to the undiscovered country of insanity. Rachel, Jean, and Tina will be accompanying us tomorrow for a change. Their interest in the old Harvard Book Store overcame the boredom factor."

"They know they can leave whenever they want to," Nick said. "Add in meeting Phil, Julie, and Katie to the mix, and we have a very comfortable gathering. Cassie expects to see hundreds there for the signing with a possibility of a thousand attending. This has been a great experience since enlisting you as my sidekick Payaso, along with sharing the signing events as Jed, my character Diego's partner."

"Jed, yes... Payaso, no, you tool!"

Nick grinned. "You know you love being Payaso, the heroic sidekick of the great El Muerto. I hope tonight's adventure doesn't get blown out of proportion, or our cover story of night research at Boston harbor will be dead in the water with the girls."

"Rachel will be so on to you, Muerto," Gus replied, enjoying what he considered a done deal with the media headlines sure to come. "If you'd skipped the picture taking idiocy, you may have had a chance. Posing with the woman, and with your foot on Kroneg's dead neck, I believe you can kiss any chance of anonymity goodbye. Rachel and Jean will be on your case so fast it will make your head spin."

Nick considered the situation with grim amusement. The thrill he felt lance through him when he choked Kroneg to death as Gus's comic creation, El Muerto, did not fade at all since the deed. His interaction with Sharon Tennington added a humorous flavor to the sanction of Kroneg beyond justice. Nick considered it a small payment for his many sins. Without payment from a sanctioned contract, Kroneg's final accounting for his sins could be thought of as Nick's own penance. Nick sighed. *Who am I kidding? I did some good. It felt good, and I killed a bad guy. No use getting delusions of grandeur.*

"I think it will end up on the back page, Gus. The media won't know what to think of it. The police will keep it on the down low because they had nothing to do with it. By the time any mention of it gets published or on the TV, Rachel and Jean will be wrapped in some other trip endeavor."

"I hope you're right, Muerto, but I know you're wrong."

"Trust me, Payaso, my doubting sidekick. All will be well."

* * *

"What the hell have you done now?" Rachel stormed into the kitchen with a very amused Jean, waving a copy of the Boston Herald.

Nick arose at five in the morning as was his custom. He had been writing continually in the hotel room suite's kitchen after walking Deke. Rachel and Jean went through their usual morning routine upon waking at nearly nine. They took a morning walk, and had breakfast, leaving Nick alone during his favorite writing time. Unfortunately, Nick could see El Muerto's adventure did not escape the Herald's front page. Deke ran around behind Nick's chair at Rachel's tone.

"You're supposed to protect me from this type of attack, Deke, you slacker," Nick told the dog, shaking his finger at him. Deke grunted, while peeking out at Rachel who dumped the paper in front of Nick, pointing at the front page pictures with headline 'El Muerto Strikes Again'.

Nick perused the article with growing uneasiness. It covered El Muerto's torture killing of Dominic Leka, the serial killer Nick had sanctioned under CIA contract. Although acknowledging his saving the two young women trapped in cages for months by Leka, the vigilante tag kept recurring throughout. The Herald did list the facts admitted to by the police concerning the proof Nick had given to Sharon Tennington, describing her ordeal the past night in detail. The paper condemned El Muerto's supposed vigilante justice while revealing that the police were investigating horrific murders now tied to Gavin Kroneg. Nick smiled at Sharon Tennington's glowing recount of her savior's actions.

"This guy, El Muerto, is pretty neat," Nick said. He pulled Rachel close, running his hand over her protruding stomach. "How is the newest member of our family doing this morning? He's kicking like hell."

"Don't sweet talk me." Rachel's tone softened at Nick's touch. "Jean and I aren't stupid. We know who El Muerto is. You're smarter than this, damn it. What the hell happened to your rules that coincidences should be avoided at all cost?"

Nick pasted a surprised look on his features with the ease of a killer who could act out a performance rivaling the greatest actors in any century. "You think I'm El Muerto?"

Jean giggled, and pulled out his black silk El Muerto mask from behind her back. "I found this in your leather coat, Dad. I planned on asking you about it, but then Mom and I found out without having to ask."

Uh oh. "You little sneak!" Nick played the outrage card as a last resort to no avail.

"You saved another woman," Jean stated. "That was a great thing. We don't want you sent to prison though. Did you take your sidekick Jed along, since the cover story was book research?"

Nick shrugged. "My sidekick's name is Payaso. Yes, he went along."

Jean gasped. "Payaso means clown in Spanish. What does Gus think about that?"

"Not much, I bet," Rachel said. "If you get Payaso thrown into prison, Tina will shoot you on sight."

"Payaso is fine with it. He created El Muerto. I'm more worried in connection to our daughter, the little snoop."

"She confirmed your transgressions, Muerto." Rachel walked to the kitchen TV. She retreated with the remote in hand, powering it, and switching to a news channel. It only took moments before finding a complete videotaped interview with Sharon Tennington.

The three watched in stunned silence. Rachel brushed away tears. She hugged Nick. "You were right. You and Payaso did real good. I'm sorry I thought about losing you first instead of considering the wonderful thing you did for Sharon Tennington."

Jean pumped her fist as they showed the photos of El Muerto. "This is so cool! You're a real superhero!"

"With a secret identity," Nick pointed out. "If El Muerto is exposed, we'll have to run for it. I don't think my reluctant sidekick, Payaso will like that very much."

Rachel leaned her head into his. "Are you really going to do this from now on?"

"It was kismet, Rach." Nick explained how he saw Kroneg in the convenience store while buying ice cream. "Although as my disrespectful sidekick Payaso reminded me after I told him it was a miracle, it's not a miracle when one serial killer recognizes another serial killer. I knew instinctively what Kroneg planned, but we did our research, and watched him. I'm using a modified version of El Muerto's adventures in the new novel, 'Assassin's Folly'. If I recognize or happen upon a similar circumstance, I will act on it within reason. Hey… I am kind of a psychopath, but I enjoyed saving Sharon. That should count for something."

Jean joined in the hug. "You're our hero too, El Muerto. I love this. I think you need a small action figure accompanying and assisting you in your duties. I could learn to handle dual daggers and be known as El Muerto's vicious sidekick, Dagger."

Rachel was a couple steps too slow to capture the elusive Dagger, who fled with Deke at her back. "Damn it! Oh, what's the use? I'm going to hell anyway. Please don't take Dagger with you on anything resembling a mission, El Muerto."

Nick shook his head in uneasy amusement at his stepdaughter's offer, knowing she was indeed deadly serious, whether it happened now or in the future. "I will not allow it, even if I have to bind and gag her before I leave. Know this though, Rach – she's hooked, and I don't have any idea how to prevent her from following through on the notion. I will train her, and my plan is to urge her to join a good ROTC college program, where she can cool her jets doing something in uniform while continuing her training. She could very likely get into West Point or Annapolis with the contacts I have. This is not your fault. It is what it is, babe."

Rachel kissed Nick lingeringly, slipping down onto his lap. She eased away after many hand explorations later by the attentive El Muerto. "It's not your fault either. Jean's not stupid, and she hates being a victim. Believe me. I remember her words when we were on the run, and you were saving our asses every other minute – 'I'm tired of being scared all the time. I want the bad guys to be scared'."

Nick framed Rachel's face in his hands. "That conversation started before you came into the kitchen that time. I admit what she said before has stuck with me since then. Jean was really mad about her Dad being killed. She said, 'Bad guys killed Dad. Bad guys are tryin' to kill us. Bad guys are why we had to leave New York. I kept wondering how come we can't just kill the bad guys before they hurt us'. I didn't have an answer until Gus hit me with the El Muerto tag. Now… I'm kind of lookin' for trouble. I can't take back all that you two have changed in me, and I'm afraid you two can't take back all that I've changed in you."

"Jean's turned me to the dark side," Rachel admitted. "I want to kill bad guys before they kill young women like Sharon Tennington, or bad women before they kill their damn kids under the guise of some psychobabbler's label of postnatal depression. This stuff is addictive, Nick. Our son will be born into a twisted world of danger because of us; but I'd rather he know every detail when he's old enough, rather than be a victim of whatever monster comes along to hurt him. You've changed everything for us. In my opinion, you've altered reality."

"Mom's right, Dad." Jean had slipped silently by design within hearing distance again. "I'll start training my brother the moment he gets to be eight. I'll be Dagger by then. Let's name him Quinn. Yeah! Quinn McCarty. He'll be the baddest kid on the planet, next to his sister, Dagger."

"We're doomed," Nick muttered, closing his eyes, and hugging Rachel tightly to him. "I don't know where this will all end, but I vow I will be with you two, and the aptly named Quinn until I breathe my last. We have to be very careful. My sidekick Payaso may have been right about my flaunting fate with allowing Sharon to take pictures. I lost track of my mind for a moment as if I were actually reading a comic book instead of getting the hell out of the park before the cops arrived."

"We'll help," Jean said. "Don't worry about all the small stuff. Mom and I will alibi you out of anything the cops get onto you for. Plus… that guy from the CIA needs you. You're the best. He'll cover for you."

Nick laughed. "I don't think so, Dagger."

Chapter Two

Family

"How many books did you sign today?"

"I lost track long ago," Nick admitted. He and Gus packed their personal bags, readying to leave the store. "Cassie went home early. I can ask the store manager if you want. I guess it would probably be in the fifteen hundred range. Jed is really catching on. Did you see Tina's face when all those women today were asking for your autograph? If not for our families interacting so well earlier, I believe Tina would have yanked you out from behind our table by your ear."

Gus shrugged. "You sure called it right with Jed's popularity. People really dig having a true to life character behind the fictional one. Tina will get over it. The family meeting turned out very well too, with Phil and Julie more relaxed in your presence than I thought they'd be after all the avoidance crap they were talking on the phone. Maybe Jamaica finally wore off, and seeing you in person again made them realize it. Katie loves Jean."

"I saw Jean reading Katie stories in the children's section. I'm glad our crew went home before boredom set in. Cassie used them as an excuse to desert us. Are you tiring of this book signing celebrity status yet?"

"I talked boats, foreign locales, and even real events in 'Caribbean Contract' when we threaded our way in to Florida again after that NSA asshole Frank blew up my boat thinking we were on board. Naturally I explained the difficulty navigating those perilous waters by using unrelated trips. I admit it, Nick. I'm hooked on this gig."

Nick saw their security guard escort approaching. "Hi Al. All closed tight and secure?"

"Yes Sir, and thank you for the bonus. There's a limousine waiting outside, but a man I didn't recognize gave me this note to give you. He said he would be waiting to take you and Mr. Nason to your hotel. Let me know if there's a problem."

"I will, Al. Thanks." Nick opened the sealed envelope. "It's Paul Gilbrech. Damn it! I'll bet the prick's going to rake me over the coals for the comic book adventure. I told you I'd probably be forced to kill him. No one respects creativity anymore."

"Calm down, Nick," Gus urged. "You're jumping to conclusions before we know the facts. This may be completely innocent. He hasn't paid us for the Leka hit. Maybe it's payday."

"Good call, Gus. I like Paul, but I keep figuring he's going to force me to remove him because I keep imagining him pulling the same crap Frank did. I have everything in my bag. Let's go see what Paul wants."

"You don't trust him because he's a psychopath like you. When explaining your take on him to me, I saw a glint in your eye. Paul's too much like you, and it throws you off your game."

Not for the first time did Nick wonder how his partner made very accurate leaps in recognizing inner thoughts Nick had not expressed. "I think you know me a little too well, Payaso."

"I better," Gus stated, "and stop calling me Payaso."

* * *

"Well, well… if it isn't El Muerto and his sidekick, Payaso," Paul Gilbrech greeted them outside the Harvard Book Store, shaking hands with each man with a welcoming smile, while holding the limousine door open for them. "Get in, gentlemen. I'd

23

like to pay off our prior debt, and discuss this new realm of activity you two seem to be exploring."

Nick glanced at Gus. "I told you I'd have to kill him."

A flash of fear streaked across Gilbrech's features momentarily. Gus patted his shoulder before entering the limousine. "Pay him no mind, Mr. Gilrech. Nick's a little edgy today. He signed a lot of books, and met a lot of people. I would advise you to avoid off the cuff references to my partner's new afterhours adventures."

"Noted," Gilbrech stated, unsure whether it was a good idea to get into the limo or not. He decided to gamble on Gus Nason's take on things. When he was seated opposite Nick and Gus, Gilbrech motioned for the driver to proceed. "Do you have your laptop with you, Mr. Nason? I will transfer payment for Leka immediately if you do. I had to wait until the video Nick took of Leka's demise reached the right people. To say they were pleased would be an understatement."

Gus arranged his laptop for Gilbrech's transfer into their account. Gilbrech did so, and handed the laptop again to Gus. After checking the amount, Gus nodded at Nick.

"Okay then, Paul. I assume our business is done," Nick said after his long silence. "Gus is right about my being a bit edgy today. I apologize, but I have the distinct feeling you're not done. I assume you are aware of Gavin Kroneg's death, and the fact Gus and I used Company resources to investigate that shithead's background. If you're showing up to give us a ride for the purpose of forbidding any future ventures I deem necessary, we may have a problem."

Gilbrech relaxed for a moment before handing Gus a packet. "There are CIA, FBI, and US Marshal credentials in the packet, Mr. Nason. We want you in with us on an official basis. It means if Nick deems it necessary for the two of you to investigate something in public, you will have the proper credentials. I know the US Marshal link is a bit beyond our arena, but because of Nick's connections with the Justice Department through Agents Stanwick and Reinhold, they have been a newly cooperative entity for us. I do not want to lose what you two have been inadvertently building."

"And..." Nick left the one word hanging in midair.

"I'm not going to pretend I have a clue about this new El Muerto and Payaso reference. Through back channels, I was able to insinuate the demise of Gavin Kroneg into a done deal we felt needed action immediately because a young woman's life was at stake. I played off the comic book references, but kept a very tight perspective on the result of this adlib. It can work. I wish we could have worked it so the FBI would have been able to claim credit for Kroneg's demise, but I can't think of a way. In any case, I believe this new perspective could garner us a number of competing entities into our corner, especially if we can direct some credit their way."

Nick stared at Paul in a way that made the CIA director look away. "You have something in mind, Paul. Let's quit dancing. I appreciate the credentials for Gus. They're long overdue, considering the missions he's helped on. He is beyond reproach pertaining to actual security. Now that we have that out of the way, what is this all about?"

Gilbrech handed Gus a USB drive. "Load this, Mr. Nason. Take as long as you deem necessary to give me your insights on it."

After fifteen minutes going over the data Gilbrech provided, Nick settled into his seat with a more relaxed posture. "This is good intel, Paul. I have no qualms taking this on. It will be the first official sanction taken on by El Muerto and Payaso. I like it. What put you on the trail of this pervert, Mel Berringer?"

"The funny part is you sanctioning that Amazon 'Book Killer' Dafar for us. It made an indelible imprint amongst many threads we follow. This Amazon 'Book Killer' phenomenon proved very interesting. I ordered a blanket audit over the known 'Book Killers' on Amazon. Only one popped out at us. He goes by the name 'Big Texas Son'. He's famous on the Internet for diving into a successful novel's reviews on Amazon, professing knowledge of plagiarism and doing a one star hit piece."

Nick waved off Gilbrech. "Hey... people do one star hit pieces all the time on the Amazon marketplace, especially on popular novels. They either don't read the Amazon preview titled 'Look Inside', or they're the dupes of other authors in the same genre. It's famous. What does this have to do with our relationship, Paul?"

"Simply put, this 'Big Texas Son' is a winner... and not in a good way," Gilbrech admitted. "He kills without conscience. The only way he came up on our radar was due to your highlighting Mohammed Dafar's involvement. He went insane denigrating your name, knowing all along it might point back at him. Dafar figured he was anonymous. Not so, my little perverted asshole."

"What triggered Dafar was your insightful revelations of Islamic Law in your novels," Gilbrech continued. "Dafar could not keep his fanatical Islamist tendencies to himself. We worked with that formula in monitoring other so called 'Book Killers', data mining for a real life fanatic being unable to resist a 'Book Killing' where the subject strikes too close to home. It proved to be an interesting experiment. Big Texas Son took exception to a number of True Crime authors portraying accurate and damaging profiles of pedophilia tied into serial killings. He went on a crusade to do one star hit pieces reviewing their material, using his anonymous avatar. It didn't take long to discover why. Berringer has a history going back fifteen years involving the disappearances of young girls in places he stays for short periods of time, very much like Kroneg, the difference being the eleven girls were never found.

26

Some portrayals in the True Crime novels listed many disturbing characteristics we think Berringer took exception to, because of their resemblance to him – hence his being unable to resist doing what he thinks are anonymous hit pieces."

"I agree with your premise. Does this guy live in Texas?

"Nope, he's right here in Boston, which was the main reason I came to see you today. Big Texas is planning something we can't ignore. A higher entity in Homeland Security just had his seven year old daughter kidnapped. We're not involved, nor do we want to officially be tied in any way, shape, or form to this case. We know the HS official is being blackmailed to reveal the names on HS's secret terrorist watch list. He's stalling, because the man knows his daughter will disappear no matter what he does. The same supposedly anonymous IP address, used on the Amazon marketplace for Big Texas Son, is also where we've traced the origin for the ransom demand. I want to know if you and Gus would be interested in somehow saving this little girl as El Muerto and Payaso. If you fail, I will find ways to obfuscate your attempt so neither of you will ever be involved. The girl will be out of time soon."

"If you don't play me, I will do anything to get the girl back safely to her parents," Nick stated. "This does look like a job for El Muerto, and his trusty sidekick, Payaso. If something goes haywire, where Gus and I get hung out to dry, the follow-up will be brutal. If you understand that, we may have a basis to discuss this op."

"I understand completely. While I have no idea what your end game is in relation to this operation, I have no one with the tactical expertise or funds to pull this off on their own, and get the girl out alive."

"Give us everything you have on this Big Texas shithead," Nick said. "We'll locate her somehow, probably by making Berringer beg me for the opportunity to reveal her location. Once that's done, we may or may not have a problem. This could get ugly. I don't halfway house these assholes when I get finished interrogating them. Big Texas will die a painful death."

"Understood," Gilbrech stated. "This guy has been on our watch list ever since your first 'Book Killer' revelation. I won't try and pretend I understand why you're doing this for us, but I am grateful."

"Grateful meaning you already know where he is, and the address. That you haven't moved on the intel means you're afraid the Company will get a black eye for operating out of their jurisdiction. I understand it, but I don't agree with it. Bad is bad. Let's concentrate on making this right. Send all the ingredients to Gus. We'll take it from there. I like the new parameters on our cooperation. It appears to only apply though if some bigwig's child or spouse is involved, but I'm okay with that for now. We'll make our own parameters for anything we do separate of the Agency."

Gilbrech handed Gus another memory chip. "Berringer's addresses are on the chip, along with the office he uses under the guise of an environmental protection consultant. He owns three places in the Boston area. This is his home base, and the first time he's ever done anything close to home. I want it to be his last, clean or messy. I'm as nuts as you are, Nick. This comic book persona is so insane as to be useful."

Nick saluted with comical delivery. "El Muerto away! Come, Payaso, we have a mission."

The driver had been parked in front of the Boston Harbor Hotel for many minutes. Nick and Gus stepped out of the limo, leaving Paul Gilbrech laughing. "What did you think, Gus?"

"I think we need to get a little girl safe and sound to her parents while destroying the Western Hemisphere if need be. We're really risking a lot doing this. I'm not convinced this isn't an elaborate trap, but the evidence is damning where Big Texas is concerned. I want to help with this girl's safe return, but I don't want to be sold out doing it. With you, getting sold out is not an option."

"Right you are. We'll need to visit Berringer first. Don't worry. If the girl's alive, we'll find her. There may be problems with the approach, depending on his security system. You let me worry about that. We have the address from the CIA flighty guy who likes our new comic book gig. We'll approach with caution, and I will kill everything in sight except Big Texas. I'm hoping he's alone, but I can't take that for granted until we find the girl. I'll need you to monitor satellite uplink at all times so we can get heat signatures, and watch my back. If he's alone, I'll have to make sure I take him alive. By the way, don't worry about me playing games with this. If it's convenient for El Muerto to leave a calling card once the girl's found, then great."

"I know you wouldn't fool around with her safety," Gus replied. "You going into the park without a gun last night was a bit disturbing though, Muerto."

"Indeed," Nick admitted. "I was caught in the moment, and I nearly cost Sharon her life. El Muerto will have to be much more attentive to his sidekick, Payaso."

Gus sighed as they entered the hotel. "I can tell I'm going to be stuck as Payaso, so I want a scary clown mask. I refuse to look like Bozo."

"Of course, Payaso."

"It's been a long day, and an even longer night. I'll get my tech gear together. Do you have everything you'll need to move on Berringer tonight?"

"Yep. I still have my bag packed from the Kroneg caper, including the 9mm Berretta with silencer I should have taken with me in the park. Do you have our jammer with your gear?"

"I do, but we have to be careful with the EMP gun. That thing is potent. Where the hell did you get it anyway?"

"It was before Rachel and Jean came along. I was supposed to return it, but I told my old dead boss, Frank, an explosion destroyed it, taking down my target. We'll have trouble informing our crew of yet another mission for El Muerto and Payaso, but it can't be helped. I'll meet you in the hallway outside the rooms in fifteen minutes."

"I'll be there if Tina doesn't sap me in the back of my head."

* * *

Nick watched Berringer's house with his night vision monocular. "He's not home. Are you getting any kind of a security system signal?"

Gus met Nick's glance with a nod from his satellite uplink screen. "He has a good one with remote cams. I count eight feeds, which he can access. Do you still want to take a chance on blasting it, and hoping he won't notice?"

"He has no idea anyone is on to him. I don't like gambling, but if I zap his system, I can wait for him inside. Then the only unknown will be whether he returns home with company or not. If he gets spooked, we'll have a hunt on our hands. It's an intelligent gamble, Gus."

"I agree. Do you have a special backup plan if he arrives with guests or cohorts?"

When Nick remained silent, Gus waved him off. "Forget I asked. If you lie down with dogs, you will get fleas."

"This is a tough one, because we're out of our element. Paul was right bringing this to us. The regular uniforms would screw the crap out of an operation like this. They'd be slow on the

30

uptake, ramrod guys in there at first to gather information who had never done it in their lives. If at the end they realized they needed an armed SWAT team, they would have hesitated to the point it would have been a bloodbath or a complete misfire. We're the front line on this, Payaso, and we know how it's done. I kill, torture, and extract info. You watch my back and make sure the info is good. We're a team now. I used to think I was a loner, but trading one liners with you, along with a family in attendance is a step beyond anything I ever imagined. It feels like all this has put me a few steps around the bend. I like it all, and you know what happens if I don't like something."

Gus chuckled. "Yeah, brother... I know. I'll monitor everything from here, so go zap his place, get inside, and let me know if there are any other problems I can help with."

"El Muerto... away!" Nick left with Electro Magnetic Pulse gun in gloved hand along with his equipment bag. He zapped everything from a safe distance away. Moving in next to the door, he picked the lock within seconds. "I'm inside, and scoping out the interior."

"Acknowledged. Be careful of hidden gifts, Muerto. You didn't put that stupid mask on, did you?"

Silence.

"Okay... fine... play the El Muerto card all the way. Enjoy."

"Always." Nick moved into the house interior with mini Mag-lite trained on each area as he passed. He paid close attention to the closets, rapping on the closet walls, searching for any hidden entry to a throne room where Big Texas would either store his mementos or souvenirs heralding his horrific past. He found it in the master bedroom closet, but it was more than he had expected. A room beyond the false wall revealed everything he expected and more. Nick's features tightened. He bent to the little girl tied and gagged within the room's interior, her face a storm of terrified emotions. Nick approached with hands cautioning his good intentions.

"Hey… don't be afraid. I'm here to set you free, honey. Payaso… help me out here."

"The little girl's name is Brenda."

Nick cursed himself for not spending the extra few seconds finding out the girl's name they were rescuing. "Let me know if we get visitors, Payaso. I'm freeing Brenda."

Brenda's eyes widened even more at the mention of her name. Nick moved to her, carefully releasing the bindings, and easing the gag sealing Brenda's mouth. He listened without interruption to her sobbing appeals, finally just gathering her into his arms, hugging her tightly.

"I have you now, Brenda. I won't let anyone hurt you again. You will be with your Mom and Dad very soon."

"Really?" Brenda's joyful face nearly upset Nick into a killer mode best left in the darkness. "That's a really great mask. You…you're a good guy, right?"

"I am El Muerto!" Nick patted her hand. "I'll get you out of here right now, and then-"

"Incoming, Muerto! They arrived an instant ago. There's four of them. I see Berringer. He has three Middle Eastern guys with him."

"After I intercept my guests, I'll bring Brenda out to you, and make Paul send someone for her. I need to do some information gathering before I settle with Big Texas for his sins."

"Understood. Do you need any help?"

"No thanks." Nick smiled at Brenda. "Please stay here for a moment, Brenda. El Muerto has to arrest some bad guys, and then I'll get you out of here, okay? Don't be scared if you hear noises."

"You...you really won't leave me, right?"

"I'll be back real quick, honey." Nick patted her hand. He made a shushing motion to Brenda before closing the false wall.

"They're at the door," Gus said.

"I'm in position." Nick knelt into a shooter's crouch, calmly taking aim at the entryway.

* * *

"When will you have the information?"

"Soon," Berringer told him. "My security system is down. It's important I take care of this. We can take no chances. Once we have the Homeland Security list of suspects, we can build and alter everything. If they have no clue about your cell, Hamas and Isis will strike back at will when needed."

Berringer checked his system, but could not detect what triggered the shutdown. He opened the door, and held it for his companions. "This is crazy. I paid a fortune for this system. At least we'll be able to go over our plans for Boston Harbor. A strike there will-"

The muffled silencer shots, downed his three companions instantly, grabbing their knees while writhing on the floor in agony. Berringer fumbled to open the door, only to have shots smash into both of his shoulders. He pitched face first into the closed door, and down to the floor. He rocked there, hands crisscrossing to his wounds. A masked figure approached. He shot into the feet and knees again of each man. Berringer pleaded as the smiling masked face leaned toward him.

"Don't! We have money! What is this about?"

"Just the usual, Big Tex – justice, retribution, and penance for your sins."

Berringer's mouth tightened at the mention of his Amazon 'Book Killer' alias. "Who are you? We need to make a deal! This doesn't have to happen. Who do you work for? We can deal!"

* * *

"Do you hear this prick, Payaso?" Nick cinched each wounded man with plastic ties at wrists behind their backs, and at the ankles. He confiscated their weapons as well. He then added duct tape to the mouths of each one, cutting down on the noise level considerably. "We have more going on than we thought. It seems Big Tex is a traitor as well as a pedophile. It's going to mean extra time in hell for his companions too. I'll be out with Brenda in a moment."

"I'll call Gilbrech, and let him know what's happening. I'll make sure he sends someone discreet to take Brenda. Damn fine job, Muerto."

"It's going to get even better shortly, Payaso, but Brenda still alive is a gift I do not take for granted."

"Nor will her parents. I'm parking in the front right now."

"Be there in a few." Nick hurried into the master bedroom, ignoring the duct taped mouths whining for something Nick knew they would never get: mercy. He opened the false closet wall, catching a terrified and sobbing Brenda into his arms. "It's all over, little one. I'm going to take you out past the bad men, and to my partner, Payaso. He will have someone to take you to your parents within minutes."

"I…I'm glad you're okay, Muerto."

"I'm fine, honey. The other guys... not so much. Close your eyes if you like. I'll carry you past them quickly."

Nick reached the entrance with the moaning victims of his assault an obvious sideshow for Brenda. She didn't close her eyes. Her mouth tightened into a firm grimace as she recognized Berringer. Brenda pointed at him, while patting Nick's shoulder excitedly.

"He did it! He took me, Muerto!" She sobbed suddenly, tears streaming down her cheeks as she buried her head into Nick's shoulder. "He hurt me... he's bad, Muerto."

Nick glanced down at Berringer, the cold blooded psychopath rising within him in anticipation. He smiled, meeting Berringer's wide eyed look while patting Brenda's back. "I know, honey. I wish there were some way I could erase what he's done, but I can't. I promise you this, El Muerto will never allow him to do it again to any other little one like you."

Brenda pulled back as Nick crossed the threshold. "I don't want you to get into trouble, Muerto. The police won't put you in jail, will they?"

Nick closed the door behind them. "You don't worry about any of that, Brenda. My sidekick, Payaso, is a great guy. I'll leave you with him. Payaso will make sure you are reunited with your Mom and Dad real soon, within hours."

Brenda hugged Nick tightly. "I'd like that so much. I...I never thought I'd see them again."

"You will soon, little one."

Gus met Nick and Brenda only a few steps from their vehicle. "Hi Brenda. I'm El Muerto's long suffering sidekick, Payaso. Don't be afraid. I have someone coming to pick you up in no time at all. We have to allow El Muerto to find out a few things from the people who took you."

Gus opened his arms, and Brenda transferred into them without hesitation, looking back at Nick. "I hope I see you again, Muerto. Thank you! Be careful."

"I'll be careful, Brenda." Nick could not remember a time he wanted to interrogate anyone more than Berringer.

"I love you El Muerto," Brenda called out in Gus's arms.

Nick raised a hand in acknowledgement. "I love you too, little one."

Nick returned to the house, shutting the door behind him, knowing Brenda would soon be in her parents' more protective hands. He smiled with grim intent while listening to the muffled pleas. Nick stepped carefully from one to the other. Pointing at the one in the middle, Nick nodded at his instincts. "You're my bitch, partner. I can tell in your eyes you want to help me with my info gathering. If you cooperate like I think you will, I won't have to do this."

Nick used his stun gun on Berringer's groin area. Big Texas Son screamed a high pitched whine emitted through the duct tape, thrashing violently in his restraints until he passed out. Nick shook his head sorrowfully. "Gee whiz, I guess Big Tex didn't like my demonstration. Anyway… are there any questions? If anyone has any doubts whether I will do this until I get answers, speak up."

Energetic head shakes indicating no questions were all Nick received in answer to his question. He removed the duct tape from over the man's mouth he had picked out to interrogate. "Don't disappoint me with stalling crap and denials. I heard your conversation coming in the house. You bunch have already picked a target. I want to know all the details, and if I think I'm not getting all the details, I will fry the balls right out of your nut-sacks. You three death-lovers can get a quick bullet right between the horns when I get my info, or you can resist. Then you'll find out El Muerto is a very bad man, and that he enjoys his work. I confess I take particular pleasure when asked to interrogate you woman mutilating and baby killing pieces of shit."

Nick put his hands out while standing in front of his captive audience. "Please don't help me willingly. I need to work out some issues. I promise to make your passing into hell a journey you will scream for with pleasure when it arrives."

The man with short trimmed black beard Nick picked for his informant wanted nothing to do with Berringer's experience. "I will talk! Do not torture me! Are…are you allowed to do these things? Are you not supposed to supply us with a lawyer if asked?"

Nick patted his face. "I'm not getting into discussions about my tools. I'm the last man on earth you see in this country, Pookie. When they call me in, they're real worried, and they don't give a shit how I find out what blasphemy you plan to do. They wish only for me to make sure whatever you have planned doesn't happen. Here I am, my little third world troglodytes. I am the last stop on your America tour. Enough about me. Make me happy right now, kids, or I'm going to get busy with Mr. Sparky here."

When Nick fired an arc from the stun-gun in his hands, he noticed all eyes watched with horror, especially the one with questions. Nick's bleak side considered all the possibilities associated with torturing them no matter what they said. It registered in his eyes and mouth despite the El Muerto mask.

"No… do not do this! I will give you the information you seek!"

"Oh… believe me, you will give me all the details in this latest excursion into trying to murder my fellow citizens. What you don't know is if you don't make me very happy, I'm going to show you the dark side of America. It's the side where we more realistic citizens exist for only one reason: the annihilation of our enemies. See… I don't care about your brain washing techniques, your mutilation and subjugation of your women and children. I just don't give a shit what your reasoning is. After 911, I would have wiped your putrid race off the face of the earth… but hey… I'm a psychopath. We psychos see facts clearly in black and white. Every act of terror on earth is being perpetrated by your cult of murderers. Therefore the solution is remove you assholes from existence."

The man on the left began a dark, eyebrows drawn whining hum of obvious disagreement with what Nick had vocalized. Nick smiled and made calming gestures to him. He removed the duct tape from the resistant one. "Ah… look here… we have a dissenter. What's the matter, Pookie? Did I disturb you with my bad words?"

The one Nick had pulled the duct tape off began immediately to thrash from side to side, his head rocking to the tune of, "Allahu Akbar! Allah will protect us! You will not survive his rage, you infidel dog!"

"Oh… I like you already. I bet I survive your ass." Nick patted his first choice again. "Don't worry. I'll be back at you in a few moments, Pookie. I have to entertain your cohort. He seems to think he's better than you, and he's proffering a short sided denigration of your helpful offer. I'm going to show him the error of his ways. You may want to look away, Pookie."

Nick pulled down his new target's pants, smiling at him and meeting his horrified gaze with speculative awareness of what his deliberate actions were doing to his other captives. "I don't believe for a second you murderous morons have the ear of God, but if you do, Allah will surely hear you now.

Nick applied the juice to his second subject with cold expertise. He did it in short excruciating applications, gauged to inject a horrifying promise of what he would do without pause or cause. Only when his alternate choice passed out did Nick glance over at his other guests. Big Tex had regained consciousness, and curled in complete terror, wincing at each scream of agony.

"Well, boys? Want to play my info game with all the details of your plans, or would you like me to tickle your delicate areas until you pray to Allah for me to stop just so you can tell me?"

"Do not touch me with that! I will tell you everything I know," the already nicknamed Pookie stated with fervent plea. "We are planning to blow up the USS Constitution. Our diver already has the C4 in place on the hull!"

Nick's eyes darkened in recognition of an obvious but effective tactic. "I believe you. Here's what we're going to do to prevent that, Pookie. Give me the diver's name and location, what events would trigger it, and most importantly of all, who has the trigger. Are you getting this, Payaso?"

"I've already networked Paul in with us, Muerto," Gus replied. "He has someone on the way to pick up Brenda only minutes away now. Your collar cam is loud and clear, picture clear. I'm recording everything."

"I have a guy I trust in Homeland Security," Gilbrech's voice came on. "I've already put him on alert without any indication of what or who my source on this is. Find out what you can, and I'll send a cleanup crew in to cleanse Berringer's house. You can leave him for the cops later, but his cohorts will go bye-bye without a trace. This is a hell of a lot more than we bargained for."

"Acknowledged." Nick turned his attention to the men still conscious staring at him. "Okay, boys… let's begin. Make this exciting for Muerto or Muerto will make this exciting for you, only in a very bad way."

To accent his point, Nick fired off an arc. After nearly forty minutes, with few follow up questions needing asked, Nick could tell his guests were beginning to repeat themselves. He noticed Big Tex remained quiet while the other three men, including the one regaining consciousness, competed with each other to be helpful.

"That's enough. I've heard a lot of good stuff, boys, especially about the old school signal detonator for doing the job. What I haven't heard is who holds the trigger blowing up the Constitution if your Hamas bosses want a statement made."

Nick saw the three look at Berringer. "Well, that's interesting. Hamas puts the trigger to blowing up a United States monument like the USS Constitution in the hands of a white child molester, serial killer. Who better to take the rap for it if things go wrong, and Hamas decides they don't want to take credit for it. What did Hamas promise you, Big Tex, that Hamas agents would scuttle you out of the country if they had to use you as the fall guy? You would be their Timothy McVeigh, huh? I have to admit, that is clever. I believe we're done here, except of course for the trigger man."

Nick went into Berringer's kitchen. It took him only moments to find a plastic wrap dispenser for covering foods. He rejoined his captive group, and sealed their mouths again with duct tape. "Sorry, boys, I don't have any hotshots for you. Your passing will have some discomfort, because I need to make cleanup in Big Tex's house as easy as possible, and you guys have already been bleeding all over."

Methodically wrapping each man's face tightly in plastic wrap, except for Berringer, Nick waited for the death throes to end. He then dragged Berringer to the kitchen, before cinching his hands and feet together, and taking the duct tape off his mouth. "I have to tell you, Mr. Big, this is not going to be a fun passing for you. I'm a psycho a lot like you, but in a different vein. Brenda told me you hurt her real bad. That means I'm going to hurt you real bad. There are some people who don't believe that torture works. Unfortunately for you, I know it does. First order of business is the triggering mechanism. Where are you keeping it?"

"Think about it, man! If you're going to torture me to death anyway, why should I tell you anything?" Berringer avoided looking at Nick while making his plea.

"Where are you from originally, Mr. Big? I know it wasn't Texas."

"Berkeley." Berringer risked a glance at Nick's face. "Why?"

Nick kicked him in the groin so hard it took Berringer's breath away, his scream sounding like a tea kettle past the first boiling indication. "No reason. When you can speak, tell me where the detonator is or I kick you in the nuts again."

When Berringer could make coherent sounds again, he began sobbing. That earned him a second kick as Nick promised. This time when he could breathe enough to speak, he stayed on subject. "Behind the...the seascape picture! In...in the living room! There's a safe!"

Nick again duct taped Berringer's mouth. Armed with the combination, he emptied the safe. It contained the detonator in a foam encased shielded box, along with nearly fifty thousand dollars, passports, and a set of memory chips in a plastic case. "I have the detonator along with passports, and eleven sixteen gig memory chips. We already have the diver's address. I'll find out if the memory chips carry the location of the girls' bodies. If not, I will find that information out before posing Big Tex."

"Understood," Gus said. "Are you still on with us, Paul?"

"Yes. That is very good news. I already have a team of divers ready to sweep over the hull of the Constitution put together by my HS contact. I'll let them know you have the detonator. It will be tricky work without the diver's firsthand knowledge of his installation. If HS takes him into custody, he won't be cooperative. I know you two have been-"

"We know what's at stake," Nick interrupted. "We'll take it."

"Thank you," Gilbrech said. "Will you be leaving Berringer with El Muerto's calling card?"

"Yes, but I'll find out where his past victims are, one way or another." Nick retrieved a quart container along with his full featured tablet out of the equipment bag after jamming the money in it from Berringer's safe. He inserted the memory chips one after another. They contained the horrific endings of the eleven missing girls with detailed map locations.

"It's all here on the memory chips he kept of everything, including locations. I'll leave them next to Berringer's body for the cops. I'll leave the other contents of the safe for the cleaners in an obvious spot by the Hamas dupes."

"Understood," Gilbrech replied.

"You can stop recording, Payaso. I'll call when I'm done."

Nick returned to the kitchen, where Berringer writhed in agony from his shoulder wounds, and Nick's interrogation method. He ripped the clothing apart covering Berringer's chest, and opened his pants. "I found what you have done. I can't spend the time I'd like with you, but I'll make due with quality over quantity. El Muerto leaves a distinctive feature behind with predators like you, much like you left on those memory chips. I missed out on my last one because the victim was there. Such is not the case this time."

Nick took a sheathed scalpel from the inside of his jacket. He watched the terror emanating from Berringer's eyes, as they remained transfixed on the scalpel, while Berringer shook his head violently from side to side. "El Muerto has examined you, Big Tex, and found you rotting inside. I have something to make you sparkling clean again. El Muerto is something of a surgeon, and the doctor… is in."

Without hesitation, Nick eviscerated Berringer. He poured bleach over the piling intestines. During the fourth application, a blood vessel popped inside Berringer's head. Nick left the plastic case with the memory chips on the side of Berringer's head. After making sure he had his equipment in the bag, including his bleach container, Nick went to the door. He knew Brenda and the other little victims wouldn't feel any better, but Nick did.

"All finished, Payaso," Nick said. "Dr. Muerto has another appointment yet. We have miles to go before we sleep, my treasured sidekick."

"That's creepy, quoting Robert Frost, Muerto. I'll be there in five seconds."

"Goodbye, my friends," Nick waved with grandiose style toward the dead. "El Muerto… away!"

"That's even creepier."

* * *

John Mazdaki awoke with sluggish certainty he was in trouble. Before opening his eyes, John tried moving his arms, legs, and twist at the waist – all to no avail. He could flex his fingers, and move his head, but was otherwise immobile. John opened his eyes, squinting slightly in the low light illuminating what he recognized to be his kitchen. He cursed under his breath, realizing he was duct taped to a kitchen chair. In four hours' time, John would have flown out of Boston to first New York, and then France. A masked man with what he thought looked like a homemade Zorro mask crouched slightly nearer to peer into his face.

"Hi honey, I'm home. It's El Muerto, your host for this early morning's procedure. Dr. El Muerto hurried over to your little bungalow from his last surgical case to discover a few things from you."

"This must be a misunderstanding. I have done nothing wrong. Who are you? If you're here to rob me… do so and leave. Take anything you want." John saw nothing in the masked man's face resembling interest in anything he had to say. John shut up.

"What I need from you John is the exact location and number of explosives you attached to the USS Constitution hull. Before you insult my intelligence with meaningless lies, let me show you something. Pay close attention. I filmed Mel Berringer's demise a short time ago. He mutilated and murdered little girls along with selling out his own country. El Muerto made him pay for his sins. Watch."

John watched the evisceration and bleaching on the tablet screen for only the first two minutes. He looked away, vomiting violently.

"Sorry… El Muerto should have brought a barf bag with him." John felt himself pulled away from his spew. The masked man peered at him once again. "I don't think you wish to die like that, John. Since you don't murder little girls, help me out so I won't have to end you in the same way."

John spat the bile sideways, his mind grasping for something he could sell to keep on living. The masked man gave him a drink, holding the cup to his mouth. "Can…can I live after I give you what you want?"

The man patted his shoulder. "I'm a psychopath, but not a liar. I brought something along to make your passing painless, since you're just a traitor. If you delay any longer in helping me, I'll start considering the innocent men, women, and children who would have died when the Constitution blew into pieces from your planted explosives. That will bring out Dr. El Muerto. The good

Doctor will find out everything, and you will die like your pal, Berringer."

John hung his head for a moment, before looking up again. "The plans and locations are on my laptop computer in the bedroom. They are in a file labeled Caspian Sea. My password to get into the computer is Avesta."

"Let me go make sure you have been helpful, John. I'll be right back."

"There is a pint bottle of Stoli in my freezer. Can I have some before you kill me?"

The masked man went to the freezer, opened the pint bottle he retrieved, and gave John a long pull off the vodka bottle. John coughed a little, his eyes watering. "Thank you."

"De nada."

* * *

Nick opened the laptop, entered the password, and within minutes accessed the 'Caspian Sea' file. "It looks good, Payaso. I have internet here so I'll send the file to our drop immediately. If it looks as good to Paul as it does to me, I'll send Johnny boy on his way, and we can go home. I see no indication in the diagrams of secondary triggers or traps. I'll keep him alive until Paul can get a second opinion. On the way to you now."

"I have it, and so does Paul. He's on with us again now."

"Give us half an hour to go over this, Nick," Paul said. "Great work!"

"Thanks. I'm keeping my Berringer movie. I believe it will help in negotiations with scum-bags, and cut down on the time factor for info gathering."

"Small doubt about that," Paul agreed.

"El Muerto awaits."

Nick returned to Mazdaki. He gave him another swallow of Stoli while they waited. Mazdaki, already a little buzzed, thought Nick needed conversation. "Would you like to know why I turned on my country? When I grew up in Chicago, I-"

"Tut tut, Johnny boy," Nick cut him off. "I believe you have me confused with someone that gives a shit. I'm a killer not a priest. I'll give you another gulp of Stoli if you entertain yourself internally."

"I'll take it."

Nick tipped the Stoli bottle for him a couple more times until Gus confirmed the info. Nick jammed the hypodermic into Mazdaki's neck. "There you go, Johnny boy."

Nick watched eternity arrive to claim Mazdaki a moment later. "All done, Payaso."

"Don't say it!"

"El Muerto... away!"

Chapter Three

The Wedding

"Do you think Dad's okay?"

Rachel paused in helping Jean with the back of her dress. Gus and Tina's simply planned wedding ceremony, only hours away, seemed more complicated the closer it drew near. The only two not stressed were Nick and Gus. They had been joking with each other while trading one liners with married life the main subject. She knew the two men had been involved in saving a little girl, who claimed over and over a superhero named El Muerto rescued her with his sidekick Payaso, the dark man. Rachel suspected a terrorist act rumored to have been avoided had also been Nick and Gus's doing. For plausible deniability, Rachel and Jean kept silent reluctantly, keeping their questions to themselves. They speculated on the quirky adventures of El Muerto and Payaso with much amusement, but only while watching the news, and only to each other.

"Give me a hint. What is it you think isn't okay with him?"

"He used to let us in on more of what he does. We're his team. I thought since he did so much for the government agencies lately, Dad could tell us more."

Rachel put her hands on Jean's shoulders, shaking her slightly. "Do you really think the Company is receptive to Nick creating El Muerto? He knows if we start tossing his new goofball creation amongst us as a joke, one of us will slip in public, and we'll all be in trouble. If he knew we were speculating while watching the news, believe me, he wouldn't like it. I'm happy he's not taking jobs overseas. I look forward to going to Europe someday, but I'd rather it was on a book tour than as a mission cover. I do think he's more uneasy about your interest. He doesn't want you to be an assassin. Come to think of it… neither do I."

Jean's face reflected the ongoing war within her when considering how much she could safely confide in her Mom concerning her future plans. "I can't be exactly like Dad, but I can help people, and get bad guys. If I do find my way in writing novels, I need real life experiences. Maybe someday I could tour with Dad while on a mission together."

"You've certainly managed to scare the crap out of your old pregnant Mom."

"Oh, I forgot to mention taking Quinn along as my apprentice," Jean replied.

Rachel pointed a finger at her now giggling daughter. "Oh… you laugh now. Wait until you have a child of your own. You'll think back on these days with commiseration for what you're putting me through. Quinn will listen to his Mama, and be a good boy."

"He'll follow in the footsteps of his heroic older sister. I'll make sure he calls you at least once a week."

* * *

Screams from the room next to where Gus and Nick were drinking coffee, brought the two men scrambling in to witness the headlock and noogie being applied by Rachel to the squirming Jean. Both were fully dressed in their wedding outfits.

"Ladies!" Nick shouted.

Rachel stopped her assault, panting while still retaining a firm grip on Jean's head. "She started it."

"Did not! Get her, Dad. She's out of control," Jean said from her head-locked position.

48

"Honey?" Nick walked over to soothingly rub Rachel's shoulders. "I'm sure Jean didn't mean to upset you this much. Remember now, we have Gus's wedding to attend as honored guests. This is not the behavior of friends on a wedding day."

Rachel released Jean reluctantly. "She got me on my last nerve in an instant. You don't know her Nick. When this little Jean the assassin grows up, she'll drive us into the mental ward."

"Uh oh. I thought we discussed this, my beloved daughter." Nick drew Jean in with his other arm. "We were to work all aspects of education and training so you will have a myriad of options to choose from before college, always sparing your poor Mom from confrontations of this nature.

Jean rubbed her head. "Mom gave me a noogie on Gus's wedding day. She should be punished."

"Why you…" Nick tightened his hug on Rachel to prevent a reengagement of hostilities.

"Easy, Rach, I know there's some tension with the ceremony. Let's call a truce. I have a feeling the rapid flow of events these past days on tour are beginning to wear you two out. If this is getting to be too much of a strain, I can order a couple first class tickets home, and I'll keep Deke with me."

"Actually, the tour's fun, but we'd like to be more in the El Muerto/Payaso adventure loop," Rachel said. "Dagger is getting into trouble, because she's projecting the unborn Quinn to assassin status, under her supervision, while on missions overseas with El Muerto."

"In that case you deserved the noogie. I'm thinking of giving you one myself for that outrage, young lady," Nick threatened.

"You can't stop Dagger. She is a force of nature." Jean folded arms over chest with chin up in distain.

Gus ruined the solemn upbraiding of Jean with suppressed laughter from the next room.

"I heard that, Payaso," Rachel called out. "Maybe after the wedding, I'll take this brat with me to Charleston to see Rick's Mom and Sister. We'll visit for a week before your book signings there. It will give us a chance to cool down while you and Payaso close out the East Coast stops. Are you sure Deke will be okay? We can take him with us."

"He'll be fine. Deke's been getting three walks a day, and dog specialty foods. He's in doggie heaven. I think you have a great idea about an early start for the family visit. I'll miss you two, but Charleston is as you said, only a week away. El Muerto and Payaso are on an official break, so you won't miss anything. Our hotel is moving Tina and Gus into the wedding suite, and it is fabulous, right Gus?"

Gus emerged from the room he eavesdropped from. "It is incredible. This would be a great time for you and Jean to scout out our hotel surroundings in Charleston while visiting family. I'm sure Nick has us booked into the best available, and you have to admit this tour in first class everything is an addictive treat."

"I can't argue with you there," Rachel admitted. "I miss our place in Pacific Grove though. It's the best place I've ever lived in. Hell… I even miss waitressing at Joe's."

Nick embraced Rachel. "The simple life is incredible, and I share your passion for it, my love. I knew we were soul mates the moment I saw your picture."

Rachel pushed away. "Wait a minute. The first time you saw a picture of me was when you were issued a contract to kill me."

Nick shrugged while Gus and Jean enjoyed the moment loudly in amusement. "Well… yeah… there is that. I think you destroyed my soul mate moment, you Philistine."

Not even Rachel could comment on that statement for many moments with both Jean and Gus succumbing to Nick's one liner.

"Okay… we all have smiles on our faces. Can we now show up for the long suffering Gus's wedding without any further distractions? We're his crew today. We want Tina to have a wonderful moment before Payaso ruins her dreams."

It took an intervention by both Dagger and Rachel to intercede between Gus and Nick.

* * *

"I can't understand you," Rachel whispered. "You claimed to outgrow being called Danger Girl, and then you embrace an even more comic book nickname, Dagger. What is going on in that mind of yours, child?"

"Shush, Mom. We're not supposed to talk," Jean whispered back.

"I'm curious, damn it. First, you're all grown up, and suddenly you're in fairytale assassin land complete with killer nametag."

"Do we have to talk about this now?" Jean's hushed question did nothing to unfurrow Rachel's brow or embarrass her into silence. "Besides, Dagger is a great name. I'm excited with all this stuff Dad and Gus have been doing. You saw Brenda talking about being saved on TV."

"I did," Rachel hissed out the side of her mouth as Nick glanced back at the two. "I also heard what happened to the girl's attacker. I don't think you could do that. Dagger's not a force of nature, but Nick surely is."

Jean stared at Rachel, trying to perceive what induced her Mom to begin the conversation so suddenly at Gus's wedding. "Are you worried about leaving Dad?"

The question startled Rachel. She grasped Jean's hand, brushing away a tear beginning to form with the handkerchief in her other hand for the wedding. "Yes… damn it. Sorry to spring the Dagger thing on you. My hormones are racing thanks to your brother Quinn. I thought visiting your Grandma Mona before Nick arrives in Charleston seemed like a great idea, until my imagination kicked in. Do you think El Muerto will run amok once we're gone?"

Jean shook her head. "Dad promised they're taking a break. He said it's too hot in the news for playing superhero. Muerto went viral on YouTube with the pictures and headlines spliced together with that eerie song 'Mad World' playing in the background. One of the crime scene photos from the way that guy Berringer died was leaked. It's on the clip too."

"I hope Gus can remind him to keep playing author on tour until he meets us in Charleston." Rachel took a deep breath, exhaling slowly. "Nick's terrifying, but I can't think of life without him."

Jean leaned her head against Rachel's shoulder. "That makes two of us."

They waited in the small chapel, where a Justice of the Peace would preside over the small ceremony. Gus's brother Phil escorted Tina in to give away the bride. Rachel acted as Maid of Honor, with Phil's wife Julie and Jean next to her. Nick would be Gus's best man. Katie Nason, Phil's daughter followed Tina and Phil into the chapel with a small flower bouquet. Nick and Gus awaited the bride with welcoming smiles. Phil passed Tina's hand on cue from the Justice of the Peace to Gus. The nerves, hesitation, and uneasiness ended a short time later after what turned out to be a touching ceremony.

Congratulations rang out long and loud after the kiss. Family and friends drove Rachel's dark thoughts into her mind's recess for the time being, but the conversation made a lasting mark on Jean, who watched Nick uneasily. She couldn't keep from wondering if maybe her deadly step-dad would indeed succumb to his new quirky creation. The strains of 'Mad World' played on in her head while watching Nick hug Gus and Tina, a living illustration of a paradox. Jean knew no matter how Rachel or Nick tried to dissuade her, she planned to follow in Nick's footsteps. She smiled, knowing making her Mom mental would be detrimental to future plans. Nick turned toward her suddenly, pointing at her with a grim expression. His sudden notice, as if he had read her thoughts, shocked Jean out of her reverie. Nick walked away from the group.

"You worry me girl when I see that look on your face. I see Jean the Assassin skulking between your ears. If you continue with this, you're going to drive your Mom insane."

"How…how did you know I was thinking that?"

"Your first lesson will be the poker face needed not to display everything on your features to someone who knows you like an old marked deck of cards, Dagger."

"Mom's worried El Muerto will go off the deep end if we leave you here alone."

"I'll talk to her. Besides, Gus will be with me."

Jean giggled. "Lately, Payaso has been like your own personal sock puppet."

"You take that back, you disrespectful bowl of Coco Puffs."

53

That comeback took Jean moments to overcome. "Okay… I take it back, but you and your sidekick have to take a vacation from the superhero trail if you want to keep Mom sane."

Nick guided Jean into the midst of the celebration. "I can't do that right now, Jean. I'm working through a few personal items. You concentrate on having a great time with your Grandma. I may not get anything on the radar anyway before we leave. Gus made me realize there's no going back. I plan on doing right, but pretending I'm a pedestrian following street signs blinking when to walk and when not to - is just out of my range."

"You weren't kidding with me about training, and giving me a chance though, right?"

"Absolutely not. If you keep pushing the Dagger nickname though, one of these days you'll regret it."

"If you can be El Muerto, I can be Dagger."

Nick smiled, clasping Jean tighter to him. "Remember what I said, Dagger."

* * *

Outside, the police were waiting for them in the anteroom of the chapel. Nick stepped forward immediately. "Hello, officers. How may we help you?"

"Are you Nick McCarty?"

Nick smiled with friendly intent at the huge black police officer with Stallings on his nametag. Jean instinctively gripped Nick's hand, looking up at the police officer with concern. "I am indeed, Officer Stallings. How can I help you?"

Jean's physical interjection made Officer Stallings pause, seeing the little girl grasping Nick's hand with both hers staring at him unblinkingly. "We did some background checks on you,

54

because of providing security for the book signings in Boston, after what happened to you in New York with that Kader family member attacking you. Ah… I…I've talked with Sergeant Dickerson in Pacific Grove. You know him, don't you, Sir?"

"Yes," Nick answered, enjoying Jean's very effective ploy. "Sergeant Dickerson and I have become friends after some difficult happenings in my chosen hometown."

Stallings smiled. "He claims you're Pacific Grove's 'Castle' like in the TV show."

Nick laughed. "Yeah… I'm Castle in that I bought the police force in my chosen hometown an expresso machine. I doubt he considers me a go to source for solving crimes."

"I think you'd be surprised by how much substance Dickerson credited in your thought processes regarding those 'difficult happenings'. The way you handled the media trying to destroy you was an effort I admired very much. The faceoff at your house… that was the best. I know you can take the heat, and there will be heat on this one. I also know now you hold FBI and US Marshal credentials, and they're not honorary. That surprised the hell out of me. Anyway, what I'd like to ask is if you'd take a look at a woman police officer's murder with us?"

Nick was tallying the caveats in his head Stallings alluded to. *At least Rach can see I didn't create this situation.* "Sure, I'd be happy to help if I can. We're in the middle of my best friend's wedding aftermath though. Is this something that just happened?"

"No," Stallings admitted. "I'm sorry we interfered today. This was the one place we knew you'd be as sited in the newspapers."

Stallings handed Nick his card. "Please call me when you're free. I'll send a car for you. If you could keep this to yourself I would be grateful."

"We'll keep a lid on it, Sergeant. I'll call as soon as possible." Nick shook hands with Stallings, and watched the officer retreat to his squad car with the two men accompanying him.

Nick turned to see his entire band of merry wedding attendees staring at him with big frowns, except for Gus, and of course Jean. "What?"

"You could have blown him off," Rachel pointed out. "I think you may be confusing the concept of doing right."

"Doin' right ain't got no end," Nick quoted from 'The Outlaw Josie Wales'.

"That was a bad guy who said that in the movie, Dad," Jean said.

"So... what's your point?"

* * *

After saying goodbye to the participants not staying at the Boston Harbor Hotel, Nick immediately turned to Gus. "Hey buddy... when should we bring the champagne and finger foods for that exquisite hot tub you have in the wedding suite?"

Gus roared with laughter. Only after seeing Nick standing there staring at him with a hurt expression did Gus respond. "You're serious? You ain't comin' up to our room, Muerto. I'll call security if you force me to."

"Payaso!" Everyone enjoyed Nick's open mouthed surprised expression. "How could you say that to me, your mentor and friend?"

"You're not my mentor. Take the family down to the hotel pool and hot tub. Enjoy. See you in the morning. Thanks for coming. Goodnight."

Before Gus could get on the elevator with Tina who was on the verge of hysterics, Nick grabbed his arm. "Couldn't we at least come visit for an hour or so to see the wedding suite?"

Gus carefully picked Nick's hand off of his arm. "I have your e-mail address, Muerto. I'll take pictures, and send them to you."

Nick grinned as Gus ducked into the elevator, leaving his partner with a little finger wave. Rachel and Jean were of course enjoying the Muerto/Payaso interaction to the maximum with actual hoots of glee. "Oh... I see now. It's a good thing Muerto is needed elsewhere."

Nick's statement of intent shut off the laughter within seconds.

"You're not thinking about consulting on a murder case, are you?"

"What would you have me do, Rach? I'm a little exposed here in Boston. Come on. We'll talk about it in the room for about thirty seconds. Then I'll need to go help the police if I can."

"Can I go with you, Dad?"

"Sure, if you want me in jail for child abuse." Nick led the way onto the next elevator to their floor. "You two can come with me while I walk Deke."

"Pass," Rachel said.

"Ditto," Jean echoed.

"It's no damn wonder Deke likes me better than you ingrates."

"We made him a homemade Nick doll. He chews on it while you're away," Jean stated.

"He's very attached to it," Rachel added. "He cries when we have to take it before you see what he's chewing the shit out of."

Nick watched them scurry down to the hotel room, wondering where he lost his edge. When he reached the hotel room door, Deke was waiting outside of it with his leash in his mouth. Nick went up to the door. "Really?"

Hearing the snickering inside, he leashed the very appreciative Deke, and walked him to the elevator. He had a waste bag dispenser built into the leash handle. "We're going on a long walk before I collude with the local constabulary, Deke. I need to clear my head from evil thoughts in regard to your original owners."

Deke leaned into Nick comfortably as the elevator descended toward the first floor. It stopped on the fourth floor. A young couple entered the elevator, cringing to the corner of the elevator furthest from Nick and Deke, who never moved from his seated position next to Nick. The man was Nick's height, with long dark hair tied in a ponytail, and a glowering expression. He wore a muscle shirt with very effective presence. His companion, an auburn haired beauty in black miniskirt and red halter top huddled next to him.

"It's okay folks. Deke is very friendly. Deke… shake with the lady."

Deke walked over, sat in front of the woman, and held his right paw up. The woman at first panicked, but as Deke kept his pose, she giggled. Kneeling down, the young woman gripped Deke's paw with obvious enjoyment.

"You are so cute!"

"I hate that they allow these flea infested mongrels to stay at this hotel," the woman's companion said.

nothing comes for free – not life, liberty, the pursuit of happiness… or freedom.

Stallings pointed a finger at Nick. "You're a killer. I know it. I can feel it. I can see it in your eyes. I don't know how in hell you acquired the position you're in, with the credentials you have. You're a hell of a lot more than a novelist."

"Let's stop dancin', Barry. Tell me what you really want from me."

"The woman police officer who was killed… she was my niece. Her death will probably kill my sister, because Cinny was her only child. I know the guy she was seeing knows who killed her."

"Now… tell me how you know Paul."

"I… that is…" Stallings threw his hands up in the air, obviously angry with himself. "I vowed to Paul I'd figure a way to ask you to consult without mentioning him. We served together in the Marines. Would it be possible to keep this between us, no matter what you decide?"

Nick smiled. "Sure, Barry, but unless you plan on never seeing Paul again, or talking to him, my advice would be to tell him the truth. Your powers of deception lack passion. That's okay though. Tell Paul no blood, no foul. He'll understand. I'm sure he had his reasons for not bringing this to me directly. Give me the Reader's Digest version of your niece's death. If you managed to get Paul involved enough to give me as a referral, there's something more to it than a tragic death."

"You're right. Paul's eyes glazed over until I told him the undercover assignment Cinny died on involved the Isis jihadi cult. She spoke Farsi and Arabic. The FBI recruited her to infiltrate a cell operating in Boston. Paul thinks they were linked to another group with a plan to blow up the USS Constitution."

Stallings reached into his jacket pocket, and retrieved a plastic encased memory disc, handing it to Nick. "I received this yesterday. Cinny sent it to me hours before she died. It's an audio recording of a meeting she infiltrated. My guess is that she didn't trust whoever was handling her with the FBI. Paul guaranteed me he'd find out who when he gave me your name to contact. I don't know if I can trust anyone in my precinct either. Any paranoid crap I babbled about would land me a suspension, or a direct order to stay out of the case."

"Is the boyfriend a suspected member in this Isis cult?"

"Yes. He was the first contact she attracted while attending services at the Islamic cultural center of Boston. Cinny worked slowly over many months to gain trust and familiarity. Ebi Zarin began paying close attention to her. They dated under the stringent code under which she swore to abide in her conversion to Islam. She recorded everything that went on inside the Center."

"So what made her suspect this Ebi Zarin?"

"One of the guys she saw him speak with at the Center was James Sherazi, a main FBI suspect in the Isis cell. They were to get a search warrant covering Zarin's communications, bank accounts, and surveillance. Cinny disappeared the day after. They found her in the Charles River Basin. She'd been shot in the back of the head with a .22 caliber. Zarin had an airtight alibi, of course. He played the heartbroken lover card."

"Were they living together?"

"No. It would have blown her cover. I never got to talk with her during the assignment. Cinny was to have been shunned by her family for being interested in Islam."

Nick listened to the parameters the poor dead girl abided by, only to be murdered anyway. He had no doubt Stallings was right about Zarin. With the threats made promising attacks by

64

hidden cells inside America by Isis and Hamas, Nick could understand why Paul steered Stallings his way, but not the circumstances. Gilbrech had something else in mind besides justice, or helping out an old Marine buddy.

"You do understand I don't serve search warrants or bring people to justice, right?"

Stallings nodded. "Believe me. Paul made that abundantly clear. He told me if I was desperate enough to call you, and wanted to remain breathing when this ended, I was not to interfere or remember anything concerning your actions."

"How do you feel about that, Barry?"

"Like I'm in way over my head, but I want this guy dead. I'm a cop with a family. The FBI already questioned Zarin. He gave them nothing. I don't have a clue what course I could take to get the real killer that wouldn't put me in prison. In addition to my wanting to avoid prison, I have no experience with terrorist cells, or interrogations. I expected when Cinny was killed, there would be FBI agents tearing her murder case apart. Instead, they brought in Zarin, asked him a few questions, and went away. Maybe you could tell me what the hell happened."

"I'll check the disc and get in touch with you later."

"It's in Farsi, I think."

"I speak Farsi, Arabic, and Pashtu. I'll call if I find something new. If not, I'll have to question Zarin. I probably will anyhow, but I'd like to have some information before I do. I'm glad you didn't let them sweep this under the rug. If an Isis cult is linked to the Hamas group blamed for the USS Constitution bombing threat, it means Boston is still a target."

"Thank you. Call me at any hour, Nick."

The men shook hands. "I will." *No, I won't.*

* * *

Rachel and Jean with Deke at their sides boxed Nick in as he sat at the room desk with his satellite linked laptop. He ignored their coughs, mutters, and throat clearings while his fingers sped across the keys, causing constantly changing windows of information and mug shots. Rachel bopped him in the back of his head, drawing a giggle from Jean, and a sigh from Nick.

"So much for the break in the action, Muerto. We want to know what you have to say for yourself."

Nick turned in the chair, taking Deke part way on his lap, scratching the dog's rear end as he liked. Nick chuckled as Deke put his nose in the air with contented ecstasy. "Okay, Deke's happy. Would you like me to scratch your butt too, Rach?"

It took a few moments for Nick's fem force to recover from his comedic offer with Rachel faking a full blown choke hold on Nick. That ended quickly as the happy Deke turned feral at the cause of his rear end scratching being curtailed. He had Rachel's right hand in his mouth gently with an all business snarl within seconds. Rachel disengaged, pointing at her dog with tight lipped angst.

"You traitor!" Rachel accused, as Jean enjoyed the moment loudly. "Muerto won't always be at hand to protect you, pal."

Deke calmly sat down, and offered his paw. Rachel turned away, arms folded across her chest. "Apology not accepted."

Deke watched her for a moment, then dropped his paw, and perched into rear end scratching position on Nick's lap to much amusement from everyone, including Rachel.

"We want you to go swimming with us down at the huge indoor pool they have, Dad. C'mon. We leave tomorrow morning for Charleston. Can you take a break for a couple hours, swim, and hit the hot tub with us?"

66

Nick suppressed the excuses foaming to his mouth with an iron will. His research into the case had him in a vice of considered future mayhem, and myriad ways to bring it about. One look at Jean's pleading face though and he was lost. "Of course I can. I have one condition though."

"Booze, right?"

"Very perceptive, my love," Nick acknowledged. "I think I will need two bottled waters with our orange flavored drink packs emptied into them. Then I will swill enough to add a double Bushmill's Irish into each. I believe I will be ready for the pool if those terms are met."

"Agreed," Rachel stated. "What about Deke?"

Nick patted Deke down. He stood and went to the everyday pack he always shouldered while walking Deke, or moving from one place to another. He took out a huge beef bone he had procured from a butcher's shop. Deke smelled it immediately as Nick unwrapped the prize, eyes glued to the treat with deadly concentration. "I have something to keep Deke's attention, while cementing me into his number one human slot."

Nick gave over the bone to a deliriously happy, tail wagging Deke. Nick laughed at Rachel and Jean posing in arms over chest disapproval.

"That's bribery!"

"Good one, Dad," Jean admitted. "If it gets you down to the pool with us and your drug of choice, I like it."

"Then the hell with national security, terrorists, and mass murdering cults… down to the pool I go. I would take this time to remind both of you the reason we have not gotten near the pool together is your Mom's nearly manic adversity to being seen in a bathing suit. How is it she's happy to go there now? Did you two find her a burka bathing suit?"

Rachel gasped in indignation, but received no support from her daughter, bent over at the waist enjoying the burka dig. "Yes... I look very matronly in my bathing suit. Now let's go before you pop my self-esteem bubble completely. I find it rudely inconsiderate of you to make fun of my looks when I'm carrying your child."

Nick and Jean did a dual gagging response in reply to Rachel's whine. "Fine! Let's go before you two turn me into a closed in pariah."

Jean high-fived Nick's held up hand while Rachel's back was turned. "I heard that smacking of disrespectful hands! You two are dead to me! Dead... to... me!"

Chapter Four

Isis

Nick glanced down at his iPhone from his surveillance of a Roxbury, MA warehouse. He had taken Rachel and Jean to their flight, walked Deke twice, and kept pursuing the angles derived from correspondence between Zarin and James Sherazi. Nick hit pay-dirt at a huge warehouse on Clifford Street. He hit the speaker button while still keeping sight on the warehouse.

"A little busy here, Payaso. Don't you have something better to do where you are, like enjoy your incredible hot tub with your lusty new bride?"

"Damn it! I knew you'd go on mission without your trusty sidekick! What the hell?"

"You were only married a couple of mornings ago, Payaso, my unromantic stooge. You should still be sweeping the lovely Tina off her feet, while living the dream in your plush suite. Unfortunately… you've decided to harass your hardworking superhero friend: El Muerto. For shame, Payaso… for shame!"

"Are you done now?"

"Of course not."

"You do know I've FaceTimed you, and I can see you ignoring me, even from the seat, right?"

Nick kept his night vision range finders on the surroundings of the warehouse he had under surveillance. "You're only a touchscreen away from talking to empty air, my bored friend. It wouldn't be because Tina has been with you so long, the wedding suite opulence has already worn off to be replaced with her caustic boredom, would it?"

Silence. Crickets… and then Gus's muttering curses. "You've made me into an action slut. Thanks to you, even my honeymoon seemed less enthralling than the murderous missions you coerce me on. I even miss being called Payaso. I'm sick! I need help!"

Nick nearly lost his bearings listening to his old friend. "Enough. I have to keep you safe from this one, my faithful sidekick. It's too dangerous. I am surrounded by people wishing me harm: police, terrorists, CIA, FBI… hell even the Boston Firemen will be calling for my head by the time I get done with this unauthorized op. I cannot speak more without risking discovery, Payaso. Go forth, and do good deeds."

"Please! There… I said it. He'p me… he'p me."

"What about Tina?"

"What about her?"

Nick laughed. "Okay… you got me, Payaso. I'll call you from the room if this goes to the next stage I'm following."

"Acknowledged. If it takes more than a few hours, your brave sidekick may already have perished by self-inflicted wounds."

"Damn… Payaso?" Nick held in laughter with every fiber of his being. "You're making me doubt your humanity, your loving nature, your bonding with Tina as your soul-mate, your-"

"One more word, Muerto, and I slash my wrists!"

"I'll be talking at you soon, Payaso." Nick disconnected, noting Gus would be invaluable with him on this. He had stayed rogue by choice, fielding and laying off Sergeant Stallings' calls.

Nick noticed from his first admission Stallings wanted 'justice'. He wanted a terrorist cell frog marched out of a building to face the American peoples' righteous anger at their planned dastardly deed. Nick didn't do 'justice'. He killed bad guys now exclusively, and no one on earth did it any better when Nick embraced a job like he did this one. He had listened to one of the Isis Islamists in a cave somewhere talking to a terrorist enabling Al Jazeera dupe, claiming on the news earlier in the day that their acolytes would bathe the American people in blood. Nick grinned. *Yep, gonna' get me some of that.*

Then within minutes of Gus's call, Sherazi arrived with a half dozen goons at the warehouse Ebi Zarin had already entered. Nick dutifully filmed everything while texting Gus, narrating the time, the participant he recognized, and the location, as he had done with Zarin. He left immediately. He had a cam in place, and listening devices already implanted. Nick arrived at the Boston Harbor Hotel moments later. He laughed, seeing Gus waiting out front with a 'Go Bag'. Nick popped the lid on his rented Ford Edge. Gus threw in his bag, and slid into the passenger side seat with his satellite laptop in hand.

"Payaso… my old friend."

"Shut up, Muerto. What are you up to, and who do I have to kill to get in on it?"

Nick drove toward the warehouse again, but stopped a few blocks away from the hotel. "Take the wheel, Gus. What did you bring?"

"Flash bangs, your MP5 with silencer, your Glock with a silencer, and that Italian Stiletto you like so much."

"I love you, man!" Nick traded places with Gus, but retrieved implements from both Gus's bag and his own, laughing out loud when he found a full head evil clown mask. He placed his earwig in place as did Gus. Nick also fastened his cam into place

71

so Gus could follow his every movement. He had already put on a Kevlar vest before going on his surveillance run. "Nice mask, Payaso. How did you know I was coming back to the hotel?"

"Gut feeling from your text. I knew you were within a short time frame to act. We have a book signing in Salem the day after tomorrow. When you brought me on board, I figured it would be tonight. You're going Ronin on this job, huh?"

"Not quite," Nick replied. He explained the basic parameters including Cinny's death, and that she was Stalling's niece. "Several agencies know this Isis wing has been marked for sanction. The main guy to get alive is James Sherazi. Several factors filter in if that ever gets done. I'm not sharing with Sergeant Stallings. He's an above board police officer with impeccable service record. He's lost his niece to these bastards, and he knows his sister won't recover from her daughter's death. I'm going to close this one out myself with your help, Payaso. Want a piece?"

"Hell yeah, Muerto!"

Nick smiled. "Good, because so do I. Cinny will get justice, but whether James Sherazi will live through it will be in God's hands. You're in my ear, Payaso. Pay no attention to anything other than warnings going out to the police. This warehouse isn't anywhere near a housing district. Thanks for coming in on this, my friend."

Gus reached over to grip Nick's shoulder without looking away from the street ahead as he followed the GPS screen. "You're doing right, Muerto. I got you into this crap while whining about you doing bad things in retirement. I see a hell of a lot more good you've already done since then. I'm happy to be a part of it. I don't much give a damn how you do it."

Nick glanced over at Gus with a grin. "That's good, Payaso, because when I get inside the warehouse with those bastards, only divine providence will allow Sherazi or Zarin to survive. If they do survive, then my plan starts. I need to take them somewhere to get answers. It won't be pretty, but I plan on making this Isis/Hamas cult combination extinct. The damn government keeps letting the cell members of these cults in, as if they're simply poor immigrant trolls. Jesus… God in heaven, I'd like to know why."

"You and the rest of the country. I've been thinking about it. It's possible these idiots have a number of explosive materials in there with them."

"I'm counting on it. That's the part I'm rolling the dice on as to whether the right guys survive. I hate these bastards, Gus. I have many contacts and friends in the Middle East. You met a few of them when I did the hit on Abdul Nazari. I'm willing to deal with these clucks in the Islamist murder cults on a one on one basis like Isis and Hamas when they're not here trying to blow us to kingdom come. The turds get let into America, making headlines in return for our generosity by claiming they will bathe us in our own blood, and I figure bypassing the idiots who let them in is the only way to deal with them."

"I hate to say it, but I don't see any other effective way. The damn people in charge are so busy being politically correct, they'll sacrifice us plain old American citizens in any number necessary to be thought of as being down with the Islamic struggle. Good God, brother! Now, you've triggered my media induced Islamophobia!"

Nick chuckled. "You're screwing up the media word application saying that. Islamophobia means 'fear of'. We need a new term. How about Islamist-interfectorem?"

"It has a nice ring to it. What's it mean?"

"Islamist killer. Interfectorem is Latin for killer."

"The term fits better than phobia for sure," Gus agreed. "We're not in fear of these murderous jackasses, cutting the heads off American citizens with dull knives. Americans want them handled like the chicken-shit cowards they really are."

"Save it, Payaso. I'll give you some closure with these hyenas on our target list. One of these days though, I'll probably go mental, and snatch someone highly positioned in government. The need to know why we keep allowing immigration from the Middle East will finally overwhelm my common sense."

"I can tell you the answer without the need for interrogation of the narcissistic pawns in our government. It's the money. They buy off politicians, and they're damn good at it, the Saudi's especially. Back to business, Muerto. We're on Clifford Street. How do you want to do this?" Gus parked on the roadside.

Nick retrieved his satellite uplink laptop from the back seat. In moments he had his cams on line. "We're already within range. I couldn't get a cam inside without killing someone in this short of time period. I did manage two cams aimed at new arrivals. Before I texted you, I filmed our two main guys entering with a thug posse. I'll send the video to Paul so he'll be able to cross off the corpses. I'm going to recon the place before I do anything. I planted an audio pickup I'm listening to right now. Unfortunately, I believe they have an underground chamber where they're doing their dirty deeds, shielded from any audio pickup. If I can get inside to confirm my hunch, I may be able to toss down some party favors into their playroom. It would depend on whether they're stupid enough not to have a sentry keeping watch. I need you to keep the head phones on, network the audio so we both can hear. With the headphones on you'll be able to hear anything down to a pin drop inside. If my recon or entry cause a commotion, you'll be able to alert me."

"Sounds good. How far away do you want to start your approach?"

"Fifty yards should do. If they have motion detectors, I didn't trigger them the last time. I think they feel pretty safe."

"I know they wouldn't simply leave a door open for you," Gus pointed out. "I'm betting they have more than a deadbolt on their doors."

Nick turned the laptop so Gus could see the screen. He cued up a video clip. "HD baby."

Nick zoomed the screen to the entrance doorway, making the electronic keypad on the frame fill the screen. Gus watched as the first man approaching the keypad entered the code. Nick slowed it down, so Gus could see the numbers and sequence perfectly.

"That's cheatin'."

"So… I'll finger in the code, enter, and wait for you to listen. If you don't hear anything, I'll find their underground terrorist toy cellar. Wait until you hear what I have planned for the contestants who survive my initial greetings. Your new mask will fit right in."

"Somehow, I don't like the sound of that." Gus left the lights off on the final approach, moving slowly toward their destination while still hugging the roadside. "It seems like a sure way to become incarcerated, Muerto."

Nick sighed. "I was only incorporating a great way for you to try out your neat new mask, and have some fun."

"What kind of fun?"

"The kind where murdering jackals end their lives in comical form."

"You thought eviscerating Big Tex and pouring bleach on his intestines was comical," Gus replied.

"So what's your point?"

* * *

"I'm ready," Nick whispered.

"I have my ears on. Do it."

Nick used the code. The green light blinked on, and Nick went in with the MP5 with silencer ready to fire. Only red safety lights illuminated the interior ground floor with a dull eerie effect. Nothing moved within Nick's field of vision. He knelt next to the now closed door, using his night vision ocular to scan the inside with patience attained in many past deadly encounters. He resisted the impulse to move his scan quickly, even though the warehouse area near the entry seemed empty of anything other than some shelving and crates. Waiting for Gus to report on any sign of discovery audible on the audio pickup he had installed earlier, Nick moved away from the entrance.

"Nothing so far, Nick. I'll let you know when the five minutes pass you specified."

"Acknowledged."

After hearing the allotted time had passed, Nick checked the entire warehouse perimeter for anything out of the ordinary. He did brief inspections into crates on shelves near the walls, but found nothing. Working his way around the outer circumference, Nick kept the interior in sight also, searching for anything from his vantage point resembling a downward access. He inspected the warehouse in diminishing circles, paying close attention to shelving and crates. Near the end of his third circle, Nick spotted the hatch. Its cover of tattered canvas revealed the sharp corners of an entry to something below. Inspecting it, Nick found the cover canvas, dirty and grimy with grease and oil, to be a prop glued onto the hatch cover.

"Found it. Take the headphones off, Payaso. This may get very loud."

"I'm set, Nick."

Nick pulled the pin on the military tear gas canister first, opened the hatch, and threw it down inside what he could see was a well-lighted area below. He knelt on the hatch, grinning. A military grade tear gas canister is nothing like anything civilians imagine. In an enclosed space, the formula causes projectile vomiting, amongst numerous agonies not common knowledge to the general populace. Picture a slightly downgraded version of nerve gas. Through the cover, Nick heard screams, panic, and distress without remorse.

"Oh ye soldiers of Islamist murder, here comes baby."

Nick pulled the pin on a military concussion grenade, popped the hatch slightly, and threw it down into the chamber. This time, Nick ran for it, unknowing of whether it would set off C4 charges capable of leveling the block. He was crouching with the entrance door open when the blast projected only a muffled whump noise. He returned to the hatch.

"I believe we'll have live ones, Payaso."

Gus took a deep breath, allowing the pent up adrenaline rush to seep out slowly. "Damn, that was a miracle. Why don't you think the explosives went off?"

"Maybe they're innocent Muslim lambs, meeting underground to exchange ideas on the passages from the Koran."

It was many moments before Gus could speak after Nick's reply. "Okay... okay... how long before you can check on the banditos?"

"I'm putting my mask on now. I'll know what's happening in a couple minutes. How's my button cam working?"

77

"Perfectly. I've recorded everything since you entered the building without a hitch. They sure didn't leave anything in the main warehouse to be detected. I'm watching, so give me a view of everything when you go down into that hole, partner."

"Will do. I'm certain they have first class ventilation down there, so clearing away the aftermath of my party favors should be in progress right now." Nick finished fastening his oxygen breathing apparatus into place. He opened the hatch to the smoky interior, descending with his MP5 ready.

The chamber below, complete with writhing and comatose figures in various positions strewn where they gave up any semblance of recovery, brought another smile to Nick's face. He investigated the lower realm with cold efficiency, noting the small arms armory, ammunition, and explosives within sight. Nick then went from man to man.

He fired a three shot burst from his MP5 through the heads of each man not either Zarin or Sherazi. "Not you… not you… not you… hey we have a winner." Zarin was unmoving. He had passed out during his first moments after the concussion grenade went off. Nick used his plastic ties to restrain him. "I have Zarin still alive and breathing, Payaso. I'm moving on."

　　　　* * *

Gus cringed in spite of how he felt. He knew each burst meant a death. It was a false positive. The underlying thread of completion stabbed into his brain. He rejoiced in their deaths as if he were on a battlefield with life or death choices. He knew every life Nick took represented an enemy unable to plot the demise of a country Gus embraced above even life. That America unknowingly employed a quirky cold blooded killer without remorse or mercy to correct mistakes its hierarchy made in policy no longer bothered Gus. He and Nick were soldiers. They didn't invent the problems, but Gus guiltily enjoyed being part of the bloody solution.

"Oh man, Payaso," Nick complained in his ear. "It's a good thing you aren't down here with me. What a mess. I have to rethink using the tear gas grenade in the future. Thank God we have the tarp in the back. I found Sherazi. I should add Fabreeze to my equipment bag. This boy needs a shot of April fresh scent."

Gus laughed. "I see how well your prep work did with the risk factor. There's no gun battles after you use that military duo. How come they don't do use the dynamic duo in combat on house to house situations?"

"Probably something ultimately idiotic like the sensibilities of our enemies. When I was with Delta, we used the duo, but only if we didn't have some CNN traitor or other media embed to film the grisly effects. There is a shit load of everything imaginable down here. We'll need Paul in on this. I believe all will be forgiven for my rogue op when he sees the treasure we've uncovered. Network him in with us, Gus. I don't think this can be turned over to the locals this time, including the FBI."

"On it."

* * *

Nick dragged the unconscious Zarin and Sherazi into a clear area. He tested the air and found it bearable so Nick put away his mask, and put on a different black mask – that of El Muerto. With no intention of dragging both men up the stairs, Nick washed away the residue from their faces before slapping each of them into blinking, agonized consciousness. "Hello, boys. You naughty little terrorists have been very bad boys. I'm here to help you pay for your sins. I am El Muerto."

Zarin blanched at the mention of El Muerto, his eyes widening in horror. "You... you tortured Mel Berringer to death... in horrible fashion! You can't just kill us here in America!"

79

It was then as Nick looked on in amusement, Zarin and Sherazi took note of their dead cohorts with pooling blood. "How can you do this? Why do you wear a mask?"

"We're learning from you chicken shit bastards," Nick replied to the vocal Zarin. "When we know a bunch of you assholes need to be tortured and killed, we make a game of it with our own masks. How do you like it?"

That woke Sherazi to consciousness. He was incensed. "Torture and kill? This is not a game. You have no right to do this! I am a citizen!"

Nick chuckled. "Not anymore. I've revoked your rights. You two are so cute. Do you think I don't know you murdered a young woman sent to infiltrate your cult? I'm the one you get when you don't allow our regular law enforcement agencies to work. The really bad part for you two is when they call me in, I bring hell with me. Welcome to hell, brothers."

Sherazi turned away. "He is bluffing. Arrest us, and turn us over to the proper authorities. We have nothing to say to you."

Nick pulled his stun gun from his bag, firing off an arc. "This is only to remind you I am not the regular federal authority."

Nick forced Sherazi screaming to the floor surface before backing out of reach, and zapping his groin area in a continual arc for ten seconds. Sherazi passed out. His comrade Zarin did not. "Did you get the message, sweetie, or do you need a personal demo?"

Zarin stared into the eyes appraising him with amusement from the mask holes with abject fear. He saw no feeling or hint of compassion so ingrained by American movies portraying the idealistic side of America. This man would do anything within imagination to him without hesitation. "I will tell you everything! Do not torture me!"

Nick unloaded his stun gun with a smile by zapping his fingers in between the electrodes, jolting upright for a split second. "Man... I can't get enough of the charge. Well now, Ebi, that all depends on what you have to say. If I'm not impressed, the game will be afoot as a Sherlock Holmes fan might say. That's when things get really unpleasant for you, pal. Start talking, buddy, or I start exploring your nether regions with Mr. Sparky. I promise you this. I will not add extra pain if you give me a name for who killed the young woman infiltrating your group. I am excellent at determining a lie. Don't lie to me, bucko, or we'll start partying right now."

Zarin looked down. "I killed her. Mr. Sherazi found out she was a plant, trying to infiltrate our cell. Since I was the one who fell for her lies, her death was left to me."

"That leaves only the gory details about this grievous wrong you two hoped to perpetrate here in Boston. Keep talking Ebi. If I don't think you're being truthful, or complete in the telling of this horrible story, I will have to give you an adjustment. We don't want that, do we?"

Zarin shook his head with vehemence. "We will not live through this, will we?"

"I'm afraid not. I promised the murdered girl's uncle you would pay for what you did with your life. How much pain goes with it, I'll leave to you."

"Nick... I'm networked in with you," Paul Gilbrech said. "Gus told me it was an Isis cell."

Nick held up a hand to stop Zarin. "I'm working with Zarin now. If you have intel I don't, ask your questions. I'll relay them. We have the warehouse to ourselves, so time is not a factor. Payaso is watching the front door, so there won't be any surprises."

"Can I have these two after you finish?"

81

"Nope. You involved your Marine buddy Stallings. I gave him my word, and El Muerto does not break his word."

Gilbrech muttered something. "Okay, Muerto, it's your show. Let's get started."

Over the next four hours, Nick covered every possible thread in the Isis network leading into America. He then took Zarin through the Isis network's connections with Hamas in America. Zarin hung his head, while avoiding either looking at his cohort, Sherazi or Nick. Nick had duct taped the now conscious Sherazi's mouth, warning him not to make a sound during the questioning. The insights surprised his interrogators. The Isis cell had filtered in through the Les Jardins-de-Napierville crossing between New York and Canada. A terrorist halfway house for the network existed in Champlain.

"I have told you everything I know," Zarin said finally when Nick asked another question about contacts in Canada. "I was given papers overseas to get me from France into Canada. We were moved from there to the border immediately without stopping. I am sorry about the woman. I cared for her."

"Who ordered her death?"

Zarin hesitated, but inclined his head toward the suddenly very animated Sherazi. "He ordered her death at my hand. Nearing my time I have no illusions. I have wasted my life."

Nick unfastened his ankles, and helped him to his feet. "Do you have any booze in this dump? My experience with you true believers is you swear to have no alcohol pass your lips, and then do the opposite. I'll help you have a few if you'd like."

"I would like a few very much. As you surmised, we have booze as you say here. May I show you?"

"Of course." Sherazi made violent movements, rolling around on the floor. Nick kicked him in the head. He quieted immediately.

"I don't much like your partner," Nick admitted, allowing Zarin to guide him.

Zarin glanced back at Sherazi. "I do not much like him either. I offer no excuses. I have been as a lamb led to the slaughter from the very beginning of my life. It has been a life filled only with death."

Nick began getting his quirky idea mode going. In spite of everything he knew, and what Zarin had confessed during the interrogation, he couldn't help liking the young man, especially his fatalistic acceptance of his death sentence. Paul had heard everything said. Nick continued following Zarin to a set of cupboards in a makeshift kitchen. Zarin pointed with his foot towards a closed cupboard door. Nick checked, and found an entire selection of booze.

"What can I get you?"

"The Jack Daniels would be very good," Zarin said, backing away from the cupboard to give Nick room. "It would taste very good right now. Thank you for your kindness."

Nick took out the bottle of Jack Daniels, and found a set of glasses in the upper set of cupboards a few seconds later. He poured a triple shot for Zarin into a glass. He gave Zarin a gulp, watching the distaste at first, followed by grim satisfaction.

"Yes. That is very good." Zarin accepted another healthy gulp of Jack Daniels. He looked into Nick's eyes. "Could you simply shoot me in the head after I finish this drink, Sir? I have nothing else to tell you. If I did, I would say so."

Nick helped him gulp down the rest in the glass. "Let's talk about that. How would you like to find God in something else than death?"

Zarin's eyes widened, but he looked down immediately. "Please do not play with me as a cat does a mouse. I know what I have done is beyond redemption in your eyes. If I could but get a quick death, I will be done with this living death sentence."

"I'm not playing a game. I could use someone like you. It will mean an abstract change in everything you've ever been taught. More importantly for you, it would mean survival."

Zarin shrugged with inebriated smile. "I am happy if I can live. If you can let me live, I am your man."

"It will probably mean at times fighting against the people you are now working for. Trust will be earned at a slow pace, and you will be averse to many of the things I do."

"What? Did I hear right? You're recruiting? Are you out of your El Muerto mind?" Gus's rapid fire questions at significantly louder volume had Nick cringing.

Nick held up a finger to Zarin. "Would you please tone your discourse down, Payaso? Calm the hell down. We need a guy with us not too thrilled with being brought up in the death cult."

"For God's sake, Nick, what if he's playing you, dimwit? Sorry... sorry," Gus said. "That's uncalled for. I know you have excellent instincts, but being wrong in a circumstance like this would be horrific. What do you have planned, taking him home like a lost puppy?"

"What he said," Paul added with amusement in his voice.

"We'll work this slowly, monitoring my new recruit," Nick said. "I don't think he's playing us. A new life where all you've known is death can be an incredible life changing experience, right Ebi?"

Zarin shook his head in the affirmative with vigor, all for the cam's view Gus and Paul had on their screen. "I swear a blood oath! I am your man from now until death. If I could cleanse my soul of innocent deaths I am responsible for perhaps... I might find peace."

Nick removed the plastic tie binding Zarin's wrists at his back with Gus muttering comical forecasts of doom in his ear, accompanied by muffled laughter from Paul Gilbrech.

"You're going to feed him and clean up after your new pet, Muerto. I'm not taking care of him for you. Deke won't like him. Mark my words – he'll bite the hand that feeds him. You can't teach old dogs new tricks. Lie down with dogs, get up with fleas, Muerto."

"Please stop before I come out there and shoot you in the head. Get your clown mask, and black hoodie, Payaso. The ending to this grim tale is at hand. My new recruit is going to film us as I take care of the one who ordered Cinny's death."

By the time Gus arrived down in the terrorist's chamber, Nick and Zarin had lined the dead Isis cell members in a bloody grouping by the wall. Sherazi knelt in front of them, his ankles and wrists plastic tied at his back with duct tape over his mouth. Nick was in the process of showing Zarin how to record the movie with his iPad.

"This is my partner, Gus. He'll be a little standoffish for a time, Ebi," Nick said. "We'll need to give you a new identity, Eb. Gus will help with that. What name would you like?"

"How about Johnny Five," Gus volunteered.

Zarin, who had been averting his eyes, smiled at Gus. "That is from the movie 'Short Circuit'. I liked it very much."

"How about John Groves," Nick suggested, having enjoyed Gus's movie quip.

"It would be easy for me to remember."

"Good. It's set then. Okay, John, I need you to tell me if Sherazi knows more than you about this cell or what you've already explained to me."

The newly named John Groves considered Nick's question carefully before answering. "He knows who runs the operation near the Canadian border. If you will allow me, I can go there and infiltrate their operation. I will arrive with news of this cell's destruction after your video clip is released. That man knows me. If I am ever to help you in public, he must be killed. Sherazi may have the man's name on the laptop he brought in the briefcase near his desk in the corner."

John gestured at the desk. "It is password protected. Anyone trying to access the information will initiate a virus which will destroy everything on the hard drive."

"I like your thinking, John," Nick replied. "You could make it much easier to erase this Isis thread from Canada. I see doubt in Gus's face."

"I'm willing to give new John the benefit of the doubt, but sending him North to take down his own former comrades makes me doubt your sanity."

"I agree," Paul added, still networked in with his out of control superhero. "I have people working right now to give your new recruit credentials. I'm liking what I see and hear, but infiltration North feels like one step beyond with a new turn."

"We'll do the video statement I have in mind," Nick replied. "Tomorrow, Gus and I have a book signing to do. That will give the media a chance to go completely insane labeling El

Muerto a monster, while the rest of the country scramble to run him for President. It's going to be fun, Boss. Relax and enjoy."

"You really are as psycho as I thought I was before I met you. I'm an altar boy compared to you. Count me in. Stash new John somewhere tomorrow, and I'll special delivery his credentials by messenger during your book signing. Let's get these assholes."

"On it, Boss." Nick put an arm around new John. "You're going to be uncomfortable with what I do. Don't interfere, and don't waver. We have a step on these people, and I like your idea in the North. Gus and I will go with you for backup. We'll be in position to end a significant threat. We're making a statement today. It will give you some cover for fleeing North."

The former Ebi Zanin turned to look Nick in the eyes straight on. "I am your man. If I may be permitted to have a life here, anything you need done, I will do. There is something else you should know: James Sherazi's name was Mohammed Abin. He does not know I found out his true name. He had my parents and sister killed. I was taken and raised in a Madrasa within the Palestinian State. Always, I have dreamed of this day. I thought my dream died when you captured us. I prayed to Allah that I could see this jackal die before me."

Nick watched Sherazi's face, seeing utter horror lance across his features. It was clear Sherazi had not a clue of Zanin's identity. Zanin knelt in front of Sherazi, clutching the man's hair with his left hand, and jaw in his right. "You will die now. I will record your death for all to see, coward. I will pay for my many sins in the future, but I will take comfort in watching you die."

John glanced at Nick. "May I have your stun gun, Sir? I will make this mongrel talk. He will tell us the name he knows, and the password to open his laptop."

Nick exchanged glances with Gus, but put the stun gun in John's hand with Sherazi whimpering behind the duct tape in spite of Gus's energetic head shake in the negative. John ripped off the duct tape sealing Sherazi's mouth, enduring a cacophony of denials, accusations, and pleadings. John shook Sherazi's head almost with joy on his face.

"Please do not speak. Be a brave soldier of Allah," John urged in Arabic, pushing Sherazi onto his side while positioning the stun gun again to his groin area."

"You...you will torture me anyway," Sherazi cried out.

"I will not. I have vengeance within my grasp, and a new life ahead, Allah willing. Give us the name and the password. I will then allow my new friends to end your life without further action on my part. Refuse, and I will use this to make you scream until you cry out the name and password. Do so now. You have three seconds: one... two..."

"Wait! It is Ahmed Abaza. The password is 9111456789."

John gripped Sherazi's hair tighter, obviously disappointed Sherazi volunteered the information. Nick put a hand on his wrist.

"We always honor our word, John. Let us have a moment to find out if he's been truthful about the password. I'm sure my boss is working the Abaza name right now."

John released him. "I saw you murder my parents and sister. I am shamed I was so weak I allowed you to order the girl's death. I should have killed you then immediately. It will be a sin I am forever in debt for."

"The name checks, Nick!" Gilbrech's voice echoed the excitement streaking through him. "He is number three on our Isis list of wanted players. Turn him over to us now. I'll send a team to collect him. Hold Abazi there. I'll-"

Nick broke connection with Gilbrech. "How's it look, Gus?"

"I'm in, and the password worked."

"Outstanding. Let's get our movie made. The hierarchy thinks I'll let this scumbag survive because he's near the top of our Isis list. That is unacceptable to me. Put your clown face on, Payaso. It's show-time."

John hurried into position for filming the execution, while Gus donned mask and black hoodie. Nick put on his full face El Muerto black mask. He had a voice altering device in place to alter his sound pattern. He held up his hand, making sure Gus was in place, before giving the sign to begin filming. When given the signal from John, Nick saluted in at attention form.

With voice adapter in place Nick proceeded. "You see before you an Isis cell, bent on the destruction of America. I am El Muerto. The man on the other side of this kneeling Isis terrorist is my partner, Payaso. I am an American citizen as is Payaso. My identity for all to see here on my mission is El Muerto. Payaso and I protect America everywhere within our reach. We will deal with serial killers, terrorists, or anyone who thinks they are above the law. We'll find you. Today we have Isis terrorists. I saved one for the message I have for Isis terrorist cells in America. Our leaders may be stupid enough to let you in. I will not be stupid enough to allow you to live. I will use this terrorist enclave as an example. As you can see, all but Ahmed Abaza are dead. When El Muerto and Payaso find terrorist scum, we kill them. We have an added pleasure in relieving this moron of his life. He personally ordered the execution of a young woman police officer. Here is his payoff."

Sherazi dropped face forward onto the surface in front of him, wailing about his rights, his persecution, and his torture. Nick let the monologue go on to the end. He then grabbed Abin's hair, hauling him to a kneeling position with Abin's head tilted upward.

"Hey..." Nick said, putting his smiling face next to Abin's for the camera. "This is what happens when underground America finds you, Isis. Watch closely. Not all of us capitalistic swine, infidels are adverse to giving you bastards a wakeup call. Consider this a warning. El Muerto is on your trail no matter who you are, or what you do. Enjoy.

Nick jerked Sherazi's head back, with Sherazi still begging for his life. With a quick swipe Nick cut his throat. Arterial blood projected outward, in the midst of Abin's final plea. Nick held him immovable by the hair, retaining a full frontal death sequence playing out across his features. Gus stood silently on the other side with evil clown mask and hoodie on. Both men wore gloves. Abin/Sherazi died within minutes, his body writhing violently in Nick's grasp. The final stillness swept over Sherazi, leaving only the feeble twitches into darkness left. Nick allowed the corpse to fall across his dead compatriots.

Nick gestured at the bodies with a flourish. "And there ends an Isis cell in America. This demonstration is brought to you on behalf of the American people who believe in Old Testament justice – an eye for an eye and a tooth for a tooth."

Nick nodded at John, who stopped recording. "I think I poked the hornet's nest enough. I'll bounce the signal all over the world, and send our tape out to all the news outlets. We'll also hit the news blogs on the Internet. After it simmers today on the grill, we'll get John on his way North to hook up with our Isis players there. Gus and I will attend my book signing, and then follow you up there to set things right. You'll have only enough time to collect some of your personal items from where you were staying, John. Then I want you halfway to Plattsburg, okay?"

"Yes. I will do it immediately. I can rest then."

Nick retrieved a burner phone from his equipment bag along with a thousand dollars in an envelope. "Pay cash from now on if you haven't been." Nick gave him a card with his phone number. "Only call this number after you get settled on your way to Plattsburg. Will you be able to handle all we're about to do?"

90

"All that and more, Sir." The new John handed Nick the iPad. "I will not fail. Goodbye for now. Thank you for Sherazi's death."

Gus and Nick watched John hurry up the stairs. Gus then gestured at the deadly mess. "What plans do you have for all this Muerto?"

"Let the cops handle it. We'll leave the chip with our evidence tying this cell into the USS Constitution plot, along with all the computer intel John helped us get. Did the data transfer okay, Paul?"

"I have it, and it's pure gold. I will need some time to sort through all of it. I'm actually beginning to trust your judgment on the new John Groves. If his involvement helps to bust the border crossing bunch, the sky's the limit for your new recruit. Want me to handle the video clip and information release?"

"That would help," Nick answered, knowing the Company wouldn't take any chances with back-traces. "How did you like our El Muerto segment?"

"It was insanely good… insanely being the operative word. We'll all have to go on the run if your secret identities become public knowledge."

"Considering how out on the edge America is right now with this Isis cult, I'd say we need to provide some entertaining feedback for them," Nick replied. "Wait and see how these pricks react, Paul. Have a countrywide screening going after the El Muerto video goes viral. I'm betting you snag many Hamas assholes along with Isis idiots if you can talk your contacts in Homeland Security to reap the benefits."

"It's a process, Nick. Everyone walks on eggshells, but every victory like your USS Constitution op wins many backers in the game. The outlanders suspect Muerto belongs to something other than a personal vendetta, so this is a really wild experiment. I'm not backing away though. I have our analysts pouring over every thread Muerto creates. I give you my word if the Muerto gig goes South, I'll give you a personal warning. With what you've done so far, I hope Muerto becomes the present day Zorro."

"I admit I've become infatuated with this El Muerto guise. I hope you're not thinking of interfering, Paul. That would be a mistake."

"Nope. Not happening. You've caused a wildfire with nothing but positive results. I'll work my end of this. If we bust their infiltration out in the open, maybe… just maybe, we can get stepped up enforcement to really stop this Middle East immigration debacle. There have to be citizens wondering what the hell we're thinking allowing all these assholes in here with an ongoing war. It's insane."

"Agreed. Can I kill everyone responsible for it?"

Nick heard Paul breathe deeply. "I wish to God I could, Nick. If ever I discover one of these government freaks selling us out at every opportunity, we'll destroy them. I know from scouring your past you pulled off something far more intricate before. It was so good, I won't even mention it on the phone."

"We won't talk about the past again," Nick stated with finality. "I like your aggressive idea with these people who keep exposing America on numerous fronts, endangering troops in the field along with the American populous. I'm sick of it. I have a family and friends to protect. I will not hide my head in the sand when I get an opportunity to make a difference."

"Every instance I am aware of I can allow El Muerto loose, I will. If this goes bad, I am with you to the end."

"I may have to test that sometime. In any case, Payaso and I are on our way out. We'll be in touch."

"Until then." Paul disconnected.

"Are you ready, Payaso, my cherished sidekick?"

Gus glanced around at the bodies. "Yeah, I'm ready. You are a very bad man, Muerto."

"Indeed."

Chapter Five

Revolution

The book signing turned into a Jed love-fest, as a few boat novices tried to challenge Gus on his being the model for Jed, questioning him on what it took to navigate Caribbean waters. They were so shocked to hear Gus expound on landings, navigation, and treacherous waters, the fans in line spread out as an audience in the book store. Nick took the opportunity while Gus spoke to sign everything, while circulating amongst the growing audience. More than a few made Gus sign their books too. The hours passed quickly, with only one small glitch, when a man in line mentioned El Muerto while Nick signed his book.

"Did you see the headlines about this character, El Muerto?"

Nick kept signing a personal note with his autograph, then met the man's eyes directly while returning his book. "I have read about El Muerto. The authorities have confirmed the men he killed were indeed an infiltration unit, plotting terrorist acts on our homeland."

"So you believe in vigilantism?"

Nick shrugged. "I'm not sure what you want for an answer. I was in Delta Force. I have a more than sympathetic leaning toward anyone taking out the enemies of our country."

Nick's response garnered loud affirmations. He could tell the man was less than pleased about his reply.

"Yes, but won't this El Muerto's actions cause a backlash against innocent Muslims?"

"Frankly... I don't care," Nick said, evoking yet another loud chorus backing his take on the question. "I keep reading and hearing about innocent Muslims, yet every act of terrorism and worldwide violence can be traced to Islamists acting out on the world stage. Perhaps it would be good to put pressure on these so called 'innocent Muslims' to do something about their brethren. If they don't speak out, they're inviting retribution."

The loud applause at Nick's words caused the man to scurry out with his book.

"Sorry, folks. I didn't mean to make the gentleman mad. I'm not very liberal in terms of America's safety. I tend to put our wellbeing in front of everything or everybody threatening it."

That statement caused an even more outpouring of agreement. The remainder of Nick's book signing event went very well. Gus answered many more seafaring questions, which took the load off Nick's time, and widened the discussions amongst the people waiting. Then the inevitable happened. Nick grinned, pleased with having figured the question would come up sometime.

"Mr. Nason," a young woman with book in hand addressed Gus. "Have you ever piloted a boat on a covert mission?"

Having been prepped by Nick that it would happen, Gus was ready. "Yes, I have. It may seem like I'm avoiding specifics, but I can't talk about any covert operations I've been a part of."

The young woman became animated in a good way. "That...that's great. Were any of them in the Caribbean?"

"Yes, they were," Gus acknowledged uneasily, noting how pleased Nick was at the question he had predicted would be asked.

"Can you please sign my book too, Mr. Nason?"

"Sure, young lady." Gus did as requested under Nick's signature, along with his mention of being Jed in the novel.

Later, as Nick and Gus packed up to leave, a man approached before the store closing. He gave Nick a wave with the large envelope he carried. Nick went past the security personnel. The man gave him the envelope, and turned away without another word. Nick opened it once he was next to Gus. It contained the new identity papers and cards of John Groves. Nick examined each one with a professional eye. They were perfect.

"Once we get clear of the Canadian border cell, these will integrate the new John into our small cadre."

Gus waved him off. "I'll withhold judgment until he does what he professes. I like him, but I have a hard time believing the new John is the real thing. Have you heard anything from Rachel and Jean?"

"Yep, and it ain't good. That's why we'll need to wrap up our border problem quickly, and hit the trail to Charleston. It doesn't seem to be a real big deal, but Rachel's mother-in-law has some bad neighbor problems."

"Damn it! You do know the mine field of working a domestic dispute, right?"

"Of course I do. I'll be careful, but family is family. I'm hoping my two loved ones don't decide to take a hand in something without allowing us to get there. You can bet Jean will be working the intervention mode in a way we may not be able to extract her from. Unfortunately, a third party observation is not in place on their excursion. Did you have an alternate suggestion as to what I should do, Gus? Speak up. Don't be shy."

"Sorry, I didn't mean it to come out like that. I know what a bear family is sometimes. What kind of dispute is it?"

"It seems Rachel's Mom in law has a drug dealer for a neighbor. He doesn't deal out of the house, but he has the whole entourage thing going on big drug money supplies – all night parties, vehicles wheeling around at all hours of the night and early morning, and the usual denizens such inhabitants bring with them. A neighbor called the cops on them a number of times. Her house burned to the ground mysteriously. It only took one of those thug lessons to hush everyone in the neighborhood."

Gus coughed in short interrupting snorts. "Ah… may I point out what would happen if El Muerto suddenly showed up in Charleston along with you visiting the relatives, along with doing a book signing."

"Oh come on, Gus. This isn't my first rodeo. El Muerto's on vacation after the border problem ends. I think I can handle a small domestic issue without bringing El Muerto into play," Nick explained with some disdain at Gus's inference. They'll still be looking for him up in Plattsburg. We'll already be in Charleston when the headlines hit."

The two men loaded into their vehicle, the nighttime's heralding dusk making the quaint Cambridge surroundings picturesque as lights came on around. Unlike their New York arena, it was a much easier place to get away from without being seen. Driving toward the Boston Harbor Hotel, Gus continued his reasoned pleas to keep Nick from his present tendency of grandiose killings.

"All I'm saying is any bodies found belonging to the house where the drug dealer lives, and I guarantee the cops will be at your in-law's doorstep."

"I have it all worked out. I'm thinking a tragic gas leak," Nick replied. "No survivors."

Gus laughed, knowing Nick's off the cuff offering was bait to get him to take a bite. "Very funny. That would be quite a solution to obliterate the entire neighborhood in order to save it."

"You've been hanging around with me too long, Payaso. I can't get a little burp of outrage from you anymore. Let's go get into a bar fight."

"You're really on edge in a funny way. The domestic feud in Charleston is really bugging you. Did you ask Rachel to try and stay clear of it until we can get there?"

"Of course," Nick answered. "She said Jean wants to pepper spray and stun gun the thugs hanging around immediately."

"Uh oh. Dagger's on the warpath, huh? Can Rachel tone her down for a few more days?"

"If Rach wasn't in her last trimester with the Devil's offspring, I wouldn't have any worries. There's nothing we can do about it tonight. You go take care of your bride. I'll walk Deke around the harbor with my flask, and have a couple of Bushmill's Irish for medicinal purposes. We've had a couple of rough days with more ahead. Enjoy tonight. I have a feeling after today's El Muerto news coverage, John will be welcomed in with open arms. They'll want first hand news about what happened. If John sticks to the script, he may be able to find out enough to make our setting this cell up easy."

"What script?" Gus asked worriedly.

"He called me after arriving halfway to Champlain in Queensbury. I explained he should pull the vengeance card, claiming he'd do anything to get revenge for the death of his cell. If he makes an impression, John will probably get put in on something they plan right away. We'll arrive tomorrow night with the El Muerto/Payaso road show."

"That actually sounds convincing," Gus admitted. "What else do you have in mind?"

"I have a new Remington Modular Sniper Rifle I've been working with. It has an AAC Titan noise suppressor. I'll retrieve it from the plane before we drive to Champlain. It fires a 7.62 Nato round, which I thought was not what I wanted, so I have .300 Winchester Magnum loads for it. It's dead on to about 1500 meters. I'm thinking of terrorizing the terrorists."

"How do you know we can find a nest from where you can shoot?"

"I'm banking on them having a place out in the boonies, where they can filter these guys into the country without a lot of observation," Nick replied. "Don't worry, I'll have plenty for a plan B if that doesn't work out."

Nick's phone rang. He answered as Gus neared the Boston Harbor Hotel. "Hello, Barry."

"Can I talk to you?"

"Sure. I'm taking my dog for a walk twenty minutes from now. Can you be in front of the Boston Harbor Hotel by then?"

"I'll be there, Nick." Sergeant Stallings hung up.

"Stallings knows you're Muerto." Gus drove into the valet parking zone. He and Nick exited with their bags in hand. Gus gave over the key to the attendant, tipping him well. "You promised to kill his niece's murderer. Instead, you recruited him to work for us."

"Keep in mind it was Sherazi who ordered her death. New John didn't want to kill her, but you can bet he either had to kill her or be killed himself. I killed the one who ordered it done. Yes, there are a few complicated threads. I'll tell Barry the El Muerto character beat me to the punch. If he doesn't believe me, it won't matter. I'll handle him. You have a good time with the lovely Tina. Can Tina entertain herself for possibly a couple days, or would you rather stay with her? I can handle the op in the North."

"I'm coming with you," Gus whispered while they entered the elevator. "You need a spotter. I've worked with you before. I couldn't go with you on the Abdul Nazari hit in the sand, and it bugged the crap out of me waiting for you to return. Besides, there's only so much honeymoon shopping a man can endure. She'll have plenty of money. Do you think we'll be gone more than a few days?

"We'll be in trouble if it takes more than a couple. This has to be a fast extermination. We need to make copies of everything, or have some people Paul trusts go through this base camp on their own. I want to head toward Champlain tomorrow, and maybe wait in Queensbury until John gives us the low down."

The men reached Nick's floor. Gus held the elevator door. "You're falling head over heels in love with the new John. Are you sure that's wise."

Nick chuckled. "He's a key I've been looking for in this terrorist mess. You'll have to trust my instincts, and know I will not put anyone else in danger with experiments. John will prove his mettle North in this op. He will undoubtedly know or get to know some of the cell operating out of Champlain. After the border cleansing, we'll both be sure, okay?"

Gus nodded. "I'll talk to you tomorrow."

* * *

Nick exited the hotel with a very happy Deke. He had behaved beautifully until getting into the fresh air. Nick smilingly let him leap around for the amusement of passersby before bringing him to heel. Stallings only approached when Nick began the walk with Deke. Nick motioned him to his side without slowing.

"You're El Muerto, and a bloody cold blooded killer," Stallings stated while striding in step with Nick and Deke.

Nick gave up on pretense. He could tell Stallings didn't want to pretend. "I'm all of that and more, Barry. Our mutual acquaintance made that clear to you. I don't take orders from Paul. He will be saddened by the loss of an old Marine buddy, but he'll get over it. Let's not put him through that. At this time you are not involved at all, and I am only a guy you asked for a consult. Leave it at that. Start bleating about me and El Muerto, and it won't go well for you."

Nick's cloaked warning caused a momentary loss in stride for Stallings. He hurried next to Nick as Deke marked territory, pausing in the cold air, sniffing at new smells with the soul of the hunter. "You…you're threatening me?"

Nick paused by the railing with Deke, looking around the picturesque harbor with a smile, making sure no one was walking nearby. A second later, Stallings was down with Nick's Italian stiletto pressed against his Adam's apple. "Nope. I'm promising if you don't forget all about me except the debt you owe me, you will awaken one night in your bed with me at your side, only I won't be holding my sharp friend at your neck. It will be lodged upwards into your brain. The only reason you're still alive is because I like your Marine buddy, and he likes you. Any questions?"

Deke sniffed at the goings on and snorted, sitting silently, a watchful sentinel. Nick grinned. "Deke thinks you're okay. Don't force me to make an adjustment."

Stallings looked up into Nick's eyes with the horror a normal human being has in the presence of death. He saw nothing behind those eyes and slight smile, but his own dark eternity. The

101

finality of how quickly Nick put him on the ground in position to die did not escape him. "I understand, Nick."

Nick's stiletto disappeared, and he gave Stallings a hand to his feet. "That's good, Barry. Don't ever forget your understanding. I have very little of a human element built into my makeup. Taking anything for granted and unimaginable things may happen around you. Deke and I have a long walk ahead of us. Turn around. Leave the way we came."

Nick once again allowed Deke to prance ahead. He dropped down, pivoting and pulling his silenced 9mm Berretta pointed back at Stallings' head. Stallings' hand dropped away from the inside of his coat where he had been reaching for his own weapon.

"Your word seems to be questionable, Barry. Perhaps your wife Beth and the kids would want you to show a bit more sanity in what you do, partner."

"I…I'm done, Nick! Nothing more… ever!"

Nick straightened. "I hope your word is better this time, shithead. I don't do take backs, if you know what I mean. Take your weapon out, put it down in front of you, and back away until I'm out of sight. You don't even want to know what I will do if you don't follow my directions."

Stallings slowly extracted his 9mm Glock with the thumb and finger of his left hand. He set it on the deck bordering the harbor before backing away from it with his hands in the air.

Nick waved. "You're welcome by the way, you ungrateful asshole. Be careful what you wish for in the future. It would be best to never let me see your face again, pal. I'm not one to forget someone who craves justice, but pulls up their skirts when the time arrives for justice to be done."

The two men traded stares. Stallings turned and walked away.

Nick looked down at Deke. "Good Lord, Deke. I hope I don't have to kill him. Don't worry though, buddy. It's my fault. I'm screwing up with my El Muerto identity. I admit it's the most fun I've had in years."

Deke snorted while resuming their walk ahead as if he understood.

"Just between you and me, Deke, I'm worried about Rachel and Dagger in a situation they could be killed in an instant. Life is not a bouquet of roses, my canine friend. I have a thin line to walk. Taking out this Isis cell threatening the country we live in has to take priority, right Deke?"

Deke kept marking territory, not really into the subliminal part of his walk.

Nick nodded. "I get it. You're first dog. You only handle threats within your jaw's reach. I need to order you a steak tonight from room service, my friend. Keep it on the down low or I'll have to answer to those absentee owners of yours."

Deke glanced back while Nick talked with a canine's observance of things said, but when it didn't fit into his repertoire of recognized commands, he kept going. Nick decided to forego his flask until he reached his hotel room. They did an hour's walk. By the time they returned, Nick saw Paul Gilbrech waiting for him.

"Damn, Deke, this guy must have a teleportation device. Hi Paul. Did Scotty beam you here or what?"

Gilbrech shrugged. "What can I say? With so much happening in Boston, I decided to check in with you before your trip North."

"Come up to the room, and we'll sip one or two. You can tell me all about your whiney friend, Stallings. Are you sure you guys were in the Marines together and not the cub-scouts?"

"Sorry about that, Nick. Barry's a good friend, just not too smart."

When the two men were settled in Nick's room, with a happy Deke chowing down on a steak Nick had in the suite refrigerator, Nick poured them both a double. He served Barry, and sat across from him. Nick held up his glass.

"To smarter friends."

"And dumber enemies," Paul added.

They sipped together. "Did your crew collect anything good from the former terrorist hangout?"

"I have a team working on everything gathered from the warehouse as we speak. Nick, are you really going to do this El Muerto gig on every mission? At some point, people will put two and two together, and come up with El Muerto. Your work with the NSA as a contractor was impeccable."

"I might point out Frank wanted to have me killed when my novels became bestsellers. Then he incorporated my author status into missions. I enjoy the hell out of writing, and I enjoy doing this El Muerto. The closest I've come to screwing up is shutting down this Isis bunch with your buddy Stallings in the know. I hope my talk with him has an effect on what he lets spew out of his mouth, or your pal and I are going to have a problem."

"No worries there," Paul replied. "I talked with him. He doesn't want to see, hear of, or talk about anything to do with either of your identities. When you mentioned his wife by name and his kids, after showing him compared to you, he's a novice with a weapon, Barry's sorry he ever approached me."

"Some of my shit rolled downhill, huh?"

"I don't do touchy-feely well. In that, you and I are alike. I honor commitments, and friendships that are real, but only when they intersect with something like the Isis connection. Barry will get his head on straight or else. We have a country to protect. The media blitz is on with El Muerto and Payaso. You've been too busy I'm sure to sample it. El Muerto and Payaso are the subject of every talking head show, not to mention print headlines across the country. Internet bloggers keep heralding the video clips on YouTube to the point El Muerto clips are being viewed in the millions. Right now, you're hotter than crazy cat videos."

Nick enjoyed the crazy cat video comparison for a moment. He finished his drink, and poured another. Paul held out his glass for Nick to add more. Nick sat down, contemplating whether to tell Paul about Charleston. He sipped a couple while enjoying the view through the suite's window. "I have a personal situation in Charleston I need to handle. If for some reason I need cover, can I get it?"

"A personal vendetta? Will Muerto be involved?

"Nope. I have a book signing in Charleston. If I did a Muerto hit down there, I may as well pin a nametag on my chest. I may have to make a couple of drug dealers and their cronies disappear from my wife's former Mom-in-law's neighborhood."

"Family's a bitch, but I'll look into what I have in place there. No videos or pictures though on this neighborhood adjustment, right?"

"Exactly. If I can do this without any exposure I will. I am familiar with the Charleston area. Unfortunately, I'm thinking making this look like a gang retaliation would be best, but I need to get down there to scope out the situation."

Paul shrugged. "Sucks to be them. If I have anyone in authority on the hook, I'll let you know before the op in the North is done. I'm staying close here in Boston while this Isis cell in the North gets handled. If you need me to provide violent backup, let me know. I've already moved some pieces into place near

105

Champlain. They know to steer clear unless called in. I don't want you hung out to dry there. This is too big a cancer to allow to grow. Erase it in any way you wish, including the El Muerto touch. If you scope out something needing a team, I will get you one, and damn the consequences. We both know those pussies in the FBI and HS won't deal with this threat. They'll set up a surveillance team for six months as Isis spreads infiltrators across the country. If you hit the mother lode on info at their place, let me know. I'll get a team to slip in and gather what you find before the regular yokels arrive."

"I think we're on the same page on all counts. I'll handle the Charleston mess with kid gloves. Those toads don't have a fort they hole up in. They can't resist stepping out to party. When they do, I'll snatch them. They'll be found in the usual arenas, bound and gagged with a hole in their head. For the operation North, do you want a network connection?"

"If it's possible, I would like to monitor the op."

"You've earned it, Paul. We'll hook you up when the time comes."

"Are you taking Deke with you?"

"Yep. Deke's been with me in bad places before. He'll be fine. I'm thinking of putting a black cape on him with a black mask. His secret identity will be Fang the Ferocious."

Many moments passed while Paul recovered from the introduction of Muerto's newest sidekick.

    * * *

A huge gray barn structure stood at the property's front where New York State Route 9 bordered it. A long well maintained access driveway wound toward a two story structure with three attached garages over a hundred yards from Route 9. No trees or other structures obscured the house. Only a huge expanse of mowed grass covered the area between the barn structure and the house. Gus slowed as they passed by as Nick captured the entire area on video, paying close attention to any movement around the seemingly empty barn. The partially cloudy day enhanced the late afternoon visibility.

"John's description was spot on. I can see why they would attract no attention whatsoever set that far away from Route 9. He told me they do not travel even in pairs. Each stopover is thoroughly screened, poked, and prodded. When the time comes to transport them to where they are stationed, they have first class identities, and even passports. I'm afraid we have some people working in government who don't give a shit they are selling their own country out to a murderous stone-age cult. Something must be done to right this wrong, Payaso."

Gus snorted his half amusement and annoyance. "It's incredible to me citizens living in the greatest nation on earth embrace scum bent on the destruction of everything they're taking for granted. I wonder sometimes what they think will happen if they finally succeed. I'd bet this Isis cult would have mass executions as a reward for the traitors. Anyway… we ain't letting it happen, Muerto."

"Right you are, Payaso. Truth, justice, and the American way will win out," Nick replied, joking only in his tone. "There will be blood. I'm glad they took in John. He must have given them a hell of a performance. With the headlines generated by our last escapade, if he arrived in a state of disarray, sincere about reassignment to another live cell, John may have had enough cover to sell his act completely. Hell, he was one of them, so it's not like he'd be diving into a foreign environment. John's in the danger zone, but he's doing it for atonement. I plan to keep him breathing if I can."

"You thought they'd kill him the moment he showed up, didn't you?" Gus suddenly realized the last piece in the puzzle he couldn't figure out with Nick and the new John. "You psychopathic prick! You figured John was dead meat!"

Nick shrugged. "I'm not his mommy. He made his choice of atonement, and I gave him the chance. Think of the alternative, Gus. He would have been shot right between his eyes, and he would have never experienced the death of his family's killer. Sorry, but I have been above board in this recruitment package, Payaso. Now, thanks to me, he has a chance to be a hero, and join our superhero squad. What could be better?"

"Only you could invent a tagline like that," Gus said, shaking his head. "Okay, I'm thinking I see your nest. What's your plan?"

"If you figured the old barn, you're dead on right. I'll have you drop me off around midnight for my first recon. I wish you could be my spotter, but I may need a ride out faster than anticipated. You're more valuable watching for signs on the road, and being ready to zoom in and pick my ass up immediately if need be. You'll be in my ear throughout this op. In the meantime, we take our sidekick Fang for a long walk in the wonderful countryside here before we get a few hours' sleep."

"How's John doing? You didn't say anything about his call, only the fact he was in position, and the location of this Isis cell. By the way, Deke hates his new nickname."

Deke grumphed from the back seat when hearing his name. He stuck his nose in between the seats to get petted by Nick before relaxing again. "Deke knows it's a secret identity, so he plays it cool. John's fine. He's gone this far without a single whine. He'll be in position to text us when I start the party later. I'll need him to pinpoint the head honcho, Ahmed Abaza, so we can give Paul a target rich environment for the Isis cells the guy is feeding recruits into. That should be enough to keep HS and the FBI busy, so we don't have to hear about the poor terrorist rights that are about to

108

get violated. See, El Muerto knows how to navigate these politically correct waters."

"Oh sure you do," Gus replied. "Is this really going to be an El Muerto/Payaso finish?"

"That's up in the air right now, depending on how things go after I start killing people. Tonight will be a test. We have a man inside, so if I put a bullet into an Isis dupe's head tonight, we can kick back and watch how they react."

"I get it!" Gus shook his head, reminding himself he was working with one of the most dangerous men alive. "They can't go to the police. They'll post guards, run around like chickens with their heads cut off, and you'll simply pick them off. They won't know who the hell's killing them. For all they know, you could be the Feds."

"That's how I figure it, Payaso. At some point, the fools will figure I'm picking them off from the barn. When they move on me, I'll sanction the attackers from another position. We will hold up while they scramble around in terror. At that point, we'll lie in wait for a vehicle exiting their place. We'll take it out immediately."

"Damn, Nick, your plan sounds good, but when are you due in Charleston?"

"I called Cassie. We have another week to bring this op to fruition before we have to be in Charleston for the three book signings."

"What if you clip one, and they abandon ship immediately? They could head for the hills after the first shot."

"Such is life. They have to try and escape in a vehicle," Nick replied. "I don't like their chances. I'll do the stakeout. It will take them a while to figure out the shots aren't stopping. When they finally move on the barn, then things get interesting. Should I take Fang with me on this op?"

"Sure… if you want Rachel to kill you in your sleep, Muerto."

* * *

Nick exited the slow moving vehicle with Gus driving, both interior and exterior lights off. He snapped his night vision helmet into place, carrying his Remington modular sniper rifle case. In multiple pockets throughout his black weather proof parka and pants, clips for his Berretta and rounds for the Remington moved only slightly as he approached the barn. The Kevlar vest underneath the parka also provided extra warmth. Nick took nothing for granted. While approaching the barn structure, he kept his eyes on the ground, looking for anything indicating recent digging or snares close to the ground. His cautious approach was rewarded when he reached the barn entrance. The door hung off to the side, but inside the door a thin trip wire strung at shoe height revealed itself in Nick's careful observation. He used a mini-beam light to check beyond and all around the entryway before entering.

"Damn, Gus! These assholes have an explosive pack trip-wired at the door. A kid could blow himself to kingdom come exploring this old barn."

"You suspected a minefield in the front. Be glad that wasn't the case," Gus replied. "Maybe you should back the hell out and set up a nest from the grounds."

"Nope. The loft in here is the perfect spot to target the house. I will be looking for more surprises. Can you see anything from the low light cam?"

"Grainy, but clear," Gus answered. "Nothing clear enough for me to watch for something you can't see on scene though."

"Acknowledged."

Nick found the loft stairway after a significantly slowed exploration of the area around it. He inspected each step, and tested for stability until reaching the open loft covering a significant area in the upper barn structure. An open swing out hatch meant for hay baling at one time revealed a clear unobstructed house view. Nick settled in, building a sturdy spot for his Remington. He then took off his helmet, and used his night vision range finders to monitor any activity within the house. Gambling on the Isis recruits messing around until at least midnight, Nick was in position by eleven-thirty.

"Oh, Payaso, my old friend, you will never believe what our supposedly ultra-religious nutcakes are indulging in. These sinners right now gamble hideously within my vision, their gambling den of sin at a table for eight. Our new John is indulging with alacrity as I see others in the group eyeing him with malevolent looks."

"A wide range of targets for El Muerto the exterminator, huh?"

"Yep. It's lucky you were able to access a file on Ahmed Abaza. He's sitting next to John. Want to wager how many of these true believers I can hit before they duck out of sight?"

"They may be ignorant, but they're not stupid," Gus replied. "I'm thinking your main target plus one possibly."

"Game on, Payaso," Nick said. "They've been drinking."

In the next thirty seconds, Nick put .300 Winchester magnum rounds into four men before the players at the table fully reacted. He wounded one more on the target's way down out of sight. Nick watched with satisfaction as John grabbed Abaza, shielding him as if he would give his own life to protect him. *Nice touch indeed, John – well played, pal*. With deadly accuracy, Nick killed two more as they revealed themselves for more than a

111

second. He then sat back against the barn wall, his murderous side kicking in on this deadly game.

"Ah, Payaso, I killed six, with one wounded."

"Holy shit... how... oh never mind. Bolt action, and you killed six? Jesus, Mary, and Joseph... that has to be a record in the psychopathic hall of fame."

"John covered Abazza with his own body. It was so cute. Our head terrorist probably thinks John is the greatest thing since sliced bread."

"What the hell are you doing right now, Muerto?"

Nick chuckled. "I'm allowing my pot to come to a boil, Payaso. I play out the game here to the lucrative end. I'm not sure how many more recruits they have in there; but rest assured, they're crawling to the escape pods. I don't like their chances, Payaso. Checking now."

Nick peeked with his range finders. One of the garage doors opened within seconds of his surveillance. "Damn, Payaso, they're not even planning an attack on the barn. I'll disable their escape pod, and wait for targets of opportunity. This should be fun."

"Only to you, Muerto... oh fuck it... yeah... it's kind of fun thinking about the demise of yet another potential Isis cell, trying to devastate America, running to their deaths like scalded rabbits. I bet those threats they've been making taste like sand now, Muerto."

"I believe you are right, Payaso," Nick whispered, the pad of his index finger triggering the demise of the escape pod driver, the .300 Winchester magnum round passing with ease right between his eyes. The vehicle, a Ford Expedition, wobbled out of control to a slow meandering path to nowhere on the grassy lawn.

Nick targeted carefully. He spotted John, who held on to Abazza as the rats bailed out of the sinking terrorist land vehicle. With smiling satisfaction, Nick brought down three others in the vehicle, who ran for it in different directions, returning to each downed victim for a killing shot after the initial wounding. John dragged the struggling Abazza out, throwing him to the ground, and kneeling on his back.

"We are mission completed, Payaso. John has Abazzo in lockdown with a knee to his back. All other Isis badass members are in the process of finding out what lies beyond the great divide. Did you ever get Paul networked?"

"He's on. Great work, Muerto. Where are you going to film the final Isis cell accounting, and do you want me there?"

"Of course I want you there, Payaso. New John will film us with the entire dead cell around the live Abazzo. We will have to do initial inventory on what they have on site before a team arrives. I'll give you a look as I go through the place in real time, Paul."

"Perfect," Paul replied immediately. "Good Lord, that was outstanding shooting. Jesus, Muerto, you are a very bad man indeed."

"Don't suck up to him," Gus ordered. "There's no telling what he will do if Muerto gets any more positive feedback."

"Acknowledged, Payaso," Paul replied with much amusement.

* * *

The cleanup operation took very little time with Nick, Gus, and John transporting the bodies back inside the house. They positioned the already dead with the newly dead in the main living room. Nick used the attentive Deke to take care of Abazzo. Nick had trained Deke in holding a prisoner without Rachel or Jean

113

knowing, figuring at some point he would be able to use Deke's incredible patience and intelligence. Deke crouched now in front of a terrified Abazzo, every few seconds making a snarling jab within inches of Abazzo's throat. Abazzo would squeal behind the duct tape over his mouth each time Deke juked towards him. Nick suspected Deke would be a natural for this type of holding procedure, and he lived up to Nick's appraisal perfectly, actually enjoying the task.

With Paul networked into the cam feeds, he journeyed through the house with Nick, Gus, and John, noting and recording everything they found for the team he had on alert. The terrorist occupants left in panic, leaving everything in place without thought to a completely unexpected attack. Technical utensils were left exactly as found until Nick could find out passwords from Abazzo.

Nick approached Abazzo with a smiling countenance, waving Deke away. "Hi honey… miss me? Here's the deal. When I ask you a question, you'll answer it or I will fulfill your wildest dreams about torture. I kind of hope you won't go along with my plan of acceptance. Then I get to extract the info, and oh honey… you and I will make a connection then. What'll it be, Ahmed?"

After Nick tore off the duct tape from his mouth, Abazzo stared into the black masked El Muerto's smiling face, searching for any sign his captor was bluffing. In the training camp overseas, they taught no American could kill or torture them. They were cowards and children afraid of the dark. Until this night, everything taught to Ahmed had proven true. The American media labeled it a hate crime to speak out against the very enemy seeking their annihilation. He ran the terrorist dispersal house across from the Canadian border without incident since coming into the United States from Mexico. They lived in luxury on this estate without fear… until this night. Abazzo and his men had thought the trip wires in the barn and around the house would be adequate. Never did they think to be picked off by a sniper herding them into a deadly trap.

114

"Tick… tock… tick…"

Abazzo hung his head. "What do you wish to know?"

Nick accompanied Abazzo in an information gathering tour of the house, checking passcodes for the computers they found inside during the first exploration. Abazzo opened the two safes, one built into the wall behind a bookcase, and one built into the floor under the corner of a carpet in the living room. Nick left Gus and John to empty the contents with gloved hands while he and Deke took Abazzo into the kitchen. After seating Abazzo, Nick put Deke on relaxed watch while stepping outside the kitchen.

"Anything special you have for my Abazzo talk, Paul?"

Paul listed a number of items, all having to do with the specifics of how Abazzo infiltrated the Mexican border, and what stops along the way existed between there and the present location. He ended with a plea. "I need this guy, Nick. Let the team take him."

"He can finger my recruit, new John. I can't take the chance he won't get amongst his brethren to tell tales."

"I know what you're capable of," Paul replied. "I give you my word he will never see a single soul he can tell. You've uncovered the greatest breakthrough into Isis or any other Muslim group we've ever had, Nick. Please, let me put this guy somewhere he can keep helping us. Hell, all I'll have to do is show him your picture if he gets uncooperative."

Nick considered the downside of letting Abazzo live with a writer's imagination for all intricacies and tendrils which could eventually backfire. He weighed the negatives with how much information Paul could extract from Abazzo concerning Isis.

"Nick?"

115

"I'm thinking. Okay. We'll do our El Muerto thing with all the dead bodies around. I don't have to slit a throat every time. Give us a half hour, and we'll be out of here. The trip wires around the house are disabled, but the setup around the barn is still hot. Everything from the safes has been emptied where they can be seen."

"Thanks, Nick. I'll send them in forty-five minutes from now. We'll pick it clean, and leave some damaging items for the police to back El Muerto's claims."

"I'll call you before we leave for Charleston. I'm naturally skipping the interrogation with Abazzo, but he'll be tied down, and ready for plucking. If you find someone else you don't want to give over to HS or the FBI, let me know."

"Acknowledged. Talk at you later. Thanks, Nick!"

"Stay straight with me, Paul, and I'm with you at every step."

"I know that, and I'd betray my own Mother before I dropped a dime on you."

Nick chuckled. "That's the spirit. We'll be in touch."

Nick walked into the kitchen once again. "Good news, my little terrorist buddy. The higher ups want you alive for now. I'll cinch you in place for them. They'll arrive shortly. My contact told me I can have you back if you don't cooperate. We wouldn't want that, now would we?"

Abazzo shook his head with fervor. Nick duct taped him solidly to the chair at each ankle, arm, waist, and chest. Lastly, he sealed his mouth again. "Stay here Deke, while Payasso and I get a few pictures."

John stood uneasily outside the kitchen. "Can we not kill that one too? He knows me."

116

Nick put his arm around John. "Now listen. You let me worry about identities, danger, and details. What was our haul from this excellent venture?"

"The safes held nearly $150,000." John seemed confused. "Do they let you keep the money?"

"No, but we do anyway, right Payaso?"

"Hell yeah," Gus answered. "You risked life and limb going undercover on this John. He deserves an even split."

"I think so too," Nick agreed. "Get the cam out, John. Payaso and I will get into character, and act out this video clip. Then we'll do a few stills, okay?"

"Sure."

Once they were ready for filming with voice altering added along with Nick's full face black mask, Nick gave John the nod. "Hello, my fellow Americans. It is I, El Muerto, here with my deadly sidekick, Payaso. We're near the Canadian border because we finished shutting down a major infiltration center for the Isis Cult. These dead Isis Cult members were on their way to cells throughout the United States. El Muerto will not allow such things. Payaso and I are on the job, America. We will not succumb to this death cult. No mercy."

John ended the scene. He then took still pictures of Nick and Gus posing over the bodies in various stances of distain for the victims. They finished the photo and video shoot, collected what they wanted in money, and left the scene together. Nick passed fifty thousand dollars over to John in a bag retrieved from the Isis house, along with a set of keys, and a folder.

"Take the money, rent another vehicle, and drive to my other property in the Carmel Valley. Keep a low profile for the time being, John. I don't want you picked up for anything by police or anyone else. Relax, and enjoy. You've earned it after this bust. Call me with the burner phone if you have any problems. Our book tour ends in Charleston. We may be involved for a time there depending on some personal issues."

"I could help in Charleston," John said. "I could keep a low profile until you're sure I will not be needed."

"I appreciate that, but it would be better at this time to drive across country. Take your time, don't speed, and stay wherever you like on the trip. Do not attract any attention whatsoever. Gus and I will make contact with you when we get home to Pacific Grove."

"If you need my help, please call, and I will be there," John replied, trying to contain the shock at Nick's orders, and generosity.

"I'll call if I need you, but I think Gus and I can handle Charleston. It's a couple of book tour stops, and a bit of family business."

Chapter Six

Expect the Unexpected

"Don't go out there, Jean!"

"There's something going on, Mom!" Jean posed ready to bolt through the screen door. "Grandma's house is in the middle of a drug/gang war!"

Rachel hugged her violent leaning daughter. She watched her former husband's Mom at the end of her driveway, arguing with three young gangsters. They passed packets to drivers stopping in front of the house for money. Although Echo Avenue was listed as one of the more dangerous areas in Charleston, it also had a variety of denizens. The houses, spaced apart unevenly like a rural area in various stages of upkeep also each had a bit of land. They were not housing tract, cracker box dwellings. Her former Mother-in-law's house, a light blue painted split level place with a broad porch, presented a picturesque neighborhood family living space. On the right side of her house stood a ramshackle place appearing more like a warehouse shed than a house.

Mona, returning from the grocery store, spotted the drug transaction going on in front of her house, and stopped to argue with the pushers. Rachel could see they were more amused than angry. They made apologetic motions while retreating to the front of their structure. Mona, apparently annoyed by the number of confrontations Rachel and Jean did not know of, followed them shouting warnings to stay away. They only laughed. Mona gave up her pointless pursuit, returning to her groceries.

"Your Dad will be here in days. He already agreed to look over the situation with Gus. C'mon, let's help Grandma Mona with the bags. Do not say anything while we're out there. Do you understand me, Dagger?"

"Yes, Mom." Jean led the way, skipping off the porch to Mona's ten year old Buick. After giving her Grandma a hug, she grabbed two of the bags from the trunk.

"Do they sell in broad daylight like this often, Mona?" Rachel picked up the last bag, noting Mona was still staring at the pushers. "It seems this would be an easy bust for the police. They could do a sting operation, and catch these guys the first day."

Mona nodded, closing the trunk. At sixty-five, her lean figure, and long tied back gray hair, enhanced the no nonsense look on her features she displayed at most times. She lived in the roughest area of North Charleston. Mona did not back away from a task or confrontation, but having been warned by her upon arriving, Rachel knew she was no dummy. After outlining the neighborhood problems, Mona made sure Rachel and Jean knew there were times unsafe to leave the house.

"The police do what they can, but body bags are about all they can offer when a neighbor tries to testify against these hoodlums. The head asshole in the house next door bullies everyone. The bearded fuck is about six and a half feet tall, nearly three hundred pounds I'd wager, and has spent nearly half his adult life in and out of prison. His hoodlum friends call him Blackbeard. His real name is Gustoff Banning. He's killed at least three neighbors who tried to rally the law against him."

Mona bit her lip, eyes filling with tears. "Two were a mom and daughter living on the other side of Blackbeard. He raped the teenage daughter. Carrie had him arrested, swearing to the police she would have her daughter Lacy at the inquest to testify. They didn't have any DNA because the prick used a condom. I came to the inquest ready to testify about the goings on Blackbeard was responsible for, but Carrie and Lacy never arrived. They were hit and killed by a stolen sixteen wheeler. The driver was never found. After that episode, no one considers speaking out or calling the police, including me... damn it! The only thing stopping the

120

bastard from terrorizing us even more is the fact most of us are armed. It didn't do Carrie any good on the way to testify."

"C'mon inside, Mona," Rachel urged. "There's no need to stand here hashing out stuff you can't change. Jean and I are happy as hell to be with you on this visit. Jean has been anticipating seeing you ever since my husband agreed to the Charleston stop on his book tour."

Mona grabbed Rachel's arm as she turned toward the house. "Did anyone ever make those bastards pay for killing my boy?"

A fast moving slide show of Nick's adopting her and Jean into his lifestyle flashed for a moment in her mind. A slow smile spread across her features. She remembered vividly Nick putting her into a position to kill the one who had actually killed Mona's son, Rachel's husband Rick. "Yep. The ones responsible are all dead, including the one who ordered it."

"How…how do you know that?"

"I can't say, Mona. I can only state without a doubt they're dead." Rachel hugged her, putting the bag down. "Believe me. I know it to be true."

"That's so sweet," a gruff voice stated from only a few feet away. "You've been messing with my crew again, Mona. I warned you about that, bitch."

Rachel swiveled to face the voice that approached from her rear, as Mona's eyes widened in recognition and fear. Rachel smiled at the huge bearded man with wild beady blue eyes. Head shaved, wearing a Carolina Panther jersey, the man clenched and unclenched his fists in overdone anger. Rachel handed the grocery bag over to Mona.

"Blackbeard? I've heard a lot about you." Rachel fronted him, not allowing the man to approach Mona any closer, while

121

reaching under her blouse at the back. "What the heck's your real name? I heard it was Gustoff or something."

Seeing Rachel calmly facing off with him nearly made Blackbeard's head explode. He looked ready to sucker punch Rachel in the face. Poking his right index finger at her, his mouth tightened into instant torque causing his words to sound like they were being strained through a filter.

"I am someone you do not want to fuck with!"

"I don't even want to breathe the same air as you do, Gustoff, so why don't you waddle on back to your crew, and tell them how great you are at threatening a pregnant woman, and an old lady."

Blackbeard made a choking sound before reaching for Rachel's throat. Instead of reaching his target, Gustoff ran into Rachel's nineteen million volt Vipertek stun gun electrodes. He dropped to his back with a squeal. Rachel followed him down, zapping the big man until he stopped moving as Nick had taught her, all the while watching for his crew. A second later, Jean was at her side with a butcher knife clutched in hand. Rachel released the trigger, searching Blackbeard for weapons. She found a .45 caliber Colt tucked into the back of his waistband. She drew it out, aiming it at Blackbeard's house.

"Wow, Mom… you aced him," Jean said delightedly, as Mona knelt next to her.

"Quick, girl," Rachel said. "Check his pockets for extra clips."

"On it." Jean handed the butcher knife to Mona, and did a first class search for an extra clip. She plucked one from his right rear pants pocket. "Got one, Mom."

"Let's get in the house."

When they were safely inside with the doors locked. Mona rushed into her bedroom, and returned with a Remington twelve gauge semi-automatic shotgun with a box of shells. As Rachel kept watch at the window, two of the men she'd seen arguing with Mona earlier approached Blackbeard's unmoving body carefully. They tried to revive him without success. They hesitantly dragged him around to Blackbeard's house, which was no easy task, glancing with confusion at Mona's house.

"We're in the wood chipper now," Mona stated, loading the five shell maximum into the Remington. "You shocked the hell out of me, Rachel. Damn... that was so good. We may all end up dead, but watching you electrocute that black-hearted son-of-a-bitch was worth it."

Jean put her arm around Mona's shoulders where she sat with the shotgun in her lap. "Don't worry, Grandma. Dad's coming with Gus. These guys don't know what bad is, but..."

"That's enough, Jean," Rachel cautioned. "What she means is Nick has been around. He'll know what to do."

"I...I thought he was a novelist."

"He was in Delta Force during the war, and has worked with the CIA before. One thing Nick would insist on is no mention of him at all when he gets here. He has book signings in Charleston, because we want you to stay with us until we get this solved. I'll keep watch while you pack some things. Leave me your shotgun. Make sure all the doors are bolted. Can you pack our suitcases, Jean?"

"Sure, Mom. You'll need to call Dad though."

"I will right now, but we have to pack and get the hell out of here."

"On it. Let's go, Grandma." Jean picked up the shotgun carefully, and leaned it next to Rachel. "We'll check all the doors first."

Mona embraced Jean tightly. "Thank you."

* * *

Nick smiled at Gus, listening to Rachel's recital, describing her confrontation with Blackbeard. Gus and Tina joined him in his suite for coffee while he finished walking Deke. Already packed to leave, Nick had been watching the El Muerto/Payaso show in the news with his friends when Rachel called.

"You are one terrific badass woman, and I like your plan to get Mona and Jean into a beautiful suite at a very high profile hotel in Charleston. I'll text you the address of the place we already have suites being held for us in. Get Mona one too. We're leaving for the plane in a few minutes, so we'll be joining you shortly. Take nothing for granted. You can shoot as well as anyone I've ever taught. Don't drop your guard for a second on the way to the car. Have Mona drive. You keep everyone covered until you're on the way to the hotel. I don't have to remind you not to hesitate do I?"

"Not likely," Rachel replied. "I miss you. I didn't know how bad it was, or I would never have come here to stay in the house. I would have packed Mona, and moved her into the hotel with us. I'd call the cops, but I have a feeling it wouldn't help. They'd probably arrest me for assault."

Nick's smile disappeared. "That would not go well for them. I know this caught you by surprise. We'll work it out."

"I know. See you when you get here, my love."

"You'd better," Nick replied. "Otherwise, the murder rate in Charleston will jump at a rate undreamed of. I love you."

"Yeah, I bet. You've probably been guzzling booze and entertaining floozies ever since we left." Rachel hung up before Nick could answer.

Gus and Tina watched Nick grinning at the phone in his hand. Nick waved the phone at Gus. "We have to go now. There's trouble in River City."

Nick explained the circumstances in detail, and Rachel's interaction with Blackbeard. By the time he finished, Tina was yanking on Gus's arm. "Anything happens to my BFF, and I'm putting on a mask too. Quit grab-assing around boys, and let's hit the road."

"Do you think she'll be okay?"

"Let's put it this way, Gus, any dumbasses sticking their heads out to interfere with their getaway will likely need last rites."

＊ ＊ ＊

Jean rolled their suitcases near the door. Mona followed with one old large one with a busted wheel. Rachel glanced from her window watching to Jean. "I called Dad. He, Gus, Deke and Tina are on their way. We only have one small problem here – our escape. You two will load the car. I will make sure no one interferes. We'll keep the car between us and them. I wish we'd rented a vehicle, but no use in raking over that. Mona drives. You need to stay down once we get in the car, Jean. Let me know if you two are ready. I don't want anyone hesitating... even for a moment. Are we clear?"

"We're with you, Mom. I can haul these suitcases to the car."

"Okay, Dagger, let's do it?" Rachel tucked Blackbeard's Colt into her rear waist band with the extra clip in the pocket of her smock. She then opened the front door, propped the screen all the way against the stops. "Outside quickly, and I'll lock up before we make our run for the car."

With Mona and Jean waiting clear of the door, Rachel locked the door. When she positioned the Remington twelve gauge where she wanted, tightly against her shoulder, and in a sideways partial crouch, Rachel moved halfway to Mona's car. She kept it targeted on Blackbeard's house, sweeping the barrel right and left.

"Get loaded now!"

Mona and Jean wrestled the suitcases out to the car. Rachel moved with them, staying between the Buick and Blackbeard's house. With Jean going into hyper-drive, the suitcases were loaded in a matter of minutes.

"We're in, Mom!"

Rachel backed to the rear passenger side door nearest Blackbeard's house. She opened the window with Mona having already started the car. After propping the twelve gauge on the window sill, she nodded at Jean in the front seat next to her Grandma.

"Let's go, Grandma!"

Mona backed out of her driveway in a squeal of tires. She switched gears and left tire treads accelerating away from her house. Jean yelped in delight as they sped away.

"That was so cool! They didn't dare show their faces."

Rachel shook her head, collapsing against the seat. "Too easy, kid. Remember how Blackbeard took out the witnesses. I'd bet money he has a similar deathtrap waiting for us."

"What the hell do we do then?"

"Drive carefully toward the Belmond Charleston Place hotel, Mona," Rachel said glancing at her iPhone screen. "Do you need directions?"

"Nope. I know where that place is. You don't think they'd try and ram us in this short of time, do you?"

"I don't know, Mona. It doesn't have to be a sixteen wheeler. It could... look out!" Rachel shot forward from the rear, grabbed the steering wheel, and yanked it into a hard right at the Meeting Street intersection. "Hit the brakes!"

Mona slammed on the brake pedal with both feet, causing the Buick to slide sideways, narrowly missing an F250 Ford pickup truck running the red light. Rachel saw the driver hit the brakes and head full speed toward them. She leveled the Remington out the window and fired at the driver's side tire. It exploded, pitching the truck into first a tailspin, and then a flip onto its back. Rachel waited, taking careful aim at the truck in case she could get a clear shot at the driver, but the truck slid slightly blocking her view of the cab.

"Hit it, Mona! He may have sent more than one. Are you okay, Jean?"

"I'm fine. That was awesome!"

"You two are nuts," Mona muttered under her breath. She got the Buick straightened and moving toward the Belmond as fast as she dared. She could see cars stopping by the pickup truck in her rearview mirror. "This is like one of those 'Die Hard' movies. I hope no one saw my license number."

"You'll feel better once we're in a suite at the hotel. Your car will be in their care. Jean, you remember that brown clothes hanger bag I brought?"

"Sure. It's in the smaller suitcase. Why?"

127

"I'm going to put some clothes in it along with the shotgun. I'll carry it up to our hotel room without anyone knowing what I have. Park on the roadside about a mile away from the hotel, and I'll fix up the clothes bag with some clothes to camouflage your shotgun with for check-in."

Mona's hands squeezed the steering wheel in a death grip. "That was bad. Blackbeard actually sent someone to ram us!"

Jean patted her shoulder. "Don't be afraid, Grandma. Mom and I have been through a lot worse with people trying to kill us. We were tied up and gagged in the back of a van once by men who planned to torture information from Mom. They wanted a computer drive from a safety deposit box."

"And... and this Nick the novelist saved you?"

"He sure did," Jean answered. "By the time we have to leave, Dad will settle with Blackbeard. I bet you'll be able to go home without worrying."

"Maybe... if he doesn't blow my house up while we're gone."

"It's better than him blowing it up with us in it, Mona," Rachel reminded her.

"Amen to that."

* * *

Nearly six hours later, the door to Rachel and Jean's suite opened. In leaped the delirious Deke, nearly flying over the furniture to tackle Jean. In moments Deke pinned her into a lick fest, his tail whipping everything within its reach. Rachel knelt down to hug their canine friend while glancing at Mona with a big smile as Nick, Gus, and Tina followed Deke in with their bags.

"This is our other partner in adventure, Deke the dog."

128

Deke held up a paw to Mona while sitting across a groaning Jean's chest. Mona shook it solemnly. "Pleased to meet you, Deke. I've heard a lot about you."

Rachel moved into Nick's arms. "Good Lord I'm glad to see you."

"I don't know, Rach. Another day, and you would have probably exterminated the pest problem at the rate you were going today." Nick held her while gesturing at Gus and Tina. "Hi, Mona. I'm Nick McCarty. This is my partner, Gus Nason, and his lovely wife Tina."

Mona shook hands with Gus and Tina. "I feel better having you all here after what happened today."

Tina walked over after shaking hands with Mona to embrace Rachel. "Damn, girl, you sure got your Rambo on today."

Rachel nodded. "I may have run off at the mouth a bit more than planned. I admit it. I provoked him."

Jean crawled out from under Deke, but stayed next to him with an arm around his neck. "You should have seen that big ape when he ran into Mom's Vipertek. He went down like someone shot him with a cannon. Mom did just like you taught us, Dad. She zapped him until smoke came out of his ears."

"Did not." Rachel waited for the enjoyment of Jean's incident report to die down. "That guy is huge. They're running a drug operation in broad daylight out of his house. I'm not sure how many precincts there are in the city, but the one that has Mona's area can't be very diligent, if you know what I mean."

"They come when I call," Mona said. "It's just that they never catch them doing anything. After the killings, my neighbors are too afraid to say anything. They have to work during the day. They don't want to come home to find their house burned to the ground by a mysterious fire. I'm hoping mine will still be standing when I get back to it."

"When Nick first told me you had neighbor problems, I don't think he mentioned killings," Gus said. "He promised we'd sip a few together, while we heard the whole story. Do you like your suite, Mona?"

"It's wonderful! I do love my place though. I wouldn't mind having a couple belts with you. I'll tell you all I know about the situation. I don't know what the heck you can do about it though."

Gus guided her to a chair at the huge suite table. "Sit right down while we gather refreshments. I'm certain we can find a solution to this."

Five minutes later, they were all seated with refreshments, and Deke a huge soup bone. Nick raised his glass. "To family, and being here with people I care about."

"Amen," Rachel said, as they clinked glasses together. "When do you have your first book signing, Nick?"

"Two days from now. I contacted Cassie, and everything is in place and ready. All I have to do is show up with the Ancient Mariner, and we're golden."

"Why you… no good… he's just mad because I'm getting more popular at the signings than he is," Gus retorted. "I have to carry the whole signing now with insights into Jed's partnership with Diego in the novels. Readers like having the real life illustration of what a fictional character is based on."

"Gus is right. The book signings have taken on an entirely different flavor since the write-up about Gus being my model for Jed in the novels. It's a hell of a lot more entertaining with the real deal next to me."

"Yeah, but you're the real..." Jean shut-up as Rachel grabbed her wrist. "I mean... the novels are so much more now with readers knowing Gus. That write up in the New York Herald Tribune with all the details really made it work. Mom showed it to me. The picture with the article was a good one of you, Gus."

Mona sipped her drink, knowing she was on the outside of something important concerning Nick. She suspected knowing the truth would somehow put her in danger. "I don't want my troubles to become your troubles. I know those book signings are important. Thank you for coming to visit. Even if Blackbeard wins this round, I appreciate having this time with all of you."

Nick smiled while reaching across the table to cover Mona's hand with his own. "I have a plan, Mona. It will get a little tricky in parts, but I believe everything will work out in the neighborhood so that people there will be able to have a bit of peace for a change."

Mona laughed in uncomfortable acceptance of what she considered her reality. "I'm grateful, Nick, but I doubt you can do anything about Blackbeard. We ignored the problem until it became too big. Eventually, the police will not be able to ignore him. Rachel's had the news on since we checked in. There's no mention of the truck she shot at or the crash. That's weird. I thought the police would be hunting for us by now, but it's like it never happened."

"I was surprised when even the local traffic reports didn't mention the crash," Rachel added. "There wasn't any traffic at the time. I'm wondering if the driver called it in as an accident. What else could he say? He couldn't admit he missed ramming us, and had his tire shot when he tried a second time."

"I'm glad this Blackbeard guy didn't have enough time to send a sixteen wheeler after you," Nick said. "Excuse me. I need to make a call."

131

Nick walked into the bedroom. Paul Gilbrech answered his call right away. "How's my trail from Boston?"

"Clear so far. The media is going nuts, calling it a serial killing spree. They're not letting anything get in the way of loving terrorists. The people are ready to vote El Muerto and Payaso onto the Presidential ticket though if man on the street interviews mean anything. The talking heads on the news shows I've heard are making fools of themselves with terrorist love. I've filtered the truth to our other outlets with the reality of averted danger, so things will settle down. Is everything okay in Charleston?"

Nick explained the circumstances, including the attempt to have Mona's car rammed. "If not for Rachel having a twelve gauge shotgun in the car with them, they'd be dead. I have a plan, Paul. There will be no survivors, but except for Blackbeard who will be disappearing, the other deaths will be non-violent. Do you have anyone in the know that has any information on the police department in Charleston? I did a quick check. They separate the parts of Charleston to patrol teams. Patrol Team One has the area from Calhoun Street north to the North Charleston city line. Can you find out if there's anything suspicious going on with any of the Patrol Teams?"

"Sure Nick. I'll work it and get back to you. Great work on the border. We are flush with new leads and threads thanks to what we took out of the Isis dispersal house. Abaza mentioned you confiscated the house money from the safe."

"I have no idea what he's talking about," Nick replied.

Paul chuckled. "Yeah, that's what I figured. I'll call you shortly."

Nick returned to the table. "I have my friend looking into the status with the police in your area, Mona. Gus and I will drive over there early tomorrow morning. We'll look over your house and grounds. If everything looks okay, we'll stick around and

132

observe your neighbors first hand. Maybe I can spot something we can use officially."

Mona's eyes widened. "If Blackbeard sees you, he'll kill anyone at my house. I don't want anything to happen to you guys."

"We'll be careful," Gus said. "We have to start somewhere. Besides, we'll go over there real early before the punks get up."

"Can I go with you, Dad?"

"Sure... if you want your Mom to kill me in my sleep."

"Anymore jokes like that, and you'll be twenty-one before you get out of your room," Rachel added.

* * *

Cloudy, muggy, and nearly sixty degrees, the early dawn smelled musty with an overture of rain. Nick and Gus road together toward Mona's house in their rented Dodge Caravan. At five in the morning, only a slight hint of daylight glowed redly against the horizon. Echo Avenue, devoid of traffic, was lined with a wide variety of structures with varying distances between them. Gus drove while Nick studied the odd ramshackle places in spots, mixed in with neatly kept homes.

"You've been quiet," Gus remarked. "I hope it's because you really do have a plan. I've been trying like hell to think of a way this doesn't become a loud bloodbath, but I'm nowhere near an idea. You have that look on your face like when you're writing a scene. How long did you write last night?"

"From seven when we ended our sipping conference. I wanted to put Diego into something similar to our San Francisco caper with Al Mady's yacht, Shalimar. Jed pilots the craft as we did to get Al Mady. Since no one knows what happened, I can write the scene very much as it happened with the usual Diego and Jed

133

interaction – with Jed whining nearly every moment while Diego tries to calm him down."

"Funny… you prick. How many words?"

"A couple thousand last night. I'm nearly at the fifty thousand word mark now in spite of all our extracurricular activities. Guess who else left me a text at our on-line drop."

"Fifty thousand, huh? Damn, Nick, you're really moving on this one. Okay, I'll play. Who decided to risk their sanity to contact you?"

"Grace."

"Uh oh. The last time Grace and Tim messed around with you, Grace said she never wanted to see you again, except in a picture on the back of your new novel." Gus flashed on recent history when their US Marshal contacts, Grace Stanwick and Tim Reinhold, lost a partner along with their boss in brutal fashion to enemies trying to get a dangerous 'Hack Chip' Nick held in his possession.

"She wasn't very appreciative of my actions on her behalf. It so happens our collaborative action landed them in charge of the US Marshal's Office for the Western USA or something. See, Gus, that's the problem with doing good deeds – they're either ignored or they come back to haunt us. I unearthed the traitor in the DOJ, and what happens? The Attorney General couldn't do anything to her but fire the bitch. Even with the testimony from those two accomplices, Faulkner and Sadun, I put in their arms, Pettinger's lawyer claimed it was a whistle blower setup to keep her from talking to the media, and the Grand Jury wouldn't indict."

"There's Mona's house." Gus pointed as he did a drive by. Blackbeard's property with a dilapidated split level house, and two small house trailers, gave off an ominous aura in the dusky dawn light. At the side of the trailers was a freshly wrecked truck with a shredded tire. "Neat looking drug den. Now we know where the truck carcass Rachel shot the tire on ended up. So, what did Grace mention the sacred Department of Justice wants you to do with Nancy Pettinger?"

Gus kept driving until out of sight from Blackbeard's property. He then turned off his lights while turning around.

"Same old, same old. They want Pettinger to cough up everything she knows and then disappear without a trace. Imagine that." Nick watched Mona's house with his night vision ocular as Gus eased the Dodge down the driveway. Then he saw it. The front curtain jiggled slightly. "Mona has company, Gus. I want you to open your door, stand behind it while gazing at the house. I will slip across behind you. When I tell you to, turn your high beam headlights on. I'll slip off to the side, making my approach to the rear. Stay in position for a couple of minutes. Then shut off the lights, close the car door, and approach the house slowly."

Gus did as told. "I'm bait again... really?"

Nick chuckled as he slid across and onto the driveway behind Gus. "Hit the lights, Payaso, you big whiney."

Gus turned on the headlights, flooding Mona's house front while gazing at it with a look of curiosity. He heard Nick whisper testing into his com unit. "Loud and clear, Muerto."

Nick picked up speed, vaulting the wooden fence divider. When he reached the back door, he moved to a position where he could see inside. It was busted inwards, hanging by one hinge. With his night vision ocular, Nick approached the house while keeping sight of the inner area of the rear entrance beyond the door. Slipping inside the damaged door, he loosened his 9mm silenced Berretta in its holster, but took out his stun-gun. Nick wanted to see who he had inside Mona's house before doing anything permanent.

"Shut off the lights," Nick whispered.

He moved silently to a position where he could see the inside front part of the house, using his night vision ocular to examine every approach and room on the way. He smiled. A huge bearded hulk of a man watched the outside through a corner of the curtain with a sawed off shotgun in hand. Nick moved behind the distracted Blackbeard without his notice. For the second time in a couple of days, Blackbeard received the dance electric. As thorough as Rachel had been the day before, Nick applied the blue arc with grinning appreciation while watching Blackbeard hit the floor, his shotgun clattering to the floor beside him. Nick crouched into a position next to Blackbeard covering any approach from the rest of the house, his Berretta at the ready. Silence only accompanied the small snorts and movements from Blackbeard with his captor waiting patiently for any reaction within the house. After five full minutes, Nick straightened.

"Clear, Gus. I'm opening the front door now." Nick unlocked, and opened the front door.

Gus came in and locked the door behind him. "Damn, Nick... you've got the big fish. Nice catch. I bet you gave him an exciting introduction to reality."

Nick shook his head. "Nope. Blackbeard will be getting his intro to a separate reality shortly. He altered my plan a bit by breaking in to slaughter Mona and everyone with her, but I can make this work easily. BB will be telling us everything he knows about his supplier, his operation, and the people he's paid off to be able to deal drugs in broad daylight. I'm really interested in his answers. Once we have them, we'll see if Paul would like to get some DEA people intrigued with this backwoods operation."

Gus picked up Blackbeard's sawed off shotgun with a gloved hand. "He planned to execute Mona, Rachel, and Jean if they came back to the house? Good God, Nick! How do you get the clout to do something like that? I mean... hell... even the police would be forced into some kind of action."

Nick plastic tied Blackbeard's hands behind his back. He then pulled the man's pants down to his ankles. "I figure BB planned to use the shotgun and surprise to cart them off somewhere else where he could exact his revenge. He probably has a killing ground somewhere nearby. Mona disappears, and everything else with her becomes someone else's problem. Instead of that simple, but very effective plan, BB has me to deal with."

Gus watched the cold blooded killer surface as Nick finished his chore and straightened. "There's no use in pretending, brother. I'm going to make BB pay for his intentions while finding out everything I want to know. There will be no Muerto masks or video clips. By the time I get done with him, BB will wish he'd never been born, and that's only if he does tell me what I want to know. This may be a good time for you to go sit in the car after you help me get BB into a chair."

"Rachel's my sister, and Jean's my niece," Gus replied without looking away from Nick's steady gaze. "I'll keep watch, but I don't move out of here until we take BB away for burial."

Nick grinned as he took a black plastic garbage bag from his equipment bag. "We're not going to bury him, Gus. His buddies know where he is right now. We need to make him into a mystery."

"Oh boy... I don't like the sound of that. What is it you have planned for him, Muerto?"

"Do you know your history, Payaso? What famous happening still exists as a monument in Charleston, my friend?"

Gus's eyes widened. "Tell me you don't mean Fort Sumter. You don't really plan on-"

"Exactly, Payaso! It's so good to know another American who understands the basics of history. I see doubt and anxiety creeping into your features, brother. We'll keep it simple. I will leave BB's carcass at the gate as if he's sleeping peacefully in front of a national monument. The toads next door at his place will be lost. First, they'll wonder where he is. Then they'll hear about it, and they'll think 'wow, man, Blackbeard went nuts'."

"And what of his friends?"

"I'm afraid they're going to be so heartbroken over the loss of their leader, they'll pull the pin on the heartbreak grenade. They'll decide to have a wake right next door for poor old Blackbeard, get some good drugs, play some good sounds they have, and unfortunately for them – overdo it and die. The cops will find our group of grieving gangsters at their final rest. We, of course, will be doing book signings, and keeping Mona with us until this blows over."

"What about Pettinger?"

"We'll have to study her for the time being. Besides, I need to hear about Nancy from Grace and Timmy at a neutral spot. I'm not blasting into a DOJ setup with guns blazing. Bring one of those plain kitchen chairs here. Put it inside the garbage bag."

Gus brought the chair, put it inside the bag, and helped Nick put Blackbeard on it with his bound hands over the back. Nick went to work with the duct tape, making certain their captive would not be moving a muscle. By the time he finished Blackbeard's head was lolling from side to side as he regained consciousness. As his beady, reddened eyes blinked, and focused, Nick added duct tape over Blackbeard's mouth. The eyes widened. Muscles tensed from his feet to the top of his head. Nick and Gus watched the transformation with grim, smiling appreciation. When the chair began jumping to Blackbeard's frenzied attempts to break free, Nick zapped his groin area. The violent reaction sent the chair over backwards.

"Gee, Gus, I think BB isn't happy with his circumstances. I should have held the poor guy's chair so he wouldn't pitch backward, but I might have received a slight residual shock. We can't have that."

"There definitely would have been enough residual to probably knock you on your ass," Gus replied while helping Nick get the chair righted again. "You dinged him that time until I thought his hair would catch fire."

Nick went into the kitchen. He returned with a glass of water, and threw it in Blackbeard's face. Gustoff Banning spluttered and choked his way into consciousness, the duct tape hampering his attempts to draw breath. The kitchen chair bounced perceptively in response to his agonized waking.

"Rough waking. Maybe if you took the duct tape off his mouth," Gus suggested.

"Now why didn't I think of that? Sorry, Gustoff. Here." Nick tore the duct tape off the man's mouth with attitude. "There you go, buddy."

Banning's eyes wildly took in his surroundings, and the two figures in front of him. He wasn't stupid. He had done this and worse to people for no other reason than enjoyment. Gustoff saw in Nick's eyes nothing he did or said would ever get him free again. Without a bargaining ploy, he knew all he had left was either bluster to entice his captors into making a mistake, or giving them something worthwhile for a quick death. Blackbeard gambled all in and lost.

"You pussies! Afraid to take a man on one on one? Undo me, and I'll fight you both at the same time. Both you cunts can even have knives! I'll still maim you chicken-shit cocksuckers, cut your nuts off, and shove them down your fucking throats!"

It was many moments before either Gus or Nick could speak. Nick waved a hand at Banning in pleading fashion. "No... no more. Oh my, you're a real treasure. Let's see. You threaten a pregnant woman, who toasts your marshmallows, and leaves you sobbing for mercy at her feet. Then you send a truck out to ram a grandma, mom, and young pre-teen daughter to death, and you're calling us pussies? Oh Gustoff... you idiot... I know you've had other victims in similar circumstances. The trouble with you is when they offered anything you wanted for a nice death, you refused and tortured them anyway. I know cockroaches like you inside out. If you had been smart, you would have begged to tell me anything I wanted to know, in return for which I'd send you to the great beyond with a minimum of pain. I'm really happy you didn't. My partner here is going to show you something. After he finishes the video demonstration, I think you might have a change of heart. See... I'm not like you. I'm goal oriented."

Gus played the video of Big Texas Son's journey into darkness for Blackbeard. It was enough to demonstrate how fearful an ending he would have after the info extraction. Nick watched Banning's acceptance of reality with less pleasure than he admitted. Rachel was the love of his life, a thread so incongruous to what he was, she remained a mysterious ingredient to his own psych. Rachel made him believe he could care. Jean reinforced the feeling with depth he thought untouchable prior to their meeting. Nick watched Gustoff's viewing with an anticipation of doing exactly that to his captive. That Blackbeard represented an already attempted murder ploy of two people he cared most about, highlighted his innermost struggles. Until he found Rachel, nothing on earth evoked more than a slight whimsical memory. With Rachel, Jean, and Deke the dog, reality shifted in every part of Nick's life on a day to day basis. Knowing the man in front of him missed killing his new reality by seconds made Nick deal with yet another decision. He knew Gus wondered what he would decide too, no matter what Gustoff said.

"How'd you like the movie, BB?" Nick decided. "Want to go out with a smile on your face, or screaming for a few hours while watching me pour bleach on your exposed intestines. There is a plus to going the hard way. Hell won't look so bad when you arrive. You will tell me everything you know either way."

Gustoff was done. "You did that shit in the clip?"

"More than once," Nick replied. "I have the technique down to a science. I overdid the bleach a couple times, and the first guy I practiced on passed out too quickly. Time's a wastin', BB. What'll it be?"

"What do you want to know?"

"That's the spirit."

* * *

At first when people saw the huge bearded man sitting against the flagpole at Patriot's Point, they figured some homeless guy decided to camp there for the night. Because of Blackbeard's size, no one approached him until the police were called. The first designation of death by the coroner called to the scene was suicide or accidental drug overdose, because of the syringe still clutched in Gustoff Banning's hand. Nick and Gus watched the discovery and recovery of Banning's body with detached interest.

They returned to Mona's house after Banning's body was taken away. The second part of Nick's neighborhood cleanup program would take place late in the evening. For now he and Gus worked on whatever mess they had made earlier, along with wiping down any sign of Banning's presence from his ill-fated visit. Nick then called Rachel.

"Hi Hon. Guess who was waiting for Gus and I at Mona's house."

"Blackbeard."

141

"Yep. Plan A has been completed in my neighborhood revamping project. We'll complete Plan B tonight. You three can see some of the sights safely now, but I'd stay away from Patriot's Point where one of the ferryboat's take tourists to Fort Sumter. If you have time to keep track of the news about a mystery man found near the flagpole this morning, jot some notes for me. I'll call you later."

"I love you. We're going with you to the book signing. Mona has never been to one."

"I love you too. It would be great for the three of you to come along. As always there will be transportation away if the book signing gets boring," Nick replied. "Cassie's arriving tonight. She'll be staying at the same hotel as we are. If she stops by, tell her Gus and I stayed to make some repairs on Mona's house, but we'll see her tomorrow morning. She really shouldn't have any publishing agent type stuff to talk over with me. This will be more of a monitoring visit by her own description."

"Be careful... okay?"

"Always. We'll be done tonight. Then we can enjoy the rest of our Charleston stop together. How's Dagger and Quinn?"

"Dagger's chomping at the bit to be with you and Gus of course, while Quinn's been reminding me of his presence nearly every second." Rachel turned away, walking into the bedroom out of hearing range with Deke following close behind. "I need you with me. You know what my pregnancy's done to my hormones and... you know... other needs."

Nick smiled, remembering his earlier thoughts about Rachel, Jean, and Deke. "I have a vivid imagination, babe. I will do my best to make up for this unfortunate absence."

"I will hold you to that. Bye for now. Wake me no matter what time you get back, okay?"

142

"You bet I will. I love pregnant women, especially you," Nick joked.

"I better be the only pregnant woman you love."

"Your will, my destiny," Nick answered, getting only a giggle as Rachel hung up.

* * *

Jean waited anxiously outside the bedroom. "I know that was Dad. Everything's okay, right? I heard my secret identity mentioned. Did he ask about me?"

"Of course," Rachel answered while roughing up Deke's head. "Yes, he mentioned you too, dog. We need to turn on the news, paying particular attention to anything about a mystery corpse found at Patriot's Point."

"Yes!" Jean pumped her fist, ran into the main TV viewing area, swiping the remote from Mona's side. "Sorry, Grandma, we need to check the news. We'll watch the rest of the movie tomorrow."

With Deke halfway in her lap and Rachel next to her, Jean blinked through channels until she found a woman in mid-sentence reciting something about Patriot's Point. A stark photo of Gustoff Banning against the flagpole was discreetly on display behind the newswoman. She made reference to the discovery, along with what facts observers were willing to share at the time, noting the mystery man's identity was being withheld pending next of kin notification. The video clip obtained for viewing, showed a closer profile of the bearded man, which evoked a gasp from Mona, and a giggle from Jean.

"That...that's Blackbeard," Mona whispered. She listened to the newswoman's stating of police and coroner's initial theory of suicide or accidental drug overdose with open mouthed

143

amazement. "Why in the world would he commit suicide? I mean sure... I'm happy as hell the bastard's dead, but-"

Jean reached over and patted Mona's hand. "Don't worry about it, Grandma. It looks like part of your neighborhood troubles are over."

Mona clutched Jean's hand, but leaned around her to meet Rachel's smiling demeanor. "You were talking to Nick. He told you to turn on the news. What the hell's going on here, Rachel? How can this all be happening?"

Rachel reached over to cover Mona's hand with Deke getting into the act by laying his chin on the human hands. "It's okay to react like you're doing with us, Mona, but you need to get a grip on your reaction. This isn't a game where we blurt out anything that comes to mind amidst strangers or the media in particular. Like the woman's saying, it was probably a suicide or accidental drug overdose."

"But-"

"But nothing, Grandma," Jean stated. "Don't take this so hard. When we had bad people after us, I found out sometimes no one can help us... at least no one in police departments and those stupid government agencies. Blackbeard would have killed you... and us. Now he's dead. Well... that's just too bad."

"Good God, girl, you're only nine," Mona remarked with dawning realization. "We can't condone murder!"

Jean stood, with Deke jumping down at her side. She stared into her Grandma's face with a shrug. "My Mom, Deke, and I wouldn't be alive if we'd depended on the police. Some things don't work, Grandma. When things don't work with dangerous stuff that will kill us, we have to depend on someone. We depend on Dad. Without him training us, you'd be dead. He taught us how to survive. He cares about us. Because of us, he cares about you."

"Jean's dead on right, Mona," Rachel agreed. "We all have to express remorse if asked about Blackbeard's death. We'll play that card anytime it's needed. Jean and I love you, but please don't assume we'll allow you to mess with Nick. If you want us in your life, you'll have to accept some difficult facts. Now would be the time to blurt out anything you have a problem with. Later will not only be unacceptable, it will be dangerous."

Mona embraced the feeling of relief Blackbeard's death clip had brought to the surface. She met Rachel's eyes without hesitation. "In for a penny, in for a pound."

"That's real good, Mona," Rachel replied. "You won't regret it. Remember this though: Jean, Deke, and I don't play games regarding Nick. If you want us out of your life, say so. We want you in our lives, but we're with Nick... period."

"Oh yeah," Jean said, reinforcing Rachel's statement. "Anyone messing with Dad, messes with me, Mom, and Deke."

Mona allowed a slow smile of acceptance to spread across her features. "Understood."

Chapter Seven

The Fixers

"How'd the troops take the news?"

"Very well. I knew Rachel and Jean would be coming undone without something to do, so I put them on the news watch. They'll check the main gist of anything reported. Plus, it was a great way to let Mona in on reality without any straight forward comments. She looks steady, but the troops will ease her into the facts of life in case she starts blurting out touchy-feely crap about her former neighbor who wanted to kill her."

Gus shook his head while holding Mona's rear entrance door in position for Nick to shim the bottom for reattachment. "I get it. You figure once the threat's diverted, Mona will start beating her breast for the poor dead gangster unfortunates that have been terrorizing her."

"Exactly," Nick replied. "Okay, I think this is perched perfectly. I'll fix the hinge, and the deadbolt. Then we'll kick back and wait for the clowns from next door to drift over for a chat about what happened to their fearless leader. Wait until you see my performance, Gus. You'll want to put my name in for the Academy Award."

"Under what category, Muerto?"

"Good point, Payaso. I don't think they have a category for me."

Nearly an hour later as Nick and Gus drank a beer out on the front porch, three of Blackbeard's posse walked down the driveway toward them. Nick had his 9mm Berretta under a newspaper setting on the small table at his side. Gus perused his laptop while holding his own Smith and Wesson 9mm automatic on the table behind the laptop. The three men, of varying heights just below six feet tall, and a little above it, stopped at the porch. Nick immediately dismissed two of them as wasted pieces of human debris living from one fix to the next. The middle one, a lean faced six-footer with a smirk looked to be the only one in the trio capable of firing a shot. He had tied back black hair, light blue eyes, and a perfectly trimmed goatee. Nick waved.

"Hi guys. Nice day, huh?"

Goatee spoke for the rest. "It sure is a nice day, friend. Our buddy stopped over here last night, and we were wondering if either of you had seen him."

Nick sat up with a concerned look. "Why no… we arrived early this morning. We're doing caretaking chores for the owner, Mona Charen. My partner and I only found a backdoor off its hinge. We fixed it, but didn't see anyone else around. When was he supposed to come over?"

Nick's question stymied the leader for a moment. Nick stood. "Sorry fellers. Would any of you like some coffee?"

"No… but thank you," the leader replied. "I guess he decided not to come over. You guys have a nice day."

Nick grinned like a redneck with a double cheese Big Mac in hand. "We sure will. Good to meet you. Do you have a number I should call if your friend stops by?"

The leader hesitated, but took a card out of his wallet. "Here's where I can be reached. Thank you for your concern."

"You bet," Nick replied, taking the card in hand. "What does your friend look like?"

"He's a big guy with a black beard. You'll know him if you see him."

"We'll watch for him. Ya'll have a great day. If we hear from your partner, I will sure get back to you on it."

"Yeah… okay. Thanks." The three walked off the way they had come.

"Damn. You should be on the 'Blue Collar Comedy Tour'. What the hell does a drug dealer's business card look like?" Gus accepted the card from Nick. "Name and phone number. Straight and to the point. Maybe you should have suggested they turn on the news."

"It's more fun this way, Gus. You haven't seen the second part of my act yet," Nick replied.

"Oh c'mon, Nick… you're not going to run over there all excited, and tell them to turn on the news." Gus studied Nick's face. "Oh crap… that's exactly what you plan to do. Have I told you that every cell in your body is rotten?"

"Not lately. It's nice to be remembered. I'll wait about fifteen minutes."

"How compassionate you are. I'll get the button cam. I suspect you're doing this to get a look inside their place for me to record."

"Very perceptive of you, Payaso. That is indeed what I have in mind plus a little more."

"A little more what? You're getting impatient. Anything you do right now will be messy. I know how much you like creating your murder scenes using unknowing gangbangers and drug dealers. What was wrong with your plan to give them all a hotshot to hell in the middle of the night using your famous stealth mode?"

"I'd like to go out to dinner tonight with our ladies, sip a few after dinner beverages, walk the Dekester, and get rested for our book signing. I need your help to do this adlib though, Payaso. I can't have your usual negative vibes throw off my intricate plans, my reluctant sidekick."

"Okay... spell it out for me. I'm at least three steps behind you on this." Gus sat down, motioning for clarification with a resigned look.

Nick took a deep breath. "Sorry, partner. I have this thanks to Rachel."

Nick showed Gus Blackbeard's .45 caliber Colt she confiscated. "I carried it with me for a contingency in case a few pieces fell into place. The guy with the goatee showing up with his crew illustrated who he has for backup, and what their competence level is. I'm knocking on their door all excited with news I heard on Blackbeard. They let me in. You, my faithful sidekick make noise at their back entrance. I need only a second to make this work perfectly. With the targets' attention drawn to your rattling at their chamber door, I will shoot goatee through the head, and stungun the crap out of his two cohorts. Then I can fix my scene of a tragic gangster falling out."

"Gee, that's wonderful, Muerto." Gus cringed slightly at the dispassionate attitude of his chosen brother. "You just talked to that pleasant man only moments ago, Muerto. Now, you're plotting to walk right in, shoot him in the head, and create a killing field with his crew. You are a very bad man."

"What's your point? Are you going to help me, or do I have to cut up your Payaso mask, and make poor El Muerto into a lone avenger?"

Gus laughed, standing and motioning at Nick in distasteful form. "You cold blooded prick! I'm in. I figured a more discreet ending for those murderous rubes, but I'm not bucking your record of creating police worthy scenes of death, involving only the targets. At least we already have the boss's name from Blackbeard.

149

Have you had time to trace this David Huxley's name, or did Paul find out anything about him?"

"Paul told me he's above legal suspicion, but has suspicious ties to Columbian financial interests. He owns a string of high end mercantile stores in Charleston simply called 'Huxley's'. He'd like me to consider sanctioning Huxley like I did in the old days. I'm thinking about it, but we don't have much time scheduled for Charleston. Maybe I should pass on Huxley. It's past time for law enforcement to earn their pay. Let the FBI have it. They'll stake the guy out for six months, and then contaminate something, letting him go free. If he's dangerous enough, Paul will come lay the big bucks on us to do him."

"I'm surprised you'd consider not doing everything yourself. I like it. Anyway, one step at a time. We should get on with this fabulous Plan B you're in love with."

"Good deal. Let's do this. I only have one more caveat to add into my plan I haven't mentioned. I'm going to call the police, and report hearing gunfire anonymously somewhere between here and the hotel as we flee this soon to be horrible shootout."

Staring in open mouthed amazement, it took a few moments for Nick's added ploy to sink in. Gus didn't hesitate. He remembered Nick saving his ass on a whim before. "I'm happy we're recording this shit, Muerto. Indeed, let's get your plan in gear."

* * *

"Son-of-a-bitch!" The goatee paced the room after he and his three colleagues entered Blackbeard's main place again. "Where the fuck could he have gone? I wonder now if he got a call, and had to take a meeting with the boss over this latest crap."

His cohorts looked bleary eyed at each other. They sold dope. Sure, they'd cut someone up if they needed to, but they didn't get into discussions about strategy or problems. They did what they were told. Period.

"He'll be back," one answered after many moments passed. "No one can take Blackbeard. Man... I don't want to stick my nose in his business. Did you call him?"

"Fuck yeah, I called him," goatee stated. "He ain't pickin' up."

The knock at the door startled the trio. They could see Nick waving through the screen door at them. They hadn't closed the main door. "Shit, it's that rube fuckin' around over at Mona's place," goatee said.

Goatee walked over to the door. "Hey... what's up?"

"The news," Nick said excitedly. "I think they have your friend on the news!"

Goatee smirked at Nick. He opened the screen door, wondering if maybe he would have to take care of this retard. "What the hell are you talkin' about? What's this about the news?"

Nick walked in with intense concern, never wavering from his eye contact with goatee. "Sorry... sorry... turn on the TV. I think they're still showing it on channel five!"

One of the drug-bots turned on the TV, using the remote to change the channel to five. It replayed the flagpole finding of Blackbeard in detail, along with the discovery of his name. Nick watched the rapt attention paid to the TV enlightenment with inner enjoyment while gripping Blackbeard's .45 caliber Colt at his waistband.

"Oh my God!" One of the street thugs exclaimed. "That's Blackbeard! Damn... what the hell do we do now?"

"Nothing, you moron," goatee said, still staring at the screen, and listening to the accompanying news banter. "What do you think we should do, idiot, go collect the body. He was next door waitin'. I can't believe it, but maybe that pregnant bitch got the drop on him. I can't figure it out. I have to think."

Gus banged on the rear door. Every head turned toward the noise. Nick drew Blackbeard's Colt, and shot goatee in the temple over his left ear. A split second later, Nick was stun-gunning the two drug-bots into unconsciousness. He then searched goatee for a weapon. Goatee carried a Ruger .40 caliber automatic. Nick put on his black Nitrile gloves. He aimed the Ruger with goatee's left hand, because he had noticed the weapon was positioned for a left handed draw. Nick shot both drug-bots in the arm, a leg, and the head.

"That'll teach you minions to mess with me, the Goatee."

After making sure the two drug-bots were dead, Nick wiped Blackbeard's Colt clean. He positioned the drug-bot nearest to goatee with the Colt in hand, and fired at goatee's shoulder, making sure the gunpowder residue would be all over the firing corpse's front.

"Take that, Goatee! We are avenged."

Nick held up the corpse's gun hand, and let it fall. The hand hit the floor, and the Colt jolted free near his fingers. Nick surveyed his scene with satisfaction before striding to the rear entrance. He unlocked and opened the door to a very tense Gus awaiting the conclusion of Nick's gang cleansing.

"Good timing, Payaso. It worked to perfection. Let's go into town, find a public telephone, and call 911. I believe there was a gun battle here."

152

"You are without a doubt the coldest bastard I've ever seen or heard of... even in the movies. Do I want to know how many murder scenes you've staged?"

"Not if you want to sleep at night."

"I'll take your word for it then. Let's get out of here," Gus said. "It's lucky the distance between places will keep people from noticing or reporting the gunfire, especially with the trouble people have had here with these dealers."

"Yep. I believe we're done here. Let's go find a payphone. That task in itself will probably take an hour. My ploy will be when I heard the gunshots, I took off in the car until I could find a public phone. The reason being, I didn't want the drug gang to know who called the police."

Not for the first time did Gus wonder about Nick's cold logic, placing each action into a pattern reinforcing his endeavor. "On it, boss. Let's go."

"I don't think you're very accepting of this fine ending, Gus. No matter. Let's adjourn to our pleasant hotel where we will put this problematic day behind us. Don't feel so bad, Payaso. No animals were hurt in this video. Let's have nothing but positive thoughts for our neighborhood reclamation project. The shootout didn't attract any nosy neighbors. We will have to stay a bit longer after the book signings to ensure we don't have to make any more adjustments. I'm hoping the one who drove the truck was in the group I helped into the afterlife."

"Oh no, say it isn't so. The great Muerto forgets to find out an important fact. This is a tragic day scarring the El Muerto legend."

"That's just mean, Payaso."

* * *

153

Gus called in an anonymous 911 call to police, warning of shots fired at Blackbeard's address at a convenience store halfway between Mona's house and the hotel, claiming fear of retribution as his reason for not giving his name. He and Nick drove to the hotel in time to take Deke for an early evening walk, and accompany their group to dinner. Rachel, pleasantly surprised at Nick's earlier than expected arrival, watched for any telltale signs indicating trouble on the horizon. She decided the direct approach would be more productive while they dressed for dinner as she stripped to get into the shower.

"You haven't said a word about your excursion to Mona's house. Is everything okay there now? I figured we should have been issued a news watch order by now."

Instead of answering, Nick began stroking Rachel's bare skin moving his hands in such a manner as to evoke a low moan of pleasure. In moments, his attention escalated into a rather lengthy delay in their showering. By the time they walked to their in room shower, Rachel was glistening with sweat, her breathing returning to normal slowly.

"God Nick… I appreciate the nice hello. What brought that on?"

"You looked too sexy for me to allow your showering without giving you a reason for needing one. In answer to your earlier question, we completed the neighborhood renovation a bit differently than anticipated, and here we are back early. We'll check the news before dinner. Did you talk to Cassie at all yet?"

"She hasn't called or anything. Maybe she won't be arriving until later," Rachel said. "I hope Cassie checks in early enough to get a good night's sleep before the signing tomorrow. I like her. She enjoys the signings as much as you do I think."

Nick led the way into the shower, setting the water temperature before pulling Rachel in with him. "Her eyes beam in a cash register type glow when she spots a line of hundreds waiting to get into the signing. I doubt she sleeps much before a signing. She goes on a caffeine high. When it implodes, I see her start to drag."

Nick began soaping Rachel down in a less than utilitarian way. Before his cleaning ministrations ended they had jointly found another reason for showering. Only the pounding on their bedroom door pierced into the erotic shower scene Nick had created.

"Hey! Anybody home in there?" Jean's screech carried through over the water noise. "I'm hungry! Quit foolin' around in there, and come to dinner, Damn it!"

Rachel clung to Nick, gasping for breath and laughing. "Did Dagger just cuss us out?"

"I believe so." Nick shut off the water. "I can hear Gus and Tina chortling away out there too. I guess we'd better dress for dinner before Jean leads a break in to get us."

Rachel kissed him with lingering breathless frenzy. "Jesus, Nick... that was a wonderful shower. What the hell got into you?"

"Just a little bit of life for a moment, Rach," Nick answered, thinking *I am El Muerto. Damn if Gus didn't get that nametag right as rain. I wonder if I'm getting caught up in this giving and taking life to an unhealthy level. It's starting to invade my reality.* He noticed Rachel watching his face as he dried her off. "What?"

"Nothing. I sense El Muerto invading our conversation."

Wow, we've been together long enough for her to start reading my mind. Scary. "You're starting to know me too well. I'm not sure how comfortable I am with that revelation."

155

"Yes!" Rachel pumped her fist, looking like an older spitting image of Jean. "I can make the deadliest killer in the universe uncomfortable. I can't wait to hear the news. I'll bet it's the stuff of nightmares for bad guys. I have only one question – is there any more targets on this visit?"

"Possibly one. We know the boss's name from what Blackbeard told us. We're allowing Paul to sort through everything. If he thinks we can divvy the network into parts for local and federal authorities, I'm leaving the next steps to him. If he thinks the boss has a chance of fleeing or beating out anything we have to pin him with, I'll handle him while we're in Charleston. It has turned out to be more than just a neighborhood drug problem."

Rachel hugged him. "I'm so proud of you. Thank you for fixing Mona's situation."

"Hey… I'm only a cleanup tool. You practically aced out the whole gang by yourself. I can't tell you how juiced I was, listening to how you handled Blackbeard, and the truck episode. I sure as hell chose the right time and person to make me into a family man. It seems like you serving me at the diner while in the witness protection program happened a hundred years ago."

"I know! It doesn't seem possible with all that's happened," Rachel agreed. "C'mon, Muerto, let's get you dressed."

"Want to give me a little taste first?" Nick made inappropriate erotic nuances, making Rachel gasp.

"Damn it, Nick! Now I won't be able to think of anything else through dinner. I hate you! Couldn't you have kept your perverted tendencies to yourself until we returned to the room?"

Nick massaged Rachel's shoulders. "I believe El Muerto's work is done."

"Not hardly."

* * *

In the Charleston Grill they were all seated with prompt courteous attention. Nick immediately ordered appetizers Jean found suitable. Once they were delivered post haste, Jean quieted down. Mona, Rachel, and Tina ordered a Merlot they thought sounded good, while Nick and Gus stuck with a favorite: Bushmill's Irish Whiskey.

"I saw more news today, Nick," Mona kept her gaze on the table after the drinks were served. "There was a shootout in the drug house next door with three men dead. They apparently disagreed about something, and it ended in all of them dead."

"It's really sad when people adopt such a dangerous lifestyle," Nick replied. "It was advantageous they had a falling out at this time, and you'll be able to return to your home without worrying about those dangerous thugs."

Jean giggled while gobbling down varied appetizers with relish. Silence followed with everyone sipping their assorted beverages. Mona seemed on the verge of saying something more, but when she looked at Rachel, she received a headshake warning her from more speculation. Gus and Nick toasted each other without notice, sipping strongly from their double Bushmill's.

Nick spotted his agent, Cassie. He waved at her. "We have company. It's Cassie. When she nears the table, let's all shun her on my cue."

Gus laughed, but Rachel gasped in displeasure. "Don't you dare!"

Nick grinned. "Relax. Even Gus knew I was kidding. I believe you're wound a little tightly my dear. Sip your wine. Is Quinn making his presence known with his feet again?"

Rachel sipped a bit more Merlot while nodding. "Yeah, he's letting his poor suffering Mom know he's nearly ready to do an Alien stomach burst on me."

"Eeeuuuuuwwwwhhhh… Mom!" Jean crinkled her face in displeasure. "That's not funny. You're already drugging him with wine. Quit insulting him."

"Why you…" Nick had to clamp down on Rachel as she readied to launch across the table. "Your moment of despair is on the way, little missy!"

"Calmness," Nick urged laughingly as Cassie arrived at the table. "Let's keep this a fun dinner. Hi, Cass. The only new face here is Rachel's Mother-in-law, Mona Claren. Mona… this is Cassie Sedwick, my agent."

Cassie reached over to shake hands with Mona as a server added a chair to their table. "I'm happy to meet you, Mona. Will you be going to the book signing?"

"Yes. I'm very happy to meet you too. Visiting with Rachel and Nick has been an eye opening experience. My Granddaughter Jean has grown so much. I don't know that I've ever been as intrigued with people visiting as I have been this time. I'm looking forward to going to a real book signing for the first time."

"You'll have a good time." Cassie sat down. "I think we'll break some records tomorrow. I heard on the news there's been a gang shootout in that nasty 'Union Heights' area. Three suspected drug dealers killed each other in a gun battle inside a house on Echo Avenue."

"It's next door to my house, Cassie," Mona said. "They've been dealing drugs there for a long time."

Cassie couldn't hide the shock at Mona's admission. "Sorry, Mona, that's horrible."

"They've been terrorizing the people who live in my neighborhood so we were all afraid to call the police or testify. I'm hoping this will mean better times."

Nick changed the subject as a waiter brought Cassie the glass of wine she ordered while sitting down. "How's our renowned publisher doing since the New York tour stops?"

"Linda was deliriously happy on the phone, Nick. I spoke with her before leaving on the plane. I guess you haven't checked today, but Caribbean Contract is now the number one best seller on the New York Times list. Congratulations. Linda has dropped any pretension about trying to mold your writing to fit whatever goofball liberal flavor of the month trend they come up with. I think she finally realizes there is fiction, and pulp fiction. You've never hidden or pretended your work is anything but what it is: pulp fiction. Apparently, contrary to what the publishers keep harping, pulp fiction is a viable and sales worthy genre."

Nick accepted the toasts and well wishes for owning the number one novel in the country with good natured acceptance. "Thank you. This has been a great book tour for me to experience too, especially with my partner Gus playing a larger role. It certainly bumped sales incredibly well. I'm glad the added notoriety with the Kader factor didn't mar the results. I'm very happy with how this road trip has progressed. I know some unexpected happenings helped, but you did an outstanding job organizing and guiding us. Thanks, Cass."

Cassie acknowledged the toasts to her ability with aplomb, laughing a little at the circumstances mentioned. "Yeah… you stopping a murderer back in Pacific Grove, and dealing with his relatives on this book tour garnered enough publicity to make the whole trip worthwhile. Mostly, I schedule boring authors who write exciting literature and fiction. With Nick, I get exciting reality going along with the fiction – the best of all possible worlds. Your fight with the Kader relative outside the New York book signing launched a thousand positive blogs."

"I'm glad it didn't turn into a riot," Nick replied. "The police did a great job checking into the family of the guy in the book signing line, Alex Kader. Gus and I stay aware when we attend anything in public now. I'm glad for Dimah's sake the more psycho members of her family don't live near her."

"People are sick of being hung out to dry by fundamental Islam," Cassie agreed. "I hate even dealing with the controversy, but your helping Jean's teacher in Pacific Grove bolstered you into a position defending women in general against Sharia Law. Our women's groups for the most part in this country defend nothing unless it has something to do with liberal causes. They have been strangely silent about Sharia Law goons doing honor killings, female genital mutilation, and the near enslavement a woman goes through as a wife in Muslim countries."

"That El Muerto guy I've been reading about is brutal," Mona said. "He's killed a bunch of those Isis stooges, and stopped two terrorist plots, along with two serial killers. He and his partner, Payaso, seem more dangerous than the ones they've killed."

"What about all the lives they saved by killing the bad guys?" Jean stared at her Grandmother with furrowed brow.

"We have laws, honey," Mona replied, gripping Jean's hand. "We can't take the law into our own hands or we're no better than the bad guys."

"I'd rather be worse than the bad guys until they're dead, Grandma. Wouldn't you want to have an El Muerto and Payaso take care of the bad guys in your neighborhood?"

"But where does it all end if our laws don't work? We have to trust in justice. Otherwise, innocent people could be hurt. I know it's hard to understand, Jean, but vigilante justice seems great until the wrong man is murdered. Lynch mobs in past instances of vigilante justice vented their supposedly righteous rage on targets of opportunity."

Jean received the Muerto stare from Nick when she glanced at him. She smiled. "I understand, Grandma, but some folks just need killin'."

Mona gasped, but when Jean, and everyone else laughed at the movie cliché, she sighed. "Good one, Jean. You had me there for a moment. Where did you hear such a thing?"

Jean shrugged. "I watched the movie 'Sling Blade' last year when I wasn't supposed to. Mom didn't want me to see it, because I was too young. I liked it though. It was sort of vigilante justice too."

"Let's have a toast to our justice system. May it eventually be as effective as we all hope and pray it will be in the future," Nick toasted, trying to end the comments on a positive note.

Jean made a face. "May as well wish for world peace, Santa, and the Easter Bunny."

* * *

The line moved along with humor and good natured kidding. Readers from all over the area had arrived in mass at the much publicized event. Gus kept a running dialogue going with yachtsmen interested in his sailing expertise. Others bore into Nick with literary questions concerning scene creation, and humorous outtakes involving misuse of pronouns. Anything relating to editing Nick handled without malice or bad temper. He issued the same statement to any reader questioning his word usage and literary judgment with a lowering of his head, and an angry bass voiced acknowledgement that 'editing is the devil'. His response elicited laughs rather than confrontations over what every writer knows deep in his or her heart – writers write alone, and writers

161

edit alone… with many times unwanted guidance from editors without a clue as to the nature of the message a scene seeks to carry. Everyone in line within hearing seemed to enjoy the Nick and Gus show.

Mona watched the goings on with Rachel, Jean, and Tina, trying to grasp the questions and answers given to the readers. They sat near the main signing table, but far enough away, so as not to be a distraction whether they chose to leave, stay, or take a break. Mona seemed genuinely perplexed Nick didn't answer back harshly when criticized for what he had written or the way he had written it. After a particularly long exchange about his using dialogue to move a scene or show action instead of describing it in detail, Nick simply answered he wrote what he loved to read. That provoked a whispered exchange with Rachel and Jean.

"Why doesn't Nick simply sign the books and say thanks?"

"Dad likes interacting with the readers. He doesn't care what they think about his writing," Jean answered. "He told me the important thing is they're still reading his novels no matter what objection they have to the way he tells the story."

Mona stared at Jean in surprise. "Doesn't he write according to what sells?"

The question caused Jean to laugh out loud, which she tried to muffle with some success. "No! Dad writes stories. I don't think he'd care if anyone read them or not. He loves to write. I've watched him. He smiles, laughs, bears down as if he were in a fight, and generally acts out everything as he goes along. In what I've learned from him, or seen his reactions to, the stories mean everything. The way Dad creates the stories he leaves for someone else to judge. I like it. He loves what he's doing. I guess the readers like it well enough too."

Mona clasped Jean's hands. "Your Dad was a lot like you… I mean your real Dad. Rick took a different read on anything he

162

was exposed to. He never cared what anyone thought about what he did, or how he did it."

Jean hugged Mona. "Mom told me. He loved his work. She told me he was the best at what he did. Nick is the best at what he does, and sometimes it goes way beyond writing. Don't think he doesn't pay attention to every word the people in line say to him. He really does. I've already started writing stories, and I plan on writing my first novel before I'm a teenager."

"That is incredible! Is that what you want to be, Jean… a writer?"

Jean's face warred with her first instinct to tell Mona everything about what she wanted. She had learned the hard way about trust. "It's one of the careers I'm considering. Mom's okay with most of them."

Rachel gripped Jean's neck in a playful choking hold. "You better be careful, girl. Maybe you had better take a closer look at what you're edging towards, and redirect to being a doctor or engineer."

"I'll be fine," Jean stated adamantly. "I can do more than one career at a time. Sometimes you need a day-job like Dad says writers need starting out. One thing I know, I'll have to earn a living before I launch off into what I truly want."

"And what would that be, young lady?" Mona patted her hand.

Jean giggled through the dead silence at the table. "I think I'd like to be a movie star. I have to pretend with my Mom so much, I may as well get paid for it if I get a chance."

Rachel laughed, but then she launched. Tina, not fooled by either the pretenses or reactions to pretenses, caught Rachel at the waist, pulling her down into the seat again. "Rachel… not the time or place for child discipline, girlfriend. You need to calm down. Jean is eating your lunch with this stuff."

Rachel stewed in place like a fast boiling roast. She pointed an index finger at Jean while nodding and smiling with grim intent. "Every electrical device you own is mine once we get back into the room… every device! If you have any playing cards, you better bone up on solitaire, because your gaming license has been revoked!"

The horrified look flowing down over Jean's countenance caused inadvertent snorts and chuckles. Jean shifted her attention to Tina, only to get a smiling shrug.

Tina took stock of Rachel's tight lipped glare fixed on Jean with grim determination. "Looks like you tugged on Superman's cape once too often. I'm afraid it's time to pay the piper. You'd best plead for leniency, and throw yourself on the mercy of the court. Otherwise… I sure hope you enjoy playing Frisbee with Deke, because you'll be doing a lot of it for entertainment."

Jean crossed her arms, returning Rachel's unrelenting stare. "I don't bargain with terrorists."

Mona listened with amusement. "My daughter and I had much the same give and take when she approached double digits in age. I hate to tell you this, Rachel, but it gets worse."

"How is Celia?" Rachel gave up on the stare down with Jean. "Is she going to visit while we're here?"

"She just reconciled with her husband, Ed. I'm glad too. Celia went through that unhappy phase where nothing pleased her. Luckily, she didn't go through with the divorce all the way. Ed Dalman is a great guy. He's an IT specialist for a string of stores in the Charleston area. She works as a manager at one of the stores. Saturdays are their busiest day of the week, so both of them are working. Ed left me a message earlier they would try and meet us for dinner tonight. They would love to give the Charleston Grill a try if you don't mind eating there again."

"I love their food," Jean piped in. "I can't wait to see Aunt Celia."

"Celia will be shocked when she sees you, Jean. You look twelve, and you talk like you're eighteen. That teacher of yours Nick helped – is she letting you keep up on your studies while making this trip?"

"I've scored all A's on my papers, Grandma," Jean stated, turning to Rachel. "Of course that means nothing to some people."

Tina laughed as the Rachel/Jean staring war began again. "We've been making sure all her homework and papers get done while we've been away. Ms. Kader has a website where we can find out what's due, and take any tests on-line. Nick likes to check on how she's doing too after everything that happened. She promised to let us know if any of her other psycho relatives arrive unexpectedly."

Jean spotted a sullen looking man next in line to talk with Nick. "That tall, thin guy with the brown ponytail is trouble, Mom."

Rachel watched the man waiting impatiently, his hands clenching Nick's novel, Caribbean Contract with white knuckled concentration. Dressed in tan Dockers, with a light brown cashmere open necked sweater, he looked like a college professor. His brown eyes glinted angrily as he stared at Nick without glancing away for a second. "I don't think he's trouble, but he sure has a chip on his shoulder. Nick's already glanced at him twice, and I see Gus smiling at him. I think the boys have been scoping Mr. Dockers for longer than we have, Jean."

Jean hunched forward. "This is going to be good."

"This bookstore doesn't have the security force for a book signing like they do in New York. Even here in a large city like Charleston, I doubt the Barnes & Noble book store thinks much beyond shop lifters as far as crime goes," Mona said.

"That's okay, Mona," Tina stated. "Nick and Gus do."

* * *

In between fans, Nick kept an eye on one of the people in line. "You see that guy with the sweater, Gus?"

"I've been watching you watch him. He's next after our approaching little gray haired lady. He has a bug up his ass about something."

"As long as he keeps a choke hold on my novel, I'm not concerned," Nick replied. He stood up slightly with Gus as a woman possibly in her late eighties or early nineties approached the table with a walker, and Nick's novel in the carry basket. Nick went around the table to help her get seated, while shaking hands with her. She settled in with a wry smile on the chair while Nick took her hardcopy of Caribbean Contract to his table side. "I hate you, Nick McCarty."

"You do? How can I make what angers you better?"

"You can't. I love your assassin series. The moment a new one comes out, I read it two or three times in the first week I have it. You need to write faster... damn it! I love Jed as Diego's sidekick. He's been alone too long. Jed really livens things up with the added humor in their exchanges. Oh... and the first time through the novel I can't even sleep until I get to the end. You're messing with an old woman's sleep time."

Nick and Gus had been enjoying the old woman's diatribe with appreciation. "What's your name, young lady?"

"Don't you call me young lady!" The old woman bristled. "I've earned these years, you young punk! My name's Gladys, and I ain't the lead singer in 'The Pips' either."

Nick made calming gestures with his hands before launching into a heartfelt note to Gladys in her book front. "Very well, you old bat, I'll find something to say to you in here. Do you have an e-mail address?"

Gladys cackled appreciatively at Nick's disrespect. "That's more like it. Give me a pen and paper. I'll write it down for you."

Gus was ready with pad and paper. Gladys wrote down her e-mail address in efficient form. She peered into Gus's face with affection. "I've been listening to your answers to the at sea adventure part. I could tell you're no phony. My late husband and I sailed back in the day when there were very few ports. Repairs were a bitch, and we never headed on a voyage without a bunch of repair parts on board."

Gladys took a moment, laughing over an old memory. "There were pirates back then just like now. Brad and I had hand weapons, but we also had a thirty caliber machine gun. When we were approached, we called out to state their business. If they didn't, we fired a pattern in front of their boat. That did the trick."

"I'll bet it did," Gus said.

"I'm going to send you the raw chapters as I write, Gladys," Nick whispered. "You can be privy to the book as it gets written. I'm working on Assassin's Folly right now."

Gladys reached across and gripped Nick's hand in both hers. "God bless you, Nick. Your banter in the books, and humor, make me laugh all the time."

She released him and stood up. "I'm not taking any more of your time. These kind folks have been waiting too. Thank you."

167

Nick hurried around to hug her. "Thanks for coming, Gladys. You don't have to drive or take public transport do you?"

"Hell no. I have a driving Miss Daisy pal. See you, Nick. Take care of him, Gus. Don't let him take any unnecessary chances like killing that idiot school teacher predator."

"I'll do my best, Ms. Daisy," Gus answered with a wave.

Her driver arrived for escorting duties while Gladys waved to everyone in line. He was black, a few inches over six feet tall, and wore a huge smile until the assumed professor at the front of the line moved toward her. The smile disappeared, and unadulterated danger radiated from the driver's face. Nick saw the professor move toward Gladys. He moved with him, but backed away with a smile at sight of Gladys's driver.

"That's close enough, Sir," the driver stated. "Can I help you?"

The professor stepped back as Gladys smiled and gripped her driver's arm. "Luke handles all my light work. Back up, youngster. You've got nothing to say to me. Go take your turn, and quit holding up the line."

The laughs at his expense sent the professor toward Nick with naked rage in his face. Nick had already sat down in his previous spot, trying with Gus to keep from enjoying Gladys's comments too much. The professor sat down in front of Nick, slamming Caribbean Contract on the desk. Nick reached to take the novel for signing without comment. The professor slammed his hand down on the book."

"I want to know why it's so damn difficult for you to use a pronoun correctly. Your books drive me crazy. It's like nails scrapped over a chalk-board. I'm not leaving this seat until I get an answer. I have a master's degree in English. I'm asked many times to edit academic papers of great importance. Please don't hide behind your publishing editor! Everyone knows they live in fear of you big time money guys."

"Are you referring to dialogue, Sir?" Nick sat calmly through the professor's spiel without interrupting.

The calm question caught the professor by surprise. "Yes, and I'm sure you'll defend it with crap like people don't talk that way. They should, and novelists have a duty to influence our future students with correctness at all levels."

Nick gestured at Gus. "Me and Gus disagree."

His common, but extensively misused use of the pronoun me received loud enjoyment of Nick's illustration. "Me and you don't have to argue about this. You and me can be friends without letting grammar get in the way of our friendship. Me and-"

The professor's chair pitched back as he jerked to his feet. "Stop it! It's not a joke!"

"Calm down, professor." Nick went around the desk once again to put a comforting arm around his critique. "Think about it. Maybe in your circles, no one makes a pronoun mistake while speaking everyday dialogue. Such is not true in everyday life. People inadvertently use the wrong past tense or pronoun usage, or God forbid, sneak in the mortal sin of more than one negative in a sentence. We all are guilty of some grammar misuse at one point or another. If you're reading my novels, you must be reading for entertainment, right?"

"Well... yes, but-"

"No buts about it. If you like the story, why concentrate on the grammar rules while reading. I understand some common dialogue usage can bother purists, but have you ever read any of William Faulkner's works, such as 'The Long Hot Summer'? He had an ear for dialogue. So do I. In my works of fiction, I use real

169

life dialogue. People in certain instances use pronouns along with the entire English language wrongly."

The professor was aghast. "Surely you don't compare yourself to William Faulkner."

"Nope. I entertain millions more people than Faulkner ever did. Perhaps the answer here is for you to stop reading my novels. It's a great solution. You'll be less pissed off. You won't be stalking me at book signings, and you can use me as an example for your students. You are a teacher, right?"

"I teach English," the professor admitted. It was clear Nick's use of William Faulkner's works had toned down the outrage. "I'm not the professor from Gilligan's Island. I'm Matt Sagan. I guess I have been obsessing over this to a rather ridiculous degree."

"No problem, Matt. I'm glad you enjoyed the stories. Would you still like me to sign your book?"

"Sure… uh… could you sign it to Matt, the grammar Nazi just for fun?"

Nick laughed along with many in line within hearing. "I sure will."

Nick signed a personal note, handed the book to Matt again, and shook hands with him. "Thanks for coming by, Matt. You're a good sport. Don't let the grammar rules overshadow your life, my friend."

"I'll try to be a more tolerant grammar Nazi, Nick. Thanks for the dialogue."

After the English teacher left, the conversations turned to sailing and weapons. Although less humorous, the wide range of questions kept the line entertained, and not feeling as if they were being rushed. The bookstore manager had tagged the end of the line to within fifteen minutes of the allotted time. Nick could see Cassie discussing sales with the manager, while his family and friends were close to eye glazing boredom time.

"I'm looking forward to drinks and food. I'm talked out," Gus said. "It was an enjoyable day for me. First thing when we return home, I'm taking the 'Lady' out on a long sail. Want to come?"

"Sure. We have to empty the freezer in Carmel Valley." Nick finished putting away his notebook computer, and his notepads.

"Damn... I forgot all about that. Yeah, we need to do some housecleaning there. John can give us a hand. The more I've considered your new recruit, the better I like the idea of having him with us. You'll be able to take another contract in the sand easier with John."

"Not likely. I'm staying the hell out of the sand. I have to talk with Grace about the Nancy Pettinger deal. We've been a bit busy lately. I suppose she'll be figuring I'm ignoring her, but Pettinger should have been a slam dunk. Here comes Cassie."

His agent hurried to her stars, giving Nick and Gus jubilant hugs. "The store manager said we set the all-time record for sales on signings. I did two interviews for Charleston papers during the signing, and they plan to do a complete feature on you. I filled them in on your military record, along with current events. Can I work on you doing a couple of signings in the near future out west... say maybe Los Angeles and San Francisco?"

"Sure, Cass. This has been fun, and fit right in with some other personal things we needed to do. Gus and I would love to do some West Coast stops. We'd maybe even sail down there if the ancient mariner here is agreeable."

171

"Damn, Nick, that sounds real good," Gus said, wondering immediately if there was an ulterior motive on Nick's radar.

Cass grabbed Nick's hands. "I will set them up right away. Let me get some dates and places for you to consider."

"No problem. Did you want to have dinner with us tonight? I believe we're planning on returning again to the Charleston Grill."

"I wish I could, Nick. I'm taking a late flight back to New York. Your tour has stirred up a hornet's nest of publicity. There are even calls about a 'Caribbean Contract' movie."

Nick grinned. "I wrote the screenplay for 'Caribbean Contract' on my Final Draft software. I convert my novels once in a while if I think they may draw attention. I'll send you the PDF screenplay when I get back to the hotel. You, of course would be my agent for that also if you'd like."

"Oh my God! You have it already converted into screenplay form? Jesus... Nick... that's awesome. Let me get back to New York with the screenplay already written, and I'll hit that angle full bore with the interested parties."

"It will be in your inbox tonight, Cass. Have a safe flight home."

"I will... you bugger. Gus... guard this gold mine with your life," Cassie ordered while moving to the exit with a wave.

"A movie, huh?" Gus nudged Nick as Cassie streaked out of the bookstore. "We should play ourselves."

"I don't think so, Payaso. Let's gather our crew, who made it through the entire signing without a whine. "I feel a good night's sipping coming on, brother."

"Don't change the subject. I want to play Jed in the movie. Make it happen."

The two men laughed together, enjoying what they knew could never be.

Chapter Eight

Extenuating Circumstances

"Hi, this is Celia and Ed Dalman," Mona introduced the pair sharing a large table at the Charleston Grill while waiting for Nick, Gus, Rachel, Tina, and Jean to join them. "Celia's my daughter, and Ed my son-in-law. It seems silly, but it will make this go quickly to get past the introductions."

The reunion went well with Jean overjoyed to see her Aunt again. Handshakes and hugs rounded out the initial greetings. Ed Dalman, an affable, red haired six footer carrying only a small paunch at his waist, hugged his wife Celia with affection Nick considered a genuine thankfulness for still having her in his life. Celia, a brown haired beauty in the five and a half foot range carried a few extra pounds with aplomb. Nick smiled with admiration for a couple who even with problems, decided life without each other was not an option.

"I'm glad you and Celia could join us, Ed. My publisher's handling all expenses, including dinners, so please be our guests here. It's all paid for," Nick said. "Gus and I, after a long day acting out our fantasy lives for readers have decided on a few Bushmill's Irish whiskies to enjoy the day's end with. Please order anything and everything you two would like."

"Thanks, Nick," Ed replied as they all took their seats and the waitress hurried over. "I'm the designated driver tonight, so I'll have a Diet Pepsi. God knows if I'd had the inkling our drinks and dinner were on the expense sheet, I would have taken a taxi over with Celia."

"Have whatever you like, Ed. I'll have a limousine take you and Celia home, and bring you back in the morning to pick up your car," Nick said as the waitress waited.

"Well… okay then. I'll have a double Scotch with water back," Ed stated to much amusement from the group.

After the orders were taken and the waitress on her way to fill the orders, Ed leaned back happily in his seat. "A limo, huh? You must be doing pretty well with the book sales, Nick. That is awesome. Does it ever bother you that people don't recognize you like they do movie stars?"

"That's a blessing," Nick replied. "I have no ambition to be recognized on the street. I like meeting the readers at book signings, but dealing with fans in everyday life would be tricky. Most of the parents at Jean's school know me and what I do back home. They don't make a big deal about it. Most of them have never read a Diego novel. Thankfully, writers and movie celebrities are a lot different as far as notoriety goes."

The waitress arrived with their drinks. Nick proposed an instant toast. "To family and friends."

After Nick's toast, conversation drifted to everyday life, occupations, plans, and troubles in Charleston. Nick and Gus kept silent as the recent demise of Mona's worrisome neighbors was recounted and passed over. Jean explained their vacation details, illustrating with words all the sights they had seen in both New York and Boston. Jean held the other adults' attention with her passion, and intricate attention to detail.

"You would make a wonderful writer, Jean," Mona said. "You describe everything in such entertaining detail. You're a natural. Isn't she, Nick."

"That's what I've been telling her, Mona. By the time she hits her late teens, she'll have a bestselling novel."

"Yep," Jean agreed. "I need to get real life experiences. I've already had a bunch of them, but now I need to be an assassin, a

175

private detective, and a politician so I'll know the slimiest thing on earth I can be. I need a baseline."

When the group recovered from Jean's adlib, Rachel came around to hug her. "You are without a doubt the most perplexing child within my meager knowledge."

"Does this mean my electronic devices ban is lifted?"

"What's in it for me?"

"I promise to stop baiting you."

Rachel grabbed Jean's hair, shaking it slightly. "You do know if you're putting me on, I will make your life miserable on a 24/7 basis, right?"

Jean hung her head comically. "Yes, Mommy… I know my life is forfeit if I screw with you. I won't do it… although the effort will curb many of my creative talents."

Rachel perused her nine year old daughter with adult angst. She knew intimately what Jean had already survived because of her. She felt Nick's hand clasp hers. "Okay, you brat, but you mess with my head again, and there will be blood."

"Agreed," Jean said. "Under protest."

"One more word, and I melt down every electrical device you have into plastic pulp," Rachel stated, shaking Jean's head with attitude.

Jean gave Rachel a thumbs up without speaking to much amusement.

Rachel sat down. "Sorry everyone. Jean and I had to define the future war zone parameters for a moment. Ed, Mona's son, and my first husband Rick worked in accounting and IT for the Tanus Group in past times. That must be an amazing opportunity with a large string of stores involved. I bet you're on call 24/7 to counteract problems."

Ed sipped his Scotch while nodding with a smile in agreement. "You have it down perfectly, Rachel. It doesn't seem to matter how well trained my managers are, I always get involved no matter what measures I have in place to counteract problems. I answer only to the store owner, David Huxley. He understands the glitches in IT departments so I never have to worry about nitpicking oversight. I explain everything in detail as problems arise."

Nick and Gus exchanged a poignant moment of recognition at the mention of Huxley's name with Nick shaking his head slightly.

"I know how important having an understanding boss is," Rachel replied. She did not miss the silent exchange between Gus and Nick, nor did Jean. "The Huxley's chain must be a sure thing. Are they like Walmart?"

"We try to please a broad consumer clientele like Walmart," Ed hunched forward, obviously excited by his job. "We only deal in the furnishing, lighting, and appliance type products. It's an incredibly competitive field. We have to keep up on market trends and competition on a daily basis. Dave loves the challenges and competition. He says it makes us stronger when cutting costs, and doing specials, while keeping our expenses in mind."

"I don't think I could handle a job like yours," Nick said. "I bet the market fluctuations in products must drive you nuts."

"Yes!" Ed became animated in spite of Celia's calming hand over his. "We adapt almost on an hourly basis in some respects. You and Rachel seem very knowledgeable about franchises like Huxley's."

"We have some common ground," Rachel said.

"There's an understatement," Jean tagged the conversation with a nine year old's lance.

Nick immediately thwarted Jean's attempt at a backdoor end around her Mom. "This chain franchise has always been a mystery to me, Ed. The hierarchy and chain of command must be intricate in design as well as implementation. How far does an owner like Mr. Huxley stay in the background? It would be incredibly tempting to try and run everything no matter how competent the people handpicked to run the operation."

Ed settled with a noncommittal wave of one hand, and his Scotch in the other. "You're right. There are overlapping intrusions, depending on the market, and the product involved. Dave keeps a tight rein on furniture shipments around the country, for example. Although they represent a small portion of profitable sales, Dave is in love with the movement of his company's products to the far reaches of not only North America, but also overseas. We try to stay as cutting edge as we can get with designs and materials."

"Markets overseas must be a scary entity in these times. I'm surprised Mr. Huxley feels they're so valuable. I wouldn't have thought furniture to be an overly profitable venture in these times. What's your best market overseas?"

"Europe," Ed stated. "We have an Avant-garde living room set that has caught fire there in sales. Dave is personally overseeing all aspects concerning that market. He checks constantly from when the shipment is loaded into the container to when it leaves the dock onboard a ship."

"Dave stopped over our house last night," Celia said. "He was upset about something, and wanted Ed to go over all the details for the container ship leaving port on Monday. He asked Ed if we'd like to accompany the shipment this time."

Nick frowned as he pictured what accompanying the shipment meant. "Isn't that rather unusual? I mean a container ship is not exactly a pleasure boat."

"It would mean seeing Europe on the company's dime," Ed replied. "Dave wants me to oversee all deliveries. It seems like a big deal, but it's more a reward. On the business side, I will meet with all our contacts overseas on a personal basis. One on one relationships with our business associates at the delivery level, instead of flying over on a chartered corporate jet where I'd meet with other suits in a boardroom, Dave believes will cement our position in over there."

Nick watched the excited glow emanating from Ed's features as he discussed the venture. His actions against Blackbeard and his gang had stirred David Huxley into action, worrying the shipment leaving port in less than two days could be at risk, because of what might have been found by the authorities at Blackbeard's place. That meant to Nick that Blackbeard had been in charge of more than what he had claimed. *I must be losing my touch.*

"You look a bit grim, Nick," Celia commented. "Is something wrong?"

"No, not at all." Nick realized he had allowed his alter ego to surface for a moment. *This is what happens when I stop being a psycho, and start allowing family life to invade my other reality.* "I didn't mean to put a damper on our dinner get together. You know how it is. I started thinking about sales, publishers, book signings, and the end of a long East Coast tour. I think it's wonderful you and Ed can make a European tour with your company's merchandise. I hope the merchandise will not be mishandled, my friends."

The waitress arrived, took their orders and left. She returned with drink refills as Jean sensing something ominous in the prior conversation tried directing it with her own interrogation.

"Uncle Ed. What would you do when the ship gets to port. How would you know who to contact or what to do?"

"Good question," Ed answered, appreciative of Jean's interest. "I have a number to contact when we're nearing port. Dave said I'd be meeting with not only the dock crew responsible for accepting the container, but also a couple of our European connection's people in charge at the retail level."

"That must be a big container," Jean continued.

Ed chuckled. "Actually, it's four containers, honey. Each one has twenty of our living room sets packed so no harm can come to them."

"Wow. I thought with all the terrorist threats, the authorities would check everything," Jean said, leaning forward in an interested posture. "Don't they rip your packing all apart before it ever leaves the docking area?"

"Most docking facilities have infrared scanners, but also scanners able to detect explosive materials. When they see furniture crates, they do a quick check during docking if they do it at all. They also have the offloading area under 24/7 surveillance. Besides, the containers have already been loaded awaiting departure."

Jean smiled. "That's good. What about drugs? Aren't the port authorities, especially overseas, always inspecting for drugs? I've seen those movies where people in charge of railway stations, ports, and airports, frame people for extortion overseas."

Jean's observation amused the group, Ed in particular, but Nick and Gus not so much.

"I like your thinking, young lady," Ed complimented her, "but we don't ship drugs - just furniture. I doubt they'd plant drugs in our containers. I realize they do it all the time in the movies. The

180

idea would make a good book though. Don't worry, Jean. We'll be fine."

"I hope so, Uncle Ed."

Tina saw Gus taking tiny sips of his drink with a big smile. "I figured you'd be on your third double by now, Gus. The signing's over. I thought you and the famous author would be tossing them down. Soon, you two will be sitting on Otter's Point beach with charged up coffees."

"Gus and I are taking it easy on the sipping tonight," Nick replied. "We're thinking of going sailing when we return home. We need to make a couple of check lists for the trip."

"That sounds like a good idea," Rachel agreed, noticing the undercurrent of purpose in Nick's tone. "We'll have a movie night with Mona tonight on the big-screen in the room, if that's okay with you, Tina."

"Sounds good to me," Tina replied.

"This tour business is pretty tough, huh?"

"Yeah, Ed," Nick answered. "Sometimes our schedule gets a bit hectic, filled with unexpected twists and turns."

"And a Twilight Zone moment once in a while too," Gus added.

* * *

Alone in the room's office like décor area, with their female cohorts watching movies with popcorn, Nick poured two doubles. He called Paul with his secured satellite phone. "Did you find out anything, Paul? Gus and I did."

"Quite a bit actually," Paul answered. "I've been following your style on the news. That was really convenient of those bad guy neighbors to kill each other like they did. As to Blackbeard's info, it seems he was entrenched in Huxley's empire deeper than I figured."

"Wait. Let me guess. Huxley had Blackbeard escorting a furniture shipment to Europe, right?"

"That's damn good, Nick. I hate coincidences, but lay it on me."

"Rachel's sister-in-law, Celia Dalman, and her husband Ed work for Huxley. In fact, Ed is one of his area managers. On top of that cute coincidence, Celia and Ed were asked to sail with the shipment leaving Monday for Europe. The containers have already been loaded with avant-garde furniture bound for buyers in the old country supposedly. Is there any chance of getting the shipment hit before Rachel's fall-guy in-laws board with Huxley's drug shipment?"

"How certain are you the drugs will be stashed with the furniture?"

"I haven't done one of the DEA's two year stings, but I probably have as good a chance as if they had. Tell them to have the dogs sniff Huxley's containers. I'll bet they get excited. I'm more interested in what plans you have in mind for Huxley."

"Are you worried about the in-laws? Huxley's already stressed with his main man, Gustoff Banning found dead of an apparent suicide. A mystery like that coupled with Banning's men suddenly having a shootout will have Huxley in a state of shock."

"Gus and I figured the same thing," Nick replied. "He's putting the Dalmans in a spot to take the fall in case the shipment gets hit overseas. Who better than an area manager with access to the entire product line. What I don't want is for the shipment to get hit here before it leaves, and Huxley put out a contract on the Dalmans, thinking they fingered the shipment."

182

"What action do you have in mind?"

"It will have to happen shortly after or before the container search."

"Today's Saturday. Even the famous El Muerto would be taking a chance with such a task. I know Banning told you where to find him, but he skipped explaining the fact he ran the dock operation. We found his extensive overseas trips, where Banning worked the dock, shipped out with the container ship, and then flew home after delivery. I'll do what I can to back your play. Any ideas on where and how?"

"It would be a fluke to catch him before the shipment hit," Nick admitted, "but after the hit, he'll be heading for the tall grass. He'll know his ass will be on the no-fly list. Gus and I are looking for a little known place he owns where Huxley could lay low for a time. It will mean a slight gamble, but if he arrives at the place I stake out, it could mean a chance to sanction him without any aftermath. I could make it so no one knows about Huxley's demise, or fix it so his body's not found for a week."

"Not bad, but what if you're wrong?"

"I'll have to do something more subtle," Nick answered. "If not for the Dalmans, I'd let the cops handle Huxley any way they wanted. Family life's complicated. What can I say?"

"I'll let my DEA contact go ahead with the shipment raid then. I've heard on the grapevine your US Marshal friends are reaching out to you about Nancy Pettinger. Did you decide whether to deal with her for them? That's a tricky one, Nick. The DOJ will throw you under the bus in a heartbeat if somehow you become a suspect."

"I know. Any chance of you keeping her under observation. I'd like to know where to find her once I'm enlightened regarding the parameters my two rogue Marshal friends have in mind."

"I can do that. Let me know if I can help with Huxley. If you locate a target area, I'll open a door for you to access satellite data on your own. I know how you feel having more than us in on this, so I'll send you a code access for a bird covering the next few days."

"I appreciate that, Paul. It'll help with our accelerated planning. I'll be in touch."

"Good luck, Muerto. Be aware with your notoriety, there will be heightened attention to anything done in the Charleston area."

After Paul disconnected, Nick grinned at Gus. "It seems the higher echelon want frontier justice out here in the field, Payaso."

"They sure are helpful. I like Paul. I know he's playing his own angle, but I like the fact he distrusts letting more people in on this than absolutely necessary. If we find any property Huxley owns in the boonies, we'll still be at risk for interception."

"Are you trying to insult me, Payaso?"

Gus shook his head. "Sorry, Muerto. Let's find the information. We'll retrieve the satellite data on the target, and you'll plot out where an interception team would stake you out from. I remember how you screwed the crap out of Frank and his NSA rogue unit in Colorado. You aced his interception team before killing the Senator."

Nick bit his lip. "My Rachel told you too much, Payaso. Did she share the whole Senator deal?"

"She did, but only because Rachel needed to convince me trust is an ongoing project. I kept my mouth shut until now. Let's assume I know what you're capable of, and get on with this project planning sorry for the brief delay."

"I've already found a place he invested in," Nick related, turning his laptop screen for Gus to see. "Mr. Huxley has a beautiful mansion/farm estate. It's located in out of the way North Charleston along North Highway 17. We start tonight if you're in, Payaso. We download the data on our target. We move into a position I pick for both an intercept team, and for taking a shot when the time comes. You'll hate every second of it. You'll refuse to follow orders. You'll whine every second you're in the field, and you'll make sarcastic remarks about my leadership. I don't know whether to shoot you in the head now, or give you a chance to prove me wrong."

By the time Nick finished outlining his predictions, Gus was roaring with laughter, and pushing the rest of his drink away. "I should have known you would create instant havoc. I can't wait to see the home-folks' faces when you plop this mission on their heads."

"Rachel and Jean will love it. This will be just like old times. I'm looking forward to you interacting with Tina if you decide to come with me."

"I'm the master of my house. You'll end up promising Rachel things for her complicity costing you years into the future. I'm in, and I'll remember this sacrilegious denigrating of my manhood."

Nick hung his head in saddened form. "We will see the true emasculation after you tell Tina you have to go out tonight, and won't be back for a while. I'll probably have to intercede before she puts your collar and leash on."

Gus gripped his pushed away drink again, downed it, and slammed the glass on the table. "Payaso wears no one's chains, Muerto, you dog!"

* * *

"You can't be serious!"

"I explained many times I may have to leave unexpectedly, Dear," Gus replied. "Tonight is one of those nights. Nick and I will be back as soon as we can. It's an 'Adam's Family' early Halloween Special. You can even ride along with Rachel and Jean to drop us off."

"C'mon, Aunt Tina," Jean urged. "Dad and Gus are the good guys. They had to wait until Grandma Mona left to spring this on us. They need us to drop them off, and do a pickup. You're part of the team now."

Tina glared at Gus, but her expression softened at Jean's words. "Okay, I get it. I soldier on. Is this where I tell Gus to come home with his shield or on it?"

"No, Tina," Nick answered. "You tell him you love him, and say thank you for being one of the guys who will never be known, who help protect this nation."

Nick's words quieted everyone. "Gus and I are going to pack up. Anyone wanting to come along on the drop-off is welcome. We're the Adam's Family, except our Wednesday Addams is a blonde, and Pugsley's still a bun in the oven. I know my Rachel will be behind the wheel – the perfect Morticia. I'm walking 'Thing', I mean Deke, before we leave. When I get back, those on this mission be ready to go. Those in opposition will silently stay watching movies. C'mon 'Thing'. Let's go clear our heads. These family meetings are very trying."

* * *

The cold droplets began in a wet spattering pattern in the night as Nick and Gus approached the position Nick had perceived would be the logical place an interception team would appear. Nick led Gus toward the nesting position decided on, quickly at first, but as they drew nearer to Huxley's house he slowed their approach to

186

a literal crawl. Gus remained silent, enduring the pauses and excruciatingly slow pace Nick moved toward their chosen observation nest. Nick picked the position after an hour of studying satellite footage covering the entire Huxley holding. Gus kept a tight rein over anything he felt like saying, trusting implicitly his partner's cold blooded killer instincts and expertise. Nick brought him along as a training exercise. Gus was sure of it. He had spotted for Nick before, but never on a stealth approach.

Gus concentrated on moving every hand and foot as Nick did. He doubted anyone could hear an approach in the rain beginning to come down, or see in the now pitch black darkness. He and Nick had night vision gear, but Nick pointed out they could be spotted from a distance when wearing them. They approached with active GPS readings. Nick stopped suddenly, holding up a hand. He turned to Gus, moving close with a whisper.

"Smell that, Gus?"

At first, Gus couldn't imagine what the hell there was to smell other than ozone, wet vegetation and mud. Then he smelled it: tobacco smoke. *Son-of-a-bitch*! "No wonder Rachel hates you, mutant."

"Remember what I told you long ago. Nothing travels further or pinpoints a human being better than tobacco smoke," Nick whispered. "They're close. They can't hear us, but I can smell them. We'll follow the smell to a better vantage point than I picked out. Neat, huh, Payaso?"

"Are they amateurs then?"

"Not necessarily," Nick replied. "Pros have bad habits too, and develop the worst one of all – overconfidence."

"Do you think they're American agents?"

"Don't know, don't care, Payaso. They were sent to wax my ass. If I had to guess, I'd say no. You'd laugh or take me through a ten minute diatribe of why I'm nuts."

Gus grabbed Nick's arm. "Spit it out, Nick. I don't laugh at anything you dream, conjure, or predict. I'm here to learn how the deadliest asshole I've ever met thinks."

"Sorry, partner. I've smelled that brand. It's not an American blend. I've smelled it before in the Middle East and Europe. It's a British American brand. I don't believe they're amateurs. What I think is they've underestimated the job. I've worked with guys like that in the past. None of them are alive now. Stick with me, Gus. You're doing real well."

Gus followed Nick in every movement. They crawled, crouched, and at points ran when the thunder and lightning started. Gus smiled inappropriately as even through the rain, he could now smell the smoke. The wooded area provided pitfalls where missteps could make a distinguishing noise, but they also shielded the rain to a point where the smoke could still travel. Then he saw it. The red glint through the trees of an inhaled cigarette. In the absolute darkness, it was like a beacon. Nick stopped, and quietly positioned his Remington MSR.

"It's okay to spot now, Gus," Nick directed. "Watch for any attention in our direction. There are two targets. I want everything from you. Give me what I need, Spotter."

Gus read off the particulars. There was no wind – the distance negligible. Nick eased into position, only making slight adjustments from experience while sighting in on his rearmost target. "Watch the guy in front. When he looks anywhere away from his partner, say now."

"Acknowledged." Gus watched the front spotter exclusively. The man checked the area in front of Huxley's house, sweeping slowly, point by point to his left. "Now."

Nick squeezed off a silenced hollow point .300 Winchester Magnum round. It dropped his target with barely a sound. Nick shifted to the spotter while working the bolt action load into firing position. He put the next round through the man's shoulder, which he knew would pass through part of his back on its way out.

"He's down, and not moving," Gus said. "The other guy's head is pulped. Did you have a question for your survivor? I know you didn't wound him by accident."

Nick was already packing up the Remington. "I know Paul wants to find out who the hell has the inside track in his department, and has been selling us out to the highest bidder. Unfortunately for the survivor, I can't take 'I don't know' for an answer, even if it's true. It would be big if this guy knows who the traitor is, and how Huxley's drug empire is connected with CIA assets."

The two men jogged toward their dead and dying adversaries while stopping at intervals to check out the area. When they reached the two man interception team, it was obvious the one Nick shot first was dead. His partner writhed on the wet ground, his silently agonized features making it plain Nick would have a difficult time accessing information. Nick knelt next to the man, putting on Nitrile gloves, and moving him into a position Nick could look directly into his pained features.

"Hi. I'm Nick, and my partner here is Gus. You and your dead buddy were sent to kill us. Would you like to make your passing less painful by telling us who ordered this?"

In the intervening seconds, the man controlled the pain lacing through his body. "Could I buy my life with a name?"

"You can if it's a name you can prove," Nick lied. "Give me a name I can check with my admittedly vast resources, and my partner and I will load you for hospitalization. We will have to make you disappear into another country though. If you expected

189

to get a vacation spot here in the USA, that ain't going to happen. Let me know if you agree so I can make the deal with my handlers. If you're going to make this into a 'Let's make a deal' con I will disembowel you and piss on your entrails."

Nick's hushed recitation, coupled with the waves of pain from his wound, convinced the man a gamble of any kind was far better than the hinted at torture. "Ken Schilling. We were told… to anticipate a sniper team… getting into place for a shot at David Huxley when he arrived."

Taking the opportunity provided as his victim paused to deal with pain in a tight lipped, face contorted grimace, Nick texted Paul at an on-line drop known only to them. Moments later, he received a reply allowing for the possibility. Nick removed a syringe from his pack, and injected the wounded man with part of what it was filled with, causing instant unconsciousness.

"Okay, Payaso. This is where our duty gets tough. Remember the spot I had picked out to kill Huxley from?"

Gus used his range finders to sight in the spot with a clear field of fire at Huxley's front door at a slight angle, nearly a hundred and fifty yards away from the house. Nick's choice of a sniper's nest to take out Huxley lay nearly a hundred yards distance from where they were now. Gus cursed. Instinctively, he knew what Nick had in mind.

"That's a long way to drag our dead corpses."

"I didn't kill this guy. He needs to be alive when he kills Huxley, Payaso. Unfortunately, we will not be able to drag him either. I'll patch his wound. We'll leave his buddy in place, but without that fine looking M110 rifle the boys brought to snuff us with."

Nick carefully took the aforementioned M110 Knight's Armament Company rifle away from the dead man, handing it to

190

Gus. He then put the still alive spotter's range finders near the dead man's nerveless left hand fingers. Gus kept watch around them while Nick took a black plastic bag out of his pack, cut a head hole in it, and put it over the wounded man.

"You get the equipment, and I'll pack our soon to be Huxley shooter. I'm going to take a roundabout way to where I want us to wait for Huxley. I'm hoping Paul can find Schilling. I don't like being in position, waiting for my shot with a loose end like Schilling free."

"Understood." Gus shouldered the equipment. Nick positioned the wounded man with Gus's help into a fireman's carry position.

Nick led the way, trying to move toward his intended position leaving as little sign as possible. It took him nearly twenty minutes to arrive at his chosen sniper's position with Gus following closely behind. By the time they reached it, the wounded man groaned nearly constantly. Nick let him down on the ground, and used the syringe once again to render the man unconscious. He then checked his surroundings with satisfaction, while breathing deeply.

"Yep, this is the spot, Gus. We have a clear view, but great wooded cover from here all along our line of retreat. I'll text Paul to have the shipment hit immediately. If we're lucky, our man Huxley will head here the moment he hears about the raid, and the rain will keep falling."

"Remind me never to go camping with you, Muerto."

"Oh crap, you're not going to start whining already, are you?" Nick began setting down his ground cover. "I have to take a few practice shots with the M110. Try and keep the whining down to a minimum, Payaso."

* * *

David Huxley sat in the back seat of his BMW 7 series sedan, his fists clenched in fury, listening to the news of a major DEA raid on his container ship. Tipped off by the container ship Captain, Huxley called in two of his most trusted lieutenants. They packed everything he would need for an extended visit to his estate until the lawyers he paid a fortune for, straightened the container ship fiasco out.

The three men left immediately with the news helicopters circling the container ship as the pre-dawn raid continued into the early Sunday morning hours. He knew something very wrong had happened when Banning was found in the ludicrous position by the flagpole, seemingly having committed suicide. There was no way in hell that self-centered idiot would take his own life. Then Banning's crew gun each other down. Something beyond his grasp was in play, and Huxley needed time to figure out what it was. He figured to call Dalman Monday morning. He needed a scapegoat now more than ever.

The Sunday morning sky, streaked with red reflections over slate gray storm clouds, washed the streets with a steady light rain. They passed only two cars heading in the opposite direction along North Highway 17 while approaching the estate. The wet morning muggy drabness added a prophetic flavor of trouble yet ahead to Huxley's seething thoughts. Someone had crossed him.

"Craig. I need answers. Is anyone new on the docks? You and Banning used the same guys to stash the drugs in the furniture crates at the warehouse before loading, right?"

"We used the same guys, boss. All eight men are handpicked cartel soldiers. They'd slit their own throats before messing with a shipment. What about the couple who work for you? Do you think they nosed around the warehouse, and saw something?"

"Fuck no! Dalman runs retail for my chain. The guy's never even been in the warehouse. I was only thinking of having

192

him and his wife go along with the cargo to Europe because of the Banning fiasco. You know damn well Banning didn't croak himself, but I couldn't take the chance of sending someone knowledgeable about our entire operation to Europe. Dalman and his wife were perfect patsies. If the shipment had been hit overseas, I could have dumped on the Dalmans, and bribed my shipment free. We have to find the leak. I'll take a major hit on this as it is! I don't care what we have to do."

"Do you want me to go back after we drop you off? I'll start at the very beginning, tracing every step, and every person who touches the product or loads it for transport."

"I'll be fine at the estate. No one knows I even own it. You and Santos go back together. I like your idea. No phone calls, not even a burner phone. They'll be watching everything: every phone line, warehouse, and residence. If you have anything to report, do it in person."

"I will, boss," Craig agreed, as Santos steered to the front entrance down Huxley's winding entrance drive. Santos shut off the car. "We'll be back to report in a-"

The 7.62 high velocity Nato round crinkled the safety glass, passed through Craig's head, Santos's driver's seat, and into the driver's chest area. The next five rounds pierced Santos in a tight pattern, sending the rest of the rear glass plummeting in small pieces everywhere over the seat. His body danced at each hit, tossing him against the steering wheel. Huxley dived down into the blood pooling quickly under Craig's head. He pulled his own 9mm S&W automatic with a shaking hand. He had sent enough pros on jobs to know a contract hit.

Huxley crawled in a turning motion, carefully keeping his head down while facing rearward. He took a split second to see over the rear seat, trying to determine if anyone was approaching or determine where the bullets originated. His second quick glance earned another 7.62 round, which clipped the top part of Huxley's left ear off. He screamed out in pain, dropping his pistol, and clutching the side of his head with both hands. Blood seeped between his fingers, as he looked around in wild panic for his S&W auto. Before he could find it, his door opened. He looked into the face grinning down at him in terror. Huxley knew death when he stared it in the eye.

* * *

"Damn, Nick… you took his ear off!" Gus had been reading off data after making it plain to Nick as the BMW wound toward them which position Huxley occupied in the car. His partner's shots after the driver shut off the BMW gave Gus the immediate impression Nick was not firing wildly into the car. The first shot killed the rear passenger, and went through the seat, paralyzing the driver for a moment. The following shots worked both to kill the driver, and send a message to Huxley.

Nick dropped his unconscious puppet he had been positioned over, and broke cover at a dead run. "Pack our gear, Payaso. Watch sunny-boy for me. I have to collect a prisoner."

"Oh boy," Gus muttered to no one in particular. The moment they realized a car had entered the long drive to Huxley's estate, Gus brought Paul on line with them while spotting for Nick. "You get that, Paul?"

"I sure did," Gilbrech acknowledged. "He is impressive, and driven. I didn't say a word about leaving Huxley alive. Nick seems to intuitively know when to keep digging no matter what the danger or the situation. I'm damn glad you two didn't blunder into an interception team's trap. I was only guessing at the leak. It looks like my suspicions were unfortunately true. I'll let you in on something, Gus. The powers that be, supplying the money on these excursions you guys have happened into on this tour, want to write you boys an unlimited budget. When a hint of Isis is involved, they want Muerto and Payaso involved. It's a new day in the neighborhood where these Islamo nut-cakes are involved. Tell

194

Nick if he gets anything out of Huxley, send it to me, and you guys go about your business. I don't really want you two involved in DEA stuff. My contact is untouchable. I will get anything Nick finds to him. I'm not stupid. I leave final decisions to your partner."

"Always a wise decision as I've found out numerous times in the past. I need to work. Hang in with us, and Muerto will go over the line as usual."

"I can hear you, Payaso," Nick reminded Gus as he reached to open the BMW rear door.

"I'm bored. I'm cold. I'm wet. When you finish with Huxley, put a shot in my head too."

Gus listened to both Paul and Nick enjoying his adlib as he plastic tied their scapegoat shooter. He grinned. *Payaso strikes again*!

* * *

Nick watched through the door window as Huxley flailed around in the passenger rear compartment, trying to staunch the blood flow from his mangled ear while searching for what Nick figured to be his gun. He opened the back door. "Hi, sweetie. I'm the angel of death. The only choices from here are how you wish to journey into the afterlife. I have door number one where you cooperate fully, and you get the painless angel. I have door number two where you don't cooperate, and you get the full Monte – pissed off angel of death. Be careful what door you choose here, David. By the way, I have confirmation in an instant, so if you're thinking lying will buy you time, that ain't happenin', pal."

"Who the fuck are you?" Huxley tried to resist as Nick dragged him out of the car by his nose to no avail.

"You've been a very naughty boy. Your operation has cost countless lives I'm sure, but that's not why I'm here. I'm not much

195

into anything touchy-feely. I see you as having information to save many innocent lives. Let's help each other. I'll help you by not torturing you beyond your wildest imaginings, and you in return help me by informing on your whole organization. I hate negotiations, so you have sixty seconds to agree to help. If you don't, I begin introducing you to hell on earth before I introduce you to the real thing."

"You're kidding! I can make you rich beyond imagining. We can cut a deal!"

"Forty-five seconds, bunky," Nick said, looking at his watch.

"You can't be serious." Huxley knew the truth though. This man would do unspeakable things to him no matter what he said or did. Huxley also knew he could give pain, but he could not take it.

"Twenty seconds."

"You haven't even restrained me."

"That's because you haven't yet stopped holding your injured ear with both hands," Nick pointed out. "Not to mention if you tried something with those hands I would break them off at your shoulder. Ten seconds, bunky."

"You know what... Fuck you!" Huxley gave Nick the finger with one middle bloody digit. Nick broke it, then kicked Huxley square in the groin.

"Told you. I'll give you two more minutes, because sometimes lessons take time to sink in," Nick warned, shaking his head in silent disappointment. At the end of two minutes Nick moved to kick Huxley in the groin again. His intentions were begged off by a squealing Huxley, his uninjured hand clutching his injured groin, and bloody hand with broken finger held up pleadingly.

"Don't… I'll talk… I'll talk!"

With Gilbrech on the line, Nick took Huxley through the details of his operation, including names, places, contacts overseas, and the supplier shipping the drugs for distribution by Huxley. Once crosschecking of information Banning had given him was completed in comparison to Huxley's, Nick restrained him with plastic ties.

"Last thing. I'm going into your house. I see you have an entry panel. Give me your security code. Also, I'll want the location of any safes inside and the combination or security code for them. I'm very good at finding hidden things. If there are any special hidey holes you've neglected to tell me about, I'll introduce you to my special electric shock treatment to your balls. It works the opposite of electroshock therapy. After my treatment, people remember things from their lives they hadn't thought of in years. Tell me all about your house."

Huxley did so without hesitation, including codes for the safe room built inside the house where both the safe, and his computer storage backup were kept.

"Very good, Dave," Nick said. "Maybe you'll be able to start your next journey pain free. I'll return as soon as possible."

Nick entered Huxley's house, checking video with Gus and Paul. Once video clarity was established, Nick searched the estate with care learned from past experience. He found the safe-room to be the only hidden and sealed area in the dwelling. The security panel opened the room after Nick located the release for the bookcase covering the entrance. Upon opening the safe, Nick started laughing.

"Jackpot, boys. This is better than winning a lottery. I guess we'll have to initiate an offshore account for Paul too, Payaso." A gold coin collection, prominently displayed at the safe's side, shared a spot with stacks of cash. A laptop computer, and a small case housing sixteen gigabyte memory chips stored in small plastic cases shared the safe's other side.

"I… uh… already have an offshore account," Paul admitted, eliciting amused responses from his two networked companions.

"You dog, you," Nick said. "Payaso and I will find a way to pad it for you once we arrive home. I'm afraid we'll be confiscating this beautiful gold coin collection though."

"Thanks, Nick. As you know, in this business, it's nice to have a trapdoor into another life. Trapdoors are expensive."

"Amen to that, brother Paul. I don't think you'll have to send a team to clean the place. I'll pack it out, and you can send a courier to get the laptop and memory chips. Once I finish with the scene outside, Payaso and I will leave it all in place to be found at a later date by some innocent or not so innocent party. How goes your scramble with the Schilling name?"

"In custody, and calling for lawyers, witness protection, whistle blower witch hunt protection, and demands to be taken before Congress to testify. Instead, Ken will be going to a special place overseas where we will have our own rendition. I wish I could drop him off with you, but I have a couple guys with him who will get the job done. I'll turn everything else you've found at Huxley's place over to the DEA after I have everything cloned for our own records. Outstanding work, gentlemen. If anything troublesome happens, call me. I will intercept any authorities sticking their noses into your lives instantly."

"Thanks, Paul. We'll be in touch."

Nick filled his pack with Huxley's safe contents, closed the safe, and resealed the safe-room with its bookcase cover in place. He set the security system on before rejoining the groaning Huxley, rolling painfully side to side. Nick helped him to sit against the open rear car door. He then injected Huxley with enough from his syringe to render the man unconscious.

"Do I have a clear shot, Payaso?"

Gus, who had been watching everything from where he stood over the wounded shooter, crouched to where Nick had made the initial shots from. "Clear view of Huxley where you have him positioned."

"Good." Nick shouldered his pack. It took only moments for him to reach his sniping roost. He set aside the pack for the time being. After positioning the unconscious original interception team member with the M110 rifle in place, Nick lay over him, put the man's finger on the trigger, and aimed at Huxley's head. "Now don't jerk the trigger this time you rascal. We don't want to be here all day while you miss the target."

Nick squeezed off the round, striking Huxley between the eyes. Nick clapped the man on the shoulder. "Excellent shot! That'll teach him. Our work here is done, Payaso."

Nick injected the interception team member with a little more from his syringe. He rearranged him in a sniper's prone position with hands correctly on the M110. "Let's go take the final shot, Payaso."

"With what? I thought you weren't using your rifle for this."

"I'm going to have the first sniper I killed shoot this one with his handgun. I noticed he has a holstered .45 caliber ACP."

"Bullshit! That's a hundred yard shot."

"Are you going to insult me or are you going to help me carry our stash to the other nest?" Nick didn't wait for a reply. He led the way with Gus following while shaking his head.

At the interception team's nest, Nick arranged the corpse in a prone position with the dead man's hand on the .45 caliber ACP automatic. Nick slowly covered the man with his own body, angling for a shot with Gus spotting. He pulled the trigger with slow pressure.

"Nice. You hit him in the back," Gus said.

"Okay, asshole," Nick said to the corpse, shaking him a little, while taking aim again. "You were off low that time. Do it again."

The next shot struck the man in the head. Gus kicked Nick's foot. "You are one scary individual. Want me to check the body?"

"Definitely," Nick replied. "No loose ends or possible loose ends. I'll put a couple of final touches on this exceptional crime mystery. We have a lot of Sunday left, partner. Maybe we should go see one of those 3D Imax movies."

Gus kept the conversation going on their link while jogging toward the man Nick had just shot. "After spending all night with you in the rain, the only thing I want is a dry spot with a good view, and a bottle of Bushmill's Irish at my side."

"Or we could do that," Nick said. "You know how women are though. They'll want to go out, and we'll say we have headaches, and they'll say if you ever want to get romantic again get ready to take us to a movie."

"Gee, Muerto," Gus replied while checking the man with a hole through the rear of his head, and missing a large part of his forehead. "When did you lose your balls between the shot blowing the front of this guy's head off, and deciding to let the women lead you around on a leash with Deke the dog?"

"You're just mean, Payaso."

Chapter Nine

Graceful

Nick and Gus trudged into the hotel suite with less than energized ambition for facing anything other than downtime. Instead of finding an empty suite, signaling the girls had left to do another Charleston exploration tour, they found everyone in the entertainment room of the suite with a plus two: Grace Stanwick and her US Marshal partner Tim Reinhold.

"And you thought we weren't a couple of lucky ducks," Nick muttered while petting down the deliriously happy Deke. He waved as the group stood to meet the arriving men. "US Marshals Grace and Tim, long time no see. Oh… wait a minute… I just saw you two coppers. Let me think. I believe Grace mentioned wanting only to see me again on the back of my newest novel."

Rachel and Jean were already sharing an amused enjoyment of Nick's greeting as both Grace and Tim hung their heads comically. "C'mon, Nick. Give them a break. We'll watch a movie while you and Gus catch up with Grace and Tim. We owe them."

"No we don't," Nick said, never looking away from Grace's face. "I like Rachel's idea, Grace. Come with Gus and me to our neat bar. We've been exploring my future book scenes, which will have Charleston aspects to it. We're tired, wet, and less than sociable – plus, I can tell by Deke's over the top greeting his owners have yet to take him for a walk tonight. Gus and I would like to sip a couple of Bushmill's Irish doubles while winding down from a long information gathering sojourn before my Deke walk. Come along with us to the bar, or say see you later to our crew."

Grace walked by him without a word until she passed closely. "You're not very nice to old friends, Nick."

"You haven't seen anything yet, Gracie."

Mona, who had been monitoring the greeting after already being introduced to the US Marshals, looked at Rachel for some explanation or guidance.

Jean took her hand. "It's time to watch a movie, Grandma. Don't worry. Dad won't hurt them... at least physically."

"I heard that," Nick called out while leading the way to the bar.

Nick poured two doubles, placing one in front of Gus. "Would either of you two government complex minions like something to drink?"

"I'll have a small one of what you're having," Tim said.

"Same here," Grace added. "We heard a big name in the Company went bye-bye due to being a sellout. Care to comment?"

Nick served them and sat down. "Maybe we should start with why you two arrived at my hotel in Charleston. I already acknowledged your message request."

"We're in the same bit of trouble the Company's in," Tim replied. "We're afraid anything implied or otherwise will be leaked. We don't take your involvement lightly. No matter what Pettinger gets away with, she'll never be in the DOJ again. The information garnered from her could be a key to reworking our network, but we don't want you entrapped getting it."

"Tim and I decided telling you face to face that our earlier request can no longer be safely done. We didn't want you agreeing to it, and then being named in the press, thinking we threw you under the bus. Pettinger has been bleating to the media she was framed. The people willing to go a few steps beyond, now that she managed to get free, know they don't have a prayer of silencing her."

Nick relaxed the wariness he first experienced, after seeing the two Marshals in the suite. "We were to meet in a neutral place to discuss this once I decided. Why come here?"

"Grace and I didn't have a clue how this sanction thing works," Tim admitted. "We knew how our request for assistance must have appeared to you."

"I wondered if you would use your resources, find Pettinger, get her to talk, and then bury her somewhere," Grace continued. "Tim suggested we clear this mistake with you before we read Nancy's obituary, followed by the release of information she threatened the Attorney General's office with if she were hounded any further."

Gus chuckled. "You thought Nick would do Nancy on the hint DOJ wanted what she knows in an e-mail drop?"

"It sounds silly when you do a one sentence repeat of intentions like that," Tim said. "In any case, we wanted you to know Nancy has hinted at a DOJ revelation, involving many political heads in Congress and the Cabinet using the DOJ as an enemies list type threat to cower political adversaries."

It was Nick's turn to laugh. He finished his double, and poured another, refilling Gus's in the same action. "Gee, kids... I don't know how to tell you this, but I doubt there's ten people in the entire country that don't suspect exactly that. I don't suspect it. I know they do it, along with using the IRS as a weapon against conservative political figures and groups. What I didn't know was you little lost lambs being ignorant of it. Gus is right of course. I don't work like that. The 'Hack Chip' fiasco we were all involved in turned viciously dangerous. It had to be handled in a rough manner after I brought you both into the mix. Once the chip was in your hands, and on its way to the Attorney General, I made sure to keep you two alive."

Grace took a deep breath. "So you never had any intention of taking the Pettinger job then. Did you already know it would turn into a clown show?"

"I made some assumptions," Nick replied. "Once I met with you, the first order of business was how many people were in the know, and their identities. Organized crime I could trust to keep anything in the sanction realm secret. The DOJ ordering the sanction of a former employee would be like taking an ad out in the newspaper. You must suspect the Attorney General's office contaminated the presentation to the Grand Jury, which is why Pettinger was freed to begin with, Grace."

Grace and Tim exchanged surprised glances to Nick's amusement.

"Well at least you lambs figured that out. So here we are. I appreciate the face to face. No, I didn't plan to do anything to Pettinger on a whim, and if the job involved anyone but you two, I would have walked away. I thought perhaps my brutal information gathering had been so temptingly easy, maybe the honorable US Marshals Tim and Grace decided to work outside the box. Not so, huh?"

"We knew what happened," Grace said. "It was the main reason we floated the idea by you. No one knows about our idea but us. We'd have to be insane to even suggest such a thing to anyone beyond you. I know it was stupid for us to hint it might be official, but I wanted to know your feelings on it. Now, with all the back and forth leak threats in the DOJ, this could get real ugly if what Nancy claims to be holding is released to the press. One thing I do know – I didn't want you caught in the middle believing we somehow screwed you."

"First off, I don't have feelings."

205

"I can vouch for that," Gus piped in.

"Secondly, I'm impressed. I never for a moment thought the notion of interrogating Nancy, and then making her disappear came from my little US Marshal lambs. It is a good idea to find out what the bitch knows, so I'm open to out of the box thinking. You two know what I do, and what I'm capable of. I trust you clowns, but my patience is running thin with outside authorities if you know what I mean."

Grace reached across to clasp Nick's hand. "We've been through a lot. Tim and I trust you implicitly. We know you're a cold blooded killing machine; but you not only have a heart, but you do know right and wrong."

"We know the damage Nancy can do," Tim added. "Our system doesn't handle people like Nancy who know everything and everybody to skirt rules, laws, and damn it… right and wrong! We contacted you for guidance. Grace and I are bonded to doing what's right. I could tell in our last encounter that's what you want too."

"You do know in for a penny in for a pound… right?"

Grace added her other hand clasping Nick's. "This goes beyond petty crap, Nick. We're talking leaks betraying our country, our citizens, and the fabric of our nation. We will never betray you, but we need your help. We're lost. Payoffs, political favors, and selling out the nation for money or favor is turning America into a third world cesspool. We don't know how to stop this shit. Do you?"

Nick drained his refill with the hand not clasped in both of Grace's. He put the glass down, and patted Grace's. "That's plain enough for me and Gus. We needed to make sure we were all on the same page of insanity."

"We can work through this," Gus said. "I hear your dedication. We know about the promotion in the US Marshal's service to oversight in the Western United States. We're happy for you. It means nothing if you two are willing to accept political orders. Nick calls the shots. He has a bullshit Geiger counter meter beyond anything ever imagined. I'm happy some normal people are on our side I can relate to. It can get eerie being the only one on the inside with Nick."

Gus's pronouncement met with hilarity, except for Nick, who glared in outrage at his partner. "Suddenly, amidst government sellouts, government traitors, and government lambs, it's 'last resort Nick' to the rescue. Gus and I will need real intel at a moment's notice once we decide to find and question Nancy. The risks will be great. Everyone has to worry about the fallout. Okay, that was funny, partner, you prick. I don't want anything happening to my lambs, so we'll look into it. Any clue where she ran off to after the Grand Jury let her go, and she made her first veiled media threats?"

"We were ordered to drop the matter when the AG's office lost in the Grand Jury hearing," Tim answered. "She left DC. That we do know. We were ready to trace her every movement until the order came down not to proceed."

"It's just as well. I have a Company contact interested in my out of the box thinking. If it's doable, and Nancy is located somewhere inside your control area, Gus and I might need a small look the other way type happening. I am after all an official US Marshal."

"Don't remind us," Grace said. "We'll back your play. What did you have in mind in the way of help?"

"I'll let you know."

"Gee, that sounds ominous, doesn't it, Tim?"

207

"Best to keep your smartass side in check, Grace," Tim replied. "Let's part on good terms with our compatriots, shall we? That way we can all either find common ground in the future, or simply part company as friends."

Grace looked to be on the verge of firing off a salvo, but Nick's grin ended the temptation. "Point taken. Let's say goodnight to the softer side of the Twilight Zone, and hit the road. Thanks for a wonderful evening, Nick. Let's do it again real soon."

"She just can't help herself, Timmy," Nick said.

"Welcome to my world."

* * *

Jean insisted on going along with Nick and Gus as they walked Deke. The rain stopped pounding the pavement for a time, leaving the three dog escorts carrying umbrellas for no apparent reason. The black skies showed glimmers of clearing near a foreboding full moon, which peeked in and out of the cloud cover.

"Why don't we play superhero crime fighters tonight? Deke can be our hellhound hybrid who can sniff out evil anywhere. You'll be El Muerto, Gus will of course be Payaso, and I'll be Dagger."

"Didn't Gus and I explain clearly enough the bad things that can happen if you accidentally call us El Muerto and Payaso in public? You've even went and outed Fang the Ferocious."

"Sure, Dad, but we're not in public. Fang loves this game, right, Fang?"

Although unaware of why he received everyone's attention, Deke played to Jean's tune perfectly, leaping around her as if answering the question with a resounding yes. Nick watched the display suspiciously, while Gus enjoyed the show.

"Quit showing off, Deke," Nick ordered. "This act seems rehearsed to me. In any case, we're not running around in the dark looking for trouble, young lady. I'm surprised at you, Gus. Don't encourage our young vigilante."

"I tried to show my displeasure at this ridiculous and dangerous suggestion of a game," Gus replied, finally able to speak. "It was Fang who ruined my display of outrage. I may be laughing on the outside, but I'm very disappointed on the inside at our canine companion in particular."

As if embracing his new role as canine vigilante superhero, Deke hunched low to the ground, snorting at the air, and issuing a warning growl. Nick noted a group near the intersection of Meeting Street and South Market Street, wearing black hoodies. They paused often together, but stayed out of any illuminating light, huddling close to the buildings they passed. Because it was only 8:30pm in an upscale area of Charleston, Nick didn't think much about it other than trusting Deke's sixth sense for unsavory situations.

"Deke's convinced me. Apparently, we don't have to hunt for trouble very hard tonight. Let's go in the opposite direction on South Market."

Jean crouched with Deke, her arm wrapped around the dog's neck. "Fang and Dagger want this mission, Muerto. We need to shadow these guys, waiting for the proper moment to strike. We'll catch them red-handed, right, Fang?"

Deke immediately embraced the mission, leaning his head into Jean's. "See, that's two votes, Muerto. How about you, Payaso? Fang and I will run point on this op."

"And how exactly did you plan on doing that, Dagger," Nick asked. "I have plastic ties in my jacket right now. How would you like to have your little butt frog-marched back to the hotel, where you will be questioned and accused before the Grand Inquisitor?"

"C'mon. It'll be fun. Help me out here, Payaso," Jean pleaded.

Gus snorted in amusement at Jean's assumption Gus might side with her. "You must be kidding. In all this time we've been together, Jean, have I ever went against, Muerto?

"I thought maybe you might step up for a change, Payaso," Jean retorted with a giggle."

"Now you've done it," Nick complained, seeing Gus go into laughing fits at Jean's upbraiding. How dare you call my partner Payaso's manhood into question? This outrage will not go unpunished."

Jean grabbed Nick's coat, yanking on it with a violent tug. "They're on the move. Fang will be our perfect cover if they spot us. We're just a family walking the dog."

"We are just a family walking the dog," Nick reminded her. He saw the group move to the corner of Church Street and North Market. Nick, having been around the proverbial block many times, knew whatever this bunch planned, it would not be a good deed. "These youngsters do plan some kind of dastardly act, Dagger. You have good instincts, but we will be skipping the superhero trail tonight. I have Fang's tennis ball. If you show it to him, you'll really see some excitement."

"You and Payaso are both packin'. I saw your holsters in the back under your jackets," Jean said. "Let's follow them, and call the cops when we see the perps act out."

"I'm warning you, Payaso. Stop laughing at her 'Bad Boys' clichés," Nick said, pointing at Gus with emphasis.

Gus raised his arms. "Okay, but I don't see the harm in following the hoodlums for a while. I have my range finders in my jacket." He shrugged off Nick's look of death as Jean began clapping her hands with delight. "We wouldn't have to get close. We'll stay in the shadows, and far enough back not to be noticed. I'll keep an eye on them from long range."

"Yeah, that always works. How many doubles did you have before dinner, Payaso. I think I hear the booze talkin'. Remember, friends don't let friends drink and be idiots."

"Let's do this, Muerto. I'm fine. Hell, they probably aren't doing anything, but slouching around, acting like they're gangsters."

Nick considered all the ways he pictured Jean's superhero play could go wrong. Seeing Jean's face perked into a pleading, twisted mask of nine year old angst, Nick folded. "Do exactly what I say. We stay at least fifty to seventy-five yards back on the trail. Gus scopes out what they're up to if anything, and we either return to the hotel, or call the cops if needed. If I say abort, it ends instantly. Understood?"

"I'm Payaso the feared tonight," Gus tweaked his partner's patience.

"Don't I get a vote on operations now that we're mission enabled?" Jean added a corkscrew jab into Nick's last nerve.

"One more word out of either you or Payaso, and I frog march you both to the hotel with Fang on guard duty."

Jean and Deke scooted ahead with Jean slinking along in a stealthy crouch next to Deke. Gus followed, using the range finders every other minute to check on their prey. Nick shadowed the three, moving into different firing positions, wondering how the hell he agreed to this obvious folly. He smiled watching Deke get into stealthy tracking mode, hunching down along with Jean as they moved ahead.

As the hoodies rounded the corner onto Church Street, they huddled under the green awning of a store. From the distance, Nick couldn't tell what they were doing. He allowed Jean and Deke close the distance to fifty yards before whispering a halt to the expedition. They waited quietly in place. Nick took the lead. He leaped over a short barrier, with Deke leaping over after him. Jean vaulted the wall as did Gus at the rear. Using the cars parked in the lot to shield their movements, Nick stopped at the barrier directly across from the half dozen young men. They remained motionless, but watching in all directions.

"I don't know what the hell they're doing," Gus whispered. "Maybe you were right about this being a fool's errand."

"Stay calm, partner. They'll be revealing their bad choices shortly."

"I love this," Jean whispered happily. "This was a great idea. We're even closer than fifty yards. What do you think they're doing, Muerto?"

"Nothing good. They're watching the area to see if they've been noticed before they make their play. We have a barrier in front of us as a shield. Now we show the patience of superhero stalking. Stay quiet. This is what you wanted to learn, Dagger. The first lesson is never lose control over your anxious side during the takedown. The quickest way to die while stalking any prey is to rush into a blind situation, where facts are missing. We don't know what the hell these guys' objective is."

"It looks like they're robbing the store, Sherlock." Jean stifled a giggle.

"I don't think so," Nick replied, suddenly very serious. "They're spreading out around the corner, blending in against the darkened building. What do you see, Gus?"

Gus looked away from his night vision range finders. "They're all packing. I can see a weapon on display by every gangsta' except one. He's standing in front of the plate glass display window with a brick."

"They're cop killers," Nick said. "After setting off the alarm, they remain in place until the police arrive. Then they execute the police sent to the scene. Usually only one car is ordered to check a routine alarm call, because there are so many false alarms. There's a driver somewhere around here with a van to pick up the cop-killers the moment they fire on the arriving police. Watch what they do when the bricklayer busts the front door handle, setting off the security alarm. They won't run."

Three minutes later, they heard the brick smashed into the door handle until the alarm went off. The security alarm, loud enough to wake the dead, blasted out its wailing tune. The so called bricklayer, got into position away from the entrance on the North Market Street side, moving to a distance of ten feet to the rear of his nearest accomplice. With all six lined in the darkness, next to the brick wall, they awaited the arrival of police in the shadows. Nick smiled. The group of thugs aligned along the building wall reminded Nick of ducks at a shooting gallery.

"Heh... heh."

"First off, I hate that you're smiling, Muerto," Gus said. "Secondly, I hate when you go heh... heh in a life or death circumstance."

The scene awakened the cold blooded killer skittering just below the surface of Nick's mind, in a shadowy damp refuge of mayhem and murder. He glanced at the grim faces in the darkness, and Jean's arm around Deke's neck. Nick whispered with a

213

sarcastic edge. "This wasn't my idea, kiddies. I'm here, and I don't plan to allow these jackasses to execute a couple of cops. We should have followed my directions, and walked to the hotel instead of playing Dudley Doright and Scooby Doo meet the Backstreet Cop-killers. Now that we're here, we have no choice."

"We could warn the police," Gus said. "Don't surrender to that deviant mind of yours, Muerto. I know you've concocted a weird plan to somehow take out the gang using your giant intellect or should I say ego."

"What do you have planned, Dad?" Still clutching Deke by the neck, Jean pointed at the small shed type structure immediately behind them. "Payaso and I can hide behind the small building behind us."

"Exactly. Once the shooting starts I want you both heading to the hotel. Wait out the initial gunfire, and then head away on a path to the hotel. There will be a police dragnet to avoid. Play the dumb-shit tourist card if you get stopped, featuring that both of you heard the gunfire. There won't be a problem. You've activated El Muerto, my beloved daughter. Don't be hatin' when Muerto doesn't perform quite as expected – and don't be blaming yourself if this goes sideways. Payaso will make sure nothing happens to you or the Dekester."

Jean hugged Nick tightly as they crouched behind the wall, whispering fiercely. "I love you, Dad. I'll make sure Payaso is okay too."

Having said that, Jean whispered a command to Deke, gesturing him to her side before running in a crouch to the structure behind them. Gus turned to Nick before following his young charge and Fang.

"This is a dumb idea," Gus admitted. "Good luck. Want me to be in position for covering fire?"

214

Nick slipped on Nitrile gloves from his pocket, along with his black mask he now carried as a joke to get a rise out of Gus. "Absolutely not. If I need covering fire, then I'm in trouble. You look after Jean. I have to get going while this one act play unfolds."

Having said that, Nick went over the wall, moving silently twenty-five yards to the rear of his prey. From there, he stalked his targets, careful of every footfall in the darkness. The city sounds covered his approach. When he heard a siren in the distance, Nick ran forward with Stiletto knife fully extended. He grabbed the hooded head in front of him, pulled it back, and slit the man's throat, arterial spray shooting out.

In an instant, Nick caught the 9mm Glock the man dropped while clutching his ruined neck. Nick turned the Glock on the man in front of his victim, firing two shots into his head. From a shooter's crouch behind his first victim's twitching body, Nick executed the next three. He wounded the fourth in both shoulders, while taking wild return fire. The would-be cop-killers had no idea what they were shooting at. Panic enveloped them as they died. Two shots they fired hit each other.

With the siren drawing ever closer, Nick switched the guns, his two rearmost victims carried. He searched with calm speed, finding a switchblade in the first victim's pocket. Nick swiped the dead man's neck once with it, finishing his ploy by placing it into the second victim's free hand. Nick used the dead second victim's hand to fire a killing round into the front man he had wounded in the shoulders. Chuckling, he ran to the front man, and boosted him into an upright position, Nick could fire on the second man, he had planted the killing weapon on. With the first man's weapon aimed, Nick took aim.

"Not much time, scooter. Make these count." Nick fired a couple into the dead man, and into a couple of his cohorts. He scanned the scene and area around him. Satisfied, he vaulted the

215

wall across the street, and continued in a route taking him away from the scene. Unfortunately, because of the gunfire, two helicopters began a weaving pattern over the suspected area. They did not appear to be leaving until someone or something was found. Nick called Grace.

"I'm afraid to ask," Grace answered, seeing the caller ID.

"I need an official extraction. Sending the coordinates to your phone. You and Timmy are still around, aren't you?"

"Yes, thanks to bad karma, I guess. We'll be over in ten minutes. Our hotel's not far from that spot. Do we get to know what we're extracting you from?"

"Not if you want our slightly seedy partnership to continue. Drive to me, stop, and I'll load into the backseat. From there, you can stop by the scene of the crime like two helpful US Marshals. Flash your badges, and ask if the locals could use your help. When they say no thanks, take me to my hotel."

"Why do I get the feeling you're trying to play the innocent victim of circumstance here? We're on our way. US Marshals' service to the rescue. Hang tight, you little desperado."

"One of these days, Alice… right to the moon," Nick hissed, mimicking the Jackie Gleason line from the old TV show 'The Honeymooners'.

Grace disconnected with a laugh. Nick stayed in the shadows, avoiding flyovers by police helicopter spotlights. A burgundy SUV stopped near his position. Nick ran over, and entered the rear passenger compartment.

"Timmy. Look who dropped in. It's that famous novelist, Nick McCarty," Grace needled him while driving toward the nearby commotion, complete with flashing lights, and arriving ambulance sirens. "I'll bet those ambulances are a waste of time."

216

"Don't be impolite, Grace," Tim urged. "Do you want us to introduce you, Nick, or just refer to you if they ask?"

"Only if they ask, Tim. Very funny, Grace. I'm trying to provide my new partners with plausible deniability. Turn on your interior light for a moment." Nick checked himself for excess blood, but except for a few spots on the sleeves of his jacket, his clothing appeared clean of any other evidence. He had turned the Nitrile gloves inside out, stuffing them inside his jacket. His Muerto mask was also inside his jacket again.

"Do you have your US Marshal's credentials," Grace asked.

"Of course."

"Okay, here we are." Grace parked outside the cordoned off area. "Let's go see what Marshal McCarty got into tonight."

* * *

Grace and Tim flashed their badges and ID's at the police taped off line. The officer checked them over carefully before grinning at the two Marshals. "What the heck do two US Marshals want in a Charleston crime scene?"

"We're in Charleston on business," Grace explained. "We were driving to our hotel when we saw the lights and helicopters. My partner thought it would be a good idea to offer our help if you wanted it. If not, we'll leave you guys to do your jobs. What happened here anyway?"

"Six bad guys had a wild shootout. They're all dead," the officer explained. "I doubt we'll need the US Marshal's service in on this, but you can offer your help to the Lieutenant next to the building there. Her name's Moragado."

Lieutenant Moragado glanced at Grace and Tim with a confused expression. "Can I help you?"

217

The US Marshals went through the ID and introduction with the Lieutenant, again offering their help.

The Lieutenant thought about it for a few moments. She looked to be in her mid-forties: short dark hair, no makeup, and a cynical wry expression which appeared to be her normal feature. "I don't see how you could help, but thanks for stopping by. What business in Charleston were you here on?"

"Meeting with a colleague," Grace replied. "He'll be working with us out west soon. We wanted to touch base with him before then. We'll be flying out tomorrow."

"Have a safe flight," Moragado said by way of dismissal.

"Thank you." Grace led Tim away while both marshals watched the crime scene prep with police officers ringing the sidewalk area, where Nick left his staged gang battle event. "What do you think, Tim?"

"I think plausible deniability is a good thing."

"Don't you want to know what happened? Jesus… six dead thugs."

"Let's get Nick to his hotel, and go have a couple beers at the hotel bar."

"Good idea, Timmy," Grace agreed. "I wish he'd volunteer the info."

* * *

When Grace and Tim returned to their SUV, Nick sat up straighter. "I'd like you to drive around this block slowly, Grace. I think there's a bad guy driver staying in place because of the helicopters. We're going to help him see the light."

218

"Six dead, Nick," Grace stated. "How do you know they had a driver?"

"They were using a store alarm as bait to draw cops to the scene. Those six planned to execute the cops investigating the alarm. They would need a driver. Trust me. You'll see."

"On it, boss," Grace replied. She did as Nick directed.

Nick watched both sides of the streets they drove down, searching for the right kind of van with possibly a driver sitting in place. When they reached Hassell Street, Nick spotted what he had been looking for. A Chevy Tahoe SUV, parked half a block ahead, fit the picture he had in mind. As they passed it, Nick saw a man smoking a cigarette while in the driver's seat with the window down.

"That's my bitch. Drive around the block. Turn out your lights as we round the corner again toward him. Stop along the curb once we are about a hundred feet behind. I'll check him out."

"When you say check him out, do you mean put a bullet in his head?"

"No bullets, Grace. Relax. I'm going to nab him for you to arrest. The locals will have a guy to question about this cop-killing ploy. If you two don't care about the locals questioning him, I'll find out what their intentions were."

"Thank you for asking, but Tim and I would be glad to have this kind of collar. We'll play the hunch card when we drive him to the crime scene." Grace handed Nick her phone. "Take some pictures of the Tahoe's inside if there's any incriminating evidence."

"Will do." Nick took the phone, and began his approach on the Tahoe.

* * *

"What do you make of this," Grace asked her partner. "How does he get into shit like this? He killed six guys on a speculation they were baiting cops for killing."

"I know this much after meeting Nick," Tim replied. "However he does what he does, it would be better on the outside of the action than in the middle of it. If he's right about this guy being the driver, we're going to look real good at the crime scene delivering him. I try to concentrate on the reality of outcome with Nick. Everything we tangle into with him, he always manages to find a shady right path to completion."

"So we play see no evil, hear no evil, speak no evil, huh?"

Tim smiled. "How perceptive of you, Grace."

* * *

Nick passed the rear driver's wheel well a few minutes later. When the driver flicked his cigarette to the road, Nick used his stun-gun on the casually placed arm, moving with it as the driver jerked backwards. He passed out five seconds later. Nick flung open the driver's door, and waved to his US Marshal friends. Grace drove alongside. Tim secured the driver. He loaded him into the backseat while Nick inspected the Tahoe interior. The only items of interest he found were the eight by ten pictures of two police officers: a male and female. Nick took pictures of the two photos taped to the Tahoe interior rear hull, exited the vehicle, and photographed the outside of the Tahoe along with the license plate.

"Find anything interesting?"

Nick handed Grace her phone as he entered the vehicle, pushing the groaning prisoner over to the other side. "I did indeed. It seems two Charleston police officers have been targeted by this bunch for a reason yet to be discovered. Their pictures were taped inside the Tahoe. That item of interest opens other possibilities I'm sure either you or Timmy can conjure on your own."

"It would mean the dead perps had inside help at those cops' precinct to know when they would be on duty at the right time for an ambush," Tim replied.

"You're thinking two cops not on the take causing hard times for local dealers or crooks," Grace added. "This someone on the inside is probably getting paid to steer the two crime busters away from certain street transactions, and they're not going along with it. Hell of a bloody way to discourage their incentive."

"A random cop killing when answering a security alarm report is an easy way to provide an unspoken warning to any other police officers being overzealous in their duties," Nick pointed out. "I think you two can appear very knowledgeable and intuitive if the Lieutenant you're reporting this too isn't the one who set it up. Well, kids, are you fighting crime tonight, or searching for an escape route."

"You have a distasteful manner when cracking the whip on us poor civil servants," Grace complained. "This isn't our jurisdiction. We weren't asked in on the case, yet here we are on the verge of a possible crooked cop ring. How is it our responsibility to do anything beyond turning the clown beside you in, along with giving local police the hints you found in their escape vehicle?"

Nick clucked his comical disapproval. "Oh for shame. Are we not US Marshals? Didn't you ever see the movies with Tommy Lee Jones? We are a force of good in a bad world. We-"

"Oh barf! Okay... okay..." Grace relented, while Tim enjoyed yet another Nick and Grace sparring match where his partner came in second place once again.

"That's the spirit," Nick said. "Onward to the crime scene, Marshal Stanwick."

221

"By your command, Marshal McCarty. I knew this partnership would be trouble," Grace admitted. "I didn't know it would happen this quickly though."

"I'd bet if you get invited in on the case because of this stellar US Marshal work, you'll be able to bring in your special consultant to ferret out this blight on otherwise upstanding local law enforcement. Enter US Marshal Nick McCarty, detective supreme, to root around the suspected precinct in question, using his precognitive powers of deduction."

"You're joking," Grace stammered, having halted at the roadside curb. "C'mon, Nick. Talking about yourself in third person is annoying enough. You contemplating interference into local police internal affairs is not a laughing matter. Tim... don't just sit there chortling like a baboon peeling an overripe banana. Say something."

"I agree with Nick." Tim shrugged off Grace's immediate stare of impending doom. "You asked. We either enforce the law, or we should turn in our badges."

"Bravo, Timmy," Nick said. "There you have it, Grace. Even your long suffering partner wants you to do the right thing. Step up!"

"Oh, you two are a riot," Grace replied, amidst humorous appreciation by Tim and Nick.

"God... get me to the hospital. I've been tased," the prisoner moaned. "You...you can't do this shit. You can't arrest me for-"

Nick lit off an arc from the tool he had used to capture the man. Then he jammed it against their prisoner's groin, giving the man a momentary jolt from the electrode discharge after releasing the button. It caused the prisoner to buck into the backseat, curling into a sobbing fetal position. Nick grabbed the man's hair.

"I'd be careful about what you say, Toasty. Stay quiet, the grownups are talking now. If you behave yourself, it's possible you'll make it to jail alive. What do you say, Grace? The Pacific Grove police force actually offered to let me be their Writer/Consultant like that TV show 'Castle'. You already know I have legal ID's with the FBI and US Marshal's Service. All the Lieutenant can say is no thanks. It'll be fun. I was railroaded into tonight's show while walking Deke by Jean, who wanted to play superhero."

Even Grace laughed at Nick's admission. "Only you, Nick... only you. I'm in. Let's go see if the Lieutenant would like some assistance."

      * * *

After perusing the pictures, and hearing Grace and Tim explain following a hunch to nab the driver, Lieutenant Moragado seemed more confused than she did when first seeing the two US Marshals. "I know these two officers. I'll get people over there to secure the van. I don't know why you did it, but that was damn good work."

She turned to Nick with a gesture. "And who is this again? Did you say he was some kind of specialist?"

"It's a long story," Grace replied. "Nick McCarty has helped the Department of Justice several times in the past, finding and securing stolen high tech items, which would have been deadly in the hands of our enemies. He also helped find a leak in our Witness Protection program. He's an ex-Delta Force member, and also a New York Times Bestselling author. He has an Assassin series about a contract killer named-"

"Diego," Moragado finished for Grace. "I read one of those pulp masterpieces. It read like a damn comic book... a bad one at that. We can't have some cop wannabe working on this. I'm not even sure I want you two Marshals anywhere near our department.

223

Since you brought in the only live suspect, I considered allowing you Feds to take a whack at finding our crime mole, but I'm not interested in civilians fooling around on something like this."

"Nick has US Marshal credentials authorized by the Attorney General," Tim said. "He can find your mole if you'll let him. We should work this in private, without bringing anyone else in on it from the Charleston Police Department."

Nick kept his mouth shut during the negotiations with Moragado, although he grinned at the thought his exercise ferreting out police corruption would be a pleasant and ironic diversion. He would be working inadvertently to solve his own killing spree. The chance to identify the insider tipping off crooks to target cops interested him even more.

"You don't speak much, McCarty. I hated the novel of yours I read."

"Duly noted, Lieutenant, but we're here to help, not hinder your investigation," Nick said. "I write novels, but I think out of the box about complex situations. It can't hurt to let me help you. We're on the same side. Another pair of eyes on a strange case can't hurt anything. I've spotted and identified problems where everything appears in order, and no one else has found anything. As Marshal Stanwick explained I have been of assistance in working with law enforcement, both local and federal."

Moragado held Nick's gaze for a moment in silence. "You certainly hold yourself in high regard, McCarty."

"If I didn't, I wouldn't be of much use to you, Lieutenant. The important fact is my help benefited the agencies I've worked with. I already have a plan. Would you like to try it out?"

"A magic formula, huh? What makes you think I'm not the one tipping off bad guys?"

"You would have stonewalled us to someone else, or refused any liaison at all with the Marshal's Service. We know we don't really belong on a local internal affairs case like this, and you could have booted us aside – but you didn't."

Moragado took a deep breath. "What's your plan?"

"Call a meeting with your Department heads. Have them bring along their second and third in command with them. First, explain the situation with the attempt to lure those two police officers pictured in the bad guys' getaway car. Then introduce Marshals Stanwick and Reinhold to the gathering, letting them know the Marshals collared the driver, and found a lead into a leak within the Charleston PD. I will stay in the background and observe the meeting."

"That's it? That's your plan?" Moragado shook her head, but held up her hand as if warding off any comment. "I get it. You think you're like that character on TV... 'The Mentalist'. All it takes is a glance around the room, and nail the bad guy, huh?"

"If you don't want our help, kick us out. We won't bother you again," Nick said. "I have to leave for home soon. I'd be glad to help, but I'm not begging for the chance."

Something in the real life assassin's tone stirred Moragado. When she stared into Nick's features this time, the small hairs on the nape of her neck stood on end. She handed each of them a card. "Be at the address on the card tomorrow at 10:30 am. I'll set the meeting into action tonight. I'll call my bosses, but I won't be specific as to the purpose. Please don't be late."

"We won't," Grace answered. "See you tomorrow."

As they walked away, Grace nudged Nick. "Moragado's not right about you mimicking the TV Mentalist for laughs, is she?"

225

When Nick didn't speak, Tim started laughing, but Grace was anything but amused. "I sure hope you can pull it off tomorrow, Mr. Mentalist. Otherwise, you'll have a couple US Marshal administrators with their bare asses hanging in the cold breeze."

"Not a pretty picture, Grace," Nick replied, making a face. "I'll make sure I'm at the top of my game tomorrow so I don't have to witness anything to do with your bare ass."

"I'd take a peek if it comes to that, partner," Tim adlibbed for Nick's amusement.

"In your dreams, Timmy," Grace retorted, but Nick noticed Tim's poke had thrown Grace off stride.

"Okay," Tim replied. "I'll settle for the dream peek for now."

Chapter Ten

Consulting Assassin

Everyone waited for Nick to enter the hotel room after being dropped off by Grace and Tim except for Grandma Mona, who had returned to her home. Jean ran over to hug Nick, with Deke prancing next to her. Tina and Rachel stayed in arms folded across chests solidarity at a distance, while Gus walked over to put a double Bushmill's Irish into Nick's hand.

Nick sipped while hugging Jean. "God bless you, Sir."

"Did you take another mission from my nine year old?"

"I think Gus took it. I came along so they wouldn't get hurt," Nick explained. "I called in reinforcements to pick me up. My new pals in the US Marshal's Service arrived in the nick of time. I helped them get a big boost from the local PD in Charleston, thanks to my awesome detective skills."

"I hand you a double Bushmill's, and you throw me under the bus? Gee thanks, brother." Gus was obviously enjoying the exchange between Nick and Rachel.

"Oh, I see. It was detective work," Rachel said. "Six guys you three were stalking for God knows what reason, suddenly shoot and knife each other to death in a bizarre battle, while waiting to ambush two police officers in a scene that defies all logic. I recall some scenes like that from our cross country run to Florida."

Nick toasted Rachel with his double. "Ahhhh... good times."

"I thought we decided jointly not to allow Jean to assign two grownups, who know better, dangerous missions involving violence and mayhem."

"Define mayhem," Nick replied.

"Don't start playing 'Name that Tune' with me. It won't go well for you. We've been watching the news, Muerto. Those six mysterious deaths have El Muerto written all over them."

"I resent that inference, my love," Nick stated, as Jean giggled.

"You wore your black mask tonight," Rachel accused. "Deny it. I dare you."

"I may have slipped on my black mask for a short time," Nick admitted. "Mystery is good for the soul."

"You have no soul!"

"How dare you say that? My soul is between my God and me. Did you have to let your Mom debrief you, Dagger. Now look what you've done. An innocent dog walk has become throw Nick and Gus to the wild wolves. I need to sip another of these, Brother Gus, while I explain how El Muerto ingratiated himself into the local PD's good graces, thereby possibly saving all of Charleston."

Gus placed an arm around Nick. "Come then, and partake with me, my brother, in front of yonder excellent windowed view. These other more human souls will have to join us when they feel ready to hear about El Muerto's wondrous further adventures."

Nick chuckled. "You're getting good at this, Gus."

"I'm so glad you noticed. We should send the loose mouthed Dagger to bed early for setting free the Rachel and Tina Krakens on our butts."

Jean immediately joined with pleading tone. "But Dad, the Rachel Kraken broke me against the rocks. I was helpless before her rage despite my strong willed resistance. The Tina Kraken broke Gus by merely raising her voice above a whisper. He folded like an old lawn chair."

By this time, even the Krakens were amused, following the two men into the comfortable and scenic room with large windowed viewing over Charleston. With drinks refreshed, Nick regaled his companions with an entertaining event description, that took place after the six would be cop-killers waiting in ambush met their gory end. He garnered much amusement with his portrayal of Grace's part in his adventure.

"So now you're going into this police meeting, after all that's happened?" The Rachel Kraken was amused, but not entertained by Nick's plan to save Charleston. "Your plan sounds like a TV show. Wait a minute… it is a TV show! No… no… no… tell me you're not playing the Mentalist in the midst of a room full of upper level cops!"

Nick frowned, as Gus, Tina, and Jean enjoyed Rachel's spot on recognition of Nick's plan. "Don't ruin this for me, Rach. Sure, it may seem obvious to you and that other reprobate Grace, but the Lieutenant Irene Moragado and the meeting participants will be stunned and amazed."

"Oh man, brother, that is one bold and rather stupid move," Gus said, shaking his head in wonderment. "You have indeed crossed over the dimensional barrier of unintentional consequences waiting to happen."

Nick again frowned, this time at his partner. "Now you're just being mean."

      * * *

When Tina and Gus adjourned to their room, she grabbed his arm. "I want to make sure I understand this. Tonight, you, Nick, and Jean went on a stalking exercise, found a real cop ambush, and then Nick executed the six men responsible? Then he calls his Marshal friends, escapes the scene of the crime, and ingratiates himself with the local police. What's wrong with this picture? He admitted to all of it right in front of me. Before, it's been innuendo. Isn't he afraid I'd turn him in?"

Gus patted her hand. "I doubt there's anything on earth Nick is afraid of. When he decides to do something like he did tonight, although initially against doing it in the first place, a scene develops in his head. I've seen that slow killer grin spread across his features before. After that, it's a game he carries out as coldly as if he were pouring a glass of water. God only knows the number of dead people following after that grin. He's an assassin with an imagination, and believe me, you don't want to know what Nick's imagination developed in past situations."

"What about me though?"

"To him, you're family now. Remember, I advised Rachel not to ambush him at the door, but she has a mind of her own. You decided to become her bookend buddy of disapproval, so you heard the unfiltered happening version, although never straight from Nick. He never once admitted to anything. He commented comically about everything without a denial or admission."

"So I'm safe no matter what?"

"Define 'no matter what' to me, babe."

"Well... uh... what if we decide to separate?"

Gus smiled. "I guess we better make sure that doesn't happen."

* * *

Nick scanned the large meeting room, while watching each person entering. By the time Moragado was ready to start the meeting, Nick had picked out six likely candidates. His suspects did nothing out of the ordinary. Nick noticed what they didn't do. The others were affable, shaking hands, and greeting each other, eventually talking shop. The six people jingling Nick's warning bell were more wooden in their greetings and interactions. Two were women, and standoffish with everyone. The feeling appeared mutual, as the others avoided them. Two of the men were clearly in their middle to late fifties. Although cordial to the others, they tended to gravitate to each other as if they were old time acquaintances, and didn't much like interacting with the younger crowd. The last two men triggering his suspicions were clearly nervous. Nick grinned. *This was going to be fun*, he thought.

Moragado started the meeting on time, explaining the prior night's attempted ambush, and the bizarre gun battle leaving six dead. She also went over in detail how the US Marshals had offered to help, and actually captured the getaway driver. Nick had his man already. When Moragado outlined what the meeting concerned, one of the last two of Nick's suspects visibly relaxed. The other, a stalwart six footer, with trim physique, and longish brown hair blanched at the mention of the driver being taken into custody. By the time Moragado introduced US Marshals Stanwick and Reinhold, along with their perception of a break in the case concerning a leak, Nick's main suspect was contemplating escape. Nick watched him edging toward the door to the meeting room with amusement before setting off on an intercept course while giving Grace and Tim the high sign.

By the time his suspect inched his way in a casual manner to the door, Nick was waiting for him. The man tried to get around Nick, but was blocked.

"Get the fuck out of my way," the man hissed in a low threatening tone.

231

"I can't do that, Sir. You and I have business to discuss with your Lieutenant," Nick replied. "I see you reaching toward the inside of your jacket, Sir. Don't do it. It won't go well for you. Here come my US Marshal friends along with your Lieutenant Moragado. You're not leaving, so please put your hands in the air slow and easy."

The man glanced around at the approaching law officers, and went for his weapon instead. He was still inches away when Nick's stun-gun discharged. It pitched his suspect to the floor in a ball at his feet. There were of course shouts of outrage with armed officers reaching for their weapons. Moragado, Grace, and Tim arrived in the midst with waving arms, calling for calm. Nick had already pocketed his stun-gun and stood with hands in plain sight.

"What the hell, McCarty?"

"This is your man, Lieutenant," Nick answered. "Get me a court order for this guy's financials, a list of all his duties, contacts, and previous duty stations when he was a cop instead of an administrator/boss. I'll track the path of his descent into darkness for you."

"Damn it!" Moragado pointed at a police officer standing to the right of them. "Chuck… put the cuffs on Brandt. Get him into interrogation for now while I straighten this mess out."

"You want me to arrest Chet?" Chuck was staring at Nick.

"It was Marshal McCarty's idea to call this meeting in order to single out the guy who leaked information to the hit squad," Moragado replied. "It appears to have worked. I can't believe it was Chet, but there wouldn't be any other damn reason for him to inch his way out of the meeting, and then draw on someone stopping him. Tell me he was drawing on you, McCarty."

"You see where his hand was. It froze on the grip when I zapped him," Nick pointed out. "I asked him to wait for you to come, and not to reach for a weapon."

"You could have yelled out 'stop him'," Moragado remarked.

That statement provoked the killer. It showed in his features. "He's armed and dangerous. Did you want casualties to make you feel better about this, Lieutenant?"

A murmur of agreement rattled through the group of officers. Moragado didn't like it at all, but the logic could not be denied. "We're done with this meeting. Please keep these events to yourselves, and tell all officers under your command about the ambush plot. The order from on top is do not respond to any situation without backup. I'll get the court order within the hour, McCarty. I want your two handlers with you at all times while you investigate this matter."

"Understood, Lieutenant," Nick replied.

* * *

Moragado led them to an empty office after attaining the search warrant promised along with the items Nick requested concerning Chet Brandt. "The computer in here is yours to use, but I see you have your own satellite uplink. A consultant with local police, FBI, and the US Marshals isn't all you are, is it, McCarty?"

"They aren't the only ones I take consulting jobs from."

Moragado smiled. "I will read a few more of your novels, hotshot. You're like a bad crossword puzzle."

Nick smiled back, but Grace walked the Lieutenant out of the loaned office. "First off, I know you can't access Nick's records anyway, but why do you keep getting your panties in a bunch because he can walk the walk?"

Moragado's mouth tightened in annoyance. "Because the S.O.B. even reminds me of that arrogant character on 'The Mentalist'."

"Take my word for it, Nick doesn't mean anything personal. He's direct, and kind of a smartass, but he'll find your proof. One other thing, Irene. Nick's someone you don't mess with."

"What the hell does that mean?"

"It means there are some people in the world we work with, stay friendly with, and never cross. Nick's one of them."

Moragado started a verbal retort, only to notice Grace's no nonsense stare. "Are you afraid of that writer?"

"It's more respect than fear, but it's also fear. Keep an open mind, Irene. He'll make you a believer."

Moragado waved her off as she walked away. "I'll make a note. Let me know when Superman finds something, Grace."

Grace breathed out slowly. "Nitwit."

Inside the room, Nick was hard at work with Tim watching over his shoulder making notes. They both turned to Grace when she reentered the room.

"Did you have fun with Irene?"

"Oh yeah, Nick," Grace answered. "I think you'll have to screw her or she's going to haunt you. She has a bug up her ass over you for some reason."

Nick grinned. "That ain't ever happenin'."

"She'll change her mind when she sees what Nick dug up," Tim said. "This Brandt guy's name is linked to five of the guys who died last night. All five are listed as Brandt's Confidential Informants for years since his beat cop days."

"I'm certain they acted as his money drop," Nick added, hitting another key on his laptop and smiling. "And you two don't believe in my luck factor. Look here. The driver, Rudy Freeman, is also listed as a C.I. from way back. These guys weren't young gangbangers ambushing cops for kicks. That's for sure. They had a plan in place. You know what that means."

Grace and Tim groaned at the same time.

"There's someone in the high echelons of the PD running the narrow show in different sectors of the city," Grace said.

"Very good, Gracie," Nick replied. "Dear old Rudy is still alive along with Brandt. We play those two against each other, and I bet one of them spits out the name higher on the food chain. To back anything like that up, I will of course be inching my way through our two hot picks' phone logs. An excessive number of calls to a bigwig by Brandt, and we have another possible participant. Our problem will be whether Irene wants to pull on her big girl panties, and follow the yellow brick road with us."

"Put it together for me, and I'll sell Irene on breaking down the two in custody," Grace said. "I don't think she's an idiot. She only acts like one occasionally. Do you-"

"Oh goody," Nick interrupted. "We have a winner: Jacob Kerns, head of Patrol Team Eight. They do a little of everything. Best of all, they're the liaisons to federal outfits, including the US Marshals. I think it's time to brief the head office, Timmy. I can see many instances where a federal investigation can be fogged over by the guy in charge of Patrol Eight. Meanwhile, I'll do a nice workup for Grace to follow through with Irene, while I do an unauthorized check of Jacob's financials so we have a head start."

"Now wait a minute, Flash." Grace's mouth had been dropping open a millimeter at a time as she listened to Nick. "We can't take something like this to DOJ. If this Kerns guy covers his ass, I'll be warding Timmy off my bare ass in the breeze."

"I doubt it would be Timmy being warded off once your bare ass did hit the breeze," Nick replied. "This makes it a definite federal case, involving the US Marshals."

"He's right, partner," Tim agreed. "This department head in charge of liaisons with federal task forces and agencies called into Charleston makes this a federal case. I'll get DOJ on board for a looksee, in case the Lieutenant gets cold feet. We have to run with this, even if you have to snatch it out of Irene's hands."

Grace sunk into a chair, putting her head in her hands with elbows on the desk in front of her. "You hot dogs are killing me. Didn't we already have enough on our plate, Tim?"

"I hear the violins playing, Tim," Nick inserted. "Best talk sense into Grace before the whole orchestra joins in."

Grace popped herself on the forehead and stood. "Never mind… never mind… I'm in. Let's get 'er done."

"Neato," Nick replied. "You do look a little like that 'Larry the Cable Guy'."

Tim grabbed Grace before she launched a full out attack with Nick comically hiding under the desk.

"Can I please mention another plan which will be highly dangerous, but very incriminating? It's one of those plans you two hate. They sound like shit, and often are, but they work. It will possibly mean a lot more notoriety for me, and the US Marshal's Service though, which I'm not thinking is a bad thing anymore."

"Spill it," Grace ordered.

236

"We'll put together the initial package for Moragado, along with sweating the two in custody. Then, we'll hint I'm staying late, working on a last thread of damning evidence, and I'm not trusting it to anyone outside the US Marshal's Service. The Lieutenant passes the word to all Patrol Team heads, especially Jacob Kerns. I'll wear a cam so we can record the video of my hoped for confrontation."

"Oh… my… God… you're planning to shoot an ambush party who already knows you're coming?" Grace gave up all pretention of rage, standing with arms hanging at her sides. "How do you know they won't simply shoot you in the head as you walk out the door?"

"A hunch," Nick admitted. "They'll want to make certain I have the damning threat info on me."

"I love this plan." Grace immediately jumped on board. "Either you get the bad guys on video, or the bad guys get you on video. It's a win/win situation for us."

"I didn't say anything about bad guys getting me," Nick pointed out, figuring what Grace was baiting him for.

"Some of us still have hopes and dreams, Nick."

"Okay for you, Larry."

* * *

Nick didn't leave the assigned office until nearly midnight, calling Gus to make sure he had someone watching his loved ones. He knew Rachel capable of killing, but Gus would not hesitate to fire, no matter the situation. Although he loved tying in facts on a case, linking threads no one else noticed, Nick held little regard for bringing bad guys to justice in a court. If his ploy today worked a little of both would happen. Tim pointed out the fact his hunch about them not shooting him on sight was in fact a valid one. Nick believed they would want to know if he had stored the evidence

237

somewhere at the station, or brought it with him. He carried his satellite linked laptop with him in his left hand, and easy access to his .45 caliber Colt to his right hand. Someday, Nick figured his quirky side would get him killed, but he never wanted to die in a bed anyway.

Enjoying the cooling night air with partially cloudy skies. Although muggy, his Kevlar vest did not make him uncomfortable. Having been in many gun battles, both in combat and his chosen profession, Nick understood people in combat situations. They jerked the trigger, hesitated, or even closed their eyes when they shot, hoping they were shooting 'smart' bullets. That was the real risk in his plan. If they sent pros after him, instead of men who only thought they were dangerous, the confrontation would be tricky at best, deadly at worst. It would be deadly for the men facing him.

Nick chose to throw them off a bit by simply walking away from the station to nearby Joseph P Riley Ballpark practically across from the station on Fishburne Street. The tree lined sidewalk was wide and scenic with lighting. Nick planned to stop in front as if he were waiting for a taxi. He would have clear line of sight in either direction. Nick walked to the section where a large patio with small partitioning fence separated the patio from Fishburne Street. He stopped in the patio relief area at the middle fence.

The deadly anticipation flowed within him. Nick shared nothing with his loved ones or his partner Gus about the psychopathic thrill his taking of a human life sparked within him. Most of his contract killings and assassinations involved intricate planning so as to avoid exactly what he reveled in doing now. Only a slight twinge of regret darkened his upbeat moment – thinking of Jean believing he was a superhero, when in reality he was a cold blooded killer without pier or conscience.

He enjoyed the fact he was the best of the best at what he did, without remorse or pretense. The downside he considered more and more after collecting a family was their probable risk, and the fact he could kill anything without hesitation, honor, or testimony. Although Nick could pretend anything with believability, the moral code had seeped into his consciousness from Rachel. She had the illusionary foresight of wondering what even Nick could afford to accomplish without direction or conscience.

Nick didn't wait long. A Ford van drove alongside the fence. Nick dropped his left foot back as three men disembarked quickly, including the driver. Nick smiled. The men clustered together at the van's side, facing him. A pro hit team would have split away from each other, making more difficult targets. They were all six feet or over, husky built, wearing jeans and black windbreakers. Nick figured they were wearing Kevlar too. With hands empty of weapons, it appeared to Nick his greeting party was confident he would simply do anything they asked. The driver spoke first.

"Get in the van, McCarty. We need to talk with you about your investigation."

"Sorry, but I'm not allowed to discuss it with anyone," Nick replied, as if he were answering a serious question. "Who are you guys anyway?"

"People you don't want to mess around with. That wasn't a request. Get in the fuckin' van or we'll put you in it!"

"Uh... no," Nick answered bluntly.

"You must have yourself confused with that assassin character you write about in your novels, funnyman." The driver began to reach inside his windbreaker.

239

"Don't do it," Nick warned. "You've made a couple errors already. Don't compound your bad moves."

The three men chuckled at Nick's statement.

"What errors, funnyman," the driver asked.

"The first error is you idiots bunched together to face me, and the second error is you brought shooters not killers," Nick explained. "If you draw your weapon, I will maim all three of you for life. If you three surrender, I'll let Lieutenant Moragado know you came along peacefully, and want to cooperate."

This time the driver reached, along with his two companions. They made it as far as a hand inside their coats when Nick's .45 caliber hollow points pulped the right knee of each man, the force tearing the men from their feet into three screaming, writhing piles on the roadside. Nick watched them for a moment, momentarily thinking of junking his plan, and shooting all three in the head.

"Don't do it, Nick!"

Nick remembered the cam recording the confrontation with audio. "Do what, Grace. Calm down. Better get some EMT's here in a hurry. These boys are screaming loud enough to wake the dead. Now shut up while I disarm the casualties."

Nick kept his Colt trained on the living bundles of agony while stepping over the short fence barrier. "I told you not to reach for a weapon, Bambi, but no, you had to pretend you were the big bad wolf. Now look at you."

When he was certain the men were incapable of reaching for anything dangerous, Nick put on his Nitrile gloves. He quickly and efficiently stripped the men of their weapons, but left the search for ID's and other paraphernalia to the locals. Grace, Tim, and Lieutenant Moragado drove in front of the van, parking while Nick finished with his weapon confiscation. Moragado stalked to

Nick's side as he bagged the last weapon, reaching for his shoulder. Grace grabbed her wrist from behind.

"Don't grab him, Irene! Let Nick finish. Then you can say whatever stupid thing you have in mind."

Moragado pulled away from Grace's grasp angrily, but didn't touch Nick again. "He just maimed three suspects!"

Grace moved in close to Moragado, gripping her shirt front. "Listen, you're making a damn fool out of yourself! If Nick wanted them dead, they'd all have a third eye. He kept them alive while making sure they didn't kill him. What the hell was he supposed to do, you ditz?"

Grace's stinging retort stopped Moragado, as Tim broke in. "Grace is right, and you know it, Lieutenant. Nick faced down three men wanting to kill him, and take his documentation. He's proved our theory about an upper level guy, probably Kerns. Did you get a car watching his house as Nick asked?"

"Yes, damn it! I did as super detective McCarty directed. If Kerns tries to scramble after hearing what's happened, we'll be right on his tail."

The sirens from approaching EMT vehicles screamed out in the otherwise quiet night. Their flashing beacons could be seen now, approaching on Fishburne Street. Nick joined his standing law enforcement companions in good humor. He had been listening to the exchange with much amusement while bagging weapons. Nick stayed quiet because Moragado saw him walking to them, and put a clamp on her poorly thought out comments.

"What did you think? Pretty good, huh. Three live perps, video proof they went for their weapons, and you know damn well their phone records will show Kerns tipping them off. He may have used a burner phone, but I'll wager we can triangulate that prick's whereabouts while the call was engaged. These three will

241

be on hand to help. Best start interrogating them on the way to the hospital, Lieutenant. They may let something slip you can use on Kerns."

"Maybe you'd like to ride along with one of your victims, and torture the info out of him," Moragado replied with venom dripping from each word. "I'm sure you'd get Kerns' name out of whoever you ride with."

"Fine with me. I'll keep wearing my cam, and I'll talk with one of the screamers. Kerns' name may very well be gathered from my interrogation technique, which will not be torture. Say the word, and I'll be happy to do a ride along to the hospital."

Moragado poked a finger at Nick's chest. "You arrogant bastard! Fine! Ride with one of them. I want Marshal Reinhold riding with you though. Is that clear?"

"Sure," Nick agreed. "Tim knows I don't have to torture anyone. Right, Tim?"

"Absolutely," Tim responded, using one of Nick's buzzwords from long ago.

"I think you should accompany the Lieutenant to the station, Grace. Be certain she doesn't make any errors in judgment while using these three fellows' ID's to garner lucrative information from the system, crosschecked with known phone calls in the area."

"You son-of-a-bitch!" Moragado went after Nick, but Grace was ready. She grabbed Moragado's right wrist, bending it into a debilitating wrist hold, stopping Moragado in her tracks.

"I swear to God I will bring you up on federal charges if you make one more physical attack on Marshal McCarty, or insult him with your childish crap while he's doing his best to nail this case shut."

Grace released her, pushing Moragado to the side. "You... arrest me? You must have delusions of grandeur, Stanwick!"

"Try me, bitch!" Grace took out her cell-phone. "I have a direct line to the Attorney General. I will have your overly sensitive ass in cuffs within ten minutes. I don't know what it is with this hard-on you have for Nick, but it ends now! Go ahead. Call my bluff."

"Do what you want." Moragado spun on her heel and walked across to the station.

Grace steamed on, nearly taking a running step toward Moragado. Instead, she shrugged it off as the blaring EMT vehicles arrived, disgorging two medical teams. Tim went to meet them, directing the techs to the injured men.

"I wish that bitch would have tested me. I talked to the AG earlier about this situation. He wants what's happening here stopped. Although I know Moragado doesn't have anything to do with the cop killing ambush, or tipoffs coming from Kerns and Brandt, she's shooting her mouth off at every turn."

"Take the car, and shadow her, Grace," Nick urged. "Be professional, and keep your temper in check. Tim will go with me as she asked. I'll get one of them to roll over on Kerns. The driver is my target. Once the EMT's get them stabilized with pain killers, I'll have Tim Mirandize the one we ride with. I'll question the driver first."

"I'll go ride herd on Irene," Grace agreed, "but don't overdo the interrogation. We have these people anyway, Nick. I'm certain you have enough to indict all of them without worrying about confessions."

"Go on. I'll be careful. We'll call you from the hospital."

"How the hell are you going to get any of them to talk?"

243

Nick smiled. "I'm going to show my chosen informant a movie."

* * *

While the EMT's belted in their wounded charges onto gurneys after doing emergency triage on the mens' ruined knees, Nick cued the movie he took of his Dominic Leka killing. He plugged in headphones, and waited for the now merely groaning men to be loaded. Nick signaled Tim he wanted to go with the driver, after talking the EMT's into loading the other two men together, leaving the driver by himself.

"This one's our best chance, Tim. Stay between the EMT and my small pep talk with our bad guy. I won't do anything to him. I'm only showing him a movie. Let's get aboard the Peace Train."

Inside the cramped quarters, Nick waited for the EMT's to anchor their patient, and get an IV started. One of them then told the driver to head for the hospital. When they were on the road, he motioned the techs away from the patient. Nick crouched alongside his upper body with satellite laptop open. He put the headphones on the man. Pulling aside the right earpiece, Nick bent in closer.

"Bambi… time to wake up. You remember me. I'm the guy who tried to save your knee. C'mon Bambi… Thumper wants to play."

The man's eyes blinked open. When he saw who spoke, he looked around wildly, adrenaline dulling the pain shot he had been injected with by the EMT. "Don't touch me!"

Nick patted his arm, smiling reassuringly. "Relax. I'm going to show you a movie, Bambi."

"Don't call me that… you freak."

244

Nick lowered his voice to a whisper. "Watch the movie, Bambi. Afterward, I'm going to ask you some questions. Answer them, and nothing that you'll see in the movie will happen to you. Stonewall me, and I swear to God, I'm going to make my next movie with you as the star."

Nick put the headset in place again, and started the movie. It was a condensed version showing the brutal evisceration of serial killer Dominic Leka including the pouring of bleach over Leka's steaming entrails. The strapped down man could not look away, his eyes staring in open mouthed horror, cringing at Leka's unending screams. When the clip ended, Nick took the headset off the man.

"Any questions, Bambi?"

Bambi shook his head while gagging audibly, trying desperately not to throw up.

"Good. Would you please read Bambi his rights?"

"Sure Nick." Marshal Reinhold Mirandized the man, and received his verbal acknowledgement signaling his understanding.

"Okay then. Who put you and your other two cupcakes onto me, Bambi?"

The man closed his eyes, his mouth tightening. "Jacob Kerns."

"Good start," Nick said. "I want you to tell us every detail about this operation on our way to get you fixed at the hospital. Don't leave anything out."

The man wasn't done talking when they reached the hospital, but he had covered plenty.

"I'll tag along with him," Tim said, as the EMT's worked to get the gurney out. "Go ahead, and take a cab to the station in case they start forgetting you have the whole thing on video. This blows the whole case wide open."

"Thanks, Tim. I hate hospitals," Nick said.

"What the hell did you show him?"

"His duty," Nick replied.

* * *

Grace met him as he entered the station. "Tim sent me the interrogation. It's incredible. The driver, Douglas Collins, whether he was on pain killers or not, stated he understood his rights. That was a joke anyway. He's a fuckin' cop."

"That's the way it is these days, Grace. Relax. We have them now. Was there any miscues I don't know about?"

"No." Grace grabbed Nick's forearm. "Don't make any smartass comments, Nick. They'll be looking to bury you. You calmly dropping down to take out the knees of each man you faced tonight dumped you into the no compassion category. These idiots think we can capture bad guys, protect our asses, and produce tears of sorrow because the perps are caught. It's mind blowing!"

"Think of the fallout if I had shot them in the head, which was my first preference."

"That's not funny, killer. You can't believe the mindset of these higher up stooges. They want cops stopping the bad guys. Then they want to wail crocodile tears with the thug's family, trying to get a payoff, all while making the despicable piece of shit into a Disneyland character."

"Okay, you got me, Grace. Life isn't fair. What's chances of me getting back to the hotel in time for a little midnight delight?"

246

Grace gasped, incredulous at what Nick was hinting at. "That's sick! Poor Rachel's on the verge of having your baby you unfeeling wretch. You should be massaging her feet with your head down, not contemplating sexual perversion!"

After Nick enjoyed Grace's accusations with enthusiasm, he put an arm around her shoulder, pulling her close. "Will you please stifle yourself? Rachel loves me, and she's at a weird time of pregnancy for soon to be mothers, where she also loves my loving nature."

Grace shook her head in feigned disgust. "Let's go meet with Lieutenant Shrew before it gets any later. She towed the line for justice, and stayed on track. I came out to meet you because a gentleman arrived with so many credentials, it's hard to figure out where the hell he came from. He turned off the Lieutenant's water in an instant."

"That must have made the Lieutenant happy," Nick replied, knowing instinctively it could only be Paul Gilbrech. "It's strange my unknown friend would meet me here. It also narrows the number of persons it could be. It's been a long day's journey into night, huh Grace?"

Grace stopped, turning to face Nick with tired eyes. "I'm trying to hold all this together, Nick. You've always valued honesty. Here it is. You scare the hell out of me. The name on the guy's ID is Paul Gilbrech. I'm figuring he's an important figure with the Company. My only question would be what our present case has to do with CIA business."

"He and I suspect some of this is related to national security, no matter how trivial the thread. I am surprised he came here. That action is off the usual track. It's possible he knows something about this cop-killing bunch, but I doubt it. I'm thinking something's on his horizon concerning my getting out of here. Paul's been getting a little too assertive on my book tour... but then again... I haven't helped much with the situations I've ended

247

up to my neck in. Let me handle Paul. I'm hoping it doesn't concern the US Marshal's Service."

"That goes double for me," Grace replied, threading her arm around his. "Oh… we're off to see the Wizard… the wonderful wizard of-"

Nick snatched her free hand as it waved along with the song. "That's enough of that. You handle the Lieutenant while I trade info with Paul."

"What did you do to that Collins guy?"

"I showed him a movie. Now let's go finish this crap, and move on. You and Tim have a symbiotic relationship with me now. I appreciated the ride out of the danger zone. I will try to keep the US Marshal's service out of any fallout from this latest McCarty adlib."

"You're worrying the hell out of me, Nick. Tim and I thought we were the ones stirring your goofy life like a blender gone wild. Now, we see you in a totally new light, where you're actually short circuiting the blender on high. You do realize Lieutenant Moragado actually suspects you of killing those guys trying to ambush cops. She has no idea how you could have done it, but she'd pin it on you in a split second if she could. How did you do it anyway?"

"Sorcery."

"I believe it, you prick. There's your man in Moragado's office, smiling and winning her over by the minute. Why can't you be more like him?"

"I doubt anything I could say other than a confession would make the Lieutenant smile," Nick replied as they crossed the threshold into Moragado's office.

Gilbrech reached out a hand to Nick, who shook it with a wry smile spreading on his features. "Good to see you, Nick. I've heard a rather disturbing rendition of your assistance in finding a damaging leak in the department. Lieutenant Moragado became curious about you. She tried to access your government files, which is of course above her pay grade. I needed to discuss another matter with you personally, so I thought it better to explain your rather unique consulting role face to face."

"I understand now you also do consulting with the CIA, as well as other agencies," Moragado said. "It explains your formidable contacts and resources. Mr. Gilbrech assured me you don't work directly for the CIA, which would make it illegal for you to work inside the United States, even under the new Homeland Security measures. I'm sorry we got off to such a poor start. You produced remarkable results in a very short amount of time. Jacob Kerns has already been taken into custody at his home."

"I'm glad things worked out, Lieutenant. I promise to be out of your hair shortly. If I do another book signing in Charleston I'll drop by the station to say hello. You could meet my family. My wife Rachel thinks I'm annoying too."

Moragado laughed. "I'll bet she does."

"I need to talk with Nick before my next flight. Are you finished with the annoying one for now, Lieutenant?"

"I believe so. Marshal Stanwick and I can review the interrogation again while they bring Kerns in."

"Let's take a walk outside," Gilbrech suggested.

* * *

Outside, the men walked in the same direction Nick did earlier in the evening. "I was surprised to see you in Charleston, Paul. I didn't think a police corruption case would blow any skirts up at the Company."

249

"Do I want to know how you became involved in all this? I know by the description I read describing six cop-killers going psycho and killing each other, that it was one of your favorite scene setups."

"You're right. It's probably not a good idea mulling those pesky details over too closely," Nick replied. "It was a good deed that went a bit sideways. Charleston has proven to be anything but relaxing, Paul. I think I need a vacation from my vacation. Rachel and Jean had a good visit though with Jean's Grandma Mona. How's the fallout from my impromptu consulting job with the local PD."

"Very good. You earned big points for our US Marshal Service connection. The AG called me directly to thank me for allowing you to work this case with the Marshals. He doesn't understand how you get into all these tangled webs, but he really likes the results. Aside from all that, I didn't want anything happening to El Muerto. I wanted to give you a warning. Your new recruit called me from your place. It seems John went to the mosque in Seaside nearby, and was approached."

"Gee... there's some good news." Paul had Nick's full attention in an instant. "Did he say why he didn't call me?"

"He knew you'd be in the middle of any number of things, so he called me first. I told him I'd brief you on what was happening. John recognized one of the men at the mosque who talked with him. His name's Ansar Pasha. He's an Egyptian. Pasha came here on a green card, worked and went to school for a short time in New York City, and then disappeared last year. He's one of many we've lost track of."

"And yet we're still handing out visas. What a world. How'd John handle it?"

"He's working it. I told him to keep going to the mosque, and not to avoid them or act overly friendly. John thinks they approached because his picture has probably been circulated. I suggested staying standoffish until these guys actually show their hand. If they do, I gave John permission to tell them the truth about what happened, and that he barely escaped with his life. He can tell them all about El Muerto, and how he nearly died, but managed to get away before the police arrived on scene. After all, there is an El Muerto video out there proving it."

"Good cover. I don't want John killed before I get a chance to train him a bit, and I don't like him doing this without backup." Nick began running scenarios in his mind at rapid speed, imagining all the negatives and positives, including the nearness to his home. *I guess I should have thought about all that before I did something as public as wounding three bad cops. Jesus… I need to talk to Payaso. I think Muerto has finally rounded the bend, taking my reality with him.*

Paul did a double take at what he thought crossed Nick's features. "I didn't like that look you just flashed. If I'm shooting too much at you, say the word, and I'll back off. We can put John in hiding until things cool off. I'm with you on the importance of a freelance asset like John. On top of that, I've never had a contract killer asset so attuned to right and wrong like you. It's made a difference in the way I think, Nick. Your quirky side has admittedly brought us closer to exposure than we can afford. On the other hand, you're doing what's actually right while taking care of national security. I've made my choice. I'm backing you all the way down the coal chute. Your results are gathering a real following."

Nick met Paul's unwavering look with an acknowledging nod of the head. "Okay then… you have me on the pad, pal. I see something between us psychos besides professional courtesy. I won't abuse it. I'm happy to get the hell out of Charleston. I want to sit on my favorite beach in Pacific Grove, and sip a coffee with Payaso laced with the Irish. I'll work on ending this threat with

John ASAP. Threats so close to my home make me queasy. I tend to kill with abandon when I get queasy."

"Understood. I'm not sure what you'll face when you access the situation in person, including another one of these damn Isis cells, but if you can use any help, in any way, shape, or form, please call me, Nick. I don't want to lose you for any reason. You would be surprised how far I'd go to keep you alive."

That statement stunned Nick into silence for a moment. "You've grown fond of El Muerto, huh? This action being so close to my homestead, I will seek to be more circumspect in my dealings with these suspected wrongdoers. It's been a pleasure working with you too, Paul. I don't care to have anything happen to you either."

"Would you like a ride to the hotel? I'll bet Rachel will be glad to see you."

"I believe you're right, Paul. My Rachel has become unusually dissatisfied with her surroundings here in Charleston." Nick walked over to put a guiding arm around Gilbrech's shoulders. "Although excited at first with my tour, Rachel, Jean, and even Deke the dog have become restless. I think I have them spoiled with West Coast living, even though it's been getting a bit violent out there too. New York, Boston, and Charleston have awoken my ladies to the fact sometimes it's violent everywhere."

"Have you considered the fact it may just be you, Muerto?"

"That's hurtful, Paul... probably true... but hurtful."

Chapter Eleven

Home, Sweet Home

John threw the Frisbee for Deke, watching with glee as the dog raced through the sand at Otter's Point, snatching the black disc from the air. Nick's new recruit never seemed to tire when playing with Deke. On the other hand, Deke caught the Frisbee, and then head tossed it off to the side before joining Jean at one of the tide pools.

"I believe Deke has signaled an end to my Frisbee tossing joy," John said.

A typical Pacific Grove morning with low lying fog, gray cloudy skies, and dead calm ocean surf made for a cool morning in the high fifties. Nick, Gus, John, and Jean wore hoodies and ball caps. To Nick it was a perfect Sunday morning, complete with mild breeze, Gulls' piercing cries haphazardly upsetting the nearly silent scene, and hot coffee spiked with Bushmill's Irish.

"Have a seat then, John," Gus urged. "We're in heaven here, bundled as if trapped on an ice floe in the arctic, and wondering what the hell is so great about the beach before dawn."

"Pay no attention to this heretic," Nick countered. "He's been whining ever since I moved his ass out here to Pacific Grove. Gus like's nothing better than to complain. If we ever came down here, and the sun was shining on a crystal clear morning, he'd find something else to bitch and moan about. This is a perfect time to meet though as you suspected. Without traffic, it would be very difficult for someone to tail you here. You were unsure when we talked on the phone whether they're that interested in you yet."

"They are interested," John responded, sitting down in his beach chair. He accepted a spiked coffee from Gus. He sighed deeply as the mixture wound down his throat. "You two are devils of temptation with this demon drink you have forced on me. It is very good. I am glad you have returned. Ansar has begun calling me at night. At first it was polite conversation, wondering about my situation here. Lately, he has begun suggesting vaguely it is time to get back in the game, because they need my experience."

"Have they ever shadowed you to the Carmel Valley house after seeing you at the mosque?"

"Yes. The second time I attended, they followed me, but because of your Carmel Valley home's location, it is very difficult to do so without being seen. I can tell they are anxious to know how I could be living at such a place. I believe they have visions of making it into a training ground. I have a scenario in mind I would like to share with you. I can tell Ansar I made a connection with a true believer while in Boston. It is his land I am staying on."

"I like it," Nick replied. "He can be an anonymous benefactor to use as a cover. Damn... this could be fun. We'll let Ansar turn my Carmel Valley place into a terrorist training ground. Paul will pass out cold on the floor when I tell him about this new angle in the war on terror."

"Wait a minute," Gus interrupted Nick's psycho reverie. "Isn't the Carmel Valley place in your name?"

"Nope. I bought and developed it under a fictional business interest tied to my place in Las Vegas. The dummy corporation there pays all taxes and utilities through an on-line account. It will be perfect for what John has in mind."

"I know Gilbrech's going to ask this," Gus continued. "What the hell are we going to do with a terrorist training ground? I know I'm interested in knowing."

"We will let John play the Pied Piper, getting all the rats together. Then, El Muerto, Payaso, and the newest member of our violent band, El Kabong, will swoop down on these wrongdoers."

Gus let out the breath he had been holding. "Oh boy."

"El Kabong?" John's questioning glance from Nick to Gus went unanswered until Gus grabbed his iPad, doing a quick on-line search. He then turned it for John's viewing pleasure of an old 'Quick Draw McGraw' cartoon, featuring the goofy horse Quick Draw and his alter ego, the vigilante, El Kabong. It was many moments before John could speak.

"See," Nick pointed at John. "He likes his new secret identity."

"We'll be the laughing stock of all creation when our first violent video hits," Gus said. "Are you meaning this as an insult so as to attract a response?"

"Of course. When terrorists die at the hands of cartoon characters, it provides the right message for these assholes. Instead of instilling fear in the populace, the people will see terrorists hunted down by cartoons."

"Yes… yes… it is just so," John managed to blurt out in agreement. "It will be seen as a great insult, and it will lower their esteem when seen in this light you have planned. Do I also get a costume?"

"Of course," Nick answered. "You shall have a black mask like El Muerto, but you will have an impressive El Kabong swashbuckler hat."

"May I shop for one?"

"Sure, John. Gus picked out his own Payaso mask. We will be a famous trio by the time we get done with this new group of

255

thugs. Paul is very happy with your actions here on the coast. Did you get your credentials?"

"Yes. I have them hidden though, so in case I begin getting visitors at your Carmel house. I like it there, Nick. Thank you for letting me stay at your other home."

"It's already paid dividends. I'll contact Paul when we finish our Sunday morning beach walk."

"I should go now before I am seen," John said. "El Kabong… away!"

John scurried along the Otter's Point rock wall, waving at Jean. Deke ran to get a last pet before John reached the stone steps. Jean hurried over.

"Dad? Did you make John into El Kabong?"

"Oh… you know of the great El Kabong, do you?"

"I saw him on Nic-at-Night. He's a cartoon horse named Quick Draw McGraw, who turns into El Kabong the cartoon vigilante." Jean began giggling. "So… you added El Kabong into your gang. That is so cool."

"Remember to keep that to yourself. I have plans for El Kabong."

"I bet you do. What does Payaso think of this new guy on the team?"

Gus shrugged. "I guess it makes sense in some alternate universe. John seems to like it… a little too much for sanity's sake though."

"John recognizes genius when he sees it, Payaso."

"If you say so, Muerto."

A police car drove to the roadside near the stone wall. Sergeant Dickerson exited the vehicle, waving at Nick. "Hey, Nick, I thought our resident crime fighting writer would check in when he returns from a book tour. You're not holding up your end of this Pacific Grove PD and 'Castle' type collaboration."

Nick reached and shook hands with the crouching Dickerson by the rock wall. "Sorry, Neil, but I figured you'd seen enough of me for a while after the Kader mess. Thanks, by the way, for backing me up on the consulting gig I managed to get Gus and I tangled in with. You know my daughter Jean, don't you?"

"We met under bad circumstances when the Kader mess unfolded. Hi Jean. Not to switch topics on you, but I need another pair of eyes on a murder I'm working with other police departments to solve. Would you take a ride with me, and take a look?"

"Go on, Dad," Jean urged. "Gus will see us home. Mom should be wide awake pretty soon anyway with the Sergeant's visit. I'll tell her where you're at. I doubt she'll be surprised."

Nick got a nod from Gus. "Sure, I'll take a look, but why is everyone getting bent out of shape over this murder? It's not like you to want me to take a look at a crime scene before you're on your last nerve."

"We're the latest PD in the area to be looped into this. It's the seventh murder of this kind in the area. We have similar... oh hell... I can't be talking about this in front of Jean. Come with me, and I'll explain in detail on the way. You can fill Gus in later if you need to consult with him. Any new ideas are appreciated. Thanks for doing this, Nick. I don't expect a lot of help, but if you could shed a new light on the shared info, it would be great."

Nick noticed the underlying horror on Dickerson's face. Something was badly amiss in his chosen beach town. "Let's do it.

Gus… best take Jean and Deke to the house. I'll call you once I find out what's going on."

"On our way. C'mon, Deke, you salty dog. We need to hose you off when we get home."

Deke immediately scrambled for the furthest part of the beach, evoking laughter even from Sergeant Dickerson.

"Your dog seems to have a wide vocabulary," Dickerson said.

"You don't know the half of it. Watch this," Nick said. "C'mon, Deke. You get a steak treat later when I get home."

Hearing that, Deke comically raced to Gus's side, enduring his leash hookup.

"Damn… that's a little freaky."

"Yep, and you don't know how many words the canine brat recognizes the spelling of." Nick knelt down and roughed the fur on his canine drinking buddy. "He'll want a b.e.e.r. with the steak."

Deke immediately did leaps in the air, agreeing with Nick's spelling of his favorite beverage to much amusement from his human counterparts.

Sergeant Dickerson straightened, waving for Nick to come along. "Let's go before Deke starts talking. We could probably use a shot and a beer before you see this crime scene."

"I'm a bit ahead of you, Neil. For full disclosure, Gus and I have imbibed the Irish with our coffee. Will that be a problem?"

"The only problem I see is that I couldn't have imbibed a bit with you." Dickerson sighed. "Come along. Maybe you'll be able to make sense out of what's waiting for us. As Jean surmised,

Rachel directed me here. She wanted to know all the details before I left which I couldn't tell her. She was not happy."

"It's a tricky job, Neil. Rachel will get over it. I'm glad she's not jogging down here to interfere. Believe me, she would if she could. Spill it for us Rachel fans. She tried to blackmail you into talking with my location, didn't she?"

Dickerson grunted his acknowledgement. "Yep. She almost broke me, but I valiantly resisted her insidious ploys for information."

"She rolled you," Nick observed with a headshake of disparagement for the Sergeant. "Let's get out of here. You can share your less than stellar performance in the squad car."

"Damn it, Nick… she's good."

"I know, my friend," Nick replied, walking quickly through the sand toward the stone stairs with Dickerson paralleling his steps at the roadside. "I'll explain to her she's not allowed to browbeat the local police into submission from now on."

"That's mean, Nick. How the hell did you ever hook up with Rachel anyway?"

"Small steps, my friend," Nick cautioned while ascending the steps to Dickerson. "It would do you no good, nor would it help with your peace of mind to know the details of our unholy union. Be happy we joined as a force of good."

Dickerson laughed, but cut his enjoyment short at the solemn look on Nick's face as he reached the roadside. "You're scaring me, Nick."

"Welcome to my world."

* * *

They reached the body before the detective in charge released custody to the medical examiner. They were in a wooded area fifty yards away from Route 68. A naked young girl, Nick figured to be between nine and eleven lay posed with a fresh gardenia bouquet posed in her hands. He could tell from the discolorations she had been abused in a yet unknown number of ways.

"Okay, Neil… I held the scene in place until you arrived with your writer expert," an overweight man, six foot in height said, his butch cut brown hair and facial lines placed him in the late forties bracket to Nick's assessment. "Please tell me this isn't a joke."

Nick took the Nitrile gloves Dickerson handed him, stuffing his hands in without taking his eyes off the little girl. He stared into her wide open eyes with the psychopathic killer again welling into prominence within him. The girl with the long blonde hair looked startlingly like Jean. He moved to the Gardenia bouquet, noticing the beginning of rot from lack of treatment. Dickerson remained silent, not acknowledging the detective, waiting with jaw clenched for Nick to examine the body.

Nick looked up at the detective. "How many like this?"

"Ah… six," the detective answered, surprised at the first question.

"This would be news all over the country if the killings were happening one after another," Nick stated, feeling along the body's backside between the ground and flesh. "What's the time interval, and how did you know to find the body here?"

"We were texted her whereabouts from a burner phone."

"And the time interval between these six deaths?"

"One year to the day, but spread over Monterey, Carmel, Salinas, and as far North as Watsonville." The detective held out

260

his hand. "I can tell from your face you're no crime scene fraud. I've read a lot about you, Mr. McCarty. My name's Derek Stilling."

Nick shook his hand. "I don't like this. Have these killings only now been joined in a single hunt, Derek?"

"Yes," Stilling admitted. "Until now, the time interval, victim's spec's, and placement wasn't recognized. Dickerson saw the pattern, which after he pointed it out, seemed stupidly apparent. How the fuck can we piece this shit together? We're screwed. We have no idea why this perp does this, and the rest of the cases in other jurisdictions have been put in the cold case file. They're willing to be more than cooperative, but cooperative about what? This killer executes these girls one year apart, in different locales. They share common ages, looks, and gender, but the time between killings is a problem. We'll of course go over all old evidence for new DNA traces. We're lucky Neil thought to widen his parameters for similar homicides."

Nick straightened away from the crouch position he'd been holding since getting there and examining the body. "I know you'll check all the obvious parts of this discovery. When you say one year intervals, do you mean an exact day in March? Also, has the Gardenia bouquet been present at each crime scene?"

Stilling glanced over the notes he had made. "Ah… yes… all the victims were found in March between the 13th and 15th. There has been a Gardenia bouquet in each victim's hands. Hey… they alternate over the six year span - 13th, 14th, and 15th. This is the second murder on the 15th. Where are you going with this?"

"Nowhere really weird. I'm sure you're aware of the Roman calendar listing the 13th through the 15th as the Ides of March, as in Shakespeare's play 'Julius Caesar' where he dramatizes the soothsayer who warns Caesar to 'beware the Ides of March'. Gardenias represent a secret love or budding desire. I'm not certain what this whacko's motive is, but the dates and flowers may help nail him."

"You're certain it's a guy? We found no indication of sexual assault, nor did the other murders have any indication of anything sexual. Only the bruising is similar on the victims' crime scene photos."

"I checked the bruising around the girl's waist. Those marks were made by a very large, thick set of hands. Also, Gardenias are not common around here, and hard to grow. This bouquet was kept fresh somewhere for sale. The stems have not been recently cut. I doubt the killer grows his own, so he bought them somewhere. I don't think he'd go the on-line route, and I wouldn't limit investigating flower shops to the cities where the murders happened."

"What about this Ides of March shit, Nick?"

Nick turned his attention to Dickerson. The Sergeant had the foresight to dig deeper when confronted with the murder, or they would be ruling the girl's murder a random homicide. "I think it's part of the game. This clown doesn't care about the Ides. He'd love for you to finally get it all out in the media after six years. I'm thinking he left plenty of clues to join the murders, but they were missed until you changed the investigation's scope, Neil. The sick fuck probably wants to be called some pet killer name in the media. The gardenias and no sexual assault mean something deeper, but there's no use getting fixated on them. Once they open the other evidence, maybe that reasoning will become apparent."

"You don't have much respect for this guy, McCarty," Stilling observed. "He's managed six murders we know of with special circumstances, and we have nothing but some flowers for clues."

Nick grinned. "I have a nine year old daughter who looks a hell of a lot like the victim here. I'm not underestimating this

262

asshole. I'm merely sticking to the facts I see in evidence. Some are to mislead us. The gardenias only intrigue me because it's a solid traceable commodity. Somewhere, he bought the damn things."

"What about meeting with the parents of the other victims?"

"You do anything you want to, Derek. I'm not meeting with people devastated by an unimaginable loss. They didn't do it, and they don't know who did. I have some favors to call in with people you can't know about. I have the coordinates locked into my phone. I'll be in touch once I follow some real time data."

"What the hell is that supposed to mean," Stilling asked.

Dickerson had begun to suspect McCarty was far more than a writer living the good life in Pacific Grove. "I'll drop Nick off at home. We'll start expanding this investigation, and see if we can find more in the evidence gathered from the other cases. I know if Nick can help, he will."

Stilling gave them the wave off. "Go ahead. I don't know if McCarty can help, but I'll be on the hot-seat from now on until this ends. I'm not turning down any help that can possibly find this bastard. I don't know what favors you're calling in, McCarty, but I sure hope they help."

"I won't string you along if they don't, Detective," Nick replied. "You'll be the first to know if there's a snag, or my channels are a dead end."

        * * *

Dickerson broke the silence first as he drove Nick home. "I'm not stupid, Nick. I noticed the headlines you've been getting on tour, especially the consulting job in Charleston. Can I help you in any way on this case?"

"The only thing I didn't ask for with Stilling is I'd like to know how each girl was initially taken, and by what means. I want to know about drugs in each girl's system found during the autopsies, and what final cause of death was. Did this guy suffocate them, or did he give them a hotshot death cocktail? Anything like that you can forward to the e-mail address I gave you would be a help. I guarantee we will find this shithead."

Dickerson parked in front of Nick's house. "Does that mean find him with his head chopped off, or alive for booking him as a suspect?"

Dickerson's astute acceptance of what Nick's capabilities were, garnered a straight forward grimace. "Whatever you wish for help, I'll provide, Neil. Be very careful what you wish for though."

"Surprise me."

Nick laughed. "I'll be in touch."

* * *

Gus swung open the door before Nick could grip the knob. "Hey, brother. We're ordering pizza for our late lunch. Is that okay with you?"

Rachel slithered around Gus to embrace Nick with Jean and Deke joining into the greeting on the doorstep. Tina gave him a wave from Gus's side. "Pizza sounds great to me… with the obligatory shots and beers with it of course."

"Of course," Gus agreed, throwing open the door. "I was hoping you'd say that. Do we have a drinking problem, partner?"

"I'll have to get back to you on that, brother. For now, I'm going up on our very scenic upper veranda with my satellite laptop, sip a few, help the police, write some more Diego scenes, and munch on pizza." Nick knelt next to Deke, absorbing the immediate lick fest with relish. "Is it too early for you to have a beer, Deke?"

In answer, the dog hopped around as if possessed.

Nick took a deep breath while straightening. "Don't let them see how far you've turned to the dark side, Deke. It's just us for now, but there's no telling if your outrageous canine lush behavior will be observed by people who will take you from us. Be calm, my canine partner."

Deke immediately sat next to Nick, waiting for his next move, but glancing up at his face as if anticipating more direction.

"You've corrupted our dog, Nick," Rachel observed, as she gripped him in a tight embrace. "You have too much power over him. Your bribes have a negative effect on his behavior, Mr. McCarty."

"He's here to protect you and Jean," Nick replied, moving inside and shutting the door. "Deke will never swerve from that duty, and will give his own life in defense of yours. I would say that kind of dedication and loyalty deserves a beer."

"When you put it that way, I guess Jean, Tina, and I will be serving you males upstairs as to your wishes."

Nick kissed Rachel with no holds barred passion, but with allowance for her growing girth. It left both of them breathless as Deke broke the embrace to much amusement by sticking his cold nose up Rachel's maternity dress. She yelped in dismay, arching away from Nick. He pointed at the unrepentant Deke with attitude.

"I should disallow the beer ration for that unprovoked cold nose attack on my mate. I see though that although perceptively on the money for a cold nose attack, your intentions were innocent. Go dog, but sin no more."

Deke immediately went to his back, four paws in the air, and played dead. Rachel, along with everyone else gasped at Deke's incredible understanding of nuance. Rachel saw that Nick was not all that surprised. She gritted her teeth, pointing an accusatory finger at him. "You've been working my dog to provide unending backup for your bullshit. C'mon… show me what you've done."

"You're spoiling our moment in the sun, Rach."

"Show us right now!"

"Fine, but Deke and I are doing it under protest." Nick whistled a short two tone note. Deke regrouped instantly at his side. "Deke, sin no more!"

Deke went to the paws in the air death imitation immediately, causing much laughter. Nick whistled him up, where he crouched to hug Nick's feet. "Can we please go and enjoy this afternoon on the deck with drink and pizza?"

"Sure, Nick," Rachel said, while walking into the kitchen. "Control your dog."

"Damn, Deke," Nick exclaimed, bending down to hug Deke. "I think your wicked step mother threw your furry ass under the bus."

Gus motioned him to get moving. "C'mon, Nick. Stop soothing Deke's hurt feelings. He'll feel great with a beer to gulp down."

As if emphasizing Gus's point, the moment beer was stated, Deke ran upstairs. Gus pointed at the lightning fast Deke. "He's cured. Let's go sip a few before the pizza gets here."

"Okay," Nick agreed, standing. "It will be a working break though, Payaso. I have much to explain about our mission to assist the police in bringing to justice a young girl murdering

266

psychopath, who kills young girls Jean's age, who also look like her twin."

Gus turned solemn in an instant. "I'll grab my satellite laptop, and we'll network this puppy until we have this sucker cold. I assume you have some clues to start us with, right Muerto?"

"We do indeed. They're not the run of the mill hints at boyish wet dreams, pornography, or Mother's abuse. I'm sure at some point those facts will come out; but since we already don't care why the cocksucker does it, we really won't be doing the explanations as to why we thought he did what he did. By that time, he'll be dead."

"Amen to that."

* * *

To their credit, Nick and Gus sipped Bushmill's, drank Bud light, and nibbled hungrily at the pizza delivered for dinner. They made jokes at the proper moments, and commented appropriately in all areas of conversation. Nick and Gus also exchanged texted comments to help each other out on their screens when one or the other was asked a question. They also delved layer by layer into their serial killer, including introducing Paul into the hunt while accessing CIA assets to trace the crime scenes with satellite archives possibly covering the six crime scenes.

While Rachel abandoned all pretense to entertain Tina on her own, Jean watched the hunt with hungry eyes, devouring every keystroke with silent contemplation. Jean knew if she interrupted Nick's networked collaboration with Gus to trace down times with satellite archives, she would be exiled to the Rachel/Tina contingent. Nick glanced at her periodically with a smile, knowing instinctively what drifted through his stepdaughter's mind. An hour into the investigation he and Gus lost all jovial aspects concerning their serial killer target.

"Son of a bitch!" Gus pushed the laptop away, drained his shot, and half his beer. Then he picked up a huge slice of pizza. He ate in silence while watching Nick glaring at his screen while pursuing the unimaginable.

By that time, Rachel and Tina awaited the findings with as much angst as Gus showed. Jean stayed silent, watching Nick work an expanding query into crime databases across the country using CIA assets. He stopped nearly a half hour later, leaned back while watching the foggy tendrils drift across their porch from the usual ocean air meeting, and munched with deliberation on a piece of pizza. Nick hugged the vigilant Jean to him as he sat.

"You haven't eaten a thing, kid. Have some pizza."

Jean sat down next to Nick. "I know what you found, Nick. The monster the police want help with has been killing everywhere. How many has he killed?"

"Twenty-six, including four in the North along Oregon, Washington, and one in the Vancouver, Canada area. He also hit many beach towns on the Southern California coast. His earliest ones were along the Gulf Coast."

"How can you catch a guy like that, Dad? Even if you join all the cases, locations, and evidence to make one of your databases, he's killing with no kind of pattern. I watch all the crime shows. The bad guys have a pattern. Otherwise, the good guys don't catch them."

"I'm not that much of a good guy, Jean," Nick replied. "We'll keep this between us, because I haven't decided what to do with this bad man we're after. If I turn over what I've found to the locals; and let them coordinate a vast dragnet with task forces in every city, FBI teams pursuing because he's killed across state lines, they would all have fun with their badges. The problem is I doubt they'd find him. They'd all immerse themselves in every detail from the different cities involved, the media would give the asshole a catchy name like The Coastal Killer, and he'll have all the warning he needs to lay low."

"Do you think those dates mean anything?"

Nick finished his piece of pizza, and washed it down with beer while contemplating Gus's question. Everyone else continued eating too, but in silence.

"I think the dates are mostly for convenience. He hit all the Gulf Coast targets on alternating Valentine's Days, then our area during 'The Ides of March'. The Southern Cal beach towns were hit on April Fool's Day, and the North Coast and Vancouver, Canada on July 4th. I doubt he put much stock in the dates except to catch the media's attention in one of the areas. He's no dummy. Killing these girls over a ten year period in mostly small coastal towns has until now kept him on the down low. Waiting until the Amber Alerts die down to stage the body, before moving on to his next killing, makes it tough on the local cops to piece anything together. I'm certain we'll be getting a call from Dickerson letting us know they've found these other killings."

"Then what," Rachel asked.

"Nothing. We're not waiting for the announcement that will send our bad boy into hiding. He'll be due to hit his Southern Coast target area on April 1st, but he'll probably back off once the media deluge begins, soaking in the notoriety. I have a hunch his home base is in the North Bay near San Francisco. That there have been no targets in the North Bay Area is an omission I think means he lives there. I have a query in to check satellite footage during this latest year's killings. I initiated a separate query with names of airline passengers arriving in airports near the target areas during the killing periods. I narrowed the search down by adding boat rentals into the mix. It will take a while for the worms I've set into motion to go into the past as far as possible on all counts."

"What if he uses aliases when traveling or renting?"

269

"He can't do it without leaving a money trail, Gus. The connection between air passengers, car rentals, and boat rentals thrown in with this gardenia fixation should highlight similar names on credit card receipts. My guess is he rents a boat small enough for him to handle alone. He then snatches his victim, and takes her out to sea, only returning to pose them on the given date." Nick paused, watching the screen. "In another couple of hours we should have much smaller parameters. In the meantime, let's enjoy the view, and of course our drinks."

Jean sat down next to Nick with pizza in hand. "Those girls look like me. How do you think he got them?"

"I don't know. I plan to ask him if all goes according to plan."

"You're not allowing this guy to get caught, are you, Gomez?"

"Not if I can help it, Tina," Nick replied. "I'm thinking he may have an ignominious ending where he recants his sins, and dies in a horribly self-mutilating way. It will be staged properly, just as he has staged his victims. An added note will be in his own handwriting, begging forgiveness for what he has done."

"You're serious," Tina asked, glancing at Gus.

"Nick's serious, Hon. How are you going to handle the police angle, Nick?"

"I'll turn over everything I find connecting places, circumstances, times, and opportunities, saying I want to help them catch the guy, but I've gone as far as I can. I'll include some of the satellite footage I can garner too. Dickerson will have to hand it over to his boss. The boss will slide it onto the Feds, and that's when the massive task force parties will begin. When our bad guy surfaces after being introduced to the afterlife, there will be much posturing about the hunt closed in on him, and he couldn't bear the pressure. It will be entertaining watching all the agencies involved try and take credit for the neat kill."

"I don't care," Gus stated. "We get this guy, and I don't give a shit what you do with him. I'm going to help – tracking, stalking, I don't care… I'll do it."

"Your help will be most needed too," Nick admitted. "We also have to keep an eye on our new recruit, El Kabong. While we're dealing with this serial killer, I don't want to lose track of the newly discovered threat he's found."

"Jesus… is there anywhere around you that isn't peopled by terrorists, serial killers, and plain old thugs?" Rachel was not happy. When she couldn't get a reaction, she took a deep breath as she realized the booby trap she stumbled into. "Okay… go ahead… lay it on me. Grandma Mona is safe and sound because El Muerto and Payaso made her so."

"Beautifully put, my love," Nick complimented with tongue in cheek enthusiasm while Jean giggled. "It's good you don't forget our world has never been in the same dimension as the world most people see. We exist on our own plain of existence. Sometimes we drag others into it by their own choice, such as Tina… a welcome companion for my partner, Payaso. It is difficult in our dangerous dimension, but we seem to be attracting layers of protection to it, because official forces are finding my skills more necessary than they ever dreamed possible."

"We're doing good, Rachel," Gus agreed. "We've been through a lot together. To stay together, we have to accept the part about abnormal circumstances being our reality. There sure are a hell of a lot of pluses though to be thankful for. We have to be alert every moment, but that's not a bad thing."

Rachel hugged Gus, then pushed him away with comical intent. "I know… but El Kabong? Really?"

271

They all enjoyed Rachel's take on Nick's new recruit for a couple moments. The phone rang. Nick saw Sergeant Dickerson's ID, smiling while holding his cell-phone for the others to see. "Hello, Sergeant."

"Nick... I expanded the parameters. You won't believe what I've found."

"Twenty-six victims, from Vancouver, Canada, around the coast to Florida. I'll be bringing in a complete report on what I've found through my sources first thing tomorrow morning after I walk Jean to school."

"Good deal." Dickerson's relief was evident in his voice. "I thought I was nuts seeing how far this extended. The bad part is it will spiral out into the stratosphere of agencies diving into this, Nick."

"I know. I'll present what I've found tomorrow morning, and then back away. There's no use in me making this hunt any more complicated. I wish the best for you, and the task forces that go after this bastard."

"Thanks, Nick. I appreciate your understanding. When we get him, you'll be on my first to know list."

"Thanks, Neil. I appreciate that. Good Lord, my friend, I hope you catch this guy."

Dickerson hesitated, which made Nick smile. "I hope so too, Nick. I admit I hate the task force crap. Most of the time it turns into a circle jerk with no results. Thanks for your understanding. I was afraid you'd be pissed at not being involved."

"No way," Nick replied. "I know these circumstances have to develop in their own reality of federal agencies and local police departments. I don't envy you in all this."

"Thank you. I'll see you tomorrow morning."

"Count on it." Nick disconnected, smiling at his extended family. "Yep. The wheels of bureaucracy are in effect full bore. Sergeant Dickerson is the refreshing entity in all of this. I will actively work to get him climbing the police hierarchy. He's good, and he doesn't close his eyes to the reality of agencies jumping in to get a piece of a federal case. I wish I could come up with something in our projected bad guy's death that would somehow reflect favorably on Dickerson."

"Thanks for reminding me I have to go to school tomorrow," Jean stated with dejection haunting every word to the amusement of her company.

"It will be the best," Nick said, unable to hide his enjoyment of walking Jean to class. "Gus, Deke, and El Muerto tagging along on a great morning in Pacific Grove, kid. It's up to you to do well in school. With an escort like you get, it should be a rocket ship to doing well."

Jean giggled. "I'll do my best, but enjoyment of walks to school I have to leave to all you oldsters. I'm sure you see more in the happening than I do."

"Oldster… oldster? Do you hear this, Gus?"

"Yeah, Nick," Gus acknowledged, hanging his head. "I thought we were a welcome go to school escort. Now… I hear we're the over-the-hill gang escorting the infamous Dagger through her necessary burden. I'm not thrilled anymore. How about you, Deke?"

Deke jumped from his bowl of beer, glancing around with incomprehension as to his hoped for answer. He chose to walk over next to Gus, grunt, and take a position at his feet. Gus pointed and petted the attentive Deke. "See… you hurt Deke's feelings."

"I did not." Jean sounded a short two toned whistle, and Deke streaked to her side. "Deke knows I have a love/hate problem with school, Payaso. I'll tell you one thing, if this guy tries to grab me, he better bring more than a con job."

Gus and Nick exchanged glances meant only as a deadly unspoken pact no one would touch Jean unless they were already dead. They could joke. They could plot plans to capture bad guys placed in their sights, but the two partners had only one dog in any hunt: family.

* * *

Jean skipped along in front of Nick and Gus, with Deke doing a circular hop, prance, and attentive jump once in a while as he accompanied his human cohorts. He suddenly growled, pacing between Jean and the road as a car drove slowly by. Both Gus and Nick reached for weapons. A man inside smiled over at Jean and Deke before accelerating on his way.

"Got it," Gus said, fingering in the license plate. "It's stolen, Nick. That was our fucking guy! He's threaded into the investigation somehow."

"He's playing with us, Gus," Nick's aura changed in the morning light to cold, dead recognition of danger. "I'm not sure how, but he's on to us. He's wondering right now if we even noticed him."

"I admit that is spooky as hell," Gus said, as Jean had stopped when Deke growled. "What now, Muerto?"

"He filled in his face for me. He's a cocky bastard, and he didn't do his homework. I believe the years of killing unnoticed has played with his head a little. I never forget a face. We'll need to contact John. We can't get bogged down in the terrorist hunt right now."

"Want me to report seeing the stolen car?"

"No. Let's keep that to ourselves for now. I don't underestimate my enemies, but if we get any clues as to where the car was stolen, I'm betting he left his own in the same spot. We'll work that angle first. I want him thinking he's the sharpest knife in the drawer."

"That was him... wasn't it?" Jean's features did not show fear, but only excitement. "I bet he thinks he can take me. He sure knows you've been asked into the investigation. I want to be the bait! We'll nail him!"

"I'd slit my own throat before I let you be bait. Please don't ever repeat those words anywhere. What I would like is for you to bring 'Dagger' to the surface, and do not let anyone talk the school or your teachers into allowing anyone other than Gus or me to pick you up. You have your iPhone. FaceTime with me no matter what question you have. We will not be far away from the school today at any time."

Jean smiled. "Got it. This guy is in big trouble."

Nick patted his daughter's shoulder. "Yeah, he is."

Chapter Twelve

Educating Ollie

"He stole it from the Fisherman's Wharf parking lot," Gus said. He kept digging into any other sightings of the vehicle or confirmation it had been abandoned. "I don't see any updates about the car being recovered. It's a 2010 Mazda 3. He took a real chance taking it out of there. Hell, he'd have to pay the parking fee face to face with a lot attendant. Damn… maybe you're right. This guy seems suddenly obsessed with you being called in as a consultant."

"He's taking way too many chances." Nick turned his satellite laptop toward Gus. "We have a winner from my cyber hunt. No one matched all criteria except for this Oliver Dansing. He lives in the North Bay as I thought. I have an address in San Mateo. His personal car is a 2014 BMW 320i. Let's go see my buddy, Jerry Burkhart. He'll have a car we can borrow for checking on the parked cars at Fisherman's Wharf."

"This seems too good to be true," Gus said. "Do you smell a trap?"

Nick gave serious consideration to Gus's instinctive feeling about Dansing luring them into a trap. He normally never let anyone cloud his decisions with unnecessary threads to worry about. "We're going over to the Fisherman's Wharf parking lot, find Dansing's actual vehicle, and wait for him. I'll give him credit for probably knowing our vehicles. We'll have Rachel and Tina go into my safe-room when we leave. He won't know what Jerry will give us to drive."

"Just for my input, partner… what if he hired a crew to take you out or something?"

Nick smiled. "It won't matter, my friend. He would have hired guys wanting to get the drop on me, stuff me and you in a trunk, and leave the Fisherman's Wharf parking lot. You already know the problems with that ever taking place."

Gus grinned at his partner's take on things. "That wouldn't work for him at all. I'm overthinking this anyway. He'll retrieve his BMW in person, and believe he'll be flitting up North. He won't drive the stolen car to the Wharf, so he'll be approaching his Beamer on foot. Are you going to take him in the lot?"

"Nope. He won't even know we're nearby. I'm going to hack into his BMW's Connected-Drive in-car internet system. Then we'll make sure Mr. Dansing's BMW is at the Wharf as we suspect. We'll drive over and keep an eye on it until he goes home to San Mateo. We'll track his car to his home. First though, I need to get busy on hacking into the BMW. I'd like you to find out everything you can about his house in San Mateo, including satellite photos of his grounds, and the blueprints. After I hack into the BMW, I'll start going over the satellite footage for the crime scene. That's a shot in the dark, but it would be cute to turn in the case with damning evidence. When they arrive to take Mr. Dansing into custody, he will have committed suicide in angst over his many murders."

"That would be the best. It will get you points for being straightforward helpful with the police, plus keep suspicion you took an active hand in it at a minimum."

"That's the plan, Payaso. The only unknown factor is why the hell he's stealing a car, doing a drive-by on us, and remaining in the area for this long. Also, I doubt if anyone's helping him from inside the PD. That would mean he was watching when Dickerson brought me to the crime scene. I wonder if he heard anything. We need to revisit the crime scene, and check for a cam he planted. I know the cops weren't looking for a cam."

277

"Should we finish doing the investigating, or do you want to check the crime scene first?"

"We'll do the prep work first, then the crime scene. I'll get a trace on him now, so we know if he retrieves his Beamer before we get done," Nick answered.

An hour later, Nick's laptop warned him the BMW was being driven. "Dansing's on the move."

Gus finished putting together the last of his file on Dansing's house and grounds. "Is he headed for home?"

"Sort of." Nick turned his laptop so Gus could see. "I think he's coming to my home."

"This guy really is creepy. What do you think he's planning?" Gus watched the BMW thread its way through traffic toward Nick's street.

"Case my house for a later visit would be my guess. We'll get to see what he uses for a ploy to get inside."

Nick and Gus went downstairs with Deke in their wake. Rachel and Tina were talking in the kitchen.

"You won't believe this, but the serial killer's on his way here to the house, Rach. It would be best if you and Tina go into the safe-room for now."

"You're not going to kill him here, are you?"

"What about if he wants to kill me and Gus?"

"One thing I know, Gomez," Tina said, "killing you is not a skill this baby killer has. C'mon, girlfriend, show me your neat safe-room."

"Right this way." Rachel gave Nick a kiss, and led Tina to the upstairs safe-room. "C'mon Deke."

278

"Is he parking yet, Nick?" Gus looked over his shoulder. "Oh yeah… right out front in his own Beamer. This guy is something else. Do you really think he's casing your home? He already knows about Jean. He proved that with the drive-by."

"I know." The doorbell rang, and Nick went to answer it with Gus at his side. The man he had seen in the Mazda earlier now stood on his porch, smiling a happy-go-lucky greeting. Nick assumed his confused but interested persona. "Hi… can I help you?"

Oliver Dansing gave Nick a small wave of his hand. At a couple inches over six feet tall, with long brown hair tied back in a ponytail, he seemed in his late thirties to Nick. Clean shaven but for a small goatee, Dansing looked well-muscled in his jeans, tennis shoes, and blue windbreaker. Nick smiled politely at the wave.

"I'm here to see the owner of this wonderful house," Dansing stated in a cheerful baritone voice. "I love this porch and your enclosed upper deck overlooking everything below."

"I'm the owner. I like it too, for nearly the same reasons. Are you visiting nearby?"

"No. I'm very interested in buying this house. Are you possibly in the market to sell? I saw your place, and I felt compelled to stop. I would not have been able to forgive myself if I didn't at least ask if it might be coming on the market."

"I'm afraid not. My wife and I are very happy here," Nick answered carefully, sizing his prey for a new plan flitting through his head. "Homes in this area are escalating in value at an incredible rate. A real estate agent stated a couple weeks ago in a phone call I could expect to get a million and a half if I did put it on the market."

The figure startled Dansing, who had no intention of buying it anyway. "A million and a half? Wow… I was thinking more in the $750,000 bracket. You must have more than meets the eye here, Sir."

Nick nodded amiably, chuckling a bit for Dansing's appreciation. "Yes, I do. I have two safe-rooms built into the house, one upstairs, and one downstairs. The real estate agent was very impressed with those two additions."

Surprise showed plainly on Dansing's face. "Two safe-rooms? You mean the kind where a family may hide from burglars, and those awful smash and grab hoodlums?"

"Exactly. We are safe from nearly any threat with our safe-rooms and security system," Nick said, baiting the hook with more chum. "Well… it was nice talking with you, but I-"

"Please…" Dansing held up a hand. "I have always thought about having one of those safe-rooms installed in my own dwelling. Would it be possible to see yours? My name is Oliver Dansing. I can show you my driver's license and credit cards, or anything to put you at ease. I think it's marvelous you would protect your wife and young daughter in such an incredibly thorough manner."

Nick's eyes narrowed. "How did you know I have a daughter, Mr. Dansing?"

Dansing grinned with practiced ease. "That's easy to explain. When I came down last week, hunting for real estate in the area, I saw a young blonde haired girl playing with a dog on your porch. I of course assumed she was your daughter."

Nick visibly relaxed as Gus faded more into the background. "Yes. That was my daughter, Jean, and her dog Deke. I guess I could show you my downstairs safe-room. It's very state of the art with everything imaginable inside, including surveillance feeds from my security cams all around the perimeter of the house. I believe in security."

"As do I," Dansing replied. "How is it that you need such intricate precautions? I would have figured this area is so upscale you wouldn't even need to lock your doors at night."

"I wish." Nick sighed, and opened his screen door to Dansing. "C'mon in, Mr. Dansing. I'll show you around if you'd like. I'm a writer. My name's Nick McCarty. Perhaps you've heard of me."

Nick could tell Dansing had not garnered that knowledge, which meant his identity had not been given out by anyone on the police force. Dansing had indeed filmed the crime scene. Nick held out his hand, and Dansing shook it as he came inside. "This is my business partner, Gus Nason."

Dansing shook Gus's extended hand. "I'm sorry, Nick. I don't know many authors. I mostly read non-fiction. What is it you write?"

"Pulp fiction mostly," Nick admitted with a self-deprecating flair. "They're popular enough to warrant my extra security measures though. C'mon, and I'll show you."

Nick led his guest to the safe-room downstairs, opening the panel access, and keying in his fingerprint entry. "It's fingerprint entry. Go on, and have a look around, Mr. Dansing. I think you'll find this is everything you could hope for in regard to security."

"Call me, Ollie, Nick. Thank you." The unsuspecting Dansing walked past Nick into the spacious safe-room, unknowing he was walking into the last place on earth he would ever enter willingly.

Dansing struggled mightily at first as Nick's iron grip put him in a sleeper hold he could not break or alter. Nick jammed him down on his tailbone, slowly applying more pressure to Dansing's

281

throat until the man went limp in his arms. Nick stood, bringing over a chair while Gus watched the serial killer. Nick and Gus then plopped their captive into the chair, binding his hands and ankles to the armrest chair with duct tape. As a final measure, Nick looped a duct tape binding tightly around Dansing's middle to the chair backing. After applying a strip to his guest's mouth, Nick straightened away with an audible sigh of contentment.

"Sorry, Gus. I changed all of our plans on the fly. This prick is the whole package. I'm not letting him wander around, especially with him knowing Jean. I'll call to Rachel, so they know it's safe to resume their discussion in the kitchen. We'll stay here with Eggbert, and get a few questions answered."

Gus acknowledged the change of plan without more than a grunt. "Sounds good to me, Muerto. When he mentioned Jean, I could nearly feel the bad vibes radiating out of you. Should I contact Paul?"

"Good thinking. Yep. Put Paul in the loop. If he thinks of anything I don't during questioning, he can jump in with you to make it known. I don't often bother saying this, Payaso, but I'm going to enjoy this."

"I don't often say this, Muerto, but I'm going to enjoy this more."

Nick called by intercom to the upstairs safe-room. "You ladies can do anything you wish now. We have the infamous serial killer in our capable hands."

"I bet you do," Rachel replied. It was no use pretending she was married to Casper Milquetoast. Rachel knew the arriving killer had not a prayer of ever overcoming Nick, or bending him to his will in some unseen manner. "Tina and I will be in the kitchen if you need anything, Nick."

"Thanks, babe."

In less than fifteen minutes, Gus read Paul into the op, and put him on speaker.

"Good Lord, Nick. Thank you for this. Do you have a way to interrogate this guy and still make plans according to what you probably had in mind?"

Nick laughed. "Are you kidding? C'mon, Paul. You've been out in the field before with shitheads like this Dansing guy. The perverted fucks have the pain threshold of a girl-scout, and that's an insult to the girl-scouts."

"Good one," Paul replied. "Whenever you're ready, my friend."

Nick woke up the unconscious Dansing with a wetted washcloth. It would be the most compassionate thing he would ever experience. Nick watched Dansing groan into conscious realization of where he was. Nick then undid his jeans belt, and roughly tore his jeans down to Dansing's ankles. Dansing hummed in shock, awe, and protest behind the duct tape over his mouth. He tried kicking out, bucking up and down, wrenching from side to side, as Nick and Gus enjoyed the performance from beyond his sight, making no noise while Dansing did his chair dance. When Dansing slowed to a stop, gasping heavily while drawing in air through his nose, Nick smacked him on top of his head. Nick and Gus moved into Dansing's view then, waving at him cheerily.

"Hi, Sweetpea," Nick said. "I'll bet a big bad serial killer like yourself thought he was just the baddest thing on the planet. I'll bet you were, as long as you were killing young blonde haired girls. I'm sorry, sweetie, but those days are at an end. Gus and I are here to introduce you to the punishment phase of what you've done. Naturally, you're going to tell us we've made a big mistake, right sweetie?"

Dansing honked, grunted, jerked his head in violent agreement with Nick's statement, and finally simply hummed loudly in wild-eyed pleading form. Nick slapped his cheek gently, while ripping off the duct tape over Dansing's mouth.

"He's so cute... isn't he, Gus?"

Gus didn't play the game as well as Nick. He stared down at the killer of twenty-six young girls with unbridled hatred... and anticipation. "Yeah, Muerto... he's cute as a button."

"I'll bet you liked my daughter Jean. She fits your profile so well, it's like you were made for each other. Unfortunately for you, I'm her Dad," Nick said. "When you referenced her in a statement, you upset me. I'll have to take my pound of flesh for you making me upset, Ollie. You wouldn't want to know how anxious my partner Payaso here is for me to take that pound of flesh. He loves Jean like his own daughter. That you even mentioned her name makes him crazy."

Gus reached out, pinched Dansing's nose, and kept the unrelenting grip increasing by the second. Dansing screamed in spite of having to gulp air through his mouth. "Good Lord, Ollie... I want to help you slowly into the afterlife myself. I don't have the imagination my brother El Muerto has. I defer to him in all aspects of inflicting pain. You intrigue us, so we're going to ask you some questions to help our understanding about pathetic shitheads like you in our own minds. I'd advise answering everything willingly, or your demise will I'm sure be legendary."

Nick grinned in Dansing's face, moving into view. "Oh yeah... legendary... such a neat word, but nowhere near covering what I have in mind. Let me give you a small illustration, tough guy, serial killer."

Nick pinched the underside of Dansing's ball sack with his gloved hand, increasing pressure until Dansing's scream became a wall of abject pain. He released his ministrations. "That was your only demo, asshole! You will do anything and everything I say to do without question. Do you understand?"

Dansing shrieked his acceptance and will to do anything Nick asked. Nick abandoned his plan as he reached for Dansing again. Gus hugged his partner to him, carrying Nick away out of hearing. "You've got this, brother!" Gus whispered fiercely. "Don't lose your edge now! We need his suicide note, a few questions of clarification, and then we stage him as you envisioned."

Nick's tensed body relaxed slowly, Gus's plea filtering slowly into his head. He wanted Dansing in a way he seldom felt in intensity. Nick knew right from wrong. Sometimes, he didn't care. The background of Dansing murdering twenty-six look-a-likes for Jean, along with Dansing's face on approach at his house had triggered a safety valve inside Nick he had trouble controlling. He patted Gus's arm.

"Thanks. Dansing wound my inner psycho with his past deeds. Ollie coming here, neat as you please, to do his playacting scene made me forget for a moment what the hell we're here doing."

Nick straightened away from Gus. He approached the sobbing Dansing with absolutely no empathy at all. Gus handed him an unlined tablet with pen. "Thanks, Gus. Okay, Sweetie, here's what you're going to do. We'll release your hands for a moment. You're going to write an incredibly heartwarming note about how you detested everything you've done, but you want to make amends. Then, you're going to list all the burial locations for the victims the police know nothing about. Are we clear so far?"

Dansing began crying. It took many moments before he could address Nick. He assumed after heated thinking this was an elaborate bluff. "I want a fucking lawyer! I'm not giving you anything! I will sue your asses to kingdom come for what you've already done. This was a setup! I will own you, McCarty!"

Moments sometimes transcend reality. Nick exchanging knowing glances with Gus in this safe-room was one of them. They didn't know what exactly Dansing knew or acted on for sure, but they did know Dansing would be sharing everything… and there would be no lawyer. Nick crouched below Dansing with his gloves on as Gus grabbed Dansing from behind, pinching the area at his scrotum he had worked on before. He didn't pause for five full minutes. The chair they had Dansing bound to seemed ready to fall apart under its occupant's wild gyrations of agony. Nick released him to hoots of breath intakes and relief from pain.

"I guess you think this is a game, pussy," Nick said, slapping Dansing into recognition of where he was at. "I'll repeat my instruction again before I deliver my penalty phase punishment. Are you ready to write now?"

"Yessssss…. God yes! Whatever you want me to write… I'll write!"

Nick smiled at Gus. Neither man had any intention of easing Dansing's pain. It would be a step by step process, but Dansing's captors knew in intricate detail what he had done. They knew how to make his demise appear when found as a suicide. Nick brought the clipboard over to Dansing's lap as Gus released his hands. Nick leaned in, eyeball to eyeball.

"Yes… please try something… anything. If you do anything other than write a sincere confession as I dictate to you, I will rip each of your fucking balls out of their sack, and shove them down your fucking throat!"

Nick gripped Dansing's chin in one gloved hand. "Write what I dictate, and write it like your hours of pain ahead depend on it, because they will."

Over the next half hour, Dansing wrote what Nick dictated, his handwriting becoming a bit shaky at the end as he neared the finish. Nick looked it over with satisfaction. "I like it, Sweetie. You seem almost penitent on paper. We have to move to the next phase now, which will be much easier, as you are now aware there are no

286

last minute stays of execution. There's just Gus and I along with our boss. He has a few questions for you, right boss?"

Paul Gilbrech proceeded to interrogate Dansing in minutia concerning his decision to become a serial killer, his motives, his obstacles, and his picking of targets. Gilrech did it in such a way as to draw Dansing in on an intimate basis. By the time Gilbrech finished, Dansing appeared on the verge of sexual excitement.

"Well… okay then…" Nick said in the way of finish. "I'm ready to barf. How about you, Gus?"

"Actually… if Paul's loving interrogation hadn't ended soon, I was planning on eating a bullet right here in the room. Nice, Paul – maybe you'd like to ask him out on a date."

When Gilbrech finished laughing over Nick and Gus's critique of his questions, he waved at them from Nick's screen, "I'm done. I leave Mr. Dansing in your capable hands. Do you want transport?"

"No thanks," Nick answered. "We'll take him to his house for the final curtain. This may get a bit tricky at the end, but we'll leave them with their only plausible scenario."

"Understood. I will tidy up if necessary. Incredible outcome, gentlemen. You have done a service no one can refute. I pray you will be able to return to your pursuit of John's prey soon also. Although I know you no longer need it, a bonus will be forthcoming to cover all doubt as to my appreciation."

"Okay, Paul," Nick answered. "Thanks. We'll be in touch after we finish with the great serial killer, Ollie Dansing. Adios."

Nick turned to Gus. "Okay, we have that at an end. Let's take Ollie home, and finish the last scene in the Dansing play. Paul wore me out with those questions. What the hell was that about? Maybe he has to write a doctorate thesis on sick fucks like Dansing."

287

Gus enjoyed Nick's take on Paul's interrogation, while readying Dansing for transport. "Want me to follow you in our loaner, or you follow me?"

"We'll put Ollie in his Beamer trunk, and I'll drive him home. Once we get there, we take care of business, and get the hell back home. C'mon, I'll explain what we're doing to Rachel. She'll pick up Jean. I want every one of ours in the safe-room until you and I get back."

"I agree," Gus replied. "Maybe we should go collect Jean now, and then ride over to your friend's place to get the car."

Nick realized at that moment how much Dansing had thrown him off his game. It was only common sense to first remove Jean from school first. "Ollie has messed with my mind. Thanks for the reset. You're right. Let's get Jean, and go see Jerry. He's never met Jean. It will mean something to him when he does. Plus, if my personal business keeps progressing the way it's doing now, Jean will need all of my contact lists."

Gus cinched down Dansing with gag back in place. "You've given up on altering Jean's course, huh? That's a big step, brother."

"I wish I had a choice. Jean scares me. I never thought it was possible to make someone like me. I'm not so sure anymore. She's seen so much, and has an absolute rage when it comes to bad guys getting away with the unimaginable, I think her empathy will get her killed unless I help." Nick threw his hands up in the air, his own helplessness on display. "Jean drives me nuts. I know Rachel believes I'll be able to turn her to writing, or anything other than what I do, but I'm losing faith that will be possible. She's no psycho like me. Jean feels things at an elemental level. She wants to help people being terrorized by the bad guys. Unfortunately, she knows how well our skirting rules works."

288

"If it's any comfort, I think you're right," Gus agreed. "The way Jean idolized what Rachel did for Mona, moving to take out Blackbeard, and save all their lives, tipped her over the edge. Maybe you could blame it on Rachel."

The two partners enjoyed that pronouncement for a few moments, while they made sure nothing short of an armed intervention would free Dansing. His wild eyed persona amused Nick and Gus.

"Ollie doesn't like any of this, Gus. He thinks there are extremely bad times ahead for him," Nick said, as he and Gus moved to the safe-room exit."

"I believe he is correct," Gus commented solemnly. "The world will not miss this sadistic piece of shit at all. I'm sure he has a Mommy. He certainly had a lot to say about her when Paul interrogated him. I felt the joy. Hey Ollie, does your Mommy like you?"

Dansing indicated with enthusiastic positive head nods that indeed, he had a Mommy who would miss him.

"We'll send her a condolence card after we send your ass to hell," Gus stated. "I'm sure your demise will sadden her greatly, but Nick and I don't give a flying ass shit… you twisted prick. You're damn lucky we don't have the time to spend with you we'd like, Pookie. I'm certain my brother, El Muerto, has an ending in mind that will both look like a suicide, and also make you wish you'd never been born."

"Count on it," Nick said with conviction. "In your favor though, Ollie, the death will not be close to what I'd like to do with you. In that sense, you are blessed. Gus and I have to leave you for the time being to make sure Jean gets home safely. Because of you, I've decided to introduce her to one of my contacts, who will be providing a car for this evening's event. This meeting will be kind of a damnation for both of us."

Outside the safe-room, Nick set the special code he had installed on the door so the person inside could not get out. He and Gus proceeded to the kitchen. "Gus and I have to pick up a car, and we'll be taking Jean with us. When we get back, I'll need you three and Deke to watch a movie in one of the safe-rooms while we're gone."

"Why does Jean have to go along to retrieve your ride for the evening," Rachel asked with suspicious tone.

"My friend, Jerry Burkhart, who supplies vehicles for me now and then loves Deke, and has been bugging me about meeting Jean. It's nothing for you to get that vein pulsing in your forehead over, Honey."

Rachel slapped a hand to the vein Nick mentioned. "It is not pulsing."

Tina put a comforting arm around her. "Yeah, it is. Finish showing me the pictures you took in Boston at the wedding. I may call your husband Gomez, but he's much safer with kids than Gomez Addams in 'The Addam's Family'. You, on the other hand, are too intense for the Morticia character."

"Am not," Rachel said, on the way to the kitchen. "Nick's naming you as our Addams Family Cousin Itt is growing on me though."

Tina laughed, and followed Rachel. "Don't be hatin'."

* * *

"Well, who do we have here?" Jerry Burkhart caught the excited Deke into his arms, hugging the dog to him. "It's the Dekester, and I believe my favorite author has finally brought his precious daughter Jean to meet the infamous Jerry Burkhart."

290

Jean giggled while sticking her hand out to shake with Burkhart. "I'm happy to meet you, Mr. Burkhart. I know you help out my Dad a lot with his special cases."

Jean's remark caught Jerry by surprise. He then remembered Nick explaining how he acquired a family in the first place. "Nick tells me you're a keeper. You have a brother on the way too. I heard you picked out his name. Quinn... right?"

"Yes Sir," Jean answered happily. "I'll be his super protective older sister, Dagger."

"Then you like blades," Jerry said. "That's a bit unusual. C'mon inside, and I'll get you the keys, Nick. I'd like to give Dagger a gift if you'll allow it."

"I think I'll reserve judgment on that until I see the gift, Jer." Nick handed him an envelope full of money. We appreciate you finding us a ride on such short notice."

"No problem." Jerry waved the envelope. "Your request came at a rather good time. How are you doing, Gus. Is married life everything you'd hoped for?"

"So far, so good." Gus took the keys Jerry handed him.

"It's the old brown Nissan Sentra out in front. "Leave it in the same spot when you get back. Although I have a cover story for the car, it would be best not to flaunt it by getting traffic violations."

Jerry then rummaged in a steel bench's bottom cabinet. He brought out a case wrapped in an old towel. He used the towel to wipe the oaken case off before placing it on the towel. Jerry released the latches at the sides, opening the cover to reveal an all black set of three throwing knives. Jerry handed one to Nick.

"I'd like to give these to Dagger. A guy threw them in as a bonus on a body repair deal I made with him. You can tell Rachel I gave them to you. I know with your skill set, you probably know whether they're any good or not."

Nick handled the blade with professional care, nodding his liking for the blade's weight and feel. He glanced around the empty shop, spotting a wooden pallet leaning against another bench nearly thirty feet away. In one smooth motion, Nick flipped the blade to his right hand, and his throw buried it in the pallet's top center board. Jerry chuckled while tossing the second and third to Nick, who planted each one below the first in a line.

"Show off," Gus mumbled.

Jean watched the demonstration in open mouthed amazement. When she found her words, they were what Nick expected. "Can I please have them, Dad… please!"

"As long as you leave it as Jerry suggested with your Mom." Nick walked over to retrieve the knives. "They were a gift to me from Jerry, okay?"

"I guess those babies are as good as I thought they were. I'm glad you have them now. They'd sit under the damn bench rotting if I kept them."

Nick shook his hand. "They are indeed very good. Thank you. I'll have the Nissan back sometime in the early morning."

"That'll work," Jerry replied. He hugged Deke and Jean. "It's great seeing you Deke, and an honor meeting you, Dagger. Take good care of Quinn, and make your Dad bring him to the shop so I can see if he resembles this cluck."

"I will, Mr. Burkhart. Thank you so much for the knives. I'll show you how good I get with them next time I see you."

"You're very welcome, young lady. I would love to see how well you progress with the blades. I can tell in your eyes,

Barbi dolls are not your thing. Maybe I shouldn't have given them to you, Nick."

"There's no denying just what you said, Jer. Rachel knows Jean loves guns and now I'm sure knives. It's a competitive sport too. Maybe I can sell her Mom on an explanation that it's like playing softball."

Jerry chuckled appreciatively, patting Jean's shoulder. "Good luck with that, partner. See you on the down low next time."

Nick shook hands with Jerry again, clasping his shoulder. "Count on it, Jer. If things with the business keep taking a downturn, you damn well better call me. I don't put friends on the pad. I need you doing what you do, and don't think for a moment I don't follow your holdings. I know you live close to the vest, brother. It's a bad time for everyone except in my line of work, which you are one of a handful who know. Don't hesitate to call me."

Jerry, surprised at first with the intensity Nick displayed, then grinned, hunching his shoulders. "Thanks, Nick. I will keep you in mind, but I'm okay for now."

"Don't wait until you're not, brother," Nick stated, releasing his hand, and moving toward the door with his entourage of Deke, Gus, and Jean all waving as they followed Nick out. "I'll think of it as a personal insult if you don't."

* * *

Jerry paused. Nick's stating he was not on the pad for anything meant a lot to him. He wasn't afraid of Nick. He understood a relationship with one of the most dangerous men on the planet to be one which must be respected. Like Nick, Jerry didn't stupidly aid anyone with a dollar bill in their hand. In retrospect, he never understood Nick's motives. Nick never mentioned favors. He presented a job he needed help on without any flourish or reference to the past. Although Nick never hinted he would be upset if Jerry said no to a job, Jerry had never even considered saying no.

He watched the group laughing as they walked away. Both fear for his very strange friend, and joy pumped into his consciousness. The Nick he dealt with now hardly resembled the cold-eyed apparition, who he contracted with in the past. Although TV movies speculated what a cold blooded, psycho killer would do if his own family was in danger, Jerry resisted the thought of sheer casualty numbers if someone put Nick's back to the wall. He almost felt a lightness of spirit giving the 'throwing knife set' to Jean. Then remembering the look of adulation on her face as Nick targeted the throwing knives to perfection, followed by her jubilation at the gift, Jerry lost his spiritual moment. *Shit! I think maybe I should have given her a Barbi Doll.*

       * * *

"Can I go with you and Gus?"

Jean's question halted their progress in a heartbeat. Nick twisted to stare at Jean, not positioning his feet differently, as if he planned on lying to himself about what he had just heard. Instead, Nick stuck his hands immediately in waiting jacket pockets. He allowed his feet to turn for a more comfortable direction in facing Jean. After a short moment, Nick held his hands out in pleading form to Jean.

"Are you stupid?"

Jean grabbed Nick's hand in both hers. "Jerry was right, Dad. I don't want Barbi Dolls, or playing dress-up. I should go with you tonight."

"Don't confuse issues, Dagger. You play softball. You don't dress up unless ordered to do so, and you hate the thought of

294

makeup. Those facts have nothing in common with suddenly asking to go along on a jaunt you suspect, rightly so, should not even be mentioned between us. I've already given in to your demand I teach you how to throw a knife. Don't push me, or the closest you get to those knives will be when I cut them into pieces with my torch."

Surprise followed by fear lanced across Jean's face. She jerked her hands away from Nick's. "Don't. I'm sorry I said it. I was joking. I know you and Gus have to do something with the guy locked in our safe-room. Thanks for telling me the truth it's that guy who kills girls like me."

"I won't melt the knives down, but you better rein in the jokes. I bet Gus's heartbeat still hasn't returned to normal after that curve ball you threw at our heads."

Gus suddenly let out his breath in a rush. "You sure have that right, partner."

"Sorry... I crossed the line," Jean admitted. "So, when do we start training with the knives, Dad?"

"Madre de Dios! Get inside before I start thinking about you in terms of little girl 'Beauty Pageants', the Campfire Girls, and tap dancing."

A short horrified gasp later, Jean streaked for the door. Gus stood next to Nick with Deke at his side, fascinated by the Nick and Jean exchange.

"I learned a couple knowledge gems in that conversation - the most important is we have a few weapons to use against her when she stops acting like a nine-year-old, and begins acting like a know-it-all oracle."

"Don't bet on it. Let's get Ollie wrapped and whisked out of the house before Jean gets any more bright ideas."

"Are you planning to teach her to throw knives for real, Muerto?"

"I don't see an option, Payaso. I'm a pragmatist and realist. If one of the girls Dansing killed would have been trained in firearms, and how to throw a knife, maybe we wouldn't be making ready to go help him find hell. Maybe he'd already be there."

"Do me a favor, Nick. Don't share that opinion with Rachel. It won't go well for you."

"Agreed."

* * *

Oliver Dansing awoke in pain, his head lulling from one side to another, but his eyes blinked open. He was duct taped shirtless to one of his oaken kitchen chairs with armrests. Dansing realized the shooting pains were from being anchored on his knees, while being restrained to the chair. He tried moving, but the chair could only be slid a few inches either way, as it had another chair duct taped to it, braced so it could not be tilted. He worked on moving until the excruciating pain of his knees on the tile floor forced him to quit moving. Dansing with his mouth duct taped shut, sniffed in air through his nose in loud rasping intakes.

"Oh look, Gus, Ollie's awake," Nick said, crouching and waving with friendly fervor in Dansing's face. "We thought I'd given you a bit too much nappy time juice. I couldn't have you asleep for your big performance of redemption. I brought along a souvenir set I found on a business trip in the Orient. It's beautiful... isn't it?"

Nick held a hinged box lined with oil cloth, displaying an ornate sheath and matching blade. Dansing stared at the set with terrified eyes. Nick placed the box to the side. He took out the blade from its setting, holding it loosely on his fingers as if serving it to Dansing. The man's shoulders began shaking while he issued a tortured squeal from behind the duct tape.

"See, Gus, Ollie's sorry already."

Gus moved closer, smiling into Dansing's face. "Yep… Ollie is really sorry. I bet he'd take back all those murders he committed if he could. Wouldn't you, Ollie?"

Dansing continued his sobbing movements, but nodded his head fervently.

"I'm afraid we can't take your word on an issue like this, Ollie," Nick said. "Those girls you murdered had sisters, brothers, moms, dads, cousins, aunts, uncles, grandparents, and friends. You blistered many lives, probably in the hundreds. Don't you worry though. We're going to help you win back a small amount of redemption by helping you perform a ritual suicide, the Japanese refer to as Hara-kiri."

Nick stood to the side with blade out, waving it slowly side to side in front of Dansing's face. "Really, a bullet in the head suicide wouldn't do for a modicum of heartfelt redemption. Don't worry. We need a believable scene for the police, so I won't be able to spend as much time as I'd like, helping you with this penitence. Okay Gus, get the last three inches of the blade cherry-red."

Gus took the blade to Dansing's gas burner stove. Nick positioned himself to brace his chair restraints while practicing the movements he would need with the knife. Gloves in place, Nick waited for Gus. He checked the bindings and sturdiness of his cobbled together torture brace. Gus handed him the blade, holding it at the middle. Nick gripped the knife in the proper position for his carrying out the suicide scene.

"Grab on tight, Payaso. This will be a bumpy ride." Nick brought the red hot tip to the insertion point as Gus steadied the

297

torture brace across from Nick. "This is going to hurt, Ollie… you sick fuck."

* * *

Gus watched his partner meticulously clean all signs of duct tape from both Dansing, where he had used folded cloth between the skin and duct tape, and the chair. When Nick finished, he checked over each piece of wiped down furniture, and every inch of tile away from the staged suicide scene. Lastly, he examined the positioning of Dansing's now bloody hands holding the Hara-kiri blade in the last rip upwards in the disemboweling ritual. Stepping away, Nick made certain of every angle in the way he had allowed Dansing's body to drop sideways after supposedly completing the ritual suicide in sorrow over his murders.

"How's it look to you, Payaso?"

"Masterful, Muerto… masterful. No one on earth could possibly be better than you at staging your Kabuki theater scenes. C'mon. We have to get home without being seen, and turn over our discovery of Dansing's address to your police buddy, Dickerson. You stay here, and quietly go over every inch again. I'll sneak to the Nissan. Put your phone on vibrate. When it buzzes, the Nissan will be ready at the end of the street."

Nick saluted. "By your command, Payaso. Let's make sure we don't ruin all this nice work with a flubbed stealth exit. Don't get cocky."

Gus stopped for a moment, turning again toward Nick. "That was one bloody awful piece of Karma you delivered tonight, Muerto."

"Ollie's lucky I couldn't think of a plausible way he could have committed Hara-kiri, and poured bleach on his intestines."

"Oh yeah… lucky."

Chapter Thirteen

A Loved One Passes

Sergeant Dickerson arrived after Nick and Gus returned from walking Jean to school with Deke. Nick answered the door. "Hey, Neil. C'mon in. Gus, Deke and I only a moment ago finished our escort into school duty. Want some coffee?"

"Sure." Dickerson followed Nick into the kitchen, sitting down on one of the seats as Gus brought him over a cup. "That was an incredible workup you guys did on this killer I laid on you. We went to his place in San Mateo right after you sent us your updated file."

"Please don't tell me the prick got away." Nick pushed the small server in front of his visitor with a variety of coffee additives. "I wouldn't imagine you coming here like this without either good news, or bad news. You're killing me here. Which is it?"

"SWAT went to the address you gave us. You were right all along. By the time we arrived, this Oliver Dansing had committed suicide in a brutal way I'm not allowed to divulge at this time. We got him… thanks to you and Gus."

Nick put on his overjoyed look, with only slight reservations showing in his attitude. "That's incredible! So… this clunker had a moment where twenty-six young girl deaths either got to him, or he didn't want to be caught alive. Too bad… they would have fixed him in prison - at least one of the inmates would get a visit once too often from his kids, and decide to gut Dansing like a trout. I guess that saves the county a lot of money in extradition and court costs."

"You have no idea. That's why I called though. The FBI Agents were more than a little impressed with how you found out Dansing's address. I already showed them how an internet moron like me muddles through this crap. We need consultants who can track leads with more than nerd sense. We need people with the instincts and imagination to give us more than vague notions."

"Neil. You're recruiting for someone. I have FBI credentials already. Shame on you. Okay… which relative does this person have of yours locked away somewhere?"

"I suck at this. That Detective Stilling wants you in a new task force he's been asked to head. I told them you'd never leave Pacific Grove, but I agreed to mention it. I think they want to dissect each step you took drawing you to that address. Maybe Stilling thinks you're one of those paranormal consultants."

Nick laughed. "It's in the report. You seemed to understand it when I explained it to you. A small amount of imagination is required. I'm already consulting with the police. Where's Stilling going - to DC? He'll hate the weather. What's this about?"

"I think he would report to DC, but only go there occasionally. He's been asked to have a ready room of people who can use their imagination with technical expertise, backing up a fast moving special operations team, who can act on the data given at a moment's notice. I've agreed to be with the special ops team. We get some extra money to train and be on call if something requires a task force caliber group on anything from serial rapists to bank robbers. We would stay with our own units, but train together six hours a week."

"Sounds like a great way to get thrown into prison by the usual political opportunists who would sell their own mother to Chinese slavers for a vote. Then, of course, my dear Neil, would come the media labeling your new strike group the new 'jack booted thug militia'."

301

Dickerson toasted Nick with his coffee cup. "That's how I see it coming down too. I'll tell him you weren't interested. I may give it a shot for a while if I can keep my old job."

"I'd be interested in consulting. I won't train though. Been there, done that. I don't mind looking at anything he gets on the plate of his new group," Nick said. "Gus will be in with me."

"I'll tell him. Thank you." Dickerson stood to leave. "I appreciate your cynical nature. I would hope if we do work together, you'll let me know when I'm getting hung out to dry by someone in the 'think tank'."

"I would indeed. Thanks for stopping by."

"Great work on finding the killer. I guess he felt you coming or something, huh Nick?"

"Yeah… or something. Don't let your imagination run away with you too far, Sergeant."

"I think we can agree that ain't happenin'."

Gus waited until Dickerson drove away. "What the hell do you think of that? You murdered your way onto a special crimes task force. That is so wrong… on so many levels."

"No one says anything about murderers playing on major sports teams," Nick objected.

"They don't have your body count."

* * *

The phone vibrated next to him as Nick woke from taking an afternoon nap before meeting Jean at school. Rachel worked at the Monte Café until 6 pm. Nick answered after checking caller ID, "Paul?"

"Are you finding time to sleep finally?"

302

"Somewhat." Nick swung his legs around Deke who had been napping with him. "Deke and I are resting for our treacherous walk to meet Jean at school."

"Not as treacherous since Dansing slipped away into never/never land."

"True, but we soulless monsters must keep our eyes open for new danger. How did the investigation pan out?"

"Solidly for your suicide scene. After you put the locals into the mix finding the body, your records are being flagged by everyone. They get blocked, but I'm sure you're aware this new notoriety will make it very difficult for you to operate in any clandestine way."

"Says who? We abandoned the hermit author living his days out at the beach before you took over. I thought you liked this new paradigm."

"I do," Paul said. "The people funding us with an open ended budget believe you're attracting the right attention with credit spreading over some media damaged agencies. Because I read in a couple at the top of this black ops hierarchy, they were with you during your entire use of our Company resources in taking down Dansing. They know it would have been illegal unless funneled through you. It was icing on the cake when a trial for Dansing became unnecessary thanks to you. We can absorb a couple of mistakes with the pluses you've built since going on your wonderful book tour. Bottom line is they trust the access I've given you."

"So this was a pat on the back call?"

"Not exactly. John knew you were handling Dansing, so he's been reporting in to me, and asking advice. His new friends pressured him into turning your Carmel Valley place into a Terrorist retreat. I didn't want him killed before you and Gus could finish with Dansing. He's been in touch often, and the situation has become more relaxed since John allowing access to your place."

"That situation exploded faster than I figured. You did the right thing, as did John." Nick heard the doorbell, and walked downstairs toward his entrance. "I'll let John know he can loop me back into the mix. I'm not crazy about having that litter of skunks moving into my Valley retreat, but it will work to our advantage when we can possibly get this particular cell right where we want them."

"Name the resources you'll need when the time comes, Nick. I already have an enthusiastic go on the op if you can find a way to make your cartoon idea with El Muerto, Payaso, and El Kabong work. They loved the insult ploy to draw more cells into the open. Call me when you're ready."

"Will do." Nick disconnected, peering through his wide angle door lens. It was a haggard looking Dan Lewis. Nick opened the door. "Hi Dan. You look like hell. Come in."

Dan nodded without speaking, absently petting Deke as he danced around a familiar human. "Thanks Nick. I…I need your help. Do you have time for a coffee with me?"

"Right this way." Nick led the old man into the kitchen, where he made two cups of coffee from the already brewed pot, fixing it as he knew Dan liked. He served it, while sitting down facing Dan. That the old man didn't have his wife Carol with him sent a foreboding chill shooting through him. He refrained from speaking, allowing Dan to gather his thoughts. The tremor in Dan's hands as he brought the coffee cup into sipping position whispered tragedy to Nick.

"Right after you left, Carol began having back pain on her left side with blood showing in her urine. After CT scans showed a tumor in her kidney, she was admitted for an eight day torture session in the hospital. Even with a morphine drip, epidural, and pain pills, she needed ice on her back. They put in a drain because her lung had lesions from the growing tumor which they attributed correctly to the cancer spreading. The nurses let me stay in her room the whole time. I figured they knew what was happening before the doctors were ready to spell it out. The biopsies showed the Renal Cell Carcinoma had spread throughout her system. Carol's in stage four with Hospice nurses coming around to replenish her pain meds. They think because of the virulent way it attacked her system, the malignant cells have spread to her brain, because of her decreasing mobility. Every moment with her is precious right now. My son and daughter flew in to help me take care of their Mom."

Nick waited as the old man's lips trembled, trying to put an iron grip on his emotions. He didn't bother trying to imagine Dan's pain. The old couple were like surrogate parents to him for over a decade since he moved into Pacific Grove. After Carol had her knees replaced, she had been getting along better, without the pain. To have this strike her in so short a time brought on a blackness inside of him, Nick recognized as his only reaction to human emotion. The ache which threaded through him at the news was his only connection he could muster, even with people he cared about. It was as close to empathy Nick could get.

"She…she'd like to see you if possible, Nick. I haven't told anyone about it except family. Carol hates seeing herself through our friends' eyes. Joe came over from the Monte, delivering breakfast for us when he hadn't seen us for a month. He was in tears when he left. I swore him to secrecy. Although she's had parts of good days with the kids, she's fading rapidly. Every smile now rips my heart out. Having the kids there is a must. Experiencing this through them is the hardest though."

Remembering he wasn't the only one who cared for Dan and Carol, Nick asked the obvious question. "Can I bring Rachel, Jean, and Gus by too?"

Dan shook his head no, gripping his cup to point of cracking in his hands. "Can't do it, Nick. She wants everyone to remember her as she was. It's only the fact she keeps rereading the chapter in your first book, Diego's Way, titled End of Days. It's the passage where the woman Diego has an affair with earlier in the novel dies slowly in pain from a gunshot wound. Adara was Diego's contact in Beirut during an operation to kill an official in the government. They're trapped together due to bad intel. Carol loved that scene. She cried every time she read it, because Diego stays with Adara to the end, in spite of the danger. Now, Carol repeats the line Diego said to Adara when the dying woman gripped Diego's hands in pain and fear – 'it is a long hard road sometimes to the end of days, baby, but I will travel it with you as far as I can go'. Do you remember, Nick?"

Nick remembered. It was not Beirut in real life. It had happened in Tehran during an op to sanction a General thought to be using weaponized Anthrax. His contact's name had been Fatima. Her pain filled face jetted into his consciousness the moment Dan mentioned the chapter. Gut-shot, Fatima died hard, but as in the novel, Nick remained with her to the end. He killed her killers, and the official who had sold them out.

"I remember. I respect your request. I'll let them know it was as Carol wished. My gang will be disappointed, but this ain't about them. Something else is troubling you, Dan. What is it?"

The old man straightened in his seat. "I made an error in judgment when Carol got sick so quickly. The bills were piling, and I didn't know whether to cash in our retirement money, or get a loan. I had no idea at the time how long she would be sick. I got a loan for fifty thousand with a loan place in Salinas. They were the only ones who could get me the money fast. We didn't have house payments, but the property taxes, utilities, food, and medical bills wiped out our savings, leaving us nearly thirty grand in debt. We weren't ready for it. I didn't have anyone go over the contract with the loan people. They had a clause in there stating they could demand the loan's full amount with only two weeks grace period. I can't do anything to stop it. Taking care of Carol, I ignored mail received since she took a turn for the worse. There's only two days left. The loan manager called to make certain I was aware this morning. He claimed hard times made it vital for them to collect their money. Due to the margin I agreed to, I owe nearly sixty now."

"Don't give it a thought. Do you have the loan papers with you?"

Dan grabbed Nick's hand in both his. "I'll pay you back! I just need some time. Thank you! I have the papers in my car."

Nick came around, and helped Dan to his feet. "Don't give it a thought. I don't want to piss you off, because I know this was hard for you, but we'll work something out. Let's go get the papers, and I'll handle it from there."

Gus approached the house as Dan was driving off, waving at Gus as he went by. "I see in your face Dan's visit wasn't good news."

Nick explained it all, including the Salinas loan. "I'm faxing these papers to Paul. I'd bet he'll know someone in the Department of Justice who would be interested in a loan outfit like this. I know loan sharking on this scale is definitely illegal. Once Paul confirms my suspicions, we'll go over to pay them off. Come in. We have a few hours before Jean's out of school."

"Let's go over and shoot them all in the head. I see it in your eyes, Muerto."

"That is the reason I'm not visiting Carol until I handle this matter. If I visit her first, I may do something rash. These are petty crooks. They'd steal their own Mommy's home, but I'm not handing out death sentences to them for it."

Paul faxed a notarized 'Cease and Desist' FBI warning naming the loan shark outfit in violation of the law. Nick held it for Gus to see. "I'll have a talk with these gentlemen, and bring them a cashier's check for the amount Dan owes. Want to come along?"

"Yeah, I do. I want to be on hand when they do something stupid. Am I dressed okay, or should I change?"

Gus wore his black slacks and shirt with his black leather jacket. "You look very scary, Payaso. I believe I will shave and follow your choice in clothing. Hopefully, your wish for something stupid won't materialize. We have John now running a Terrorist camp in the Valley I haven't had a chance to explain yet to you."

"Will you see Carol afterwards?"

"As soon as I explain the situation to Rachel and Jean. Tina cares for Dan and Carol too. They'll have a hard time understanding, but we'll make one of those funny collage things on one of those digital picture frames Rachel buys but never uses. It might brighten Carol's day, and give our female companions something positive to do."

"Tina loves those two," Gus added. "That's a neat thing you thought of. I'd almost think you had a heart, Muerto."

"I almost wish I didn't, Payaso."

"I hear you. Get your black on, partner. We need to set things right in financial land where we seldom journey. I'm interested in seeing what kind of fuck writes an old man a loan like that."

"I don't like your tone, Payaso," Nick warned. "I'll leave you at home with Deke if I hear any more talk like that."

"As you wish, Muerto."

* * *

308

The building housed more than one operation. Nick and Gus entered the center shop doorway with the big vertical billboard announcing Easy Loans: check cashing, foreign exchange, reasonable loans, and instant money. A chime sounded when they walked in. Two men in business suits came out to greet them with welcoming smiles. The interior, although narrow, incorporated a complete ATM and banking tools. Forms for everything imaginable were well labeled, and marked in plain categories.

The two men were not average looking loan officers by any means. One wore black, and the other dark gray, with somber dark colored ties. Both men were Russian Mafia, matching pictures Nick and Gus had turned up as employees of Easy Loans, among others. Sandy haired, rough featured, and big in only a slightly overweight manner. They sported wide shoulders, broken noses, and Rolex watches Nick could tell at a glance were real. He and Gus had done a complete workup of Easy Loans. They did mostly expensive, but legitimate transactions, except when someone needed money right away. Bad reviews, threatened customers, dismissed court cases, and accusations of leg breaking methods abounded. Nick didn't care what they did. If he could straighten Dan's debt out, he planned to do so quickly and quietly.

"Gentlemen," the larger of the two men said, extending his hand to Nick. "How may we be of service? I'm Rod Matger, and this is my top associate, Saul Korbin."

Nick shook both men's hands as did Gus. "I'm Nick McCarty, and this is my partner, Gus Nason. We're here to settle a debt for a friend, Dan Lewis. We have his loan papers and the amount owed. I have a cashier's check for the $58,976 dollars owed on the loan. His wife is dying of cancer, so he's with her now constantly. I hope we can conclude this matter quickly, Mr. Matger."

"Of course… of course," Matger said, exchanging unreadable glances with his co-worker. "Step over to our desk, and I will get your loan on screen. May I have the papers please?"

"Certainly." Nick handed them over in a folder.

Matger gestured for Gus and Nick to sit down in front of the large desk in their right hand corner, while Korbin stood smiling with hands clasped at his waist. Matger sat down, fingered Dan's loan on screen, and then checked the details by glancing from the loan papers to his screen. After a few minutes in which both Nick and Gus realized they were about to be screwed, Matger turned to them with a sorrowful gesture.

"I am sorry, Mr. McCarty. Mr. Lewis's loan has gone into collection and forfeiture of collateral. It is not possible to take that amount in payment at this late date."

Gus jumped to his feet, fists clenched. "Listen, you soulless wanker, we're a day earlier than agreed to by that two week scam of yours. Do yourself a favor, and take the check. Write us a receipt, and we leave you two treasures alone."

"Oh… you think so," Korbin moved on Gus while Nick kept his eyes on Matger.

Korbin reached for Gus's coat front, and in seconds was on the floor in an unbreakable arm lock. Matger reached inside his jacket, only to be staring down the barrel of Nick's .45 caliber Colt. "You don't want to go there, Mr. Matger. My partner Gus and I are more than we seem. Please allow Gus to release Mr. Korbin, so we can adjust our negotiations."

"Very well, Mr. McCarty, but Saul and I are a bit more than we seem also. You cannot threaten us. He and I are old school. We never forget. Do you know what I mean?"

Nick grinned. "Yep. I sure do. Gus and I never forget either. Do we, Gus?"

Gus helped Korbin to his feet, dusting him off comically, while aching for a reason to plant the man in a more final manner. "No, we never do."

Nick placed the 'Cease and Desist' warning in front of Matger. He then showed him his FBI credentials, while Gus showed his US Marshal's Service ID. "We don't have to do this the hard way. You made a mistake. It will cost you, because we have people very interested in your loan sharking outfit. If you had chosen to take the check at an incredibly unfair profit, we would have exited your lives without a pound of flesh. Now, you take the check, make us out a real legitimate receipt, and then you take a moment after we leave to rework your operation. If you don't, there will be people to do so for you. Do we have an understanding, Mr. Matger?"

Matger took the check, typed a complete statement of the loan being paid in full, printed it out and handed it to Nick. "You have made a very bad enemy, Mr. McCarty. You should have left the old man's business alone. He would have been fine. They always have a place for old folks in this country."

Nick barely jutted in front of Gus before his partner launched in a no holds barred ending to Easy Loans. "Thank you for your cooperation. I hope we'll be able to avoid any more unpleasantness."

Matger smiled engagingly. "Yes… if I were you, I would be hoping so too. We do not always get what we wish, do we, Mr. McCarty?"

"Hardly ever, Mr. Matger," Nick admitted, moving Gus toward the door. "Let's go, Gus. We have the only legal thing we need. I want to get you, Rachel, Jean, Tina, Deke, and me into one of Rachel's digital picture frames to possibly please Carol for a moment. These two fucks behind us will die all in good time, my friend. I will have our police pal, Sergeant Dickerson, protect Dan's home officially while the forces launch on Easy Loans. You

311

and I will of course be available for retribution I'm afraid will never materialize for Matger."

Gus immediately relaxed as they passed through the doorway to Easy Loans. "We should have killed them on the spot, Muerto. I do see your plan though to be in the best interests of everyone, except now we'll be watching our backs again."

"Complacency is the root of all evil, my friend. We will be diligent. First, we will do all we can for Dan and Carol. The rest will follow as we clear out our Carmel Valley place of terrorists, and other assorted blots on humanity. We'll need some space before dealing with our acquaintances at Easy Loans, possibly in an info gathering session."

"That's what I'm talkin' about," Gus said, his tight lipped, fist clenched departure from Easy Loans, content with a promise for the future.

"Truthfully," Nick countered, "I'm more of a let the buyer beware type guy. I get sick of reading how everyone needs the government as their mommy to protect them. Easy Loans feeds off the suckers and saps who are between a rock and a hard place. Dan had a weak moment. It happens. Unfortunately for Easy Loans, Dan has us. The old man will try and pay me back every damn dime too. If he does, I'll funnel it back through to his kids."

"I admit it. I've been where Dan is a couple times. I imagine cold blooded psychos are immune to entities like Easy Loans, huh Nick?"

"No, but we usually revisit the situation with a solution."

"I'll bet."

* * *

Nick entered Dan's home, feeling the dread permeating the atmosphere in sad waves as he followed the old man from the entrance. He shook hands in the kitchen with Dan's son and daughter, whom he'd met when they visited a few years before. The solemn, tear stained features said more than words could ever express. Dan took him into the living room where Carol reclined on their loveseat with pillows braced everywhere, covered by a quilt he knew she had made. An ice water circulating pump flowed in and out of a pad Nick could see was braced between the seat and her left side. A table against the nearby wall held syringes and pills. Carol's head lay against the loveseat, her face pallid and drawn. Oxygen through small tubes at her nose, delivered from a system pump on the other side of the couch, worked to help her labored breathing.

"The cold pad's the only relief she gets from the pain in her back," Dan explained.

Carol groaned slightly, hearing Dan's familiar voice. Her eyes opened in a wide eyed stare of incomprehension at first. Dan sat on the armrest next to her, his hand gliding soothingly over her forehead. "It's okay, baby. Nick made it over to see you. Are you feeling well enough to talk?"

Nick cringed at the transformation. Dan's gentle touch brought Carol back for a moment. She sighed, but then smiled at Dan. Nick saw the old man bite his trembling lip, his eyes filling as he bent over to kiss her head. Dan held a cup with bent straw to her mouth. "Have something to drink, Hon."

Carol sipped the water, gripping the cup over Dan's hands. She pushed the cup away, reaching out to Nick, who knelt in front of her. He grasped her hand carefully, seeing the bruising all along her wrist and arm from intravenous needles. "Oh, Nick... I'm spoiled now. Thanks... for coming over. I...I've been reading your first novel again."

"Dan told me you're stuck on one of the chapters. I brought this for you to see we all miss you." Nick held the digital frame with images and sound he and Rachel had put together.

313

"My goodness. This is lovely. I'm sorry about not having everyone over. I can't do that anymore."

"Don't be sorry. They all understood." Nick remembered their digital picture creation had been halted many times with tears.

Carol leaned forward, gripping Nick's hand with both hers, features tensing as if she held her consciousness in place. "I have to know. Was there ever an Adara? I...I know writers use personal experiences. The chapter End of Days makes me cry every time I read it, but...but it's a good cry. Was there?"

Nick glanced at Dan. He made a decision before putting aside the digital picture frame, and grasped hers with both his too. He stared into her pain ridden features, trying to smile reassuringly, and failing. "Yes. It wasn't in Beirut. I met her in Tehran. Her name was Fatima."

Carol's eyes brightened, excitement overcoming the pain for a moment. "It has always been like you joked. You are Diego."

Nick allowed the cold blooded killer to surface into his own features. "As I told my Rachel, Diego's a campfire girl compared to what I am. You've made me confess, old girl. I hope it isn't too much."

"Oh no... not at all. I suspected." Carol lifted a cold hand to frame Nick's face for a moment. "You are so much more though. Will you say the line to me, Nick?"

"Sure I will," Nick agreed as Carol moved her hand from his face to her husband's hand as it rested on her quilt. Nick recalled the moment near the end with Fatima dying in his arms as if it happened only minutes ago. "It is a long hard road sometimes to the end of days, baby, but I will travel it with you as far as I can go."

Nick saw her hand tighten around Dan's.

"Did you Nick… travel it with her?"

"Yes, old girl, I surely did as far as I could go. Then I sent a bunch of guys responsible all the way with her."

Carol closed her eyes, leaning back as Dan held the cooling pad for her to rest against. Nick felt her hand release his. "Thank you for that… Nick. Please tell everyone thank you… for me."

Nick patted her hand. "I will indeed, Carol. Goodbye for now, old girl. I will see you soon."

"You'd… better not," Carol mumbled, drifting off into labored slumber.

Nick said his goodbyes to the kids, who rejoined Carol, while Dan walked him out to his car. Nick handed him an envelope from inside his jacket. "The Easy Loans thing is over, Dan. Sergeant Dickerson will have a squad car drive by your house until we're sure there will be no retaliation. I have some contacts with the FBI's financial investigations people. They're going to fix Easy Loans. You take care of yourself. I won't say a bunch of meaningless crap. Carol's the best."

"Thank you. You weren't only writing make believe stories. It's all true what you write."

"Much of it is worse," Nick admitted. "I have credentials for the US Marshal's Service, FBI, the Company, and I have consulted with all of them. It was the reason I met Rachel and Jean. I was sent to kill them. Instead, I killed the man who ordered it done. Then I helped Rachel and Jean so they could become my family. Carol deserved to know, and so do you. I'm more legit than I have been in the past, but I still can't make it public knowledge."

Dan shook his head. "That is amazing, and I am glad you told Carol. That is the most animated she's become in days. I won't ever forget what you did for me with Easy Loans. I will pay you back, Nick."

"What if I could use you for something else? You wouldn't be an errand boy. You can look like you belong anywhere. I need someone who can occasionally go somewhere, and keep their eyes open without drawing attention. I believe you could do that easily. I'd like that far more than you paying me cash. Think about it, Dan. Goodbye for now, my friend."

Dan shook his hand, and turned to walk away. "I will consider your kind offer. I could tell in there you knew you would not see my baby alive again."

"I did. Thank you for inviting me into your home." Nick watched Dan walk to his doorstep, his shoulders squaring as he neared the door. *May God be merciful to Carol, my friend, and to you.*

* * *

"Did Nick help you with Easy Loans, or should we get a lawyer?"

The old man met his son Dan Jr.'s inquisitive look with a nod. "He did. I have the receipt here that he gave me."

"I know he's a famous author," his daughter Sally said, "but why would he do something so huge for you, Dad?"

"In his way, I think he loves your mom and me. I don't know why, but we became close over the years, seeing him at Otter's Point, and sharing coffee at the Monte Café. It's God's blessing we became friends."

"I know Mom loved his novels, but she always said she didn't really know him," Dan Jr. said.

"I know this much," the old man said, "he's one of the most dangerous men alive. I must leave it at that, or betray a confidence. He made your Mom very happy tonight for a moment. That's all I care about. She was haunted by a chapter in his first novel. He

316

cleared something up for her that she thought very important. Then he said her favorite line to her. It was her brightest moment in days."

"Would you want him to come with us... I mean when..."

The old man hugged his daughter. "I know what you meant, Honey. Yes, I would like him to come with us to Mom's favorite beach very much."

"Are we going to try and move her to the bed tonight?"

"No, son. It's too painful for her. I'll sleep next to her on the loveseat. That way I'll be able to renew the ice in her pump reservoir easier."

"What was the name of the chapter Mom questioned him about?"

"The End of Days," Dan answered after a few seconds hesitation. He turned away from his kids, hands over his face, regaining control a moment later. He took a deep breath, turning back to put his arms around Dan Jr. and Sally. "C'mon. Let's go settle Mom in for the night."

* * *

Rod Matger awoke in a sweat, sitting up in the bed feverishly gasping for breath. Matger's silk pajamas, wet and clinging coldly to his body, radiated an odor of decay. Glancing at his mistress, he noticed her snoring form appeared blurred in the darkness. Rubbing his eyes, the pain began lancing through his ribcage, forcing him onto his back once again. An equally grainy form hovered over him, as his bedside lamp flicked on.

"Hi there, Rod. Remember me from earlier?"

Matger peered at the smiling face, squinting against the light. "McCarty?"

"Yep. Right the first time. My partner and I were going to allow the forces of law and order to hound you for a while over your nasty loan sharking business. Then I visited a real lady who I'd probably murder a hundred of you just to make her smile. When I left her side, I noticed an ache I could do nothing about. Then I thought of you and your buddy Saul. Although you're not feeling too good, my untouchable ache has receded slightly."

"My God! Wha…what have you done?"

"I've killed you, but I wanted to share your end of days all the way to the finish. I've already made sure Saul had a nasty accident. It seems he pitched down a flight of stairs at his apartment building, and snapped his neck. Don't worry. I stayed with him, watching life fade from his cheap thug eyes before coming here."

Matger's eyes closed, his fists clenching under his heart, pain building in an irresistible wave. "You bastard! You…you'll never… get away with it!"

"Ah contraire, my small time hoodlum. I will get away with it. Not only that, I will mark where they bury you and Saul. A couple months from now I'm going to piss on your fucking graves," McCarty related to Matger in a matter-of-fact tone. "Maybe the ache will have gone away by then. Don't worry about your girlfriend. I only gave her a little whiff of ether to help her sleep through this unfortunate turn of events."

Matger tried to curse the fading form over him, his mouth working without sound until darkness descended in a final black curtain.

* * *

At a few minutes after five in the morning, Nick and Gus sat on beach chairs, watching the slate gray horizon, crashing waves, and rocky Otter's Point beach with solemn faces. Gus

318

replenished their high octane coffee, pouring carefully into each of the mugs. In a few hours, they would walk Jean to school with Deke, who lay near Nick's side, his empathy for the humans who cared for him in tune at all times. Deke sensed frolicking in the sand was not in line with the day ahead.

Gus never questioned the mission when Nick called. "What do you think will happen when Rod and Saul are discovered mysteriously dead within the same time frame?"

Nick sipped his brew, but remained silent. He couldn't describe the ache he mentioned to Matger. Instead, Nick absorbed the unfamiliar emotion with a predator's recognition of reality. He wasn't meant to feel things, and yet now he did. His choice to wipe Matger and Korbin from existence would remain a visceral statement he would deal with at a later time. For now, he enjoyed the company he shared, and the fogging elixir in the cup at hand.

Gus sighed at Nick's silence, smiled, and leaned back. "It's okay, partner. You don't give a shit. I texted Paul to erase their names from the database. He was inquisitive about why we called Easy Loans into question at all if we planned on putting them down like a rabid dog. I merely agreed due to circumstances beyond our control Rod and Saul found out why sometimes it's just plain bad Karma to be assholes. He texted back an LOL, and that he'd fix it. I like that guy."

Nick held his cup in toasting position. Gus quietly tapped it with his.

* * *

Nick followed Dan, Dan Jr., and Sally toward the beach, watching the old man's erect form carrying his wife's ashes in a backpack he had insisted on shouldering. The Pacific Grove coastline at night surged in majestic form under the bright sliver of moon. The fog, a usual participant along the coast, took a time out

319

as if ordered by a higher authority. Nick had requested Sergeant Dickerson keep the usual coastal patrol cars away for the evening.

"It's a small thing, Sergeant."

"Consider it done, Nick. If any uniformed wankers intrude, put them on the phone with me. It won't happen, but if it does, you have my number."

"Thank you."

"It's a small thing, my friend."

So now, their cadre of mourners treaded silently down the hill. Crossing the coastal road, they approached the nearly pitch black darkness with care. Dan led the way to a large rounded rock near the low tide emptiness.

"This was Carol's rock. She could sit here for an hour without moving," Dan said, as he scraped the sand at the rock's base away into a deepened indentation. He then withdrew the plastic bag carrying his beloved's ashes from his pack, removed the small twist tie at the top, and spread some down below the rock. Dan stirred the sand, covering his wife's small occupancy with gentle strokes of his hand.

Dan straightened, and moved forward toward the ocean to a small tide pool where even in the darkness, the mourners could see the silvery glint of ocean water under the moonlight. The old man knelt, and poured the remains of Carol's ashes into the tide pool, stirring with steady strokes until all of her physical remains lay absorbed into the pool.

Dan stood again. "Carol loved Clint Eastwood movies. She never got to meet him, although we would visit the restaurant he owned at the time called the 'Hogs Breath Inn' in Carmel frequently. Once, I went there at nearly closing to have a drink with a friend. Clint was there, and I stupidly mentioned it to her. I don't think she ever forgave me."

Dan chuckled at the memory. "We saw the movie 'Outlaw Josie Wales' many times. There is a line in it she liked very much when Clint's character Josie finds his young companion has died from wounds received. I think she'd like the slightly revised line now for this moment – She was born in the time of blood and dyin', and never questioned a bit of it. She never went back on her folks or her kind. I rode with her, I've got no complaints."

The old man then knelt, his hands clasped. "If you'd like, please join me in the Twenty-Third Psalm, which was also her favorite prayer. We shared it every night for the last two months."

Beneath the moonlight, amidst the sound of waves smashing onto shore, the small group followed Dan's lead with only hushed sobs and solemn recitation. After many remembrances, and shared touching moments, the small cadre of survivors paced up the hill towards Dan's house. At the point where Nick's journey home split away, he moved forward to put an arm around Dan's shoulders.

"This is my road home, Dan. Thank you for inviting me along to settle Carol on her way. It was magnificent. Please call on me first if you need anything. I will not intrude in any way unless you ask."

Dan gripped Nick's shoulders, his eyes filling with tears. "Thank you for coming, Nick. It meant a lot to me. I will speak with you at a more pleasant time in the future."

"I understand completely. Until then, my friend." Nick shook hands with Dan Jr. before giving Sally a quick hug goodbye. "Stay well, kids. Dan has my number if you ever need anything. You have only to ask."

* * *

Dan and his kids watched Nick walk away until darkness obscured their view. Without another word, Dan started home once again, only to be brought short by his son's hand.

"Did you read the papers today? That Easy Loans guy Matger and his associate are dead. The news claims one had a heart attack, and the other had a tragic fall at his apartment. Dad, who is this guy McCarty?"

Dan glanced at his two kids with a wan smile. "Nick is someone you never want to meet in anger, revenge, or violent intention."

When their father continued on, Sally hurried next to him. "What the hell does that mean exactly, Dad?"

Dan didn't slacken his pace. "It means justice sometimes arrives in a mysterious form, cloaked in darkness. The funny part is, that particular justice doesn't give a crap what we think about any outcome it considers justified. If you're looking for answers beyond that, I don't have any. My advice, although he is a God blessed friend, leave Nick alone."

Sally exchanged vivid glances with her brother, and then followed their Dad silently.

* * *

When Nick walked into his house, he faced the contingent waiting for him. "It was simple and heartbreaking. Carol would have loved it. If you bunch are looking for something more tangible, forget it. I have some drinking to do."

Rachel walked forward with a large shot glass filled with amber liquid. "We loved Carol. She was a beautiful person without peer. We minions are here for you. I know I'd like to hear all the exchanges you must have had with her over the years. I also know you have a photographic memory to provide them. Care to share?"

322

Nick took the glass and drained it. He walked toward the stairs with Deke immediately shadowing him. "I will be on the deck, recounting tales of deception and laughter shared about one of the most impressive women I've ever encountered. If you wish to be enlightened, then follow me... with the Bushmill's bottle."

Jean ran her head into Rachel's side, wrapping her in a death grip of angst and loss, swallowing her sobs in quiet imitation of Nick. Rachel stroked her hair. "I know, baby. Let's all put our game faces on and hear what only Nick can tell. I know this about that cold blooded zombie, he will make us all cry before he finishes his retelling of interactions with Carol."

"Amen," Gus said, putting an arm around Tina, who covered her face, wracked with sobs. "It didn't take long to become someone who loved Carol. She will be missed unconditionally... and her loss... unimaginable."

Chapter Fourteen

Training Camp

"We must have more funding!"

John shrugged without stress. "I am sorry, but I have already provided you with a place to train, live, and recruit. My benefactor cannot at this time offer anything more in the way of money. He must account for expenditures with this country's IRS under the radar. If he does something stupid, we will all be at risk."

"I would meet with this supposed supporter of Allah, who wishes to serve under his own conditions," Faris Nagi stated with angry tone. "Not all moneys can be scripted to individual's preferences. Are you not dedicated to this cause?"

John reined in his initial knee-jerk reaction as Nick had schooled him to do. "Surely, with all my benefactor has done, he should not be called into question on some trivial gambit you endorse without circumstances and facts which can lead to his death. Think clearly before you go on, Faris. My benefactor protects me, supports the cause with land as well as food and clothing, and asks nothing in return. What have you done in any way other than blaspheming with your arrogant mouth?"

John recognized he would get form over substance in a second while Nagi sputtered, caught without cliché to fall back on. John waved a dismissive hand in front of Nagi's face. "Do not negate my true words with bluster. You will find you have turned an ally into an enemy."

John's strong words enraged Nagi, who poked him in the chest belligerently. "You are but a lowly stepstool in our endeavors! Are you a soldier of Allah, or are you but one more infidel nonbeliever?"

Nagi perceived he had gone too far. John's face blasted from a contemplative adherence to fists clenched rebellion in a heartbeat, Nagi did not miss in body language. "I mean only to remind you of the true path."

The true path in Nagi's vision dissipated into nothingness as John kicked the unsuspecting Nagi in his groin, followed by a kneeing into his facial region which broke everything of a fragile structure: teeth, nose, and the orbital bone on Nagi's right side. John allowed Nagi's body to fall away from him to the floor, where Nagi spit blood, and curled into a fetal position. John called Nick, enlightening him on what had transpired. To his surprise, Nick began chuckling.

"You have put up with this long enough, John. You're stressed out because you drew attention from terrorist bunglers. Then you house them under my roof in Carmel Valley, unsure what the hell to do with them. Insult upon injury, this Nagi guy busts your chops no matter what you do. End him, my friend. Gus and I are on our way. This scenario using my property is finished."

"Thank you, Nick!" John put the phone on speaker, spun to the helpless Nagi, kicked him full in the face, and then plunged the stiletto knife he drew from his pocket down powerfully through Nagi's right eye. "Allah be praised! Yet another addle headed miscreant has achieved hell. Let Maalik, the true hell's angel deal with this annoying piece of camel dung!"

"Bag him out of sight. Stay on the down low until we can help you with the others. Will they miss this Nagi guy right away?"

"No," John answered. "They are at the Masjid, including Ansar Pasha. There are five of them besides this pig I killed. You have at least one hour before they return. Do you wish to take prisoners?"

"We can't, John," Nick answered. "They all know you. I will not lose my El Kabong. We have a lot of work to do. After we question them, we'll make our first kills as El Muerto, Payaso, and El Kabong. Then we'll make them disappear. We'll let the FBI decide about this Masjid, and a continued role for you there. Did anyone else at the Masjid know Nagi and his goons were at my Valley place?"

"No. They met resistance there from the Imam, who was becoming increasingly suspicious of Nagi. Ansar went tonight because he needed to try and smooth relations with the Imam. That is the main reason Nagi stayed here to harass me about more money while Ansar handled public relations. How will you make them disappear? Do you mean to bury them on your land?"

"Payaso and I will take them out to sea far enough if they are found, the location of their deaths will be a mystery still. We'll see you in fifteen minutes."

"Yes, Muerto, El Kabong will be ready."

* * *

When the Taser needles hit into the men as they entered Nick's Carmel Valley Home, the ensuing pileup of bodies caused some inappropriate hilarity. Their three costumed captors cranked up the juice, Nick and Gus using a two Taser gun attack, while John fired on one, but kept a stun-gun in his other hand in reserve. Once their initial attack incapacitated the men, John and Gus put them into restraints while Nick watched them with his 9mm Berretta.

Nick received a text message from Paul, requesting a talk. He waited until the prisoners were restrained before leaving the room. "Yeah, Paul, what's up?"

"Egypt is most anxious to have this bunch. I'm thinking we can do a rendition without exposing you superheroes. You're all in costume, right?"

"Sure, but this is our first operation with El Kabong. I wanted him to make a statement," Nick said. "What happened with simply making them disappear?"

"I put the pictures John has been taking of the cell members out to security agencies around the world. Three of them are on Egypt's most wanted list, with Ansar Pasha the star. It would mean a few favors to be named later if we could deliver them. You have final say though, Nick. I'll send a team to get them immediately, and they would be held incommunicado until sent to Egypt if you let me have them."

Nick considered the request. His hesitation involved allowing five Isis cell members to be taken alive from his custody after living in his Carmel Valley home. "John's already killed one of them. The others haven't seen him yet, so I guess we could stay in costume. You'll be stressing my directorial role. I'll let you know whether to send a team or erase their faces off the database."

"Until then." Paul disconnected.

Nick took a deep breath. He, Gus, and John all were using their voice altering equipment with full face masks. When he rejoined his companions, Gus and John stood side by side in arms folded character behind the now kneeling, unhappy prisoners. Nick stopped in front of the kneeling men. They had all tested their voice alterations, choosing slight adjustments to suit each of them. Nick chose a more Darth Vader type voice, which he practiced before their encounter with great effect.

"Payaso. Will you record our discourse with the video recorder here in this room? We have much to discuss with these Isis loons."

"Yes, El Muerto," Gus agreed with his own reverberating toned voice preference.

John retrieved the tripod while Gus brought over their more professional digital recorder. He attached it to the tripod, making sure his lowlight setting and parameters would record the entire scene. After completing the task, Gus took the remote blue tooth control with him to again stand behind the prisoners.

"El Kabong. Please drag the body of Faris Nagi out here for our guests to see."

"Right away, El Muerto." John hurried into the room he had stashed the bagged body of Nagi. It took him only a few moments to carry the corpse and dump it in front of the kneeling men. He then tore away the bag over Nagi's face, complete with eyeless socket where John had ended his life. That action prompted a chorus of duct tape covered, muffled pleas. "Shall I remove their gags, El Muerto?"

"Yes please. Start recording, Payaso." When he saw Gus nod, Nick began his act, stepping within camera view. "You five are lucky. Your leader Nagi, and the man Ebi Zarin paid dearly with their lives for this travesty. We cut off many parts of Zarin. We will use him for shark bait. Nagi was kept intact to show you five what will happen if any do not cooperate fully."

Nick plucked the corpse to a position staring sightlessly at the kneeling men. They cringed away, only to be kneed forward again by John and Gus. He then dragged Nagi's body to face the camera, with a small addition of a Kabuki dance of the dead Nick had invented – humorous only to him, but coldly creepy to anyone else seeing it.

"This is what our newest team member, El Kabong, did to the Isis coward in hand to hand combat." Nick released the body, gesturing for John to join him. He placed an arm around his shoulders. "El Kabong joins us from the believers of Islam who do not cower down to the more vocal women beaters, blaspheming his religion. He does not shout and scream. He kills dogs like Nagi, who are only good for strapping suicide vests on women and

328

children, throat slitting tied up innocents, and causing chaos in the world. What say you, El Kabong?"

John pumped his fist, kicking Nagi's body, and spitting on it. "Many will die at El Kabong's hand. El Muerto, Payaso, and I, the deadly El Kabong will hunt these jackals down."

Nick patted John's shoulder. El Kabong returned to his place next to Payaso. "Thank you, El Kabong, my brother. These men behind me will be spared so they may betray others from their murderous cult. Whether we will have to skin them partially alive or not will be up to them."

Nick jutted his gloved finger at the camera. "We will find you murderers wherever you hide. There will not be trials and traitorous ACLU lawyers. There will only be El Muerto, Payaso, and El Kabong. The knives will be sharp, and the cutting violent vengeance on our enemies!"

Gus cut off the video on cue from Nick. Retrieving syringes from his bag, Nick stuck each of the five men, rendering them unconscious. He then called Paul. "I'm uploading the video to you. Send a team. We'll meet them away from my Carmel Valley home. Let's do it in the turnoff to Point Lobos State Park tonight. It will be pitch black, and devoid of people. I'll send you the coordinates."

"Done deal, Nick. Thanks for this. I will send my team I put on alert in Monterey. They'll meet you at the turnoff in an hour. Bring whatever corpses you have, and we'll dispose of them too for you."

"We spared the five, so there's only Nagi to get rid of. Talk to you later." Nick turned to his partners. "Let's load them in the Caravan. We can drop them at the Point Lobos turnoff in an hour. I'll bet you'll be happily rid of these clowns, huh John?"

"It is not a joke, my friends. They were arrogant, condescending assholes the entire time, especially Nagi. I looked forward to killing them. What place are they being sent?"

"Egypt. Paul said we'll get some favors for delivering them, especially with Ansar in the group," Nick answered, noticing horror sweeping across John's face. "Do you have something against the Egyptians?"

"No... I would not want to be questioned by them. Although you are a very bad man, the Egyptians employ many very bad men in their security forces – no offense."

"None taken. Sucks to be them then."

"Indeed," John replied. "We were extremely scary in the movie. You do these videos with natural talent, Nick. You could have been a director."

"Don't give his swelled head any more ideas," Gus said. "Believe me, whatever stuff the Egyptian guys can come up with, Nick can surpass it. He has an imagination unparalleled in nasty ways to extract information, from the simple to the complex. Nick-"

"That's enough out of you, Payaso," Nick interrupted Gus's praise for his torturing expertise, which had John entertained. "How did you like my killing your real life identity off, John?"

"It was most impressive," John answered with excitement. "I will alter my appearance even more with short hair, and a trimmed beard. The Imam at the Masjid will be pleased not to have these fools in his presence anymore. I believe he knew they were not believers, and only considered them violent thugs. It will probably take some time for him to look at me again without suspicion after my having befriended them. I must continue there no matter what. I will be the first one asked questions when our video is seen."

330

"It's good to be prepared, John. When Muerto posts a YouTube video, it gets a million hits in a very short time, because it usually is removed within a few days. Then we have to place it in other venues."

"That's excellent thinking, paying attention to anyone who appears overly interested in where and how our guests disappeared," Nick added. "I'm more than relieved to have those flakes out of my house."

"I will spit shine your property to remove all elements of their unfortunate presence, Nick," John promised. "I know it was a disgrace having them here. I'll go get the Dodge, and back it in close to the door."

As Gus and Nick moved the unconscious bodies to the entranceway, Gus put a hand on Nick's shoulder. "You're not thinking of turning John over too, are you, Muerto?"

Nick's mouth tightened. "Brother, I may be very close to the cold blooded robot you think I am in reality, but John is one of us now."

Gus's relieved look surprised Nick more than he expected. "I'm glad. I like John, and I believe he is one of us. Sometimes you don't always let me in on your advanced thinking. I didn't want to be talking to John one moment, and you drive his nose bone into his brain the next without some warning."

Nodding his understanding, Nick gripped Nagi's body bag, and dragged it over to join his live companions. "I get it. No more surprises as lessons, Gus – I promise. You did need one though with old Gil Montrose. Here's you - 'Oh Nick, he's fine. You don't have to kill him. He won't try anything on us. We're golden with him, you unfeeling zombie'."

Gus laughed, remembering the lesson Nick taught him while saving his life when their Company contact Montrose tried to have them sanctioned after an operation to kill Sheik Abdul Nazari. "Fair enough, brother, I don't want any of those lessons taught to me the hard way from now on, okay?"

"Understood. We're not even taking John with us to drop off our cargo. I don't want anyone to get the feeling we're having second thoughts like you just did. We need John, especially with the added exposure I've received in the media, with much of my past and present life in the headlines. We're on a course dangerous to our immediate family. Eyes and ears on an element contributing to that danger is a blessing. That's how I feel about John. We still have the Kader family to keep track of. Who better to infiltrate a threat we suspect from them than John. Let's get this shit done. Tomorrow, I'm finishing my novel, come hell or high water. In between... I have some drinking to do."

"Carol?"

"She was the best sounding board I ever had or will have on my writing from a female point of view," Nick admitted as they began depositing the bodies in the Dodge Caravan. "Special is only a word. Sometimes you have someone who changes every aspect of your future just by interacting with you. Carol was exactly that. When I received orders to kill Rachel, the first people I interacted with after seeing how much Rachel resembled an old acquaintance of mine were Dan and Carol. Their unabashed love for one another, the banter, the way Dan clasped her hand in his planted a seed within my soul. I needed something they had. I then put a .50 caliber bullet through that despicable piece of shit Tanus's head as he enjoyed the last view from his office he would ever have."

"Damn... that's deep, brother. It was something you saw between Dan and Carol that brought us all here to this point?"

"Yeah, it was," Nick replied, helping Gus with John listening intently. "I saw the two at Monte Café, and walking by Otter's Point so much with mumbled good mornings I began paying attention to them. We became friends. What they had

332

together… I wanted. I knew I couldn't kill for it, or steal it. I understood somehow I would have to earn it. I now have Rachel, Jean, and Deke the dog. God bless us, everyone. They were worth every second of the earning, including morphing into an urban soccer somebody with an SUV. It will be a sad and devastating day for anyone trying to take away what I have."

"Amen, brother," Gus said, as they moved the bodies. "Thanks for sharing that. We will continue our requiem for Carol tonight."

"I do not know this Carol, but may I join you? I would very much like to know her."

"You sure can," Nick said. "Gus and I will get the transfer of prisoners done, and then pick you up. We'll toast a few on my deck again to Carol. You can drink or not drink, but you're welcome to stay at my house. We have plenty of room."

"I would like that very much," John replied. "I hope that my partaking of alcoholic beverages offered will not offend you, or bring shame on me through your eyes."

"Not at all, brother," Nick replied. "We're all sinners. We hope in the end to tally far more blessings than sins. Gus and I plan to do much good. It will often involve the demise of monsters we find. Are you comfortable with that, Brother John?"

John hugged Nick, startling him, and bringing a smile to Gus's face. "Yes… I am your man as I stated before. We will do much good together."

Nick patted John's back. "Yeah… we will."

* * *

"These guys don't look too friendly," Gus said as he and Nick stood in the darkness outside of Point Lobos State Reserve. "You don't think Paul decided to cancel us out, do you?"

333

"No, I do not. I don't rule out one of these guys making a deal on the side. Hold your water until we see what we see. If one of them tries a quick draw on me, they didn't read my file carefully enough. You have your damn vest on, Payaso. If that's not enough for you, duck behind me while you're pulling your weapon."

"Prick." Gus had to listen to Nick's chortling while Paul's team approached.

"McCarty?" The man leading the three men designated to take Nick's prisoners paused ten feet away from Nick and Gus.

"Yep, it's me, Nick McCarty. If I know any of you, please say so now."

A tall dark, heavily built man stepped forward. "I know you, Nick."

"Doc?" Nick stepped forward with his hands outstretched.

The man rushed forward into an embrace of Nick, obviously heartfelt and beyond normal human interaction. Nick pushed the man to arms' length, his joy obvious even in the moonlit scene.

"Good Lord, Doc, it's great to see you! I thought you died of wounds, brother!"

"You carrying my ass out when you did saved my life, you psycho! I might have known the damn Nick McCarty author was the same cold blooded bastard from our outfit. Damn… it's good to see you, brother!"

The men around them relaxed. Nick was vouched for beyond bosses.

"What the hell are you into, Joe? Do the teams have a medic now on board in every team?"

"Sort of. There are live ones in this pickup, so they sent me for complications. And yes, I've taken a life when it was needed. You already know that's the only way I could make a career with the Company."

"I'm just happy to see you, Doc. I don't give a crap about anything else. We've chewed so much dirt together, I wouldn't even blink in anger if you put a bullet between my eyes."

The man Nick labeled Doc glanced around at his companions. "That won't be necessary, Nick. The guys around me know I'd do anything for them. What they know now as I say it is I will put a bullet in any one of their heads if they reach for a weapon. Truth be told, I know if anyone of them drew, we'd all be dead, except for you and your buddy there."

Nick relaxed. "Thanks Doc. They sent shooters?"

Doc laughed. "Yep. They have all killed, but I doubt they react even in these circumstances like you. I'm glad it won't come to the test. I don't want to die for a bullshit bunch of terrorists."

Nick frowned while all who were watching twitched around uncomfortably. "Did you just insult me, Doc? We draw down, and everyone in your group will die but you."

"You've overlooked the fact of friendly fire, Nick."

Doc's words launched a laughing fit with the two men slapping hands, bumping fists, and generally enjoying the odd interaction beyond reality.

"Good one," Nick said. "Would you like Gus and I to help you load our cargo?"

"Yeah, let's get this exchange done as fast as possible. I don't want to attract attention from the locals. You picked a good spot. I bet you've used it before for something nefarious."

"Guilty," Nick admitted, remembering the three contract killers he'd gutted in a van on the turnoff. He opened the Caravan. In minutes, they transported the dead and living to the other van.

Doc handed Nick a card with a hastily scribbled number and address. "We have to go, Nick. Give me your card. I'll stay in touch. If you pop in close to me call and stop by."

Nick gave him a card. "I will for sure. Anything you need an extra for, call me."

"Count me in if you have something special: patch jobs, hideouts… or anything else."

They shook hands once again, and then the Company team left. Nick grinned at Gus. "I thought Joe Downing died of his wounds. Now, I feel like an idiot not having checked on him. After the mission he was wounded on, I transferred into the NSA black ops section under Frank. I had no contact with the Company after transferring. I had a lot more freedom, but you know how that entanglement turned out."

"I remember Frank's retirement sanction very well. He made a great donation to our general fund. You never told me how the hell you tied in with his rogue outfit in the first place." Gus got in and started the Dodge with Nick beside him.

"That mission Joe and I went on in Columbia went sour. Our crew got ambushed on a snatch and grab to rescue a guy supposedly kidnapped by rebels. It was a trap to capture us, perpetrated by the guy we were rescuing. We lost three men, but we wiped out those snakes who ambushed us. They were shooters. After that cluster fuck, Frank approached me with a private contracting job for his new outfit. I would be working alone. It was a good deal for a long time. Frank lost perspective. In his defense, he did sell out for a lot of money, which we now have."

336

"That mistake did not end well for him. I think this small celebration with John is a good thing. He hasn't met our families because of that undercover gig he immediately dived into."

"It will be a good night," Nick agreed.

* * *

A few minutes away from his Carmel Valley home, Nick's phone rang. "Nick here."

"We picked up a tail in Monterey, Nick. I've called Paul, asking if he had a secondary team on our six, but he said no and to call you."

"Have your driver do a series of street turns to get you along the coastal road. Then turn toward the Point Lobos turnoff. Establish if they're following to intercept or to tail you to your destination. I'll be waiting for them at the turnoff. When you enter the turnoff spin left immediately, Doc. Do you understand? Acknowledge now."

"Acknowledged," Doc replied. "How long do you need us to stall them?"

"Twenty minutes. I need a sit-rep whether they're tailing or intercepting. Call me in five minutes."

"Acknowledged."

"That didn't sound good."

"In more ways than one," Nick said. "Speed it all the way to John. I'm calling him now."

John answered on the first ring. "Nick?"

"Get my Barrett sniper rifle case out of the safe-room I showed you. Also bring out three MP5's with ammo. We have a problem. Meet me out front with everything."

337

"On it." John disconnected.

Nick's next call was to Gilbrech. "Know anything yet?"

"I know it wasn't us," Paul answered. "That means we're being set up by the Egyptians. There must be a leak on their end. I got sloppy, Nick."

"Ditch the whiney crap. You've drawn out someone else. This bunch following our guys had better not be with Homeland or FBI. I don't have a plan for their survival."

"I covered that the moment Downing called me. I'm sending Downing's description of the vehicle to your phone. I have another team on the way from Sacramento by helicopter. ETA ninety minutes."

"Acknowledged. Be talkin' at you soon." Nick disconnected.

John awaited them as ordered. He loaded everything himself in seconds while Nick shifted to the Dodge's rear, and took the Barrett from him. Gus streaked away the moment John settled into the passenger seat. Nick worked the weapons in the rear with lightning fast expertise. He had the MP5's loaded, and the Barrett ready for action in minutes.

"Drive to the rear of the turnoff, Gus. Turn to the right, park, and both of you follow me out. I'll direct you from there. Here, John." Nick handed two of the fully loaded MP5's to the front. "Here's two extra clips for each. Have you ever fired one before?"

"Yes. I am most proficient with this excellent weapon."

"I know Gus is, so we're set. Let's get-"

Downing called. "Yeah, Doc?"

"They're tailing. No move to intercept us, and we gave them a few opportunities. See you at the turnoff."

"Have your team stay down. Do not exit your vehicle. If anything gets real hinky, execute your prisoners."

"Acknowledged. We'll be ready if things change."

"Acknowledged. Only on my order. Keep this line open, Doc." Nick said. "Fire in the hole, boys. Stay with me when we exit."

Gus skidded the Dodge into the abrupt Point Lobos turnoff. In seconds, while keeping the turnoff entrance in sight, Gus whipped the steering wheel right, sliding the Caravan to a halt. He shut off lights and engine. After taking the MP5 offered by John, the two men in the front exited, following Nick as he went to a spot with clear vision of the entrance. In seconds, Nick was positioned at the wooded perimeter, his Barrett .50 caliber rifle at the ready.

"Gus goes to our left fifty feet, John to the right fifty feet. I will tag the driver, and the driver's side tire. After that, it will get tricky. I'd like to find out what this is all about from the participants, but that may not be possible. The bad guys are in an E350 Ford full size black van, and we have no idea how many guys are inside. Anyone exiting the van once I get it stopped with a weapon in hand finds God. Are we clear?"

"Clear!" Both men answered, while jogging to their positions.

Downing called. "Two minutes out."

"Acknowledged. In position," Nick said. He watched the van Downing had picked the prisoners up in spin into the turnoff before going left, leaving a plume of debris firing into the night air.

Nick could not use his night vision scope because of the coming van's headlights. He also didn't know if the trailing van would follow their target vehicle into the turnoff. If they did, it would mean they hoped to take the prisoners. Nick smiled, still sighting on the entrance. He knew the pursuing van was overdue turning into the Point Lobos entrance. Minutes passed as hours would normally, but it appeared the pursuers needed more than a few moments to make a decision to follow, in spite of their orders.

"Nick?" Doc's voice came over their open line

"Silence, my friend."

The black E350 turned finally into the Point Lobos entrance nearly ten full minutes later. The van slowed to a crawl, its high beam lights illuminating the area in front of it in light. Nick had slipped his light dimming glasses into place. This was not the first time he had faced an oncoming vehicle with full high-beam headlights. He put a burst through the windshield that nearly decapitated the driver. Shifting to the front driver's side tire, Nick shredded it with another burst. The van dived left, heading in slow motion towards the woods. Nick then fired rounds into the front passenger side tire, and the passenger side rear, effectively bringing the vehicle to a halt on its rims.

The passenger side expunged three men, armed and firing wildly towards Nick's chosen sniper roost as they rounded the van, using it for cover. Nick knew they could not see. Shifting to his lowlight goggles, he fired at any head showing for more than a split second. Two died instantly, before the third man understood the danger, and threw his weapon to the ground.

"Nick?"

"Stay where you are, Doc," Nick replied. "I'll let you know when to come out."

"Acknowledged."

After a few more moments Nick saw the third man's hands sticking straight into the air as he appeared hesitantly at the rear of the van. Nick called out in Arabic. "Come out in front of the van. Lie down and extend your arms and legs fully."

The survivor understood. He walked around the van, and did as Nick ordered. Nick called out again in Arabic. "Stay lying face down no matter what you hear. Do not even raise your head!"

Nick then fired the Barrett incrementally across the van, tearing through the sheet metal in an up and down zigzag pattern. The screams echoed out after the gunfire silenced. Nick called out to Gus and John to flank the sliding door on the van.

"Come out. Crawl out. Stay inside, and you die," Nick shouted repeatedly in Arabic. Three more men, screaming in pain, clutching horrible wounds appeared at the sliding door. They crawled out to the ground. Gus and John dragged them clear of the opening. Nick ran to join his companions, bringing his own MP5 to bear on the van and survivors. He checked the van interior, dragging the dead driver backward, and through the sliding door to the ground. "Keep your prisoners guarded, but join us, Doc. Take a look at these guys, and help us watch them while I send photos to Paul."

"Coming now."

Seconds later, Downing and two of his men were watching over the prisoners with Gus and John. Nick then sent photos of each man's face to Paul. He didn't want to start any kind of interrogation until he received more information. While waiting for a response, Nick checked each man for identification or papers. He found nothing. The glove compartment and inside of the van were clean of anything indicating their prisoners' origin. Paul called after the search was completed.

"They're all Pakistani ambassadorial staff. I bet you'll be thrilled to know the only connection to anyone in our government is Nancy Pettinger. Two men you killed were vouched for by Pettinger's office when Homeland requested their deportation. I sent agents to her underlings' houses to speak with them in person. Pettinger engineered the blocking of those men's deportation on grounds they were witnesses in a Department of Justice investigation that did not exist. She must have a backdoor into our operations. I'll work that end. Let Downing take over from there. His men will transport all the survivors. My backup team will be there shortly. I'd like you, Gus, and John to get clear of this. Thank you for assuming control. As I said, I got sloppy. I should have sent in a combat team, but I'm shorthanded in that area at the moment. It won't happen again, Nick."

"You will call me if you get the okay on Pettinger, won't you. Our US Marshals already have an interest. I'm certain this maneuver should get some people thinking this bitch has to be stopped at any cost."

"Count on it. I will test the waters at DOJ concerning Marshals Stanwick and Reinhold being more than shadowy liaisons in matters of national security. As you can imagine, tonight's ambush, orchestrated by one of their own, is not a popular subject. I believe they'll be more receptive in the future to joint operations if we can deal with the traitor before she does anything that actually succeeds. I'll call you tomorrow. Great work!"

Nick shrugged at Downing. "The boss wants to limit my guys' exposure, so we'll have to leave you with the leftovers. Your backup team will be here soon. Keep your heads down, and trust no one until we settle with our DOJ leak. You have my number if you need independent confirmation on anything."

"Take off, Nick," Downing agreed. "Thanks for backing our play. Do you think they decided to stop tailing and attack?"

"I think so. They thought about it when you turned into here. They made a decision, or someone made it for them. If I find out anything newsworthy, I'll call you. If you don't hear from me, it's because we settled out of court."

Downing laughed. "Understood. See ya'."

Nick gave Downing a small salute, and walked over to where Gus and John had already loaded the Dodge when Downing's men took over. Gus drove near Nick, and a moment later, they were driving toward Nick's house with Nick explaining about Pettinger. "I'll lock the gear at my place until tomorrow, John. I don't want you stopped without me in here with you. Your ID is good, but the locals would take you downtown anyway if they saw what we're packing right now."

"Tomorrow's Saturday," Gus mentioned. "Do you think we can put off pursuit of traitors for the weekend? Dansing's media coverage is finally fading off the front pages. Thanks to John, we've taken down yet another terrorist cell, and we even stopped an attempted ambush. We need a couple of quiet mornings on the beach with a soothing elixir. Might I also remind you the editing is not finished yet on your new novel?"

By the time Gus finished categorizing their trials and tribulations, Nick and John were quietly humming along musically. When he finished, Nick answered in typical form. "Fine, Gus! We'll put off saving Western Civilization until after your weekend beach break, you selfish prick. If for some reason we have to speed things along due to our US Marshal duo of Grace and Tim getting orders, John and I will put to rest Nancy Pettinger's traitorous actions once and for all. It will not be the same when the famous trio, El Muerto, Payaso, and El Kabong must act on new intel without the lazy Payaso rascal."

The three men enjoyed Nick's counter to Gus's request for a holiday, with Gus trying and failing to bring a point of order. "During our small break, didn't you promise knife throwing lessons for this weekend?"

343

"Leave it to you, Payaso. We try to enjoy a small laugh at your expense, and you go nuclear on me," Nick complained. "Yes, I agreed to teach knife throwing to my incorrigible daughter, the infamous Dagger."

"What did Rachel say when you showed her the gift? I'll bet you pulled out all the stops. 'Oh dear, these are like works of art. They can't be even considered weapons. Knife throwing will soon be an Olympic event. These are beautifully made treasures'." When Gus finished his falsetto imitation of Nick's imaginary plea to his wife, Nick was glaring at him, while John struggled mightily with snorts and clamped hands over mouth to keep from laughing.

"Okay…. I did lay it on a little thick," Nick admitted. "I have a problem with you mimicking me so accurately. I think the infamous Dagger betrayed my heartfelt pleas to her Mom in comical form for Uncle Gus's amusement."

"Guilty. I interrogated Dagger in a moment of weakness behind your back, brother. My questionable source told me Rachel was not drawn into the flowery praise of throwing knives. Jean was down at the mouth about it. She suspected the knives were going to be returned before she even touched one."

"Oh ye of little faith," Nick said. "I later carried on the conversation, reminding Rachel without training, Blackbeard would have had his way with Mona, Jean, and the weapon abhorrent Rachel. With training, I pointed out, Rachel handled Blackbeard like he was a cub scout with a bladder problem. I'll be teaching knife throwing to both of my ladies thanks to the quick thinking of El Muerto, the master of deception."

"You are the man, Muerto!"

"Thank you, Payaso, you disrespectful tool. You're right though, I promised the lessons, so I'll be creating a target site in my backyard. I'll start them out with the basics tomorrow morning."

344

"Do you still wish to imbibe the devil's morning beverage at Otter's Point tomorrow morning while we play Frisbee with the Dekester?"

"Yes, Brother John, we will be walking down together tomorrow early to continue our celebration of Lady Carol. There will be a few small doses of celebration tonight as well. I admitted to her my true past in answer to her last wish. Dan knows now too. It made her smile. I'm working on getting Dan to think about helping us out somewhere along the line, listening in where only a geezer could do so unnoticed. I believe he may warm to the idea of paying me back in such a way rather than money he can't afford."

Gus remained silent, his mouth tightening to check his emotions. Nick noticed, and put a hand on his shoulder. "We did right, partner. Dan will never betray us. I couldn't refuse Carol's request. I may have reacted over the top afterwards, but don't worry about Dan knowing."

Gus nodded. "That was special what you did, Muerto. We won't overdo it tonight, because I'm looking forward to the arctic chill, and waves crashing on the rocks tomorrow, while we sip our enhanced coffee. I'm sure your knife throwing will not suffer because of it."

"I killed a man at nearly fifty feet with a thrown knife while drugged. I'll be fine."

John leaned forward from the backseat. "He was a bad guy, huh Muerto?"

Nick smiled, remembering a similar question from Rachel. "He was to someone."

Chapter Fifteen

Making Memories

Jean pumped her fist. At fifteen feet, she had buried the throwing knife in the large layered cardboard target Nick created from boxes cut to a three foot square center, attached to an old tilted pine table. Rachel, Tina, Gus, and John sat under Nick's rear veranda, watching the lessons. Jean never showed any boredom with Nick's repeated corrections to her form and handling. She ran each time her knives plunked to the ground without any indication of frustration. Nick was already worried. He sensed dedication. Although he taught with calm deliberation, Rachel bailed early from the lessons. Tina, John, and Gus had taken a few shots at the target with only Gus making progress with a few hits.

They neared the two hour mark in the lesson as Nick began to legitimately regret enjoying his Otter's Point sojourn with Gus, John, and Deke. Although the magic coffee elixir had been incredible with the stillness of both the water and his outlook, shared with Gus and John, it had taken a toll on him. He grinned over at the watchers, knowing Jean's first strike with the knife would mean more practice than he had bargained for.

"Hey... give Dagger a break. Show us what you can do with the knives," Rachel said, knowing Nick had been imbibing down at the Point. "You've been showing form, but we want some substance."

She was of course encouraged by all watchers, as Jean ran to the throwing line Nick had created with the knives. Jean understood what the joke was. Watching Nick plant the three knives at twice the distance on target at Jerry Burkhart's request, she handed him the knives with a smile. "Show them, Dad."

Nick without pause or aim, planted the knives to the hilt. They struck so close together in the bulls-eye target he had pinned to the cardboard backing as to appear staged. He went to gather the knives himself, chuckling over the remarks of awe as well as disbelief. Nick returned to the throwing line, handing a knife to the exuberant Jean. "If all you other blokes are bored, go on inside. I'll stay out here with Jean."

Rachel stood and ran over to hug him. "You may be a lot of things, but damn... you're good. I'll pay more attention to the future lessons."

"You'll have to," Nick replied, holding her to him. "I doubt Dagger will be giving this particular sport up any time soon. She's driven, Rach. It's best to accept it, and move on, rather than fight it, and alienate her."

Rachel glanced at her high fiving daughter before returning her gaze to Nick. "You're right as you so annoyingly are on a daily basis. Good Lord, Nick... I hope you're wrong."

"So do I, baby. So... do... I."

* * *

On Sunday morning, Nick wrote and edited with single minded concentration, Deke lying happily at his feet. Nick's new novel 'Assassin's Folly' touched him in a way he could not express. Although resembling his other Diego novels, this new one incorporated more of himself in it than he had ever chanced before. Diego felt things he had chained inside his being, never to see the light of day. Nick poured over it with a passion he knew originated in the happenings he had faced since his prior book tour. He glanced startled at the clock, hearing a soft footfall, combined with the musky odor that drove him crazy at times. Rachel moved nearer to him with slow steps, clutching her black silk robe around her he had purchased on a whim. His imagination of Rachel in it

347

one day, while shopping with her at the mall, had forced him with it in hand to the cashier.

"It's only six, babe. Is Quinn doing his usual stomping act on your bladder?"

Rachel smiled, allowing the robe to open while wrapping an arm around Nick's shoulders. "Of course, but I missed you in bed with me. Quinn had little to do with me traipsing down here to interrupt your pursuit of Diego's latest pulp fiction killings. I know you've finished the novel. Why this driven obsession to edit until your eyeballs pop out?"

"I edit best in the morning." Nick's hands roved in places garnering moans as well as gasps of denial. "See… even you are a quandary of emotion in the morning. Your body says yes, yes, yes, while your head calls out no, no, no. I would say my concerted editing efforts are far more reasonable than those half-hearted denials."

Rachel clutched him to her with passionate annoyance. She backed away after a moment, her small embrace of angst fazing Nick not in the slightest. "You go too far!"

Nick grinned innocently at her, his hands roving without pause. "We're married. You're having my son. There is no too far. Let's retreat to the bedroom before your protests wake Dagger up."

Rachel allowed a full surrender to Nick's manipulations as he moved her toward the stairs. "Tell Deke to stay down here."

Nick glanced down at the attentive Deke, who shadowed his new path away from the kitchen. "Don't worry about Deke. Everything we do makes him doze. He'll be in a sleep coma ten minutes after I get you into bed."

"Yeah, but he goes into his coma at the end of the bed… oh damn… okay… who cares."

348

* * *

Gus arrived with Dan Lewis in tow at 8 am. Nick met them at the door. He shook hands with Dan. "Did Gus find you wandering the streets, old man?"

"He did indeed," Dan admitted. "I was plodding down to Carol's beach when Gus intercepted me. This is my first journey out. It's a rough one."

"His kids have returned home," Gus added. "I figured since we're all walking to the ocean, we may as well walk together."

"I agree. Why not walk along together, Dan, if you don't mind. Gus and I have to walk Deke. Then I have a knife flinging lesson at 10 am with Jean. She's obsessed with it. We nearly spent three hours at it yesterday."

"Are you training her for anything in particular?"

"I hope not," Nick answered truthfully. "We have something on the horizon you may be able to help us with if you're interested."

Dan considered Nick's statement before answering. "Get Deke, and tell me about it on the walk. Otherwise, I may say yes now, and no later."

"That's fair enough. Be right back." Nick gathered the happy Deke, added a beach chair to his dual set, and his pack with thermos. He also brought along Deke's water dish and water. Gus brought the cups, while Nick could strap up to four chairs tightly to his pack, and it held snacks as well as spiked coffee. He always traveled down with his small satellite laptop.

Rachel caught him before Deke dog sledded him out the door. "Hey, Muerto, do you know what Jean's already doing?"

349

"Probably smacking the target with throwing knives. I heard her. The first part of our lesson was to teach her safety. How's she doing?"

"Let's just say if you were the target, you would not be happy. She's burying one or two every set she throws."

"She's a natural," Nick said. "How was I this morning?"

Rachel gasped and blushed, smacking Nick's shoulder. "Never mind. No matter how you were this morning, you're never doing it again, so it won't matter."

Nick kissed her, holding onto Rachel below the hips. "You always say that."

Rachel broke away from him. "Did you know all sex in or out of marriage is rape?"

"Really," Nick seemed interested. "Is that why you were screaming?"

Nick's quickness, led by Deke's intuitive nature, allowed the pair to escape through the door before Rachel could catch them. Nick and Deke scrambled down to the sidewalk as Rachel appeared huffing and puffing on the porch. When she saw Gus and Dan, Rachel remembered she only wore her black silk robe. She waved at the men, as she clutched the robe to her.

Gus and Dan waved in response. Rachel added a fist waving sequence at the unrepentant Nick. "I will have my revenge, Muerto!"

"Who is Muerto?"

Nick clasped Dan's shoulder. "All in good time, old man. All in good time."

"What did you do to anger Princess Preggo this morning?"

"Not a thing, Gus. I was my usual lovable self," Nick replied. "I have no idea what got into her highness this morning. Some people are unfortunately not morning people. Let us move past these petty squabbles with hormonal women. We need to enjoy the small good fortune of another chillingly wonderful ocean visit."

"Chillingly wonderful meaning another trek to Ice Station Zebra," Gus complained, slapping his hands across his chest as if drumming arctic cold from his body.

"You haven't grown accustomed to our brisk climate yet, Gus?"

Gus shrugged, gesturing down the hill, where gray skies highlighting drifting somber clouds, framed the ocean scene embedded with rocky escarpments jutting from white capped waves. "It's a process, Dan. I admit it is beautiful. I'd miss it if I were anywhere else… like the sandpits overseas."

"I remember you guys went overseas for research on Nick's new novel," Dan replied. "It was more than research, huh?"

"It was a business/research trip," Nick answered for Gus. "We've decided to stay out of the sand. There seems to be more terrorists here than overseas now anyway. With these new Isis bastards claiming to have cells all over the USA already, I'm wondering if we'll ever shut the damn immigration door."

Dan chuckled. "You sure are right about that. I thought Diego isn't political."

"He's getting as fed up as I am," Nick replied. "It may be seeping into Diego soon. The Kum Ba Ya crowd doesn't buy my pulp fiction anyhow, unless it's for the purpose of doing a 'Book Killing'."

"Are you contacting Grace and Tim at the beach?"

351

"Grace and Tim?"

"Gus is referring to our US Marshal friends. We're working on a case they were dumped on with. It should have been funneled down through a different venue. Their relationship with me, along with a recent case we worked has our usually reticent Department of Justice reaching into dark corners they don't belong in. Our contact with the Company will be attempting to limit their involvement after an unforeseen development."

"Is that the case you were referring to at the house?"

"Only if you're interested, Dan. We may not be able to use you. If the woman has fled the country, any part we could use you for probably wouldn't work. Her name is Nancy Pettinger. She's been selling us out from a high level in the DOJ, betraying missions, and blocking action against suspected terrorists. Nancy's on the run, but after the other night, we know she has some backdoor into operations no one knew existed. My concern is if she's already sold the backdoor to the myriad enemies we have all over the damn globe."

"What's a backdoor?"

"It's a Trojan Horse type virus used to allow access into a computer mainframe," Nick answered. "Depending on the sophistication in its creation, it may take weeks to find. Pettinger will be careful who she sells to, but she can sell an endless number of tipoffs on operations that will cost agents their lives. She's no dummy. Our traitorous Nancy slips in for an important piece of information requested for, and slips back out undetected. I'm sure the sale is for a large amount of money."

Dan slowed as they reached Carol's beach, only a block from Otter's Point. "What could I do to help? I'm an old man as you've pointed out."

"Let's find a place in the sand. I'll explain my idea to you." Nick led the way. Unlike Otter's Point, Carol's favorite beach had a vehicle turnout, horseshoeing from the coastal road entrance, and then back to the road again for exiting.

When they reached the beach, Nick let Dan show them where he wanted to sit. He led them to a rounded rock with a rocky tide pool in front of it, Nick recognized from the night with Dan and his kids.

"Anywhere here guys."

Nick and Gus prepared the beach chairs. They left Dan alone as he stood next to the rock and tide pool. Deke chased the Frisbee for half an hour in the sand. As if sensing a change, Deke returned to stand next to Dan. As Nick and Gus moved to the chairs, Dan sat down with Deke at his feet, both watching the tide pool flowing in, and round again to the ocean. Nick opened his thermos while Gus readied the cups. He passed a charged coffee over to Dan.

"It's loaded, Dan," Gus warned, "and not with mocha berry almond fudge supreme either."

"Understood." Dan accepted the cup, wiping his face with a handkerchief before sipping the coffee. "Very good. It's 5 pm somewhere."

"That's our motto." Nick also gave Deke water in his dish, and spread a small towel with a rawhide chew on it. Nick also opened his laptop. In moments, he accessed a site used as a drop, Grace could contact him without a call or a trace. After a few moments reading, Nick took a long swallow from his spiked coffee. "Uh oh. Nancy got wind of the dragnet possibly descending on her head. She's driving into Oakland Monday night, and hopping an Alaska Airline flight from Oakland International to Montreal. She'll be staying at the Hilton Hotel at the airport. Grace and Tim have agreed to be our chauffeurs on this trip to the East

353

Bay. They'll be arriving today. We have a small window of opportunity tonight. Nancy's traveling with two guard goons."

"Did Paul get them on board?"

"Yep. Apparently Paul shared our adventures the other night where Nancy nearly cost us a whole team. They have not found her Trojan backdoor into the system yet either. They figure she's on her way to Montreal to sell access into the system from out of the country." Nick leaned back, sipping his coffee, and chuckling.

In an opposite reaction, Gus sat straight in his chair, pointing at Nick. "I see that look, Muerto, and I don't like it. This is not a fun time."

"It is to me, Payaso. I have a job for you, Dan. It will clear up your entire debt to me you think you owe, and take care of a traitor. Would you like to work with Gus and I on this mission?"

"Listening to you two has made the damn pain recede for a few moments from my head. If I can barter my way into a day and night thinking about something else that doesn't rip my heart out, I'd do anything for it."

"That's plain enough," Nick said solemnly. "Your part will be very important. You'll need a walker, and a geezer attitude without fear."

Dan drained his drink, and held the cup out for more. Nick filled it. "I fear nothing, Nick. Without Carol, death, prison, or even torture don't mean a damn thing to me. The night before Carol lost all conscious thought, my daughter thought it would be good to watch a movie with her... one of her favorites. Carol smiled when Sally showed her The Wizard of Oz movie case, so I put it in. When Judy Garland sang 'Somewhere Over the Rainbow' Carol's eyes widened, and she smiled. It nearly killed the rest of us... good Lord... we muffled our cries and tears so Carol didn't notice. She was so absorbed in the song we pulled it off. Now though, every day that song rings in my head out of nowhere… and I…"

Dan lost control for a few moments, turning away as his shoulders shook. Nick and Gus remained silent, resisting the urge to interrupt the old man's pain with comforting words they knew would bring no comfort. Seemingly in tune with his pain, the crescendo of waves against the rocks increased their tempo. When he turned again to face them, Dan wiped his face once more, and drained his drink.

"I'm in, boys. Tell me what I'll have to do. I won't screw up."

"We know you won't, old man," Nick replied.

* * *

Nick answered the door, hurrying in from the all-day knife throwing activity in the back. He had talked Dan into staying with them to meet John, Grace, and Tim. Built around Jean's knife throwing obsession, Dan enjoyed the banter mixed in with knife practice Jean could not get enough of. Rachel had participated, with some success, while Gus, John, Tina, and Dan watched appreciatively. Deke at first wanted to chase the throws. A couple of beer bowls, and Dan feeding him beef jerky treats had calmed Deke down noticeably.

"Hello minions of the darkness," Nick greeted his US Marshal friends.

Tim laughed, but Grace barged right past Nick. "Damn right! I want that bitch in the worst way imaginable, Nick! It was a crappy trip. I need a drink and a plan. I don't give a shit who knows what we're doing. I pray to God you have something for us."

Nick retreated a bit, surprised for a change at Grace's initial greeting. "Well okay then. Has she been like this all the way here, Tim?"

"She's calmed down somewhat. We did not drink on the way here."

"You definitely need a drink then. Come outside with us. Our knife throwing exhibition is almost over due to temperature and darkness. I have a couple of new team members, and a hell of a plan. We need transportation, the proper room next to Pettinger and her bodyguards, and a place to bide our time afterward, until one of my team members can play out his part."

"Let me see the knife throwing contest, meet your people, and then get my cranky ass up on that great drinking deck you have," Grace replied.

"Done… and done," Nick agreed.

* * *

Dan approached the bodyguard's hotel door, the walker he used banging into the doorjam and door noisily while Nick, Gus, and John fanned out to both sides of the old man. Dan tried the wrong room-card repeatedly, cursing and ramming into the door. It soon opened, with a tall, dark, and very annoyed man of Middle Eastern descent glowering at Dan.

"What is it you want, Sir," the man asked.

"I want into my damn room!" Dan peered at him in confusion. "What the hell are you doing in my room?"

"This is not your room! Go away!"

Dan stumbled forward, his walker catching in the doorway. Nick surged around him, using a stun-gun to knock the door greeter to the floor. Gus grabbed Dan and the walker, lifting both

356

clear of the door as Nick and John rushed in with Tasers. They caught the second bodyguard completely unaware, the dual sets of needles hitting him as he sat on the bed. In seconds he was unconscious. Gus dragged the other bodyguard further into the room while Dan closed the door.

"Excellent," Nick whispered. "We'll wait a few minutes, and Dan can pull the same thing at Nancy's door. She'll call over to her bodyguards. John will answer, and tell her he'll be right over and will knock once. Nancy opens the door, and we Tase the shit out of the bitch."

"No, Muerto, we won't," Gus countered. "Stick to the plan. We don't want to leave marks to upset your psychopath scene setup."

"Fine, nitpicker. Great job, Dan. Are you ready for another taste?"

"I'm good to go, Nick. You guys are frighteningly good."

"You don't want to be in the room when Muerto really becomes creative after we get Nancy," Gus said, with avid agreement from John, who was restraining the bodyguards with plastic ties and duct tape.

"Yeah… I do," Dan answered with conviction. "Let's do this."

"That's the spirit, Dan," Nick said.

* * *

Nancy Pettinger gulped down a large portion of Johnnie Walker Red on ice, wondering what the hell all the commotion was next door at her bodyguards' room. When it quieted again, she poured another drink, smiling at the money offerings she was getting every moment on-line for her auction taking place in Montreal. Then someone was cursing, banging into her hotel room

357

door, and sounding like a mental patient. She called immediately over to her bodyguards.

"Yes?"

"Get your ass over to my room and find out who the fuck's ramming my door!"

"On our way. One knock."

Nancy disconnected, cringing each time the banging persisted. Then she heard voices followed by silence. A single knock on her door, and Nancy drained her refill and walked unsteadily to the door. She opened it, and men grabbed her while physically dragging her deeper into the room. A hand clamped over Pettinger's mouth as her arms were restrained by her wrists behind the back. A piece of duct tape was spread across her mouth as the clamping hand released her. The man who had clamped her mouth shut smiled and waved.

"Hi Nanc. I'm Nick. I'll be your escort to hell. Don't worry though. I can't do all the things I wish I could do to you. I need to make a tragic scene of death here, where your bodyguards became embroiled in a sexual scene with you. One will be the participant while the other will be the jealous lout who ruins everything. I'll give you a little something to help you into the mood, you traitorous bitch!"

* * *

Dan watched, mesmerized as Nick stripped Pettinger, placing her on the bed. Then with Gus's help, he stripped one of the bodyguards naked. They spread the clothing around in haphazard seduction form. Nick had injected the supposedly amorous bodyguard with something, and the man now lay near Pettinger with a drug induced erection. With gloved hands at all times, Nick lubricated and created an undeniable sexual scene.

John held Nancy in place during the final setting with Gus controlling the bodyguard.

Nick then produced a silenced Ruger 9mm automatic. He put it in the second bodyguard's hand, whom he had sitting on a chair, while aiming it carefully. The vocals surprised Dan; but drew clucking noises of discontent from Gus, and suppressed amusement from John.

"You bitch! How dare you betray our love," Nick said with actual angst as he fired a round through Nancy's forehead. He then shot the sexually coupled bodyguard in the back, assuredly near his heart.

Rushing over to the bed, Nick placed a silenced Glock 9mm in the sexually coupled bodyguard's left hand, aiming back at the bodyguard in the chair. "You dirty rat! You've killed me, you prick! Take that!"

Nick shot the bodyguard in the chair through the head. Dan watched as the Ruger the unconscious bodyguard in the chair held, clattered to the floor with the body. Gus took the chair, placing it in its original position at the room table. Nick allowed the Glock to fall away from the dying bodyguard's hand, standing while scanning over his scene. He waited while the bodyguard died, the final death in his macabre play. Nick checked the bodyguard's vitals, while Gus and John scoured both rooms, making sure no hint of what had actually transpired would be left behind.

"Holy God in heaven," Dan said.

"My advice," Gus said, while guiding Dan to the door, "leave the Lord out of this."

"Amen," Dan replied.

* * *

359

At their new beach, with Gus, Dan, John and Nick sitting comfortably on folding chairs, they sipped their spiked coffee with appreciation. Nick's phone vibrated. He threw a Frisbee toss for Deke and answered, noticing the caller ID.

"The fabulous and deadly El Muerto here, with his equally dangerous sidekicks: Payaso the bold, El Kabong the silent death, and OG the herald of doom."

It took many seconds for Paul Gilbrech to recover from Nick's greeting. "That... was too much."

"Says you, El Kablooey. How has our tragic scene panned out?"

"Exactly as you had envisioned, you prick. May I say without a doubt, you scare the shit out of me, Nick. With Dan playing the role of a senior citizen making a 911 call, complaining about a violent argument in the room next to him, the scene was incredibly good. How the hell did you recruit someone to work that angle so perfectly?"

Nick looked over at the old man staring into a tide pool. "I recruited him from hell."

The End

An Added Bonus Short Story
Cold Blooded Future

She saw him walk out of the gym with bag in hand. His nondescript nature and looks made her doubt everything. Approaching him seemed a bad joke. Although around six feet tall with a solid look about him, he could have been a hundred other men. His close cropped graying hair gave him a frustrated gym-rat look rather than a sinister one. The woman sobbed. Fear clutched her insides into a ball of misery. Remembering what her US Marshal Aunt had told her, she stood in plain sight, trembling with her hands empty. Only a moment passed before the man who until that second gave no indication she lived or mattered, approached her with an unhurried gait. When the man reached her, he smiled and held out his hand.

"Cindy Brighton?"

Cindy grasped his warm hand. He put his other hand over hers. "Your hand is like ice. Is your car nearby?"

"It's the Nissan over there by the curb," Cindy managed to blurt out, trying to control the tremble in her voice. "Are... are you Nick?"

Nick McCarty put an arm around her, shielding some of the wind chill blowing in from the ocean. "Yep. I'm Nick. Why don't we talk in your car with the heater on? I can tell you're nervous. Don't be. We'll talk like two old friends, and then we'll get to know each other, or part ways with a smile, okay?"

Cindy nodded without speaking, allowing Nick to guide her to the Nissan. She beeped open the locks. Nick opened her door and held it open until Cindy sat down in the driver's seat. He closed it and went around the Nissan, quickly getting seated in the

361

front passenger seat. Cindy started it, putting the heater on low blow. Nick smiled at her, his eyes direct and unblinking.

"Better?"

"Much," Cindy replied. "Grace Stanwick is my aunt, Mr. McCarty. I went to her as a last resort. I... I didn't know what to do. I thought as a US Marshal, Grace could help me get my daughter away from that cult she joined. My aunt said it wasn't something she could do anything about unless approached by my daughter Kelly."

"That is unfortunately how it works, Cindy. Grace told me your daughter called you secretly, begging you to get her out of there." Nick's eyes narrowed slightly, his facial features chilling into an uncaring mask. "You wouldn't be making that up to get help, would you, Cindy?"

Cindy shook her head no violently. She reached over to clutch Nick's hand. "No... never... Grace was my last hope. When she told me to be here at six o'clock at night to meet some novelist named Nick McCarty, I thought she had blown a fuse in her head."

Nick chuckled, his face easing out of the grim featured tone he had been casting. "I've thought that a few times on a normal basis about your aunt. I've known her well over a decade, and she's just as mental as I remember her from the first time we met. Your Uncle Tim is a saint to have stayed with her. That they pulled off remaining together as partners is a damn miracle."

Hearing him speak so familiarly about her aunt and uncle stopped the trembling in her hand. Nick kept holding the hand with a light touch. "My aunt told me if you decided to get my daughter back to me there would be consequences and secrets that could never be shared with anyone. At first... I really thought she was nuts. I don't read pulp fiction, but I know you're one of the most famous authors in the world. You've sold millions of novels about an assassin named Diego. I asked her how a New York Times

362

bestselling author could help me. I thought at first she meant you could buy Kelly out of the cult."

Nick's face darkened like a Midwest tornado forming on the horizon. "Sorry, I don't work that way. I don't much care if I could buy her out of there. I'm sure Grace explained that to you."

"Yes," Cindy acknowledged. "I... I didn't mean it like that. I just couldn't figure out how Grace thought you could help. She told me you don't just write about Diego, you are Diego."

Nick grinned, patting her hand. "Like I told my wife Rachel long ago – compared to me, Diego's a campfire girl. I also have a few partners. I brought one with me. She may make you more comfortable."

Nick's hand went to his ear. "Hey Dagger, c'mon out here." Nick laughed at something he heard before turning to Cindy. "She'll be out in a second. My daughter Jean's a little rough around the edges, but I'll need her in on this."

Cindy watched the gym door. A slim woman emerged, striding toward the Nissan with acrobatic grace. The parking lot lights flickered on her grim visage, the woman's long blonde hair, tied at her neck tightly in the back. She wore a black windbreaker, and carried a small bag much like Nick's. As she drew closer, Cindy thought she looked to be only a few inches shorter than Nick. She flung open the back door to the Nissan with suppressed anger, slamming it shut. Before she closed it, Cindy noticed the thin scar running from her right eye down to her ear, and another small one at the left corner of the woman's mouth in the dome lights dim illumination.

The woman slapped the back of Nick's head. "I told you to stop calling me Dagger... damn it!"

Nick chuckled. "Yeah... so what?"

To Cindy's surprise she saw the grim woman grin before turning her attention to Cindy.

"Who's the mark?"

"This is Cindy, Grace's niece. Her daughter's being held in a cult against her will. Cindy, this is my daughter Jean."

Cindy shook hands with Jean, surprised at the strength she felt in the short grip. "You must work with your hands. They're rough. It's nice meeting you."

"Nice meeting you too." Jean didn't comment on Cindy's observation. "Let's go over to the Monte, Dad. Mom's working the night shift with Quinn. I'm starving."

"I haven't decided yet about Cindy's problem."

"I have," Jean said. "Cindy's okay. Let's get her daughter back."

Nick's chin dropped to his chest, earning him another slap on the head.

"C'mon. What else do you have to do? This is for Grace and Tim. We owe them."

"No we don't."

Jean patted Cindy's shoulder. "We'll get her back, Cindy. Dad's a little slow on the uptake since turning fifty-seven. Don't mind him. Do you know where the Monte Café is?"

"Yes. I've lived in Fremont all my life, but we visit down here all the time. The Monte Café is one of our favorite places to eat at. Has your Mom worked there a long time?"

"Nearly twenty years. My younger brother Quinn works with her now. He was practically raised there. Mom loves what she does, so she ignores the fact Dad has more money than God. You talk to my Dad and drive him over to the Monte. I'll follow with our car."

"Okay, Jean. Thank you."

"You bet." She grabbed Nick's ear, shaking it slightly. "Say something, Muerto."

"This is about me roughing you up, isn't it?"

"Nope, but I am going to beat your old ass one of these days. I'll call Uncle Gus, and Uncle John for a meeting. See you at the Monte." Jean exited the car, and jogged over to a gleaming black sedan.

Cindy drove toward the Monte Café. "I like Jean. She must look like her Mom."

"She does. Jean's my step daughter, but closer than blood. Quinn is my son. Let's talk about how your daughter entered the cult. Grace told me it's an offshoot of those nut-cake Isis guys we finally almost exterminated. How the hell did she get introduced into a radical Muslim group like that?"

"Kelly met an intense young man in high school, named Javid Harandi. He invited her to their mosque. Kelly's always been a wild one. I didn't figure she would ever attend more than one meeting. They all stay at this ranch in Salinas, where they've converted the main building into their mosque. The outlying structures used to house farmhands, but now are part of their compound where families supposedly stay. Javid seemed like a nice kid. It wasn't until too late I found out he didn't attend school there."

"He was recruiting."

"Exactly. He was very good at it. Before I knew what was happening, Kelly was wearing long dresses and a hijab. The school began calling, accusing Kelly of disrupting classes. When I

365

confronted her, she threw a fit about the school being unclean. She left in the night. I tried to get the police to intervene; but because she is eighteen, they couldn't barge into that compound even though she hasn't graduated. Can you get her back, Nick?"

"How did she get word to you she wanted out?"

"They get deliveries there from UPS, among others. Kelly snuck a note to the UPS driver. He was nice enough to call me. You keep avoiding the question."

"I'm gathering information. I don't know if I can get her out. I'll talk it over with my partners. Jean's having them meet us for dinner. We may have to scout the place first. For one thing, we don't know where she would be."

"I'm sorry. I don't know what I thought you could do," Cindy replied. "I hope you can figure some way to help. You're my last chance."

* * *

At the café, two men sat together at a place where two tables had been pushed together. There were no other customers. Jean led the way in with Nick and Cindy following. Jean hugged a tall young man with an apron on.

"Hi, Sis. I heard you have a meeting planned. Am I invited?"

"Sure, if you want to make Mom's head explode," Jean said, echoing the same words Nick used when Jean asked to be let in on missions. She smiled as her Mom appeared with a tray of appetizers, glaring at Jean. "Hi Mom."

"I heard what's going on," Rachel said, serving the appetizer tray in front of the two amused men. She pointed a finger at them. "Don't you two start either."

366

As if prearranged, both men made lip zipping motions in sync. Nick hugged his wife. "Is Quinn torturing you again with Jean's help?"

Rachel framed her husband's face with her hands. "Yes, and I blame you."

Nick kissed her, eliciting quick 'get a room' remarks. "I'm always to blame. This is Cindy Brighton, Grace and Tim's niece. Her daughter Kelly's being held by a Muslim cult offshoot of Isis. What do they call it now?"

"Javid said they are of the Daesh sect of Islam," Cindy answered.

"That's the French word they created to be politically correct overseas. It means the same thing: Isis, Isil, Daesh – all the same."

"That's John Groves," Nick said, holding onto Rachel. "Gus Nason is next to him. The young man is Quinn McCarty. Last and certainly not least is my lovely wife, Rachel."

The others waved, but Rachel shook her hand. "I'm sorry about your daughter. Mine has decided to follow in the footsteps of her Dad, where she received those lovely scars infiltrating a nest of shitheads much like the ones holding Kelly. Nick, Gus, and John barely arrived in time to keep the bastards from slitting her throat. Don't worry, she's much more careful now, right darling?"

Jean absorbed the amused laughter in good spirits. "Thank you for the history lesson, Mom. I didn't do what I was told, and I paid the price."

"She could have the scars fixed surgically," Cindy said. "They do wonders with plastic surgery now. It would practically be an outpatient procedure."

"Nope. Not doing it," Jean said, as Rachel did an eye roll to the heavens. "When I wake in the morning, and see my face, I know not to do something stupid again."

"Let's eat while Rachel busts our chops," Gus said, digging into the appetizers. "Sit down Nick. John and I have some news about the Daesh bunch. We read in Paul on the way over. He's backing our play if we decide to help. Apparently, they're already on the radar."

Nick sat down after holding a chair out for Cindy. Jean sat down next to her. Rachel brought over the coffee pot and filled the cups while Quinn replenished the finger foods. "It's damn nice the CIA director still takes our calls."

"He never forgets how he got there," Jean said.

"You mean Paul Gilbrech, the actual Director of the CIA?"

"Keep that between us, Cindy," Nick said. "Paul likes us. We've worked together many years, since before Quinn was born. We have a habit of attracting cases involving Homeland Security. We're legal though. We consult with the FBI, DOJ, and US Marshals. I originally made contact with the US Marshals through Grace and Tim."

Cindy waited for Nick to go on, but he began eating as did the others. Rachel patted her shoulder. "Don't worry. I can see it in their faces. They'll be going after Kelly."

"I want to go with them," Quinn announced. "I'm old enough to make my own decisions. I've been trained since I was old enough to walk."

"Jean didn't work with your Dad until she finished her stint in the Marines," Rachel countered. "She'll be graduating college this year if she's still alive."

The last part of her statement drew laughter from everyone, including Jean.

After the meal, John showed the satellite footage of the Daesh compound. "It will be easy to recon the place. I am not sure how easy it will be to find out where Kelly is."

"You and I will have to go in, Uncle John," Jean said. "We'll gain admittance, while Uncle Gus and Dad watch our six until we locate her."

"I already spotted a perfect nest," Nick said, pointing at the fixed screen. "I'll have full range on everyone in the compound. They probably don't even know about the advances in sniper rifles, at least not on our level of clearance. I like Jean's idea. She speaks Arabic like a native. John will have to bluff into the place, but since he's a believer, it shouldn't be a problem. I need Gus to be the wheel man. That leaves Quinn to spot for me, because we have quite a distance to be safe."

"I'll spot for you," Rachel said. "I don't want Quinn in the mix."

"You come too, then. Quinn spots, but a second set of eyes in this case is a good thing."

"I hate you."

"You always say that, Rach. In or out, baby. You can bring your new Colt to watch over our poor son."

"Fine, but this op better work exactly the way you plan, or I might use my new Colt on you. I'm closing. C'mon, Quinn, let's get doing what real workers do."

Jean followed her Mom. "I'll help, so we can go home, and sit on the deck together."

"You guys in for a little deck time," Nick asked. "Bring the wives and kids of course."

"See you there, brother," Gus stood with John. "I'll be designated driver tonight, lush."

"Me?" John jolted to a stop as he had been walking toward the door. "Lately, we have to pour you into a vehicle, or make you walk it off on the way home, Payaso."

Gus grinned. "Yeah, El Kabong, I do need to cut back a little. How soon are we moving on this, Nick?"

"I'm thinking tomorrow. It's an in and out with casualties."

"The sooner the better," John said. "I do not care for this sect so close."

"See you in a few, guys," Nick said. "I'll walk you to your car, Cindy."

Cindy had been making some observations of her own while listening. "You're that El Muerto, and your two partners are Payaso and El Kabong. The three of you are a legend. That...that means your daughter is Viper. Oh my God!"

"Also on the down low, Cindy, along with everything else," Nick warned. "We have people in very high places protecting us. We've erased serial killers from existence no one else had a clue about over the years. We're letting you in because you're Grace and Tim's blood relative, and you have a problem only we can solve. It would be very bad for you to forget the confidentiality your Aunt Grace mentioned. Stay inside your hotel for the next couple days. We'll bring Kelly to you."

"Are you serious?"

"Deadly serious. Take your daughter, head for home, and forget all about us or anything you see in the news. Are we clear?"

Cindy gripped Nick's hand with both of hers. "I understand. Thank you."

"Don't thank me yet. Viper is a loose cannon. She was a lot cuter when she was Dagger."

"I heard that," Jean's voice called out.

* * *

John and Jean arrived at the compound at noon the next day by taxi. Jean wore all black, including her Hijab. She kept her eyes down with John leading her. He had dressed in a dark business suit. They approached the gate with confident strides. It had taken Paul Gilbrech half the night to find a connection overseas for John to use at the entrance to the gated compound. A scowling guard met them outside the gate, his hand on the gun handle at his side.

"What do you want?" The guard asked in Arabic.

"We have come from Saudi Arabia, given passage by Aaban Safar," John said. "We were told to come here."

The guard's eyes widened as his companion approached. "Who is this woman?"

"An ally from overseas," John answered. "She will be of great use because of her ability to infiltrate the nonbelievers groups. Speak woman!"

Jean kept her eyes down, while answering in Arabic. "I am Isolde. I do the bidding of Safar Aaban."

The guards relaxed. The first guard gestured to them. "Come, I will take you inside. We are in a guarded state at this time. Your help would be most valuable, especially your woman companion."

"One thing we must do is find out the problem you have with a woman named Kelly Brighton. Safar has heard she puts the entire Masjid in danger."

"I am glad to hear you say so," the guard admitted. "Our Imam's son is obsessed with her. She will never fit in. It was a mistake to bring her here. Has it come to this where her presence here threatens our plans?"

"It does, brother. We must find a way to make her disappear or convert her to the true path before any more damage is done. We have a mission!"

"Yes!" The guard turned to address John. "We must strike soon. This Kelly is a liability we do not need. I do not think she can be converted to our cause. Javid enticed her to us with hopes of a woman like your Isolde who could penetrate our enemy's meetings."

"You must take us to her now, brother. Isolde will decide if she can be used. If not, I will take her far away where our Masjid will not be held in jeopardy or our mission compromised."

"I will do so immediately!" The guard's animated anger directed at Kelly showed in every feature on his face. "It was truly a mistake to bring her here."

"Agreed," John said.

The guard led them to a quarters far from the main complex. A guard stood outside the small blockhouse. He held up a hand questioningly to the guard who had brought John and Jean.

"These two must see the Brighton woman."

"I cannot allow that. Javid Harandi ordered no one is to see her."

372

Jean drove the guard's nose bone into his brain a split second after he finished speaking.

"Uh oh," John said, as the escorting guard's head was pulped by an incoming round from Nick's sniper's nest. "Gee… that went well. It may have been better to make sure Kelly's in there, Viper."

"On it." Jean scooted through the door, ready for anything. All she found was a terrified Kelly, sitting on a cot. No one else was sharing the room with her. "C'mon, girlfriend. This is a breakout. Your Mom, Cindy, wants you in the worst way to be a good girl."

Kelly broke down in tears, rushing to hug Jean.

Jean patted her back mechanically, and shook her a little. "We have to go now while no one knows what's happening. Get your shit together, kid!"

With Kelly between them, Jean and John rushed her toward the exit gate. Men appeared and died along the way.

     * * *

"That was a great nose strike," Rachel observed. "I wonder where she learned that one, Muerto."

Quinn called out coordinates, with wind figured, chuckling at his Mom's comment. Nick pulped the other guard's head. "A little busy here, Hon. Could we wait for the retribution until after the op?"

"Of course, Dear. Jean has her out and on the way. No response yet," Rachel said. "Wait one. She called out a vector Nick turned to. He fired, eliminating the approaching man.

"Good catch, Hon. Hey Newbie, get your head in the game."

"They have a vehicle in pursuit, Dad. It's armored," Quinn said.

"That's what they think."

* * *

John and Jean kept Kelly on a zigzag pattern toward the gate. The revving of an engine behind them caused a stop near one of the structures where they were challenged by the occupants. John downed the most vocal one instantly with a throat strike. Both he and Jean peered around the structure to see the armored vehicle's driver's head get pulped, followed by shots into the driver's side tire, causing the vehicle to dive and roll.

"Hello down there," Rachel's voice echoed in their ears. "Move it, you two. What the hell are you waiting for?"

"See, John… that's why I told Dad not to bring the Snow White on mission." Jean listened appreciatively to the gasps and amusement on their networked line. "Coming, Mom."

When they reached the gate, the guards were already dead. Gus slid to a halt and the trio piled into the waiting vehicle. Twenty minutes later, they delivered Kelly to her Mom. Cindy broke down in Kelly's arms, hugging her with all her might. Kelly, her eyes and mouth clamped shut in guilty acknowledgement clung to Cindy, trying to calm her Mom. Jean grinned appreciatively, giving a backhand slap to Quinn's chest.

"See kid. Now that's how it's done."

"Damn, Sis," Quinn said. "That nose strike was awesome. Did Dad teach you that one?"

Jean glanced where Nick leaned against the hood of their vehicle, his arm around Rachel. "He taught me a hell of a lot more than that, my brother."

The End… for now

Thank you for purchasing and reading Cold Blooded Book III: Sins & Sanctions. If you enjoyed the novel, please take a moment and leave a review. Your consideration would be much appreciated. Please visit my Amazon Author's Page if you would like to preview any of my other novels. Thanks again for your support.

Bernard Lee DeLeo

Please do not be hesitant asking questions concerning any subject about writing, publishing, or characterization. My publisher, RJ Parker and I answer questions all the time on the Facebook page. Previews and release dates are updated on the fan page constantly. Thank you.

Author's Face Book Page -
https://www.facebook.com/groups/BernardLeeDeLeo/

Author's Contact Links -
http://rjparkerpublishing.com/bernard-lee-deleo.html

17640207R00213

Made in the USA
Middletown, DE
02 February 2015